Bitter Bloodline

The Clearwater Mysteries

Book five

Proofread by Ann Attwood
Cover Design by Andjela K

Printed by CreateSpace, an Amazon.com company.

ISBN- 9781704638393

Available from Amazon.com, CreateSpace.com, and other retail outlets.
Available on Kindle and other devices.

Bitter Bloodline

Jackson Marsh

One

Doctor Benjamin Quill squinted at the society pages of the national newspaper with his one good eye and smiled at the opportunity the viscount had unwittingly presented. Comparing today's announcement to the same one made three months previously, confirmed that the viscount's plans remained unchanged. In announcing an audacious reformation of his family's traditions with a gathering of aesthetes rather than clergy, he had opened his inaugural society event at Larkspur Hall to the scrutiny of the public. It was a bold gambit, and one intended to curry favour with the rich and famous of the Garrick Club, while thrusting his Foundation and his cause into the limelight.

It was the viscount's first mistake.

'Our game is not yet at an end,' Quill chuckled.

They were his words to Clearwater before he took the stand to save the man from ruin and his lover from the cells. In saving the person he had sworn to destroy, Quill had brought their first game to an end, and having placed himself in a position of power, of indebtedness, had confused Clearwater's defences.

The second game had begun just after New Year when the viscount played a bold opening gambit; the announcement of his Easter Dinner with a guest list that gave Quill plenty of opportunity for attack. Not a fatal attack, not on Clearwater at least, not yet. The endgame was far distant, but in the meantime, the taking of pieces and the gradual chipping away at defences was game enough for the doctor.

Clearwater had begun, albeit unknowingly, with a classic Slav Defence, and after a break for further recuperation, the time was right for the doctor to play his next move. If he was to use the analogy of chess, Quill was to shift his knight towards Clearwater's rook, but to complete the move and secure his advantage, a piece must be sacrificed. Quill's knight would make the move that brought into play a pawn ignorant of the tactic, and this man would be the one to take out the rook. The knight already knew the strategy, but the move would only become clear to the pawn, and more importantly, to Clearwater, when the rook fell, and that would happen during the much-publicised Larkspur Easter dinner.

The second game would be won.

Satisfied, Quill threw down the newspaper, sighed contentedly, and closed his eye to picture the humiliation. Beyond the window, seagulls cawed, tugs chugged, and an arriving steamer sounded its shrill whistle. The smell of the sea pervaded his room, bringing with it the sound of the South Eastern Railway delivering passengers to the cross-channel steamer. The ship was scheduled to depart on the night-time tide at an hour when Quill's misshapen appearance would cause less alarm to fellow passengers, and when he could slip into his berth without being recognised; not an easy feat for a man described in court reports as, 'Of a monstrous appearance.'

The hate and derision would be behind him once he reached France, and by the time he arrived in Rotterdam, everything about England would be forgotten; everything apart from Clearwater and their game.

He laughed excitedly, but as if the hotel didn't allow jollity, was immediately silenced by a knock at the door.

'Wait!' he called.

Sucking back saliva, he adjusted his pigskin mask to cover the most obvious of his facial disfigurements, righted himself in the chair, and called for his visitor to enter.

The man was as Quill remembered him; elegant, dark and with eyes that mesmerised. If he was to add a cape and top hat, he could well pass for a stage magician, but Quill had not contacted him to perform a parlour trick. His knight was far more skilled, and far too important for that.

'Dorjan,' he said, making the pretence of trying to stand.

'No, please, Doctor, stay as you are,' the man replied as he approached. 'No need for such formalities between friends.'

'Colleagues,' Quill corrected. 'I have no friends. Sit.'

Throwing his coat over the back of a chair, Dorjan did as instructed.

'May I say that you have improved since last we met, Doctor?' Dorjan said.

'You may, but it would not be true. Although I admit, some scars are healing both physically and within.' Quill reached for the decanter on the nearby table. 'But such things as pouring wine must still be done with care... No! There is no need to assist me. Not with this simple task.'

He filled two crystal glasses and having replaced the decanter with a trembling hand, cautiously lifted a glass and passed it to the man opposite.

Dorjan thanked him, and having swirled the liquid and sniffed its bouquet, they clinked their glasses before sipping. The flavour of the blood-red liquid brought a smile of admiration to the visitor's face.

'You found a Golden Mediasch,' he said, impressed.

'I am a man who keeps his promises, Dorjan.' Quill swirled the wine once more. 'I promised you this as I promised you your revenge, and as I promise you again, no-one will suspect. That is, as long as you are still prepared to follow my instructions to the letter.'

Dorjan put down his glass. 'Not wanting to appear sceptical,' he said, 'I must ask you to swear me my security once more. I am sure you understand.'

Quill nodded carefully, a gesture which involved moving his left shoulder as well as his head as the two were fused by a hideous burn.

'You said you had concerns, and I appreciate you taking the time to travel down to see me before I leave,' Quill said. 'As you know, mobility is no longer my forte. I will need all my strength for the journey ahead, as you will need to summon your deepest resolve to play your part.'

'I am more than resolved to see this through for my bloodline and my own satisfaction.'

'And yet you are anxious.' Quill shifted in his seat, grimacing. He suffered little pain, and his mobility was as good as it was ever going to be, but the pretence had to be maintained if he wanted to keep Dorjan's sympathy. 'Tell me, what troubles you?'

The man took another sip of wine, it was too good to leave aside for long. 'It leaves a bitter, but not unpleasant sting on the tongue. Will it taste exactly like this when served?'

'I am certain of that,' the doctor replied. 'I am a man of science. You are still in possession of the watch?'

Dorjan tapped the base of his glass against the fob chain hanging from his waistcoat, and Quill nodded. 'Next?'

'The man I will meet,' Dorjan said. 'You remain sure of his loyalty?'

'If correctly bought, yes. The purchase is down to you. I have told you his weakness, and I have done my research. The timing is right, and a great deal of money is owed. Once a man starts on the path to gambling, there is no leaving it, and certainly not for a man like him. I have known him for a few years, I have witnessed him at the tables, and I have never seen a man so skilled in trickery lose so habitually. He, like your victim, can see no further than his own vanity.'

Reassured, Dorjan took another sip. 'Victim.' The word rolled from his tongue on a carpet of Romanian accent, the second syllable tumbling as it fell. 'It has a delicious ring to it.'

'As does revenge, and you shall have yours.'

'I demand mine,' Dorjan's tone changed. His lips drew back, displaying straight, sharp teeth as he seethed. 'For what he plans to write and say about my people, for what he has already written and said, there is no other outcome possible.'

'I see the fire in your eyes, colleague, but dampen it,' Quill warned. 'You must keep your head level, no matter what comes, and you must stay married to the plan. Be calm, but be cautious. There will be others there who have enquiring minds. Clearwater has drawn men to him who are unknown to me. Men of courage and loyalty. Trust none of them but the one I have mentioned.'

'I understand, Doctor, but...' The visitor paused, anger quelled by lingering anxiety.

'The boy?'

'The boy,' Dorjan agreed. 'Necessary?'

'An insurance against the unforeseen.' Quill again shifted in his seat, this time to check the time on the mantle clock. 'I must prepare,' he said. 'But before we part, yes, the boy is important.

10

Should the gambler fail you, you will have a second stab at revenge, but he will not fail, and nor will you. This matter is too deeply driven into your heart to allow it. I am wrong?'

'You are not, Sir.'

'Then it will come to pass as we have arranged. Trust in me, Dorjan. Your duty will be fulfilled and your oath as *Protectori ai Szekely* will remain untainted. More, you will revel in its glory, having prevented the unthinkable. I am correct?'

'Always, Doctor. The Protectori and I thank you.'

'You can save your thanks until we meet in Rotterdam. Take the boy, put the man in play, and attend our meeting. There will be no need to stay and see the deed done, not once our pawn is aligned. Now, if you have no other concerns, we should toast our trust, and prepare for our journeys and our vengeance.'

The tapping of their glasses rang out like the most delicate of death knells.

'To trust and vengeance,' Quill said. '*Yia buyatul shi uchideh tatal.*'

'I shall do just that.' Dorjan grinned, before draining his glass and crushing it in his hand.

Two

E ven in his sleep, Silas knew something was wrong. Whatever dream he had been having scuttled to the darker recesses of his mind, scared away by the knowledge that he was alone, and the man who should have been beside him was no longer there.

He opened his eyes to the silvery glow of the mirror above the fireplace, and below it in the grate, a pile of grey embers behind the guard. The air was scented with woodsmoke and clean linen, thinly veiling traces of his lover. He reached behind to find Archer's hand, intending to pull his arm around his chest, to nestle into the security of his presence and be comforted back to sleep.

There was no hand and no lover, just a crumpled, warm sheet and a disrupted eiderdown.

When he rolled to face where Archer should have been, he saw only the clock by the light of the faltering candle. Four in the morning. The darkest hour.

Shadows painted the room. From the uneven landscape of the bed to the oak posters that guarded its corners, from the dead fireplace to the spectral glow of the looking glass, everything was dappled with a grey ghostliness. In the shifting candlelight, the corner of the wardrobe became a mountain peak projected onto the bathroom door, itself a four-panelled patchwork of uncertain furrows and highlighted mouldings, while table legs were cast like railway tracks across the floor.

A more stable light came from beyond the window where Archer stood naked in silhouette looking out across the moor.

'What's up?' Silas asked through a yawn.

He wasn't sure if he had been woken by the chime of the stable clock or Archer's absence, but he suspected the latter. It wasn't uncommon to wake and find the viscount had snuck back to his adjoining bedroom in the early hours to avoid discovery.

A powerful arm beckoned him to the window, and Silas obeyed. He collected the viscount's dressing gown on his way, his bare feet sinking into the carpet, warmed by it and reassured. Holding Archer from behind, he delighted in the feel of his broad chest and the press of his naked back, and kissed his neck before offering the dressing gown.

Archer took it but didn't put it on. 'Quill is out there,' he said. 'Four months, no word, and now, through a dream, I know he watches us.'

Silas shivered. 'Don't trouble yourself.'

'Listen.' Archer cocked his head. 'What do you hear?'

Silas heard nothing except the beating of their hearts, but reluctantly letting his lover go, he stood beside him and peered into the platinum night.

'I hear Thomas nagging that you'll catch cold,' he said. 'What is it?'

'I thought I heard…' Archer held up a finger as if he was expecting the sound to come again. It didn't. 'I thought it came from beyond the tower. Across the moor. Beyond the railway line.'

'What did?'

'Screaming. It woke me, or it may have been in my dream. It's strange…' He faltered until Silas took his hand. 'I was expecting it before it came as if someone spoke and told me to wake. I heard first the clock, and a short while after, screams.' His voice was hushed, as though he was talking from within his dreaming.

'From behind the tower?' Silas humoured him. 'Out on the moor?'

'Yes. Faint, very faint. And the bell…'

Silas took back the gown and hung it over Archer's shoulders. He put an arm around his waist and held him close, his fingers playing along the half-moon scar that ran from Archer's chest to his groin.

'What about the bell?'

His lover's gaze remained on the silent scene, his sad eyes dark beneath their brows. Wandering in his thoughts, Archer struggled to express a painful memory.

'Becalmed on the Black Sea,' he said, his voice far away. 'Coming up to six bells, three in the morning. A night like this with a weakening moon. We had been fog-bound for two days. It was the

13

second night and my watch. Quill was with me, and Hawley, we had midshipmen about, but no-one spoke. Nothing stirred. No rigging hissed, the jack hung limp, the ensign hushed. Not a breath of wind nor sigh of wave.'

A blink brought back an unsettling image, and he cradled Silas beneath his shoulder.

'When six bells was rung, all of us to a man made a jolt. We had been transfixed by the padding of the fog, it pressed on our chests as if to smother us, and yet we could breathe... The chimes echoed only briefly, the sound dulled by vapour. The ring was... funereal, and as it died, so it left behind a certainty. I knew what was to happen next.'

His hand unconsciously moved to Silas' head where his fingers curled thick, black hair.

'I felt it before we heard it. A vibration from the inside out. My breathing was crushed, but I was suddenly alert. It was wrong, the order of the sounds. The bell, a scream and then a gunshot immediately followed by cannon.' A shudder, and he was more awake. 'Sorry,' he said, his voice more assured. 'I was drifting. I expect I heard fox in the grounds.'

'Are you feeling alright?'

Archer took Silas in his arms and pressed their lips together. 'I was only dreaming.'

'About seeing things before they happen?'

'Feeling them before they happen.' Archer looked back to the moor, listening. 'Something's not right.'

'You want me to ring for James? Get Fecker to go and look?'

'No, no. Nothing like that. Just a feeling.'

'Right, well, if you're sure. It's cold, and it's four o'clock in the fecking morning.'

Silas led him back to bed and pulled the eiderdown tightly around their entwined bodies. Archer fell asleep within seconds, but Silas lay staring at the monochrome ceiling, his thoughts unsettled. Dreaming or not, Archer had been right about one thing. Quill was out there somewhere, and he had left them alone for long enough. While Archer dreamt of the past, Quill would surely be dreaming up something for their future.

Three months had passed since Silas first set foot in Larkspur. He had arrived on Christmas Eve after a long journey that began the previous October. When he thought about everything that had happened since Thomas walked into The Ten Bells in Greychurch and invited him to meet a viscount, his mind was unable to take it in. At least, not in one continuous thought. Playing each moment separately was the only way of keeping perspective. Flirting with Thomas and then meeting Archer, the world standing still as he realised something deeper than physical attraction drew them together. The business with the Ripper, being held at knife-point, the incident with the runaway train, the opera house, and then his time in gaol, it was too much at times, and he had to shake himself to break free of the past and look forward.

Christmas had been the best he remembered, but then it could be no other way considering that, until then, he had spent each one hungry and cold, alone apart from Fecker. Not only did it bring the gift of Archer's love and the freedom of his estate, but Silas came to the house to find Fecker alive and, although injured, well. Then Archer had given him something he could never have imagined. The viscount and Fecker had rescued Silas' twin sisters from more than poverty and given them employment not only at Larkspur but in Silas' own suite of rooms, conveniently joined to those of his lover. With his good friend James as his valet and assistant, there could be nothing better, and Silas' life was set on a course for... For...

'That's the thing, though, isn't it?' he said later that morning, again staring from his window to the moors that rolled into the distant mist. 'What am I doing?'

James, behind him and brushing his collar, said, 'You're living, mate, that's what counts. And you're living free.'

'Yeah,' Silas agreed. 'And that's my problem. I'm living for free. I ain't doing anything for Archie, nor for the estate. I ain't got any skills other than mimicking folk and being cheeky like I'm some kind of music hall turn. You've got a job, you have a purpose, you're alright.'

'I am, and I can't deny it,' James said, putting down the soft-bristled brush. 'Turn around?'

Silas did as asked, and James was content with his appearance.

'I got to have something to do, Jimmy.' Silas collected the brush and attended to James' suit.

There was no need for him to tidy his friend's clothes, and in any case, it was the valet's job, not the master's, but Silas was not a master. He never called himself one, and the ritual was purely to remind Jimmy that despite the roles they had to play in public, they were equals.

'What do you want to do?' James asked, straightening an arm so Silas could check the sleeve. 'You've been learning to ride and fence, that's something.'

'Yeah, Fecks and Danny have got me on a bloody horse without me falling off, but...' He sighed. 'Life was a lot easier before I met Archer.'

'What? Renting on the streets of the East End was easier than living here?' James' hazel eyes were wide in mock horror. 'You'd rather be doing that?'

'I'd rather be doing something other than sitting around reading books and being nice to posh people,' Silas moaned. 'There, you'll do.' He replaced the brush on the dressing table and returned to the window. 'Don't get me wrong, Jimmy, I love being here, and no, I don't want to go back to my old life, who would? But I do miss the...' The word evaded him.

'Sex?' James suggested as he stood shoulder to shoulder admiring the infinite view.

'Dirty git,' Silas chuckled. 'No, I get plenty of that with Archie, and it's completely different. No, I miss the thrill, I suppose. Not knowing what's coming next, who you're going to meet, how you're going to survive. I had a purpose then, see? Staying alive, mainly, but now? I feel like a spare prick at a whore's wedding.'

James put his arm around the shorter man and gave him a squeeze, something that would never happen in any other noble house. 'Tell him then, mate,' he said. 'Tell Archer you're bored and see what he comes up with.'

'I don't want to sound ungrateful, and I don't want him to think I'm only here to be his plaything either.'

'You are far more than that, and you know it. What you don't know is what to do with yourself.' They took a breath together as below on the lawn, a crow disturbed the mist and broke the

16

morning with its caw. 'You miss the excitement, don't you?' James prompted. 'We've not heard from Quill since the courtroom.'

'Don't remind me,' Silas moaned. Despite the memories of the cell, the beating and the humiliation, he managed a smile. 'But yeah, I do miss all that, not that I want him to rear his deformed head anytime soon, but I've got to have something to do, Jimmy.'

'Leave it with me, Sir,' James said, releasing Silas and standing to attention. 'I will think on it.'

'Cheers, mate.' Silas kissed him on the cheek, something else than would never happen between a viscount's secretary and his valet, probably not in any house let alone a stately one, but they were the closest of companions, and their friendship had always been gilded with attraction. Attraction that was never allowed to boil over into anything other than the occasional peck, a hug or light-hearted, verbal flirting. They both understood the rules.

'And your plans for this morning?' James asked as he collected Silas' pyjamas and draped them over his arm.

'Going for a wander,' Silas replied. 'Maybe see Fecks. I don't know. Stuff.'

He paused at the door. Although they were in Silas' private suite of rooms, there was no telling who was on the other side, and there were many secrets the servants were not to know.

Opening the door, Silas said, 'Thank you, Mr Wright, that will be all.'

'Sir,' James replied as he bowed his head.

They winked at each other, and Silas stepped into the gentleman's corridor, turning right towards the main stairs. If he turned left, he would come to the end of the passage and a stone arch; the entrance to the tower. The building rambled in a 'patchwork of styles,' as Archer called it, and on more than one occasion Silas had become lost in its passages, galleries and stairways.

One night, Archer had asked Thomas to bring a set of children's building blocks from the attic. They had been Archer's when he was a child, and as with so many other things in the house, they had never been thrown away. He had used them to build a rough layout of the estate as a way of helping Silas orientate himself to the property. Two long bricks either side of an arch represented the south façade that faced the inland moor, one up-ended brick for the west tower, and at the other end, another long brick at right angles for the east wing. Behind and below the house were a jumble of smaller wooden pieces, the kitchens and below-stairs rooms leading to a back yard and the dairy, the icehouse and the machine room. Beside them the kitchen gardens were laid out, and a plot of land now farmed by Fecker's brother, Danylo. To the west, behind the tower and beyond another jumble of blocks, were the stables, Fecker's coach house, the groom's quarters and stable-boys' rooms. The north lawn descended to the ruined abbey and its graveyard, and around it, more ruined walls where stones had been robbed out to build an extension to the house. Every viscount over the centuries had added something to the original hall; a wing, improved kitchens, a new paddock or a cottage, and even Archer, only elevated to the title eight months previously, had installed hot water and baths for not only the upstairs, but also for the servants. He had plans to electrify the property as soon as his company could address the work.

Until then, the house was lit by gas and warmed by fireplaces, though there was always some part of a corridor or room where the cold wind whistled. The central, medieval hall, although splendid with its crested ceiling and chandeliers, was permanently chilly, unless a party was arranged in which case the maids set the fire and Barnaby attended it while candelabras helped warm the stonework.

Silas descended to the hall, taking the men's stairs and arriving on the flagstone floor, where his leather shoes clicked as he doubled back to reach the breakfast room, trailing his hand over the stone pillars, as he threaded through them to the passage.

Archer had eaten and gone, Saddle informed him as he entered. The under-butler stood smart and attentive in his uniform, guarding the sideboard where various dishes were being kept warm, and where Barnaby, the recently appointed footman, waited in silence.

'Do you know where he's gone?' Silas enquired.

'To the village, Sir,' Saddle replied, turning to check the heat of the coffee pot. 'Just five minutes ago.'

'Thanks,' Silas said, making his selection from the dishes. 'How are things with you?'

It wasn't that he particularly liked Saddle, it seemed no-one at Larkspur did, it was that Silas was keen for conversation and

18

without Archer, there was no-one else to talk to.

'With me, Sir?' The under-butler managed to make the question sound like an outrage. 'All is well, thank you.'

'You, Barnaby?'

'Thank you, Mr Hawkins, aye.' Barnaby was a Cornishman. After ten years as a hall boy, Archer had promoted him to footman. Thomas had trained him well, but he had trouble controlling his accent.

'The reply is, "Yes, Sir,"' Saddle corrected, annoyed. 'Apologies, Mr Hawkins.'

Silas waved it away and winked at Barnaby. 'Be there a newspaper, Mis'r Barney?' he asked, copying the young man's accent to annoy Saddle just for the craic.

Saddle nodded sharply to the footman and then at a newspaper on the sideboard before announcing, 'If you will excuse me...' He strutted from the room, and the footman delivered the broadsheet to Silas as he sat.

'The usual stuff, I imagine,' Silas muttered as Barnaby poured his coffee. 'Court matters, farming disputes... Oh, I see we have a local branch of this new society.'

'Sir?'

'The Plumage League,' Silas read. 'Apparently, it's an organisation campaigning against the use of bird feathers in women's clothing. What do you think of that, Barney?'

It wasn't that Silas was interested, he was just lonely.

'I've not read it, Sir,' the footman replied. 'But it sounds absorbing.'

It wasn't. Silas turned to the City news section. 'Ah, I see they're opening a new theatre in town later this month,' he said. 'The Garrick. Oh, and someone called Dunlop has invented a tyre for bicycles. That'll keep the messenger boys happy.'

'I heard it's a success,' Barnaby said, standing back to guard over Mr Hawkins as he ate.

Silas put the newspaper aside and picked at his scrambled eggs. Beside him at the head of the table, Archer's place had been cleared, and there was nothing else to see in the room apart from its lavish furnishings and paintings he had inspected a hundred times. Outside, the sky was a dull grey, and although not as cold as it had been of late, the scene was still a desolate one. The back of the house afforded a view of the moors rolling down towards the sea, distant but discernible on sunnier days. Away to the west the village of Larkspur was hidden by the rolling countryside.

'Do you know what His Lordship is doing in the village?'

'Aye, Sir,' Barnaby replied, apparently shocked to have been addressed. 'Sorry. Yes, Sir. Only he ain't in the village. He's over at the dower house with Mr Harrow. Something about repairs. He'll be back dreckly. I mean, soon.'

'Barney,' Silas smiled. 'I don't mind how you speak to me, as long as you don't mind me calling you Barney.'

'I don't, Sir, but Mr Saddle doesn't like it.'

It was probably best not to confess that Silas didn't care what the under-butler thought, nor was it correct to say what a ridiculous name the man had. He liked Barnaby and didn't want to embarrass him. Plain speaking and the same age as Silas, he was a cheerful, grateful young man, far less serious than his new position allowed. 'What about Mr Payne?' he asked instead.

'Mr Payne addresses me as Barnaby, Sir.'

'Then I shall try and do the same. Where is he?'

'Mr Payne took the early train to Plymouth, Sir. He's ordered a special wine for the Easter dinner come Friday.'

'Ah yes,' Silas remembered, reaching for the newspaper again. 'It was going to be mentioned in here, wasn't it?'

'Page seven, Sir. I saw it when I were ironing it. When I was ironing it.'

'You'll get the hang of it.' Silas slipped into his natural, Irish accent. 'Sure, it took me a time to cover me accent, but you can't hide the blarney, Barney.'

The footman stifled a snigger. 'Will there be anything else, Sir?'

'No, you're okay. You get on with whatever you've got to do. I'm going to read this.'

'Right you are... Very good, My... Sir.'

'Take a breath, Barnaby,' Silas laughed. 'Remember Mr Payne's rule.'

'Stop, take stock and start again. Right you... Very good, Sir.'

Silas winked and tipped his head to the door. Barnaby returned the good humour with a grateful grin before straightening it and his back, bowing and leaving the room.

The new footman had lifted Silas' mood, for which he was grateful, and he turned to page seven with a sigh of contentment. Friday, Archer had said, was to be the most important dinner he had ever hosted, personally and professionally. If it was the success he craved, the Clearwater Foundation would secure further patronage and not just from Archer's close friends, as it now enjoyed, but from some of the leading lights of the stage and arts.

Silas began to read.

The Cornishman, Monday, April 17th, 1889
Larkspur Hall to Host Glittering Dinner

It has been some months since Larkspur Hall, the country home of the Viscounts Clearwater since 1450, has played host to a society dinner, but all that is to change this coming Easter Friday.

Following the death of the 18th Viscount last year, the Hall rested in mourning until December, and to his credit, the current incumbent, has not been hasty in hosting a celebration, no doubt in deference to his late father, a great supporter of the Bodmin and Larkspur schools, hospital and St Peran's Church, Larkspur village.

Residents of Bodmin and the surrounding area will have known the new viscount as the Honourable Archer Riddington, second son of Mathias, Lord Clearwater, and will know that he was elevated to the title on the sad incarceration of his older brother, the first son and heir, Crispin Riddington, now in a private institution in The Netherlands. What readers may not yet be aware of, however, is the new Lord Clearwater's fascination with and support for the arts.

His Lordship has, since the death of his father, spent much of his time in the Capital, but it has not been time wasted. His first grand project was to devise The Clearwater Foundation, a charity specifically to assist underprivileged men of the city's East End. The charity was officially launched at a spectacular gala at the Royal Opera House last November, a glittering event which the King of The Netherlands saw worthy enough to grace with his presence.

That evening's great success no doubt spurred His Lordship to the further raising of funds for the charity which continues to thrive in its work among the lower classes. As we know, funds are hard to come by, especially for such an unusual and, some say, socially daring endeavour, but it appears the 'Litterati' are of a different opinion.

Anyone passing through the village of Larkspur this coming Friday may be forgiven for imagining themselves on the streets of Bloomsbury or even Covent Garden itself, for, as The Cornishman has learned, a small, but important gathering of our country's finest are invited to the Hall for the Friday to Sunday, the pinnacle of which will be a dinner complete with a guest of honour.

Those invited to attend are: Lady Marshall the Viscountess Delamere (His Lordship's godmother), her nephew, Mr Cadwell Roxton, the shining star of last year's Foundation gala, Sir Arthur Sullivan, the Earl and Countess Romney and the poet laureate, Baron Tennyson of Aldworth and Freshwater.

The guest of honour is Henry Irving who, accompanied by his business manager, is returning from a successful tour of America and stopping at Larkspur on his way to a command performance (with Miss Ellen Terry), for Her Majesty at Sandringham. No doubt he and Mr Sullivan will have much to discuss, as the composer, still riding the success of 'The Yeoman of the Guard', was responsible for the music for Irving's last season production of Macbeth.

Readers aware of societal convention will have noted that, unlike previous Easter dinners at the Hall, the number of gentlemen guests outnumber the ladies. This is because the gentlemen attending this sumptuous event are all members of the famous Garrick Club, including Lord Clearwater himself.

When we spoke to His Lordship last week, he was keen to stress that the Arts, despite its occasional unconventionality, has always supported the needs of the unfortunate.

"Whether it is in employment," he said, "or the waiving of fees at charitable events, I have always found those involved in theatre, music, poetry and the other aesthetics, great patrons of those whose lives have taken less glamorous turns. Were it not for the outlet of stage, canvas and paper, many of our creatives may have gone the way of the young men of Greychurch whom my Foundation seeks to assist."

Noble words from a noble man indeed, and the sentiment gives us some insight into the mind of our new Lord of the Manor, a man who only turned thirty this March. He has already achieved so much. Since returning from his London season, Larkspur Hall has hosted the Bodmin Moor Hunt in traditional fashion. His Lordship preferred not to ride out, and instead, put in his place his Master of the Horse, a young Russian of some intrigue to the ladies of the village. Also newly appointed to the Hall is Lord Clearwater's private secretary, a man of low Irish descent. We mention this as proof that His Lordship is a man determined, as Viscountess Delamere is quoted as saying, "To put his mouth where his money is." Not only does the second son support the unfortunates through his charitable work, but he has also taken in and employed such men. How many others, we may ask, would be prepared to do such a thing?

Larkspur Hall, now 'under new management' does not only care for the 'Litterati' or the subjects of the Clearwater Foundation, but many of our own local families also benefit. On a more personal and local note, Barnaby Nancarrow, the son of a local farmer was recently promoted to the position of footman; Miss Edith Hammett and Jane Gloyne, both from Bodmin, are now in service there, and the Hall and its three farms on the Larkspur estate continue to employ men and women from the village and its environs.

The New Year saw the arrival of our new viscount, and it seems that change is the way forward, both domestically and in the wider world as Lord Clearwater seeks to bring on board some of our most talented and well-known names who will dine with him on Easter Friday. We expect to see St Peran's Church full on Easter Sunday morning with not only villagers, but also the glittering stars of the city arts scene, and we hope the event will bring much-needed attention and thus income to our area.

Much, then, is riding on the Easter Friday dinner, and not only for our county but for the 19th Viscount Clearwater of Riverside and Larkspur.

Three

Thomas was intrigued by the man travelling with him in second class. He had also boarded at Plymouth, but unlike Thomas, carried no luggage. Whereas Lord Clearwater's butler carried items needed at Larkspur as well as his newspaper and personal shopping, the man on the opposite bench seat appeared to have nothing apart from a pocket watch. This he regularly withdrew and examined as if hoping an hour had passed in the two minutes since he had last noted the time.

The man, dressed for third class and yet sharing the carriage with gentlemen, had chosen to occupy a seat away from the window, suggesting to Thomas that he wasn't a tourist come down to Cornwall to experience the newly opened route to Padstow, but a local traveller who had no need to take in the scenery. He only moved to the window when the train pulled into a station, there to look out and watch the platform until the train pulled out when he returned to sit, his head down. Apart from his watch, he only had eyes for his shoes, scuffed, Thomas noticed, and in need of repair, or at least a stiff brush and polish.

His eccentricities became more apparent as the train gathered speed after leaving Saltash where several new passengers had come aboard. The man, who Thomas guessed to be in his early thirties, shrank into his seat as unfamiliar faces brushed past him, and took a special interest in the lining of his jacket, burying his head to examine the stitching as if he didn't want to be seen.

With every passing station, Thomas became more fascinated by his behaviour and his unusually attractive features. Despite a hooked nose, the man was handsome in a strangely exotic way and had something about him that was hard to place. A feeling of loneliness, perhaps? He gave the impression of being a foreigner, and yet one who understood where he was and knew what he was doing. It was difficult for Thomas to put his finger on it, but there was more about the stranger than his handsomeness and unease.

Glancing surreptitiously so as not to make the stranger any more uncomfortable, Thomas couldn't help but compare him to James. Where his lover was blond, the passenger's hair was dark and unfashionably short at the back, parted in the middle and not well cut. Like James, he had no moustache, but unlike James, he showed evening stubble even though it was only just past one in the afternoon. High cheekbones caused further shadowing of hollow cheeks in a striking and not unhealthy way, his ears were pointed, and everything about him seemed black, from his hair to his mood.

By the time the train pulled in at Liskeard, Thomas was unable to contain his curiosity, and with the nearby seats vacated as passengers alighted, he leant forward and addressed his fellow traveller.

'Excuse the impertinence, Sir,' he said as the stranger put away his watch. 'I couldn't help but notice you seem anxious about the time. I have travelled on this line on many occasions and have never known the Great Western Railway to be late.'

The man said nothing, but returned Thomas' friendly stare with one of mistrust. He shrugged in the manner that Fecker was prone to do and returned his gaze to his feet.

'If your watch is not working,' Thomas continued, undeterred. 'I can tell you the time from mine. It is regularly wound, that being my job.'

The ambiguity of his statement drew the man's attention from his shoes, and he stared at Thomas with dark brown eyes as intense as they were large.

'I am the butler at Larkspur Hall,' Thomas explained. 'Perhaps you know it?' There was no reply, only a look of surprise. 'I'm sorry. I see you want to be left in peace.'

Sitting back, he gave up on a bad job and was opening his newspaper when the man spoke.

'I don't know it,' he said, and glanced behind.

The nearest passengers were several feet away, and the carriage was clanking and swaying on the tracks as if the wheels were anything but round. No-one could hear the conversation, but still, the stranger shuffled forward on his seat and hunched his shoulders.

'Perhaps you could tell me more about it, Sir?' he said. His speech was educated, but thickened by an accent Thomas had not encountered before. It added to his mysteriousness. 'I would be interested to know how such a grand house runs, for it must be grand to have a butler. Are there many staff beneath you? Who lives there? I hear there are great celebrations at Easter on these estates, is that the case at yours?'

They fell into conversation with Thomas answering his questions, proud to speaking from a position of authority. He outlined preparations the forthcoming dinner, his first as the butler, and the conversation rattled along like the carriage. It passed the time, but the man, although interested in the minute details, continued to refer to his watch.

'I had hoped to be at my destination by now,' he admitted when he noticed Thomas' curiosity. 'But I missed the early train and had to wait.'

'Ah, I see,' Thomas smiled back, folding away his paper. 'I hope it wasn't an important meeting.'

'It wasn't a meeting,' the man replied. 'It was…' He thought better of it and sat back.

'Thomas Payne.' Thomas offered his hand.

It was regarded cautiously as if his acquaintance thought it might in some way be dangerous, and he took so long studying it, that Thomas' arm began to ache. Perhaps it was the butler's congeniality or his caring green eyes, but the man opposite unwound his shoulders and took the hand as his otherwise downturned mouth morphed into the briefest of smiles.

'Joshua Smith,' he said. 'Sorry to be a bore.'

'Not at all.'

The hand was smooth on top, but his palm and fingertips were rough. As Thomas greeted him, he couldn't help but notice worn shirt cuffs. Ill-fitting, they showed from beneath the man's jacket which was made of rough wool and broadly stitched, it too didn't quite fit, and one button was missing.

Knowing it impolite to comment, but his curiosity running wild, Thomas asked, 'Are you from Plymouth, Sir?'

'Plymouth? No.'

'From Cornwall?'

Smith shook his head.

'I only ask because you seem uninterested in the scenery, and the climb to the moors is notable for its views, particularly in the spring.' Thomas indicated the window. 'On a clear day, one can see across to St Neot and the moor above.'

'Oh.' Smith could not have been more disinterested. Instead of looking at the view, he again took out his watch.

'It is just gone one fifteen,' Thomas informed him, glancing at his own.

Smith put his away. 'I'm sorry,' he said. 'I am anxious to make my connection, but afraid I may have missed it.'

'Connection?'

'I was told I had to change at Bodmin Road?' The place name was said with a slight rolling of the R among the foreign accent.

'Ah, yes. If you are heading further west.' Thomas produced a hipflask and unscrewed the lid. 'You are unfortunate that this train is the only one per day that extends to Padstow rather than Penzance. You will be further delayed.'

He offered the flask, and Smith regarded it, sucking in his lips as he considered, weighing up his options. If he accepted the drink, he would be entering into a friendship rather than simply chatting with a travelling companion, and apparently it was a big decision.

'You're the butler at Larkspur Hall?' Smith clarified as if accepting a drink from anyone else would be dangerous.

Thomas thought he had ben perfectly clear. 'Yes, Sir. Where His Lordship keeps a fine cellar, but this is whisky. April has not yet brought the warmer west wind. Please, if you are feeling the chill…?'

'Thank you.' Smith accepted, smiling. After a long swig, he gasped and handed it back. 'Gosh, that's rather good.'

'It is, actually.' Thomas moved forward conspiratorially. 'My master has a liking for Scotch and insisted I take this with me. It's not a particularly cold day, but he said it would, if nothing else, relieve the boredom of the journey. It seems he is correct.'

The whisky, or the gesture of offering it, had gone some way to helping Smith relax. 'I need no excuse for a decent Scotch,' he said.

'Nor a fine wine. I expect you know a lot about wine, being a butler.'

'I currently know as much as I need to,' Thomas replied. 'But not as much as I would like. I am returning from an expedition to procure a special crate of Purcari Dragasani for His Lordship. Like the Golden Mediasch his ancestors laid down, it is Romanian and very rare, but my victualler had it imported, and I went to check its resting.'

Smith said nothing for a long while, but his murky eyes remained fixed on Thomas as though looking through him to an imagined other place beyond.

When he realised he was staring, he said, 'I have heard of this Mediasch,' and Thomas had never heard the word pronounced in such an accomplished manner. 'He is fond of red wine?'

'As most men are, but the wine in question isn't for him. The Romanian wines are the favourite of his guest of honour. The Mediasch is to be a special surprise.'

'I am sure it will be,' Smith said. 'And who is the guest with such lavish taste?'

Thomas didn't want to say too much to a man he didn't know, but did allow him a snippet. 'One of the country's most acclaimed actors on his way back from a tour overseas.'

It was enough. 'I see.'

Smith lost interest, and Thomas changed the subject. 'Is this your first visit to Cornwall?'

'Yes. Are you also new to the area?'

The answer confirmed that Smith was not local, and Tom wondered again about his accent. It hid behind a veil of well-spoken English such as Archer might speak, but was not as clipped or polished.

'Not exactly,' Thomas replied. 'I was born in Kent. I moved to the city and into service when I was eight. Since then, I have been regularly at Larkspur and in the city. His Lordship has two houses. Rather, he uses two houses, the others are tenanted.'

It was a lot to share with a stranger, but the more they spoke, the more intrigued Thomas became, and the friendlier Smith appeared. Another sip each from the hipflask helped loosen tongues further.

'His Lordship is who?' Smith asked. 'If that's not a rude question.'

'Not at all.' Thomas replied. The man's mood had transformed from silent and concerned to talkative, and he adopted manners and a tone that suggested breeding. Not the highest breeding judging by his clothes, but at least some. 'My master is Viscount Clearwater.'

Referring to his best friend as his master was easy. It was just a word, a title, a form of address. They had grown up together, and despite the divide in status, had been inseparable since they were young.

'Clearwater? Not a name I am likely to know,' Smith said. 'And where exactly is Larkspur Hall?'

'About three miles from Bodmin, where I leave the train. It sits high on the moor and faces across to the sea to the north. You should be able to see it once the train leaves Bodmin Road station if you care to look.'

Smith swept his hand through his hair on one side, pulling it back from its parting before his other hand did the same on the other side. Another mild eccentricity, Thomas noted, and pointless because his hair fell back into exactly the place it had been before being disturbed.

'I don't care for travel much,' Smith said.

'You fear the railways? They have come a long way in terms of safety since they began.'

'Oh, no, it's not that. I find I suffer from motion sickness if I am too close to the window.'

The carriage rocked as the locomotive picked up speed. It was not as well sprung as the first-class compartments and not as comfortable, but was luxury compared to third. There, open to the elements and provided only with wooden benches, the passengers huddled tightly together for warmth. Second class rattled and vibrated, but at least there were windows to keep out the soot, and thin padding on the seats. Archer insisted that his staff travelled in second, even the maids. If a journey was needed, he would pay fares from his own pocket. He would have had Thomas in first if he had his way, but sometimes the butler had to put his foot down when it came to what was appropriate.

'Motion sickness can't be a pleasant experience,' he sympathised and offered the last of the Scotch, which was accepted. 'Finish it,' he said. 'I shouldn't be drinking it anyway.'

'Your master sounds very liberal,' Smith commented. 'Giving his servants his whisky.' The smile had returned.

'He insisted. It's up to me whether I drink it or not.'

'Quite.'

'Tell me, Mr Smith, as we're getting along so well...'

Thomas was about to query the man's accent when it occurred to him that the vibration of the carriage had now become a shake. The planked floor trembled, sending shockwaves into his feet, and looking from the window, he was confused to see the bushes and trees passing at an ever-increasing speed.

'Is something wrong?' Smith asked, sensing Thomas' unease.

'Something is unusual,' Thomas replied. When Smith appeared not to understand, he added, 'We're approaching Bodmin Road. We should be slowing down when, in fact...'

Other passengers had noticed the anomaly, and several had moved to the windows in the hope of understanding the reason. Their conversation, until then barely audible, could clearly be heard over the rattle and creaks as voices were raised in concern.

'Perhaps it's gaining momentum for an incline?' Smith suggested.

If that was the case, it was the first time Thomas had experienced such a thing on this part of the line. There was no reason for the driver to push the locomotive so hard.

The carriage jolted with a screech of metal on metal, and the whistle blasted like a scream of horror, but the station flew past in a blur, the brakes impotent against the momentum.

'Good Lord,' Smith said. 'Sir, you have turned pale.'

'This isn't right.' Thomas spoke more to himself than the man opposite. He peered through the glass to see as far up the track as he could, but the train was approaching a bend, and he could see nothing but the chimney smoke and fast-passing foliage. 'I don't like this,' he said, returning to his seat.

'Are we in danger?'

With the curve tipping the carriage, and the locomotive cresting the hill at full tilt, the answer was yes.

Smith could see it in his eyes. 'What should we do?' he asked, blanching.

'If I were a religious man, I would suggest praying. Stay in your seat and hold on.' Thomas rooted himself to the bench.

30

With his body trembling, and his heart pumping faster than the engine's pistons, he broke into a sweat. Somehow, he knew and expected what was to happen next, and the realisation came with a mix of fear and sadness. This was not how he expected his life to end, and he had left the Hall without saying goodbye to Archer.

The carriage tipped to the left, throwing several standing passengers against others, and the whistle blasted more urgently. Wheels hit the tracks with a metallic screech before the car bounced the other way with such force it threw people off their feet and Thomas from the bench. He was suspended in the air for a second before landing with a crash. Someone pulled the communication cord, but it made no difference.

Wheels thundered, the whistle shrieked, and a man tried to open the door.

'Am eşuat!' Smith swore and crossed himself. 'Will it slow down?'

'If it doesn't,' Thomas shouted over the cacophony. 'We're going to come off the...'

Four

Archer returned from his estate work, and having changed, left the Hall through the tower to step into a gloriously transparent afternoon. The sky was an endless wash of pale blue above the granite stables beyond the yard, and gravel crunched satisfyingly beneath his feet as he crossed the path, the sound dying when he reached the grassy slope. Heading downhill, the ruined abbey came into view, its plinths, all that was left of the once-grand nave, forming two lines either side of a flat strip of green. Broken walls and half-arches threw shadows across the grass, and the remnants of the great east window framed the horizon. Where once had been stained glass, the tracing now outlined faraway hedges, stone walls and the April sky.

Two figures danced in what was once the aisle, and the closer Archer came, the more he could hear their voices. A call of 'Allez!', the click of steel on steel, and the swish of foils through the air greeted him as he paused at the bottom of the slope to watch.

Silas was unmistakable. Less coordinated than his adversary, and much less skilled, he managed only the occasional touch with the tip of his foil. His left arm flailed where the other man's was steady and raised, and Silas seemed more intent on dodging his opponent than offering a parry. They circled each other, but the instructor was more nimble on his feet. It was clear from his actions that he was an expert with a sword, and had this been a real fight, would have cut Silas down within seconds.

'Recover!' the man called from beneath his mask, and they broke apart.

A warm wash of happiness came over Archer as he lowered himself to the grass, as yet unobserved. Tucking his knees to his chest, he watched as a second bout began.

The click and metallic tapping faded into the sounds of moorland birds as wheatears chirped and a crow cawed distantly. Archer rested his chin on his knees to admire the skilled swordsman, and remembered their meeting.

Due to bad weather in the Bay of Biscay, the Firebrand had docked at Plymouth later than expected. Forced to seek shelter at La Rochelle, it had waited out repairs following a violent storm, and once made seaworthy, had limped under sail around Brest before crossing the English Channel. When news of its arrival came to Larkspur, Archer, barely able to contain his enthusiasm, called for Fecker.

'The ship is here, Andrej,' he said. 'All is well, and my man has put your brother up at the Minerva Inn. He is waiting for you.'

The look on Fecker's face was worth every penny of what it cost Archer to arrange the journey. It wasn't that the viscount liked to make men cry, but in Fecker's case, it was an unusual sight, and one which reassured Archer that despite his strength and size, the Ukrainian was human.

'I sorry,' Fecker said, wiping his eye. 'I am happy.'

'I know, Andrej.' Archer put a hand on the man's shoulder. 'I am only sorry we couldn't locate the rest of your family.'

Fecker held him with his vibrant blue stare, studying Archer as he prepared a question. That day, his hair had been tied back in its customary fashion, but there was no plaiting. In his work clothes, he appeared as any other stable labourer or working man, but Archer knew him to be so much more than that.

'I say something now.' Fecker cleared his throat and looked around the room.

'Would you like to sit?'

They were in the library, the longest room on the ground floor with a swirling staircase up to the gallery. Every wall space was filled with books, few of which Archer had read, and overhead, two chandeliers hung like glass clouds waiting to rain light on the Turkish carpets when night fell.

'No,' Fecker said. 'I not clean.'

He had taken off his boots, for which Archer was grateful (he suspected that Thomas had insisted), and the Ukrainian's socks were not the cleanest. Like his hands and everything else about him, his feet were unusually large.

'Then what do you want to say?' Archer prompted. 'Because I have something to say to you before you go to fetch him.'

'I say this.' Fecker was known for using as few words as possible. 'We not find sister and mother...'

'We will keep looking.'

'Shush.' He also didn't like to be interrupted. 'Maybe we never find, but Danylo is come...' He blinked back more tears. 'But he is not all my family.'

'I know,' Archer said. 'But I have a man on the case in Sevastopol. After there, he will try Odessa...'

'No,' Fecker shook his head. 'I mean, Danylo is not all my family.'

'You said.' Archer was confused.

Fecker screwed up his eyes and took a deep breath. When he next looked at the viscount, it was directly and with his chin raised, sincerity boring down his long, regal nose.

'You are my family,' he said, and before Archer could react, added, 'I understand. I only working man for you. I know my place. Bolshoydick and Missis Pekar tell me, but I want that you know, Sir Chysta Voda, you are my family.'

That seemed to be the end of the speech, and it was touching, even though Fecker had referred to Thomas as 'Massive-Cock' and Archer as Sir Clear Water. Archer allowed — no, liked — the unusual use of words that Fecker employed, but he wasn't sure that Mrs Baker would be happy if she knew he called her Pekar. It might have been a literal translation of her name, but it sounded rude.

'That's very kind of you, Andrej,' he smiled. 'I'm not sure how we might be related, but I also think of you as much more than my horseman. My Master of the Horse is not a noble enough title for you, but it is all I have. Now...'

He was suddenly crushed in a bear hug and pulled to his tiptoes as Fecker landed a kiss on his forehead. If anyone in Archer's circle of friends or his servants had seen, they might have feared for his safety, but Archer had come to know Fecker well and quickly. Although he didn't show it and had never said so, he was beginning to think of the younger man as a protective, older friend.

'Bringing Danylo here is the least I can do for you,' the viscount gasped. 'We must find out what he wants to do, as in, be in the

34

stables with you, or work in the house, or even not live here at all. But we can…' He was still being held captive. 'You may let me go now, Andrej.'

'Sorry.'

'Thank you. We can look at those details when you return. For now…' He handed Fecker an envelope. 'In here is the address of the inn. You can show it to people when you get to the port and ask for directions. And this is a letter from me in case anyone questions who you are, or who Danylo is. Would you rather travel by railway, or take one of the carriages?'

'I ride Thunder.'

Thunder was a large horse and strong, but it was January, and although the blizzards that had plagued the country the previous December had faded, the temperature had remained low ever since.

'You could, but you will be more comfortable on the train, and then you will need to bring your brother back, and he'll need a mount, so that's complicated. I would advise the train. Williams can drive you to the station. Here's money for the fare, and for the inn.'

'I pay.' Fecker said, refusing the notes.

'No. This was my Christmas present to you.' Archer pushed it into his hand. 'And we will say no more about it. Go and pack, and I'll have Thomas ask Williams to be ready.'

'I love you.'

'Honestly, Andrej,' Archer said, stepping back from the threat of another crushing hug. 'For a fellow who prefers women, you do an awful lot of hugging and kissing of other men.'

Fecker smiled a goofy grin full of teeth. 'Is because you are brother,' he said, taking a step forward and not taking no for an answer.

'Well, alright, but then go and…'

The last words were squeezed from him with his breath, but Archer relished the contact and hugged the Ukrainian in return. Not because he found Fecker sexually attractive, but because he appreciated the friendship. Such manly embraces had been missing from his childhood, as had the word love, and he took every opportunity to enjoy them now he was an adult.

'There,' he said, with an air of finality. 'Be ready in an hour, and return by Monday or I shall worry.'

Fecker returned on Monday bringing Danylo with him. Apparently, there had been much celebrating and drinking over the two days he was in Plymouth. Two brothers reunited after ten years of thinking the other was dead was a good reason to drink vodka for forty-eight hours straight. Luckily, they were both recovered and sober when Danylo was presented to the viscount.

He was not what Archer had expected.

'You must riposte.' His voice was deep and commanding, and the shout brought Archer back to the grassy bank and the sight of his lover's fencing lesson. 'Show me again. En garde.'

Silas took up a position and lifted his arm ready to parry.

'Block… Don't retreat, idiot!'

'Don't call me a fecking idiot, you eejit.' Silas' riposte came with words rather than his foil, making his instructor laugh.

'Parry like this. Now you show me.'

Silas did as he was told and blocked an advance.

'And now you riposte.'

He jabbed forward too hard and stumbled.

'And there is where I cut your head from your body.' Danylo's accent was rich as his words unfolded from his mouth. His English was more assured that his brother's, but his accent was the same. 'We go again. En garde.'

'Hang on a bit, mate,' Silas said, shaking his head and bending to catch his breath. He pulled off his mask and let it drop. 'I've had enough for one day.'

'You're coming on well,' Archer called as he stood and came down the bank. 'How long have you been at it today?'

'About three bloody hours,' Silas panted.

'Just one.' Danylo stood to attention when Archer joined them, and his hand flew involuntarily to his forehead in a salute.

'There's no need for that, Danylo,' Archer said, but he returned the salute out of deference to the man's custom.

Standing to attention with his shoulders pulled back, Danylo was not much taller than Silas. Where his younger brother was six foot four, Danylo was at least half a foot shorter and not as broad. Having worked first as an infantryman and then as a stevedore, he had strength and stamina, showing no signs of breathlessness despite an hour of sport. Unlike Fecker's golden hair, his was a blond-brown mix the colour of caramel, and where his brother's eyes were gemstone blue, Danylo's were an unusual shade of amber. Apart from their voices and their love for each other, it was hard to imagine the two were related.

'Will you train, My Lord?' Danylo asked.

'I actually came to ask Mr Hawkins if he wanted to ride into the village,' Archer replied.

'Why? What's on?'

'Nothing particularly. I thought we might meet Thomas on his return and take tea.'

'Fecks has gone to collect him,' Silas said. 'You just want to see me fall off a horse, don't you?'

'I haven't seen you do that for some weeks now.'

Archer resisted the temptation to put his arm around Silas and kiss him. It grew harder to resist every day, but with the Hall bearing down behind, and with Danylo present, it was inappropriate.

Danylo was aware of the situation at Larkspur, Fecker had explained everything. How Silas and Archer were a couple in private, and why Thomas shared quarters with James. Danylo said he didn't deserve an opinion, and although he didn't understand, he accepted the arrangements and harboured no prejudice. How could he when he was a foreigner in a strange land, and a liberated man indebted to his rescuer?

'I must work,' he said. 'If there's nothing you need me for, Sir?'

Archer studied the man, marvelling at his near-fluent use of English. He had learnt it while in the military serving alongside a British battalion for several years during the Black Sea troubles, and then with British sailors in the port of Sevastopol. It was one of the reasons it had been so easy for Archer's contact to find him; not many Ukrainians spoke English.

'No, thank you, Danylo,' Archer said. 'But tell me, are you still happy with your duties?'

'Happy, Sir? Why would I not be? I live with my brat, I have this to look at...' He waved his arms towards the back of the Hall. Rising to four floors, the pitched roofs were lower than the height of the tower which kept watch majestically over the ruined abbey and grounds. 'You have given me land to work and a trade to learn.'

'And the work is what you want?'

As well as giving Danylo a plot of land where he grew vegetables for the Hall, Archer had made him the assistant gamekeeper under Jack Trelevan, a man a whose health was never at its best.

'Yes, Sir. I grew up on a farm. It is what I would be doing now if the Russians hadn't stolen it.'

'But you are sure you're happy here?'

'Why? You want me to leave?' Like his brother, Danylo was prone to jump to conclusions and be direct.

'He doesn't mean that,' Silas said, landing a hand on Danylo's shoulder. 'He fusses that he's not doing enough for people.'

'Sir,' the Ukrainian said solemnly. 'You could not do any more for me or my brat.' He bowed, but looked up sharply with narrowed eyes when Archer laughed.

'I am sorry,' the viscount said. 'It's the way you call Andrej your brat.'

'It means brother in my language, Sir.'

'Yes, I know, but it still tickles me to hear it.' Aware that the Kolisnychenko brothers were sensitive and proud, Archer added, 'I mean no offence,' clapped his hands together and said, 'Right! Vu khochete chayi?'

Danylo smiled sympathetically. 'Chayu,' he corrected. 'No, thank you, My Lord. I will have tea later. I must work the land.'

'Of course,' Archer said, and nodded, dismissing him.

Danylo collected the equipment, and after a final short bow, left the ruins and jogged towards the stables.

'What do you think?' Archer asked, when he was out of earshot.

'About?'

'Danylo.'

Rolling down his sleeves, Silas collected his jacket from where he had hung it on a broken column. 'I like him,' he said. 'I think everyone does.'

'He's adjusting to our way of life?'

'If you mean, he's got used to living among secret queers, yeah, he's about used to it as he'll ever be.' Silas rested on the column beside Archer. 'Fecks explained everything that first night in Plymouth,' he said. 'Least, that's what he told me. He repeated it all on their journey back in January in case they'd been so slaughtered he'd forgotten anything, and Danny got the wrong end of the stick.'

'You call him Danny?'

'He doesn't mind.'

'Would he accept it from me?'

Silas shook his head. 'He more than appreciates what you've done for him and Fecks,' he said, his sapphire eyes twinkling in the sunlight. 'But he expects to work in a great house for a nobleman, which is what you are, of course, but I don't reckon he's yet up to the level of acceptance as, say, Jimmy.'

'James is one of us.'

'Aye, but Danny's different. As straight as a railway track, right down the middle.'

'Tracks have curves and points,' Archer countered. 'No man is perfectly straight.'

Danylo disappeared behind the stable yard wall, and Archer felt a nudge on his elbow. When he looked, Silas was grinning mischievously with one eyebrow raised.

'Fancy him, do you?'

If truth were told, Archer did. He also found Thomas and James attractive, but no-one compared to the cheeky Irishman beside him. Silas' soft features and full, lush lips were as arousing now as the first time Archer had seen them, but behind his beauty lay a character as passionate as it was devoted, and there was no way he would sleep with anyone else. The idea had crossed his mind, but when he imagined being unfaithful, he immediately suffered crippling guilt intensified by the realisation that the man he pictured was Thomas.

'You're blushing, Archie.'

'I'm catching the sun.'

'Yeah, right.' Silas sighed and leant closer. 'Look,' he said. 'Danny's sexy, I'll give him that, and he's bloody good at what he does. I don't blame you for fancying him. You're not alone.'

'Oh, yes?' Archer queried.

'Not me, you eejit,' Silas chuckled. 'Iona. You've got one chambermaid hot to trot with him, and Lucy still sick in love with Fecks. On top of that, Karan's now got this thing for Barnaby.'

'Barnaby, the footman?'

'How many other Barnabys live here?'

'He's no more than nineteen.'

'He's twenty-one, actually. Jesus, Archie, I swear you live in your own little world.'

'So, Barnaby's not on our crew either?' Archer almost sounded disappointed.

'I thought you'd given up fancying the footmen,' Silas sniggered. 'I don't know. You want me to ask him?'

'Hell, no, but it would be good to... Never mind.'

'Good to what? Have a house full of queers?'

'Mr Hawkins,' Archer said, returning his lover's sassy grin. 'I only have eyes for you.'

'Aye, I know, but you have a bone-on for half the men on the estate.'

'I do not!'

'A big, thick and throbbing bone-on at that.'

'Don't be disgusting. No. I meant, it would be good to be able to help other men who are like us, as we do in Greychurch at the Foundation. To give similarly disposed men good jobs in a safe environment where they can be themselves without fear of prejudice.'

'You do that anyway. Whether they're as bent as us or as straight as Danny's railway track, all your staff are well looked after.'

'It's good to hear you say it.'

'It's true, Lover. And I don't mind you looking at other men, Archie.'

The words were said with a hint of sadness, but Archer knew them to be true.

'I don't want to be unfaithful to you, Silas. And I shan't be. I just couldn't.'

'But you wouldn't mind from time to time.'

'No!' It was a lie that needed explaining. 'Alright, I admit it, I do look at other men, and all I have to look at are those around me. You know Thomas and I have always been close, and being as honest as you are, our friendship, when we were young, often threatened to become something more carnal. I find James physically appealing in his angelic yet manly way, and yes, Danylo is more attractive to me than Andrej. But even if I took Thomas' elegance, James'

40

physique, Danylo's mystery, and dare I say it, Barnaby's innocence, and put them all together in one ideal man, he would still not measure up to you.'

'Yeah, well, not many boys measure up to you neither,' Silas leered. 'Not when it comes to a bone-on. Except for Fecker, of course.'

'Will you stop being so rude?'

'Probably not. Will you stop being so coy?'

'Coy?'

Another sigh, but this time longer and louder, and Silas looked Archer directly in the eye. 'We're men, Archie. We compare ourselves to each other. We wonder what total strangers have in their breeches. We wonder how we measure up, and yeah, we all get attracted to other men, even if it's only when we're young. For most, that's as far as it goes, but for the likes of us, it's… Well, it's like hunting, ain't it?'

'How do you reach that analogy?'

'I know you didn't go,' Silas continued, 'but I watched them the day after Christmas when they charged out across the moor with that trumpet thing and loads of hollering. A pack of grown men only after one thing; the thrill of the kill. I saw the same thing in Greychurch, and I don't mean the Ripper. I'd be standing there under a lamp, on my pitch, watching these blokes on the hunt. They'd be prowling and deciding who looked clean, who had the tightest arse, and they'd go from one to the other until they made up their minds. They'd go off, have their shilling's worth, and that's that. Next night, they'd be back, hunting another boy and never being happy until they'd gone 'round the block and back again if you get me.'

'That's different,' Archer said. 'And I hope you're not comparing me to anyone who picks up…' He faltered.

'Prostitutes,' Silas finished the sentence. 'You can say it, Archie. It's what I was. But no, I don't mean that.' He slipped his hand between them and felt for Archer's fingers. Hidden by his jacket, he hooked them in his. 'I love you,' he said simply and without thought. 'And if you wanted to see what it was like to hunt a different fox, then, as long as you came back to me, I'd understand.'

Archer's blood ran cold.

'You think I would do that to you?' he asked, aghast.

'No, but I do think that's what men do. All I'm saying is, I love you enough to agree if you ever wanted to do.'

'Well, I don't. And I wouldn't.'

'But you could.'

'Are you trying to tell me something?'

Silas laughed. 'Archie, mate, I've had more cocks than you're ever going to see. I don't need no more, and besides, it ain't about that. It's about trust.'

'You're starting to worry me.'

'Sorry, I ain't so good with words like Jimmy or Tom. I'm trying to tell you that I love you enough to let you have anything you want, and 'cos I don't have anything but the money the estate pays me, all I can give you is trust.'

'And love.'

'Without question.'

Their fingers squeezed harder. Silas wasn't trying to let him go or let him down, he was, in his own way, just trying to show how much he cared. The thought warmed Archer's cold concern, and he understood. Silas' openness, and his offer — which must have pained him greatly to say — made Archer love him more.

'My love,' he said. 'Thank you, but you have no cause for concern. Between you and I, it's nothing to comment on the looks of another man, we've often done it, but to go further with someone else? I wouldn't want to.'

'Liar,' Silas cajoled.

The thought had left Archer with a growing and visible erection. Silas had given him permission to sleep with other men, and the thought both excited and sickened him. A compromise was the only answer.

'At least,' he said. 'I wouldn't do anything like that unless you were with me.'

'Jesus, Mary and Joseph! You're as dirty as me.' Silas nudged him. 'Whatever you want, whenever you want,' he said. 'I know you love me.'

'And only you.'

'Apart from Tommy.'

Archer stood. 'Oh, come on!' he gasped. 'That's not fair. Tom's my best friend. Yes, I do love him, I always have, but not as I love you and never physically. I try to protect him as I do all my staff, and I like to think I give them a safe place to be themselves and live a fulfilled life. Just as you say. You need to understand that it's a different kind of love, and that's where we will leave it.'

'Thank fuck,' Silas laughed. 'You've given me a bone-on that's got to be dealt with and soon. Want to go upstairs?'

'Well, as you turned me down for tea in the village, I might as well.'

'Cheeky fecker.'

They walked quickly towards the Hall, carrying their jackets to cover their excitement.

'How do you discover these things?' Archer asked, somehow cleansed by their conversation.

'What things?'

'About Barnaby and the others? No-one gives me gossip.'

''Cos I ain't the lord of the effing manor,' Silas said. 'Unlike you, I get to spend time below stairs, and Jimmy fills me in with the rest of the craic when I see him in the morning.'

'He never says anything when he's dressing me,' Archer complained.

'Don't worry about that, 'cos I'm going to be undressing you in around five minutes, and that's all you've got to think about.'

'My God, I don't think I can wait that long.'

Archer was about to break into a run when the sound of pounding hooves stopped him in his tracks. He spun to the direction in time to see Fecker galloping across the field towards the stables, his hair was streaming, and he was riding Thunder without a saddle.

Something was wrong.

'What's he playing at?' Archer said, his sexual anticipation deflating.

Fecker expertly jumped the stone wall and drove the horse in a spurt across the paddock. Leaping the fence with ease, he drew the animal up sharply a foot away from where Silas and Archer stood open-mouthed.

'You must come,' he said. He had raced three miles, but wasn't out of breath. 'Train crashed. Thomas was on it.'

Five

Time was nothing more than images in a revolving zoetrope flashing one tiny movement after another. Weightless, Thomas hung in the air, more shocked at the horror on a stranger's face than the fact he was floating until he met the cushioned bench with a thud that jarred his back, and his teeth snapped together. Smith was falling towards him and then suddenly away as if yanked back by an unseen hand, given and taken in the blink of an eye. A suitcase bounced from his head and tumbled to the window through which he saw branches. They scraped the glass until, upside down, it shattered. A bough burst through, swiped a woman and was gone. So was she.

On his side, he wondered where the glass was until pieces cascaded over him, and he raised his arms across his face. A weight hit him in his gut winding him. For some reason, he expected the pain and thought nothing of it, but it made him uncover his eyes. He was in the clerestory, on his back and looking up at the floor. Benches hung from the wooden planks, empty as if he was the only person in the carriage. Falling again, he finally became aware of the sounds. Screams, breaking windows, cracking branches, metal grating on metal, the hiss of escaping gas, a maelstrom of noise. It intensified as the floor rushed to catch him, his head hit a bench, and it was over.

Thomas didn't know how long he lay there, but when his ears focused, the sounds had changed. The breaking and splitting were replaced by sobs, quiet and stunned, soon overtaken by distant screams as the cries spread towards him from further down the line. The carriage floor was littered with shards of shattered glass and luggage. He tasted blood.

Realisation approached like an unwanted house guest, and his first thought was for injury. Laying still and looking along the planks, he counted the prone bodies as he moved first his fingers and then his hands. He was able to shift his feet without pain, and untrusting of the apparent lack of injury, he pulled himself upright in case his body was lying, expecting at any moment to hear the snap of a bone and see it break through the cloth of his ripped suit.

The wailing crescendoed as the unconscious woke. There was no sign of Smith.

'Who's alive?' Thomas called, and the words seemingly coming from elsewhere.

The moans and screams reached his carriage as the tide of despair washed ashore in second class bringing with it shrieks that split his ears but cleared his head.

'If you can walk, get out,' he shouted, his throat choked with dust.

The air was heavy with the smell of gas, the lantern fittings were smashed, a pipe had been severed.

At the far end of the car, a badly arranged pile of legs began to untangle itself. Men in suits staggered to their feet white with fear and calling names, their blank faces streaked with blood. A woman's hand caught Thomas' leg as he lurched forward, tripping him and sending him stumbling into a bench. When he turned to help, her eyes were lifeless, her body broken and bent like a useless doll thrown down by a petulant child.

Bile rose in his gut, became unstoppable, and he bent to vomit through a missing window. Unbelievably, the carriage was upright. It had pitched, rolled and landed against trees at the bottom of an embankment.

The cries for help were lessening as he blundered towards the men at the front. They were dragging, pushing, begging women and children from the carriage, some hurling their loved ones through the window, others shouting about the gas.

Thomas assisted as best he could. His mind was still registering the images, putting them together like a badly made jigsaw. Where was the man who had sat opposite? Why was that child not replying to its father? A woman was howling that she'd lost her hat while around her, blood dripped, and limbs hung broken.

'Butler!'

The voice, the accent, it came from behind, back where he had landed, where the smell of gas was stronger and the hissing louder.

'Mr Smith?'

Thomas crouched and searched, holding his handkerchief to his nose against the fumes, only noticing when he took it away that it was bloodied. He wondered if it was his.

'Mr Payne!'

The carriage had been lit before, but where the sun had filtered in, broken branches and foliage now darkened the scene.

'Sir, here!'

Thomas found him trapped on the floor. One of his legs was caught in twisted metal that had once been a bench support, and he was trying to free it.

'Stay still,' Thomas said. 'Is anything broken?'

'I don't think so.'

Laying on his front, Thomas crawled beneath the bench only then noticing the body of another passenger on the other side. There was nothing he could do for the man, he was dead, and he had to concentrate on helping the living. If he could save one person, he might not suffer so much guilt for being spared.

'Clear the carriages.' The voice, accompanied by a whistle, shouted urgently and came with the increased sounds of hysterics and running feet, crunching gravel and the creak and grind of slowly splitting wood.

'What's happening?' Smith asked through gritted teeth.

'It's the lighting-gas.' Thomas glanced to another broken fitting. 'One spark and…'

Smith began struggling.

'No, hold still, you'll make it worse.'

The man did as instructed as Thomas gripped the twisted supports, one in each hand. They had been pushed together like a vice, trapping Smith's ankle and drawing blood. They were made of steel, not iron, a small blessing, and he would be able to pull them back if he could find enough leverage.

Suddenly, the carriage shook, and a great wave of red light rolled over it. The screams along the line increased but were swallowed by the explosion.

Thomas could only imagine that a flame from the boiler had caught the lighting-gas. The pipes ran from the front of the train to the back, bringing the flammable vapour all the way along. Once one carriage ignited, it wouldn't be long before the others followed.

'Go,' Smith shouted. 'I'm done for.'

Ignoring him, Thomas turned and extended his leg, pressing a foot against one of the metal bars. Grabbing the other with his hands, his body bent painfully, he told Smith to hold his breath.

The carriage rocked as a second explosion vibrated through, closer and more violent. When it died, an eerie silence had fallen beyond the wrecked carriage, but the ankle was free.

'Quick,' Thomas ordered. 'Ignore the pain.'

He righted himself and dragged the man free by his shoulders, pulling him to his feet while blocking out his wails of agony. There was no time for pleasantries, and their nearest exit was the missing window. He half carried and half yanked Smith to it and looked down. The ground was not so far, but there was no-one there to catch him.

'Right,' Thomas said. 'You hang there, and when I say so, roll out.'

Leaving Smith draped half in and half out of the window, he leapt from the carriage. Landing, all manner of pains shot through his body, but he was more intent on saving his companion and lifted his hands as if entreating God to throw him down.

'Out. Now!'

As Smith struggled to tip his weight from his feet, the far end of the carriage erupted into flame. The first lamp blew, and then a second following in rapid succession, with more coming closer one after the other and building in intensity.

'Now!' Thomas yelled and jumped, grabbing the man's clothing and pulling.

A weight fell on him, he cushioned the fall, and as he crumpled to the ground, rolled to protect Smith from the jet of fire that burst through the window and roared over their heads.

The next thing he knew, he was being dragged up the slope by rough hands, his eyes at boot level, sticks and foliage passing him. Stones grazed his stomach, and his clothes were in tatters. Smith was being dragged beside him, his face bloody. He was screaming, but at least they were alive.

Archer arrived to unimaginable carnage. Witnessing death in battle was not new to him, but it came instantly with bullets, clean cuts and thrusts of a sword, it was neat, clinical almost and not the human mess that met his eyes.

It was clear to see what had happened and what needed to be done. Why the locomotive had derailed at the corner, rolled and pulled its carriages over the incline was a question for later, more pressing was, where was Thomas?

The engine had fallen among the trees lighting some as burning coal spewed from the exploded boiler. Its flames had ignited the gas chambers, and the first-class carriage was burning, as were the two second-class ones where Thomas would have been. One carriage was wedged beneath first-class, both belching smoke, and the second, uncoupled, was leaning at an angle against the treeline below the embankment. The third-class truck was upside down behind it, and Archer knew there was little hope for anyone who had been inside.

The disorganised scene was enveloped in smoke, debris and panic. Splintered wood, planks, luggage, wheels, smouldering coal, steam and worst of all, patches of dark against the green-grey slope; bodies. Between them, bedraggled passengers staggered, shocked, calling names, lifting material from the faces of the dead, dropping it, finding another and falling to their knees at the sight.

Some of the injured were being led towards the station while others were attended to among the trees along the line. The fires were still burning, no-one was coordinating a rescue, and passengers were trying to re-enter the burning coaches to find their luggage as if unaware of the flames.

Having raced back to the accident the moment he had informed Archer of it, Fecker was already helping people away from the wreck. Those who could walk, he simply directed, those who were too stunned or hysterical, he lifted and carried to safety, handing them to calmer passengers before returning.

'Down here, Geroy!'

Fecker's shout brought Archer to his senses. If he was to be of any use, he needed to stay focused and alert and not let the sight overwhelm him. The bloodshed he could cope with, but if one of the bodies beneath a coat was Thomas...

Dismounting, he tethered his horse before racing to Fecker, where the stench of burning flesh and oil was overpowering.

'Where's Tom?' he shouted over the cries of despair.

Fecker pointed up the line to the near-upright coach, burning fiercely, and Archer bolted.

Thomas was sitting up, staring ahead, unmoving, a bloodied mess of torn clothes. Archer flew to him, nearly tripping on a corpse.

'Tom, are you hurt?' It was a ridiculous question.

Thomas blinked as recognition dawned, and dazed, slowly shook his head.

Unable to hold back, Archer threw his arms around his friend and held him. 'Oh my God, Tom,' was all he could say as he checked for obvious injury.

'Your Lordship!'

A cry from afar cut through the mayhem, and Archer tried to see where it had come from.

'I'll be alright,' Thomas said, his voice distant and rough. 'Help others.'

'Lord Clearwater?'

The Bodmin police had arrived. Archer recognised Sergeant Lanyon. Broad and imposing, usually as solid as a monolith, the man approached on unsteady legs as Archer rose to meet him.

'What can I do?' he asked as the officer mopped his brow and surveyed the scene. 'Sergeant,' he repeated louder when Lanyon didn't respond. 'What can I do?'

'We need to...'

Lanyon was affected by the carnage. It was beyond comprehension and turned him into a wreck as destroyed as the twelve forty from Plymouth.

Archer took charge.

'Sergeant,' he barked. 'We're not going to be able to extinguish the fires until water arrives. Get your men to search what's not alight, and take the wounded up the line to the station.'

Lanyon was still gawping.

'Andrej!' Archer bellowed, attracting Fecker's attention and bringing Lanyon back to life. 'Any more living in that carriage?'

'Nyet.'

'Move to the next. You!' He collared an able-bodied man who was heading into the trees with a portmanteau. 'Put that down, damn it, and get these people away from here.' Shoving the man towards the wounded, he yelled at others. 'You over there!' Several faces turned to him, some he recognised from the village; they were not all passengers. 'Well done for coming, men, but time is vital. Mr Sawyer? Have you your cart?'

'Yes, My Lord.'

'Start taking the injured to the cottage hospital. If you see Mr Jakes or anyone with transport, send them here. And there... You, Sir. Mr Killick?'

More people drew near, relieved that someone was doing something.

'Put yourself at the station platform, Killick. Arrange for the most wounded to travel first, organise the transport.'

'Aye, Sir.'

Both Sawyer and Killick hurried away. The drayman and the blacksmith were level-headed men, and Archer could trust them to stay calm and act efficiently. He wasn't so sure about Lanyon.

'Sergeant, is Doctor Penhale on the scene?'

'I'm not sure, Sir.'

Archer exploded, bawled the man out and shook him until he had pulled himself together. The strategy worked, not only to spur Lanyon into action, but also those nearby who stopped worrying about themselves and sought to help others. Lanyon began ordering his few men to move everyone away from the wreck and take those who couldn't walk to the railway station.

'If anyone has come merely to gawp,' Archer called after him. 'They must be ordered to assist.'

'Aye, Sir.'

James skidded down the hill from where he had left his horse, tripped and stumbled into Archer, his eyes wide with horror as he saw Thomas.

'He will be fine, Jimmy,' Archer said, catching him. 'We have him, I need you to look for survivors.' When James didn't reply, he said, more firmly, 'Mr Wright. I need your help.'

'Yes, Sir, of course.' James made a masterful job of pulling himself together. 'Mr Williams and the others are up front,' he reported. 'It's a bloody mess.'

'Go to the back,' Archer ordered. 'Get down and see if there's anyone alive under that last car.'

James obeyed without question, calling for others to assist, and swearing at them when they refused to move.

Archer knelt beside Thomas.

'Can you walk, Tom?'

'Yes, Sir.'

Silas arrived with Danylo behind him.

'Jesus, fecking Christ,' he swore when he saw Thomas' face. 'Thought I got roughed up bad in gaol.'

'No time, Silas,' Archer said. 'Horse or trap?'

'We brought the trap.'

'Right. Danylo?'

'Sir?'

'Take Thomas to the station, for now, make him comfortable there, then use the trap to take people to the hospital. One of the policemen will tell you the way. Silas. Help get Tom up the line, I will see to the dead.'

'Yes, boss.'

'Come on, Tom.' Archer helped Thomas to stand.

'Mr Smith,' Thomas whispered, raising a wavering hand to the body beside him.

'I think this fellow is....' Archer stopped when he saw the man's chest rise and fall. 'Who is he?'

'We were talking...'

Thomas passed out.

'Andrej?'

Fecker looked over from where he was lying beside James, face down and groping under the upturned third-class car.

'A child,' he shouted.

'Jimmy can see to it. Over here!'

Fecker joined them as Silas and Danylo supported Thomas, his head hanging. He was breathing normally, and no blood was flowing.

'Fecks,' Archer said, unaware what name he was using. 'Carry the wounded to the platform, start with this man.'

Thomas was taken away, followed by Fecker carrying Smith over his shoulder.

The crowd was thinning now. Injured passengers limped towards safety guided by the police officers and helped by those who could walk. The flames were dying along with the sounds of crying and horror, and the scene would have been peaceful were it not for the crackle of burning wood and the smell of death.

As Archer helped the last survivors to their feet and found them a companion to walk with or be carried by, Lanyon picked his way towards him, stepping over the obviously dead and bending to examine those he was unsure about.

'How many?' Archer asked when he arrived.

'So far, fourteen. God knows how many injured.'

'Any idea what happened?'

'Not yet, My Lord.' The policeman rubbed his red eyes, his face was patched with soot, and his jacket hung open revealing a shirt stained with the blood of others. 'The driver and fireman are both dead. We've not found the guard yet. Seems it were going too fast at Carminnow Corner, left the rails, engine dragged the rest down the bank. That's my guess.'

'Is Doctor Penhale here yet?'

'Aye, Sir. Up at the platform, and they've started taking the casualties into town.'

'Well done, Sergeant.'

Lanyon shuffled his feet, embarrassed. If it hadn't been for Archer, he would still be uselessly rooted to the spot. 'It were a shocking sight, My Lord.'

Knowing what he was trying to say, Archer saved him from humiliation.

'We are all shocked, Lanyon,' he said, kindly. 'I myself took a moment to comprehend the scale and decide on action. You have done admirably.'

'Thank you, Sir, but I was just so...'

'As were we all, Bill.' Using the man's first name made him an equal in the rescue attempt and helped restore the policeman's confidence. 'And we are still dazed, but there are people who need you.'

'I've messaged for assistance from St Austell and Liskeard, Sir. They should be here shortly.'

'Then I will leave this scene in your hands and see what I can do up the line. Will you be alright?'

Archer offered his hand to the scattering of bodies, and Lanyon swallowed and nodded.

'If Doctor Penhale allows,' Archer said, as the last line of survivors wound its way into the distance, 'I will take my man home when we have done all we can here. Meanwhile, if you need anything from the Hall, people, resources, anything, dispatch a message. Agreed?'

'Very kind, Sir.'

'Not at all.'

There was nothing more Archer could do at the site, and he was about to leave the authorities to their work when James approached, the limp body of a young boy in his arms.

'Is he alive?' Archer asked, stepping forward to hold the lad's swinging head.

'Yes, Sir. But the only one.'

'Poor bugger. No parents?'

'No-one else breathing, Sir.'

James, like Archer's other servants, had acted without thought, but now as the smoke thinned, realisation caught up with him. As inevitable as daybreak, it came with a blanched face and eyes that stared in disbelief.

'Right, Jimmy. He's your responsibility. Get him to the doctor and see if anyone claims him.'

James looked back to the carnage. 'And if no-one does? He can't be more than ten.'

'Then if he doesn't need the hospital, take him to the Hall, and we'll deal with it from there.'

'Sir.'

'And, Jimmy...'

'Sir?'

'Tom will be fine.'

He watched James pick his way through the wreckage and hoped his prediction proved correct.

Six

The first thing Thomas saw when he woke was Mrs Baker's concerned face. She was fussing, tucking him in among a faint smell of lavender and antiseptic. For a moment, he was six years old, and his mother was saying goodnight, and the next, he was a body of aches with a dry mouth, a thumping head and a hundred questions.

'Good, you're awake,' the housekeeper said. 'The doctor said you should be by now, so that's one less worry.'

'What time is it?' Thomas gingerly sat up and looked beyond her. This was not his room. 'Why am I here?'

'His Lordship wanted you in the Bosworth suite so he could be nearby,' she explained. 'You've been asleep since the accident. It's just gone seven.'

She tugged the bell-pull beside the bed as Thomas raised a weak arm and touched his face.

'I remember falling,' he said, his voice distant.

'I dare say. You were lucky, Mr Payne. There was no need to take you to the hospital like many. Doctor Penhale was happy they brought you here, but we need to keep an eye on you for a few days.'

'Gone seven? The dining room…'

'Don't you worry about that,' she said, sitting sideways on the edge of the bed. 'Mr Saddle and Barnaby have everything in hand.'

'His Lordship's dinner party…'

'Is not for another five days. You are to stay in bed, rest, and you're not allowed on your feet until the doctor says.'

'But I must.'

She ignored him, and when he tried to turn back the covers, prevented him by taking his hand.

'We will have no more of that. Now, what hurts?'

'Everything,' he said, giving in and laying back.

'There's nothing broken, though you have many bruises. The doctor didn't find anything damaged internally, but, if you start to feel worse, you must say.' She rustled about at the bedside table and held up a glass. 'This will ease the aches,' she said, passing it to him. 'It might make you sleepy too, but that's for the best. Drink it.'

Thomas was shocked to find he was wearing pyjamas, and Mrs Baker noticed because she said, 'Mr Wright dressed you with help from His Lordship.'

He managed a weak smile of thanks. 'Where is His Lordship?'

'Drink this.'

'Later.' Again, he tried to get out of bed and once more, she prevented him.

'You try that one more time, Tommy Payne and I will put you over my knee.'

It was how she used to speak to him when he was eight and first at the house, a naughty 'runagate' as his father used to call him.

'That would make for an interesting spectacle, Mrs Baker,' he said, resigned to his incarceration.

'Good to see you have your humour intact,' she replied. 'Drink, or you'll get no information or sympathy from me.'

He obeyed, and the bitter liquid burned his throat.

'That's foul.'

A knock at the door and James entered. Thomas' heart immediately leapt at the sight of the valet, smartly dressed as always, his tie straight, his suit fitting perfectly and his hair immaculate. The only difference between this James and the one he had kissed goodbye that morning was his face. Where it had been full of happiness twelve hours previously, it was now a white wall of apprehension.

'You rang, Mrs Baker?'

'Mr Wright, yes. I must go and see to the bairn.' To Thomas, she said, 'His Lordship suggested someone sit with you. There's a bed made up in the dressing room, so he will be close by. It's in case of delayed shock, or sickness from the concussion. You don't mind, do you, Mr Wright?'

'Not at all.' James addressed Thomas. 'I am glad to see you, Mr Payne,' he said. 'That was a horrific...'

'Yes! We know,' Mrs Baker interrupted. 'Best not dwell on that until he's better.' She busied herself at the table while she spoke. 'Mr Payne is to stay in bed. His Lordship will be in to see him later, and I will have trays sent up for you both shortly. He has had something for the aches and may sleep again. Even so, it's best if you stay with him. Now then, he's not to...'

'I *am* here, Mrs Baker,' Thomas complained, his eyes still on James.

'And there you shall stay until I order otherwise.' She hurried to the door. 'Ring if you need anything. Don't leave him alone, Mr Wright. He'll likely try and escape.'

'As you wish.'

The housekeeper stopped at the door, her hand on the handle, and regarded Thomas sympathetically. She sighed and swished away.

As soon as the latch clicked into the lock, James was at the bedside, sitting and leaning into Thomas.

'Can I kiss you?'

The answer came as a long, lingering pressing of lips before a cautious but passionate embrace.

'Fuck, Tom,' James said when the flood of relief had faded. 'I was so worried when I saw you. You could have died.'

Thomas wiped a tear from his lover's eye and tasted it. 'I didn't. I was lucky.'

'It must have been horrible.'

'It was...' Thomas searched for the words. The images, tiny fragments of a larger picture, swirled and danced before his eyes, none of them making sense and none of them settling into place. 'It just was,' he said.

'Maybe we shouldn't talk about it,' James suggested. 'Do as Mrs Baker says and let you sleep.'

'I don't feel tired, just lightheaded. Why am I in the Bosworth suite? And what bairn was she talking about?'

James rose and crossed to the window. The sun had set, but dusk was lingering. The moor rolled on until it dropped from sight at the crest of a hill, and a mile further away, the site of the accident. Looking at the desolate yet beautiful scene, the smoke had cleared and there was nothing to suggest the tragedy. He drew the curtains and returned to the bed, this time sitting to face the door so that he could hold Thomas' hand ready to drop it should anyone enter.

'You've been brought home with a mystery,' he said. 'Two, in fact.'

When Thomas didn't understand, James explained what had happened.

Silas was the first to arrive back at Larkspur, sent on ahead by Archer who stayed behind with Fecker and some of the estate staff, who, on hearing of the disaster, had ridden across the moors to offer their assistance. As His Lordship's secretary, and with the butler incapacitated, it fell to Silas to bring the news to the staff still at the Hall.

When Fecker had raised the alarm, it hadn't taken long for news to spread that the men of the estate were needed at a railway accident, and when Silas entered the servants' hall, he found Mrs Baker and Mrs Flintwich at the table with the maids, speculating on what had happened. They scrambled to their feet.

'Sorry to interrupt your tea, ladies,' he said, doing his best to adopt a calm manner. 'I have some news.' He nodded at the housekeeper, and the servants sat. Iona and Karan regarded their brother with a mix of concern and pride. 'Sorry to interrupt your day, but I have instructions from His Lordship.'

'Was Mr Payne in the crash?'

The hall boy's words brought gasps to those who hadn't learnt the news, and Mrs Baker scolded him for interrupting.

'In a minute, Mark.' Silas tried to smile, but he was still struggling to understand what he had seen. 'Some of you must have heard what's happened,' he went on. 'A train from Plymouth to Padstow left the rails at Carminnow Corner. His Lordship, Mr Wright, Mr Andrej and others are down there at the station helping out. The thing is, Mr Payne was on the train...'

Several louder gasps, and in particular one from Mrs Baker, accompanied looks of horror as hands flew to mouths. 'He is unhurt.' Silas paused while that sunk in. 'At least, he's not badly hurt. Cuts and bruises, the doctor said. He will be fine in a day or so, nothing to worry about.' He turned his attention to the housekeeper. 'Mrs Baker...'

She recovered professionally from her anguish and sat erect in her chair. Equal in status to Thomas, it was her job to ensure everything ran smoothly in his absence. Behind her, Saddle also appeared ready to take on any responsibility. Standing with his head held high, his grey temples were as perpendicular as his back, his small eyes on Mr Hawkins.

'His Lordship has asked for the Bosworth suite to be prepared for Mr Payne,' Silas went on. 'Given the circumstances, he would like him near his own rooms. It was His Lordship who asked Mr Payne to visit Plymouth this morning, and he feels responsible.'

'Well, that's just daft,' Mrs Baker said.

'Which is what I told him, but he insisted. His Lordship would like James and me to attend to Mr Payne when he arrives, and one of us will stay with him. Perhaps someone can make up a bed in the dressing room?'

'Will that be necessary?' Mrs Baker asked. 'If Mr Payne needs someone so close, there's an adjoining door to the next bedroom. Mr Wright could use that.'

'It's already taken,' Silas said, and the statement brought questioning looks and whispers.

'Mr Payne was travelling with an acquaintance,' Silas explained. 'He was very concerned for the man's wellbeing. In fact, I was told that Mr Payne pulled him from the wreckage just as the carriage exploded.'

The whispers became louder and more animated. Mrs Baker banged the table, and the maids fell silent.

'This man was unconscious when I left them,' Silas continued. 'The doctor has examined him and says there's no major injury. The hospital is more than full, and we were keen to do as much as we could to help. No-one knew him, and no-one claimed him, so Mr Payne was worried for this chap, and of course, His Lordship wouldn't hear of him being left on his own. So, Mrs Baker, could you have the connecting room made up as well? Have plenty of hot water and… whatever ready too. Mr Wright can find suitable clothes for the stranger.'

'May I ask…?' Saddle stepped forward.

'Yes?' Silas expected the under-butler to present some unthought-of obstacle to Archer's plan, some point of etiquette he didn't want broken, but, surprisingly, he was as concerned as everyone else.

'What can I do, Mr Hawkins?'

'Thank you, Mr Saddle. Thank you, everyone.' Silas gave them all an appreciative smile. 'His Lordship said that everyone would want to help, but the less fuss we make, the better. Saddle, you're to stand in for Mr Payne like you were doing when we were in the city.'

'Very good, Sir.'

'Then we should get on,' Mrs Baker stood.

'One more thing,' Silas said, halting her in her tracks. 'Two things, actually. First, preparations for the dinner on Friday are to carry on as normal in the hope the line will be open, and guests can get here. That's down to you, Mr Saddle.' The under-butler preened at the responsibility. 'Secondly, there's another houseguest on his way. Mr Wright rescued a young lad from third-class. We don't know who he is, and he's not saying anything, but if he was travelling with anyone, they are now... Well, he is on his own until someone claims him. His Lordship asked that Mrs Baker take care of him somewhere.'

'Of course,' the housekeeper said, concerned. 'Is he injured?'

'No, but he is very shocked, and so the doctor's sedated him. Maybe put him in a room, and one of the girls can sit with him? I'll leave it to you. Everyone should be back soon. And that's it.'

Silas was impressed with himself as much as he was impressed with the way the staff reacted to his authority. He had never addressed them on behalf of Archer, and it dawned on him that this was his job and what they expected from him. As Archer's man's man, his personal, private secretary, he was closer to the viscount than anyone else in the room, even those who had known the viscount since he was a child. In truth, he hadn't even thought about that, he had simply done as instructed, as would the servants. For someone who hardly spent any time below stairs, Archer knew his staff well.

The whispers had become gossip, and the maids were asking questions.

What happened? How many were hurt? Were more injured to come to the Hall? They were all sensible concerns, but also ones that would have to wait.

'I'll tell you everything when I can', Silas said, silencing the chatter. 'For now, there is a lot to do, and I'll leave you in Mrs Baker's hands to see it done. Apparently, you know where medical supplies are kept. We will need to re-dress some wounds, but nothing major. Mr Wright and I can take care of that. They thought Mr Payne's friend had a broken ankle, but apparently not. Like Mr Payne, he's only bruised, cut and got knocked out. Mrs Baker? Well… You know what to do.'

'Thank you, Sir.' Mrs Baker stood and began organising her troops. 'Iona, Karan, make sure the fires are lit, the rooms are aired, and the beds made. Lucy, the bairn can be in with you, you being the most sensible.'

'I'll make a broth,' Mrs Flintwich volunteered as if her cooking was the answer to all ills as chairs scraped, voices babbled, and the servants set about their tasks.

'A word.' Silas drew the housekeeper to one side as the others left. 'When they get here, they will need to be washed and changed. I think it's best if we men do that.'

'I quite agree, Sir. Mr Saddle and Mr Wright…'

'I'll assist Mr Wright,' Silas said. 'Let Saddle see to His Lordship when he gets back. He'll have to take over Mr Wright's duties for a while too.'

'Very good, Sir.' The housekeeper was relieved she wasn't going to have to undress anyone. 'And what of Mr Williams and the brothers?'

She had not yet come to terms with Fecker and Danylo's surname.

'They're fine,' Silas reassured her. 'They're covered in muck and worse from carrying the injured and… other things.' The other things were bodies, as the brothers had assisted the police in removing the dead to the hospital morgue and the butcher shop. It was the only other place with a large-enough cold storage to keep them until the police had identified the corpses, but she didn't need to know the gruesome details. 'All they need is a bath and a rest. We must get ready to welcome injured strangers and your main man.'

'I've never heard His Lordship called that.' Mrs Baker raised an eyebrow.

'I meant Tommy,' Silas said, and out of habit, winked. Mrs Baker had always been fond of Thomas.

She rolled her eyes at his cheek and bustled away, shouting at the laundry maid to start boiling water.

The carriage returned an hour later, driven by Fecker and

60

carrying Thomas and Danylo. Archer and the stable lads brought back the horses, and a short while later, Williams drove up in the trap bringing the stranger and the boy, both sedated into sleep and laying on the floor attended by James. Neither was expected to wake until the evening. Archer oversaw the arrangements as the men were carried into the house through the tower entrance, which offered the most direct route from the yards to the first floor.

James brought the lad to the servants' hall where, with permission from Mrs Baker, he carried him to the female servants' rooms on the top floor. Lucy fussed, made the bed, set the fire and turned her back while James cleaned the lad and put him in pyjamas too large for him before hurrying down to Thomas.

The older stranger was laid on the bed in the Bosworth suite and Barnaby was tasked to watch over him until the other men had seen to Thomas.

Silas, Archer and James, stood at the bedside looking at their friend. Tom's hair was matted with blood from a cut which had also painted his face and ruined his shirt. There wasn't much left of his jacket and trousers, the material being more rips than cloth, and where the doctor had pulled his shirt free to check his abdomen, it had been done up on the wrong holes.

'He won't want to see himself in this state,' Archer whispered. 'How are we going to do this?'

When there was no answer, he looked at James and saw he was holding back tears. Archer put his arm around the valet's shoulders and drew him to his side. 'He'll be fine, Jimmy,' he said. 'We haven't lost him.'

'Sorry, Sir,' James said, trying to pull away. 'I forgot myself.'

'Come here.'

Archer hugged the man, and the act brought James to tears.

'I'm sorry,' James spluttered again. 'It's just shock.'

'You take your time.' Archer patted his back. 'Better to get it out now so you can be strong for him later. And while you're pulling yourself together, we have to decide who's going to do what.'

'Can I make a suggestion?' Silas didn't wait for an answer. 'James ought to be the one to undress him, but I'm happy to lend a hand if you need me to lift. Only, I don't think Tommy would want to think that you'd seen him naked, Archie.'

'I think, in his present state, he wouldn't know let alone mind,' Archer replied. 'But I see your point. We'll see to Mr Smith while you do it, Jimmy, but we'll help get Tom down to his underclothes first. See what the damage is.'

Together, and with James recovered, they undressed the butler until he wore only his long johns. Silas' ideas about modesty wasn't a success as the long johns were as ripped as his trousers, and there was no way to cover what was on display. Silas caught Archer gawping before he looked away as if he'd just seen something he'd often wondered about. Who could blame him? Silas had often wondered the same thing about Thomas, but there were more appropriate times for such thoughts. The intimate act of washing him and changing dressings fell to James, and he was left alone to care for his lover.

In the next bedroom, Silas and Archer found Mr Smith on his back, laid atop an old blanket to protect the sheets from the dirt and soot on his clothes. The fire was alight, and an open window aired the room which had not been used since the late viscount's funeral.

Barnaby was dismissed, and they set about removing the man's shoes, socks and jacket, finding his clothes in much the same condition as Thomas', and his vest stained with patches of darkly dried blood.

'Doctor Penhale told me that his ankle is most likely sprained,' Archer said. 'It's certainly not broken, but we may as well leave on the bandage that's there.'

'Whatever you say.'

'Help me get his shirt off, then bring the water, will you?'

They removed the man's shirt with Archer holding him up and supporting his head and weight while Silas manoeuvred his arms from the sleeves, and then did the same with his undershirt. Pulling it free, it revealed a toned chest, smooth except for a few dark hairs in the centre. His stomach was drawn in showing its muscles, and the otherwise perfectly pale body was marred only by unevenly shaped bruises and scratches.

'Who is he?' Silas asked as they laid him down.

'All Tom said was that they were chatting just before the accident.' Archer told him, dipping a cloth in warm water and applying it gently to the man's angular face.

Silas took hold of his drawers at the waist. 'Shall I?' he said, pulling a worried look. 'Seems odd.'

'Silas, when I was at sea, we had to do a lot worse than undress a man.'

'Oh, aye?' Silas smirked.

'Now isn't the time,' Archer chided, unable to hold back a knowing smile. 'It'll make a change for you, getting a man's drawers off without first being paid.'

'Cheeky fecker.'

'We're all just men, Silas,' Archer said. 'This man needs help, he's not going to mind you seeing his… luggage.'

'Luggage?'

'Well, he *was* travelling. Just get them off and see if he's got any injuries on his legs that we need to see to, then turn him over and we'll wash his back. Poor chap.'

'Mr Smith?'

'So Tom said. Joshua Smith.'

'Unknown, unclaimed passenger?'

'Indeed. No-one at the scene knew him. Unless he was travelling with one of the unfortunates, he is a mystery.'

'Anything in his pockets?'

'Only that.' Archer pointed to the pile of clothes. He had been through them and found only a pocket watch. 'It's gold, so I expect he's a man of means, and someone will claim him in due course.'

'No identification?'

'Nothing but his ticket. Not even any money. Tom said he was heading west, but was on the wrong train. Lord knows where he thought he was going.'

'Oh my.'

Silas looked down on the now naked man, and his voice drew Archer's attention away from his work.

'I thought *you* were a big lad,' Silas said.

'Will you just get the poor man washed and not worry about his…? Oh, just get on with it, you dirty-minded, gorgeous beast.' A quick glance at the door and Archer leant over and kissed Silas on the lips. 'I'm so proud of you,' he whispered.

'Love you, Your Lordship.'

63

James joined them just as Archer had washed the last of the grime and blood from the man's face, and Silas was changing the water in the bathroom.

'Fuck me,' he said as he walked in.

'Not you too,' Silas tutted returning with the bowl. 'He's a man with a big dick, alright? No need to be jealous.'

'That aside,' Archer said. 'Can you help us turn him, Jimmy.'

'Of course.'

'How's Tom?'

'Clean, in pyjamas and sleeping,'

'Good man. Now, take his legs, Silas that side…'

Together, they rolled Mr Smith gently onto his front, with Archer arranging his arm, so it wasn't crushed. His back was covered in blood which gave Archer cause for concern, and he dipped a clean cloth into the fresh water to see what damage lay beneath.

James was bringing a pair of Silas' pyjamas from the armchair where he'd set them when he heard Archer draw in a deep breath, and whispered, 'Oh my God.'

'What is it?' he asked, coming around the bed for a closer look. 'Bloody hell!' In cleaning the man, Archer had revealed an inked pattern on his skin. 'Are those teeth?'

Archer revealed more. 'I believe so. And here.'

'It's a mouth.'

'Yes.' The cloth was dipped, rinsed, and more of the man's back came to light. 'No cuts,' Archer said. 'The blood must be from elsewhere. Have you ever seen anything like this?'

'No, Sir. It looks like… Is it a wolf? No, it's a dragon,' James said. 'Incredible.'

'A dragon indeed,' Archer said as he worked. 'If I'm not mistaken, it's the *Râşnov balaur sacru.*'

'The what?' Silas asked, gawping.

'The Râşnov balaur sacru,' Archer repeated, as if by doing so the others would understand its significance.

James and Silas exchanged shrugs.

'Rasnov?' James queried. 'As in Musat-Rasnov?'

Silas looked him up and down. 'You've heard of it?'

'I've heard His Lordship's full title,' James said. 'And so have you. It was read out in court.'

'It was, Jimmy,' Archer agreed.

'So what does it mean?' Silas asked.

'It means,' Archer said as he continued to wash the man's back. 'I doubt this person is called Mr Smith.'

'Why?'

'Because the *Râşnov balaur sacru* is Romanian shorthand for "The scared dragon of the family Rasnov." It is also part of the family crest, and the Rasnovs are one of the oldest houses of Romanian royalty. Transylvanian to be precise, but they and the Szekely people have been in dispute for centuries.'

'Well, blow me down with a feather. He's a royal?'

'Not necessarily.' Archer worked the cloth over the remaining blood, cleaning the last blemish away from the tattoo. He drew in a sharp breath.

'What is it?' Silas leant in for a closer look.

'He's not Romanian royalty,' Archer said.

'Make up your mind. Why d'you say that?'

'The Dragon is part of the Rasnov royal crest,' Archer explained. 'And I know that because I am distantly related to them through my mother's Hapsburg line, but not this dragon, not this pattern.'

He sat back, dropped the cloth into the bowl, and his brow furrowed in thought.

'Not this one?' James prompted.

'*Protectorul regalității Râşnov.*' Archer's words were whispered, as if he was casting a spell.

'Speak up.'

Archer cleared his throat. 'The direction makes this symbol the mark of the *Protectorul regalității Râşnov*. The Protector of Rasnov royalty. It means he works for the family, but isn't part of it.'

'Works as what?'

Archer regarded Silas, concerned. 'As an assassin.'

Seven

It took an hour for James to tell Thomas what had happened, and for Thomas to tell him what he remembered. By the time they had exchanged stories, they had finished the supper Mrs Baker had delivered, and Thomas was feeling a little better although his head still thumped, and his limbs were heavy. James sat beside him on the bed with his lover resting on his shoulder.

'What happens to Mr Smith now?' Thomas asked.

'The Rasnov assassin?' James grinned, finding the revelation exciting rather than disturbing. 'I'm not sure. His Lordship said he would come and talk about it later. He's gone back to the village to see what else he can do to help.'

'His heart's too big, that's his problem.'

'I don't disagree with you there, but it's also his duty. At least, that's what he said.'

'He said something strange.' Thomas was uncomfortable after so long in one position and tried to hoist himself up the bed. James helped.

'Who, Smith?'

'Yes. It was just before the accident. I could tell something was wrong, and I told him to hold on. I thought we would just tip as we took the corner, but at the same time, I knew we were about to crash.'

'Hey, don't upset yourself over it.' James kissed Thomas' hair. It smelt of Archer's musk oil.

'It's okay, Jimmy,' Thomas said, stroking James' hand. 'I'd rather talk and get it out.'

'If you're sure. What did he say?'

'I was right. We tipped, the carriage I mean, and one side left the track. A second later it came down with a crash and bounced, throwing us in the air. It would have been a comical sight, like those rope swings at the summer fair when you make them go too high, but it was too serious for that. Mr Smith rose at the same speed as me and fell back to his seat just as quickly. It was then he said something like "I am Eshuat." That's what it sounded like. It might have been one word, but it didn't make any sense. What did it mean?'

'I don't know, Tom. Like I said, it's all a mystery, and one we're going to look at tomorrow. For now, you should go back to sleep. Mrs Baker left another powder for you.'

'I don't want to go to sleep. I want to get back to work.'

'With that bump on your head and you feeling dizzy? Not a chance.'

James slid from the bed and rang the bell.

'What are you doing?' Thomas was shocked. 'We don't ring for staff.'

'We don't sleep in the guest bedrooms either,' James said. 'But look at where you ended up. Don't worry, I've done it before and no-one downstairs is going to say anything, they're all too concerned about you. Barnaby hasn't stopped asking after you and wants to come and see you.'

'Barnaby? What on earth for?'

'He's worried. Got a bit of a crush if you ask me. Now...' James began tucking in the sheets and tidying the bed. 'Someone will be up in a moment to take the trays. I'm going to check on our guest, then I'll be right back. You stay where you are.'

'I need the bathroom.'

'Oh.' James thought on his feet. 'I'll bring you a pot.'

The look that came back from Thomas told him that a pot was not what was needed, and there was no way he would use one in a guest bed in any case.

'Right, here we go then.'

Having helped him from the bed and into one of Archer's dressing gowns, James supported Thomas as he limped to the bathroom. Having made sure he was safe, he left him there as a knock on the bedroom door heralded the arrival of Mrs Baker and Iona.

'Can you take the trays?' James asked, nodding towards them.

Mrs Baker glanced at the bed, confused. James saw and tilted his head towards the bathroom.

'Ah. How is he?'

'He's going to be fine, Mrs Baker. Nothing to worry about.'

'And the stranger?'

'Him too. Is His Lordship back yet?'

'He's just ridden up with Mr Hawkins.'

Iona stacked the trays and left, Mrs Baker closing the door behind her.

'Your new friend wants to see you,' she said.

'My new...? Oh, the lad?'

'He's a bonny boy. You'd think he would be shocked into silence after what he's been through, but he's happy enough to ask after you. Mind you, that's all he has said.'

'Do we know who he is?'

The housekeeper was tidying the bed James had just made as if criticising his work, but he said nothing.

'No. He will only talk to you. His hero, he called you.'

James blushed. 'It was Mr Andrej who found him, but I'll go up as soon as someone comes to take my place here. Excuse me.'

He left Mrs Baker mixing the doctor's prescribed sleeping powder and knocked gently on the bathroom door.

'Everything alright?'

'Everything is as it should be, thank you, Mr Wright,' Thomas replied.

His mildly prissy tone told James that he was feeling more like his normal self, and smiling, the valet continued past the dressing room into the second bedroom.

Smith was still asleep and snoring gently. The water by the bed had not been touched, and the handbell was in the same place, standing beside a note which Archer had left. It instructed Smith to ring when he woke, to alert James in the next room. It was signed, "Your servant, Viscount Clearwater."

The room had grown stuffy, and now that night had completed the dusk, James opened the window further and left the curtains slightly parted. He attended to the fire, stoking it to counter the cold, and was about to dim the lamps when Thomas appeared in the doorway.

The light caught his copper hair, burnishing it, and Archer's silk dressing gown fit his elegant frame perfectly, shimmering in the firelight. James had lost count of the number of times he had looked at Thomas and his heart had skipped, but the excitement of seeing him never faltered or lessened. He found it even in briefly snatched glances; as Thomas crossed the servants' hall in his black and whites, or when James followed him up the back stairs, sat beside him at the table, or even when Tom was giving him instructions, the man never failed to fire his heart.

Thomas watched the sleeping stranger thoughtfully if a little sadly.

'What are you thinking?' James whispered as he crossed the room to tuck in a sheet.

Thomas shook himself. 'I was just reliving a moment,' he said, and returned to the other room.

James tidied the covers silently around the guest before retreating, leaving the connecting door ajar. When he joined his lover, Thomas was alone and slipping back beneath the sheets.

'Mrs Baker said to remind you that your boy was calling for his hero,' he smirked.

'My boy now, is he? I'll go up when Silas comes.'

'I'll be fine, Jimmy.'

'You might be, but what about the assassin next door?' James widened his eyes dramatically. 'He could be after you for all we know.'

'Hardly. We only spoke about the Hall and wine.'

'Well, I'm not leaving you alone,' James took his seat as before and put one arm around Thomas' shoulders. The other reached for the bedside table. 'Your medicine,' he said, passing it. 'And no arguments.'

Thomas obeyed, and they held hands, saying nothing. Within a few minutes, Thomas' eyes were sagging.

'Lie down,' James whispered, and when Tom was comfortable, kissed his forehead. 'You're my hero, Tommy Payne,' he said and sent his lover to sleep with a smile on his face.

The clock had just delicately chimed nine when Archer and Silas arrived. Washed and wearing clean clothes, they crept into the semi-darkness of the room where only the fire threw out a glow.

'How are they?' Archer whispered.

'Both sleeping.'

'Doctor Penhale will be pleased.' The viscount beckoned the others into the sitting room where the three could speak more easily.

'How is it in the village, Sir?'

'Fifteen now dead, thirty injured.' Silas imparted the news succinctly and without emotion.

'Do they know what caused it?'

'No, Jimmy,' Archer said. 'But it looks like the driver might have suffered a seizure, or the regulator failed in some way.'

'So, an accident.'

'Of course, What else could it be?'

Archer had sat, and invited James and Silas to do the same. They brought chairs together, and Silas sat on a backwards-facing upright, where he leant his arms on the backrest and his chin on his hands.

'It's just that Thomas told me something,' James explained. 'Mr Smith spoke just before the train left the tracks. He said… What was it?' He thought hard. 'Strange words… "I am Eshuat", or something.'

'Was it, "Am eşuat"?' Archer asked, pronouncing the words with an accent.

Surprised, Silas raised his head. 'You know what it means?'

'I do. It's Romanian for "I have failed".'

'How do you know this shit?' Silas was impressed.

'Because I read books. And because I'm a quarter Romanian on my grandmother's side. My mother's mother's side of the family were Rasnovs, generations back, hence the Boyar Musat-Rasnov thing, and why she stays there a lot. Bunica used to teach me Romanian words when I was little.'

Silas was gigging. 'Booze-knicker?'

'No, Silas, *Bunica*. It's Romanian for grandmother.'

'Makes sense to me,' James said. 'My grandma was once done for nicking gin.'

'Yes, alright, boys,' Archer tutted. 'It's just another language.'

'At least you know who your grandmothers were,' Silas said, resting his chin back on his hands and pouting until Archer swiped his fingers through his hair and kissed him.

Thinking it best to return to the subject, James said, 'So, Smith said he'd failed. You reckon he knew the train was going to crash? Was there someone on it he wanted to assassinate?'

Archer laughed. 'Calm down, Jimmy,' he said. 'For someone so bright, you're being extremely dim. For a start, there are cleaner ways to kill someone. Secondly, the order of the *Protectorul regalității Râșnov* has not been active in centuries, so his inked skin is probably only for decoration. Thirdly, why put himself at risk by, somehow, crashing the very train he was riding in? And how?'

Silas and Archer looked at James with smirks on their faces.

'Yeah, alright,' James conceded, mildly irked. 'But why get yourself painted with something obsolete?'

'Probably a family thing,' Archer reasoned. 'Keeping history alive, the same as my honorary Boyar title.' He tapped the arms of his chair. 'Anyway... It looks like both patients will sleep through until morning. I don't know about you, but I am going to have supper, a bath and an early night.'

'And I must go and see the boy,' James said, standing. 'Any news on his family?'

Archer shook his head. 'Everyone is accounted for apart from our two guests,' he said. 'It looks like the boy was travelling alone, or his parents are among the dead, poor thing. If you're going up there, Jimmy, find out as much as you can. Mrs Baker said he had nothing on him apart from a few shillings. If he had luggage, it perished in the fire.'

'Will do, Sir.' Turning to Silas, James said, 'I'll be back later so you can get to bed.'

'Happy to stay here,' Silas offered. 'Someone's got to be around in case Smith wakes up, and I want to ask him about his tattoo.'

'There is a book about the Protectorul Order in the library if you're interested.' Archer yawned and peeked into the second bedroom. 'I doubt you'll hear from him until morning.'

'Shall I see to you before I go upstairs, Sir?'

'No, Jimmy. You do what you have to do. The delightful Mr Saddle is waiting for me. And you, Mr Hawkins, don't stay up too late.'

'Yes, Dad.' Silas poked his tongue out and ducked a playful swipe as Archer and James left.

Alone, he prepared himself for a restless night keeping watch over the injured. It might have been the breeze that hissed about the casements, or the unexpected cracks from the fire-logs, perhaps because he was suddenly alone, but he was far from easy. His mind was drawn back to the image on Smith's back, and combined with Archer's words, 'A Rasnov assassin,' they made him nervous. It shouldn't have mattered, not if the order was no longer operating, and yet it did. Only that morning, Archer had been awake and worrying about Quill. Now Silas knew how he felt. It might not be Quill, but some kind of trouble was out there in the dark, approaching stealthily across the moors. Something told him it was already with them in the house, and its name was Smith.

James was unused to the female corridor on the servants' floor, but Mrs Baker had given him permission, and the maids knew he would be there. All the same, he knocked loudly and called before he stuck his head around the door. The empty corridor was a direct reflection of the men's quarters he had just walked through, except here, the names in the placeholders belonged to the girls. He knocked and waited to be called in before entering Lucy's room where the maid sat reading a magazine.

The boy was sitting up in bed, also reading, and apart from a dressed cut on his head, showed no signs of having been in an accident.

Lucy stood as soon as James entered, and the boy put down his book.

'He's been looking forward to meeting you, Mr Wright,' Lucy said with her usual polite charm before addressing the boy. 'This is the man who saved you.'

'Actually, all I did was help Mr Andrej get you out of the wreckage,' James explained. 'Then carry you to the doctor. How are you?'

The boy simply smiled.

'He doesn't say much,' Lucy said. 'He's been asking for you, but that's it.'

'Shy or shocked?' James sat at the end of the bed.

'Both, perhaps. Excuse me, Mr Wright…?' Lucy was hovering by the door.

'Yes?'

'Would you mind if I nipped downstairs? Sally's forgotten to bring me a tray, and I'm starving.'

'Yes, of course.' James waved her from the room, saying, 'I'll be here until you get back.'

Once they were alone, he studied the lad. The boy had a serious, downturned mouth, but an expectant enthusiasm in his tree-bark eyes which were highlighted by a pale complexion. The ears were at right angles to his face in the way that Thomas' were, and James found them just as adorable, though for a completely different reason. On Thomas, they were alluring; on the lad, they were comical. His hair was reddish brown and cut in a short back and sides reminiscent of an army man.

'Hello,' James said, putting on what he thought was an older-brother kind of smile. 'What's your name?'

'Why am I wearing these?' the boy asked. He was well-spoken with a hint of an Irish accent and was pulling at his pyjama top. 'Who's A R?'

'Tell me your name, and I'll tell you his,' James countered.

'Who are you, Sir?'

'I'm the one you wanted to see. I just said.'

'Your name, silly.'

The lad was confident, but covering it with mistrust.

'Well…' James moved up the bed a little and tucked up one leg to appear informal. In fact, he was unused to conversations with young people. His sister, now fourteen, was the only younger person he socialised with, and then, only when she deigned him worthy of her company. 'Most people in the house have to call me Mr Wright because that's my proper name, and I am his Lordship's valet. But you, you can call me James if you like.'

'Thank you, Sir,' the boy beamed.

'And you are…?'

The enthusiasm in the boy's eyes turned temporarily to concern and darted about the room, finally settling on his hands which he clasped together in his lap on top of the covers.

'Jerry,' he said.

'Jerry what?'

'O'Sullivan, Sir.'

'Do you not want to call me James, Jerry?'

'Sorry, Sir. Habits.'

He was a strange lad, but now that he had engaged, an affable one.

'Habits?'

The concern returned to the lad's face, but he shrugged it away and pulled at the pyjama jacket again.

'Ah, yes,' James said. 'Did anyone explain where you are?' The boy nodded. 'And did they say what happened?' The boy wagged his head from side to side. 'Just some of it, eh?' A nod. 'Well, you are at Larkspur Hall, home of Lord Clearwater, and you are a very special young man.'

'All the others are dead, Sir?'

The question's directness took James by surprise and, at first, he wasn't sure how to answer.

'Who were you travelling with?' he asked, thinking it best to be cautions.

'No-one.'

'No-one? How old are you, Jerry?'

'Nine, Sir. Last December.'

'And you were travelling alone?'

'Yes. But that's all I remember.'

The boy had banged his head and had been through a horrific experience. James decided to return to his questioning later.

'Okay,' he said. 'Well, the train crashed, and you ended up under the last car. You've had a bit of a bashing. My friend, the big, blond man... Do you remember him?' Jerry shook his head. 'Well, he found you first, and then I picked you up and took you to the doctor. There's nothing broken or damaged, apart from that cut.' He tapped the side of his own head, and Jerry felt the injury on his temple. 'But you have to stay in bed for a while. The doctor ordered that, so we have to do what he says, correct?' Jerry nodded, now listening attentively. 'We brought you here because no-one down there knew who you were, and there wasn't anything on you to tell us who you belonged to.'

'So why A and R?'

The lad cut through the gentility and came straight to the chase.

'Because, before he became Lord Clearwater, his name was Archer Riddington, and those were his pyjamas when he was young.'

He didn't explain that Archer's mother had kept most of Archer's childhood clothes in trunks in the attics all these years. It was, Archer had said, one of her more disturbing traits; to hold on to everything from her children's past in an attempt to halt her own ageing, something neither James nor Archer understood.

'They are made of silk,' James said. 'Which makes you a very special young man indeed. 'Where do you live?' The tacked-on question was intended to catch the boy off guard. James was convinced he was not telling the whole truth.

The boy thought for a moment and appeared to be trying very hard to recall the facts, and for a moment, it seemed he genuinely couldn't remember.

'I am not sure,' Jerry said. 'Sorry. What will happen to me?'

'Now that's a good question, and to be honest with you, I don't rightly know. But, tonight, you are to sleep up here where that nice lady, Lucy, can look after you. Tomorrow, I expect you will meet His Lordship, and he will decide. Maybe the police will have found out something about you by then.'

'Police?'

Jerry's concern, until them only appearing in brief moments, was intense. It stayed on his face until James calmed him.

'You're not in trouble,' he said. 'But we do need to find out who you belong to. Your parents must be very worried.'

Jerry said nothing, just yawned.

'You need to get to sleep,' James said. 'It is getting late, and you have had a horrible day.'

'Will you stay with me, Sir?'

'I'm afraid I can't.' James pulled a long frown, clown-like and exaggerated. 'Only the ladies are allowed up here.' Leaning in conspiratorially, he whispered, 'I had to get special permission.'

'I'm not a lady.' The lad's cheerfulness had returned.

'I know.' James returned the smile. 'But that's how it is. When Lucy comes back, I will go, but I'll come back in the morning, and we'll see what's what. How does that sound?'

'Will you read to me?'

James' heart was warmed and wrenched at the same time. On the one hand, the boy's trust was touching, but on the other, the request was pathetic, as if it was a desperate plea not to be left alone.

'What were you reading?' he asked, reaching for the book by the boy's side.

'The nice lady leant it to me.'

'Oh, "Kidnapped"?' James read the cover. 'I read this one last year. Are you enjoying it?'

'I've only done the first bit. There are lots of long words in it, but I am trying.'

'Good lad.' Not knowing how long Lucy intended to be, James opened the book. 'Just until the nice lady comes back,' he said and prepared to read.

'James?'

James looked up from the page. It was the first time the boy had said his name, and the use of it endeared him to the lad.

Apparently, the endearment ran both ways, because Jerry patted the bed and shifted over, saying, 'Sit here?'

The boy had been through a hideous experience, and had possibly lost his family; it would be churlish not to agree. Feeling slightly uncomfortable, but only because such a thing was new to him, James did as he was asked and rested against the headboard, his legs stretched over the covers with Jerry beside him.

By the time Lucy returned, Jerry was asleep beneath James' arm, and the valet was engrossed in chapter three.

'He's taken to you, Mr Wright,' Lucy whispered, as together they Jerry down and tucked him in.

'Poor little mite,' James said. 'Doesn't remember much. Keep an eye on him, will you?'

'I will.'

As Lucy turned down the gas, and James tip-toed to the door, he spied a pile of clothes on a chair and asked, 'Are these his?'

'They are. I meant to throw them away. They're ruined. Oh, he had some money in the pocket, so I put it by his bed.'

'Okay. I'll get rid of these,' James whispered as he collected the clothes and left.

Passing through to the gentlemen's passage and taking the backstairs down to check on Thomas, he examined the articles to ensure nothing had been missed and none of the boy's personal possessions, if he had any, would be thrown out. There was nothing in the pockets, not even a railway ticket, and the trousers, jacket and shirt were ripped and unwearable. Pausing on the stairs, he tucked the clothes under one arm, and out of a valet's habit, began folding the garments to make a neat bundle. It didn't matter they were to be discarded, clothes should always be treated with respect. He held the jacket open and shook it, only then noticing what was inside the collar; four letters stitched in needlework by hand. They were not a tailor's label, nor were they a brand or a shop.

'If his name's Jerry O'Sullivan?' James mused. 'Why does his jacket belong to someone with the initials INTS?'

Eight

For the second night in a row, Silas was woken just before dawn. Again, he was alone in a bed, but this time it wasn't Archer's absence that stirred his sleep, it was the sound of an unfamiliar voice.

It took him a moment to remember where he was, and when he did, his first thought was that Thomas needed him, and he had thrown back the covers before he realised the voice was not that of the butler, but was coming from the other room. Apparently, Mr Smith was awake and talking.

Putting a dressing gown over his pyjamas, he collected the candle from the dresser and padded barefoot across the carpet to the door. Holding the flame towards Thomas' room confirmed that Tom was asleep, so Silas approached Smith's room, protecting the flame with his hand so it didn't throw too much light. There, he stood with his back to the wall, and his head cocked to the darkness beyond the doorway. If Smith was with someone, they were not replying. Silas heard only one voice, and it was muffled as it rose and fell in volume and uneven rhythm. The words formed a pattern of sorts, and he realised that Smith was repeating lines as if he was trying to memorise a verse. Intrigued, Silas placed the candle on the floor and peeked around the corner.

Smith stood at the window in much the same way Archer had done the night before, only he wasn't looking out across the moor. His head was down, and his hands hung limply by his sides. For a moment, he reminded Silas of a schoolboy being told off and muttering his excuses while staring at his feet in shame, but then, he wondered if Smith was asleep. The voice was low-pitched, and the words growled and spoken from the throat. The syllables were discernible even through the man's accent, but they were not words he understood.

'*Yia buyatul shi uchideh tatal.*'

Smith repeated them unaware of Silas' presence as he stepped silently into the room where the words lay heavily in the gloom.

'*Yia buyatul shi uchideh tatal.*'

The candle flickered, throwing low light on the carpet, and its shadows danced, giving the appearance that the bed was swaying. A sliver of moonlight fell like a sword-slash across the floor, and broken by the space between the chair and the wall, landed on a painting as a lone, rectangular spotlight. Everything else was darkness, a shroud around the animalistic voice.

'He seeks to take the family name. He means dishonour, he means you shame. *Yia buyatul shi uchideh tatal.*'

Outside, a fox screamed, marking its territory, but even the chilling suddenness of the noise didn't deter Smith in his sleep-talking. He repeated the phrase, a mixture of English and some other language, taking a deep, hissed breath after each repetition.

It was best to leave the man alone. Smith had been through a trauma the same as Thomas, and his half-asleep, half-awake state was probably the result. To disturb him might cause too much distress.

Silas crept back the way he had come, and at the dressing-room window, stopped to look to the east where the first grey dash of dawn was fighting for life. Sunlight would soon wake Smith naturally, and it was safest to let it happen that way.

With the man's voice rumbling incomprehensibly through the wall, Silas lay down and tried to sleep, but it was impossible. Something in the words added to his already creeping unease, a meaning he couldn't grasp, an intent perhaps. After a few minutes, he rose. Thomas' room felt safer, and he curled himself in the armchair to doze against troubled dreams.

When he woke, it was to the sound of gentle knocking. His legs were cramped, and he stretched them as he unwound himself from the chair. Thomas had also heard the knock, and after a brief moment of confusion, tried to sit up.

Confusion deepened as Archer appeared carrying a tray in the same way Saddle or Barnaby would attend His Lordship.

'Good morning, Sir,' the viscount said, affecting the haughty voice that Tripp had once employed. 'I do hope you slept well.' He placed the tray on the bedside table and walked with a straight back to the window, throwing a playful wink at Silas as he passed. 'The weather appears quite clement this morning, Mr Payne', he said, drawing the curtains.

James entered carrying another tray and smiled at a dumfounded Thomas. 'Good morning, Sirs', he said sailing through to Smith's room as if this was an everyday occurrence.

'What are you two playing at?' Silas laughed, stretching.

'I always wondered what it was like for the footmen', Archer said before plumping Thomas' pillows. 'How are you feeling?'

'Out of place', Thomas said.

'Any pain, Mr Payne?'

'Very funny. I mean, sorry, My Lord. Just a little.'

'It's okay, Tom', Archer sat beside him. 'Honestly, how are you?'

'Stiff.'

'Shall I call for Jimmy to help you with that?' Silas joked, and Thomas tutted.

'I need to move around', he said. 'I'll get up and see to the breakfast room.'

'No, you won't.' Archer was adamant. 'Barnaby is doing that.'

'I must do something. I am not staying in bed all day.'

Archer lifted the tray and placed it before his butler. 'Actually, you are', he said. 'Mrs Flintwich has made you coffee and toast. There's marmalade too, and a leftover cake of some dubious description.'

'Sir, really, I can't...'

'Shut up', Archer said flippantly. 'You eat that, and then, if you are up to it, you may get up and go to your own room to rest.' He turned to Silas, staring from the window. 'Any problems?'

'No', Silas replied. 'Not a sound from Tommy. Mr Smith was sleepwalking, though.'

'I should go and see him.'

James was back. 'Your guest is awake, Sir', he said. 'I said you would be in directly.'

'Thanks, Jimmy.' Archer patted Thomas' leg. 'Tom, this is an order. You only get out of bed if you feel up to it, otherwise, stay here until you do. Doctor Penhale should be up later, so you really ought to wait until he has seen you...'

Thomas' hand on his shoulder halted his fussing. 'Archer...' He

80

whispered in case a maid was waiting within earshot. 'I'll get up in a minute and go to work. Please, it's what I need to do.'

'Could be for the best,' Silas suggested. 'Be as normal as possible. Might help you forget.'

Archer conceded and left to pay a visit to Mr Smith.

Silas said nothing about the strange sleep-talking, but he remembered the words. They had stayed with him through his dozing, and he could hear them in the man's accent. Wondering if Fecker might know what they meant — the accent was not dissimilar to his — he left James to help Thomas, and returned to his own room to wash and change.

'Mr Smith seems remarkably well,' Archer reported as he joined Silas at the breakfast table a short while later. 'I insisted he stay upstairs and rest until Penhale gets here, though. Morning, Barnaby.'

The footman greeted him in his usual fashion and immediately set about serving Archer at the table. Silas preferred to help himself, but Archer was a man of routine when it came to breakfast and always had the same thing. Barnaby had quickly learnt his master's requests, and after pouring his coffee, thick, black and Turkish, arranged a plate of eggs, bread and kidneys.

Silas was still mulling over Smith's strange words and was keen to speak with Fecker. His friend usually exercised the horses early in the morning with the help of the stable boys. Danylo, also a keen horseman, but not as skilled as Fecker, joined them before starting work on the kitchen garden and smallholding Archer had given him, and there was no point going to the stables until later.

'What time are you expecting the doctor?' Silas asked, poking a sausage around his plate.

'It depends on how busy he is,' Archer replied. 'I thought I might go down shortly and see how they are doing. Find out what's happening to the... To those who didn't survive. See if there is anything I can do. What about you?'

'Need to see Mr Andrej. And I thought I might look at that book you talked about.'

'What book?'

'The one about the Romanians.'

'Oh, well good luck with that,' Archer laughed. 'It's just one of about a thousand in the library.'

'If I might, My Lord,' Barnaby said, placing the viscount's plate. 'It would be one of four thousand two hundred and thirty.'

Archer was aghast, impressed, rather than offended by the correction from his young footman. 'How do you know that?'

Barnaby blushed and looked at Silas for advice. Silas encouraged him by pointing his fork at the viscount.

'My grandfather was the librarian at Larkspur until just afore he died, Sir,' Barnaby said. 'Sorry, just *before* he died. Then me father took over in his spare time, when he's not at the farm.'

'Your father is Mr Nancarrow?' Archer was shocked. 'Why didn't I know that?'

'I expect you did,' Silas said to cover Barnaby's disappointment and Archer's embarrassment. 'But what with the train wreck yesterday, you no doubt forgot.'

'Yes, quite.' Archer was the one now blushing. 'I'm sorry, Barnaby, it completely slipped my mind.'

'That's alright, Sir. He don't come to the house often, and I've not been above stairs long, so you and me have not much spoken.'

'All the same, I'm terribly sorry to have forgotten, old chap. How many did you say?'

Barnaby repeated the number, adding, 'And that's without those on the gallery level. Another six hundred up there.'

'And somewhere among them is a book about the Order of the Rasnov Dragon,' Silas said. 'I'll start looking.'

'And for me? What am I doing after I've seen Penhale?'

Archer glanced across the table at his private secretary who had finally decided to eat the sausage. It was halfway to Silas' mouth when he was caught, and he put it down gently.

'Without your diary, Sir,' he said, 'I can't be completely certain, but today was set aside for the Easter dinner and guest arrangements. Mrs Flintwich and the menus at three as I remember. Mr Payne and the wine list before lunch, and the table plan at some point. You also wanted to dispatch messages to your guests warning them they may have to take a carriage from further down the line because of the accident, but confirm that your guest of honour is still able to attend.'

'That sounds right,' Archer said, nodding. 'Barnaby?'

'My Lord?'

'Would you ask Mrs Flintwich if she is still free this afternoon?'

'She is.'

The voice came from Thomas, standing in the doorway in his black-and-whites. Archer twisted in his chair, and on seeing his butler, stood.

'Mr Payne, are you well enough?'

'I am not unwell, My Lord,' Thomas said, walking into the room as upright as usual but at a slower pace. 'Just a little stiff in places.'

'Not dizzy? Penhale won't like you being out of bed.'

'I am perfectly fine, My Lord, thank you. Barnaby, I will take over here.'

'Very good, Mr Payne.' Barnaby was unable to hide his disappointment, but he nodded once and smartly to the butler, and then his master, and retreated.

'Come and sit down, Tom,' Archer said once the footman had left.

'No, thank you, Sir. I would rather stand and keep my limbs moving. How is the boy? Do we know?'

'James has gone up to see him,' Archer said, watching Thomas closely as he moved to the sideboard to check that everything was in order. 'The lad seems to have taken a shine to Jimmy.'

'While you're both here and we're alone...' Silas put down his knife and fork. 'Has Mr Smith said anything?'

'Only how grateful he is to be alive,' Archer told him. 'And to thank us, ask where he is and apologise for being a burden, which he isn't. Why?'

'The thing is,' Silas went on. 'He was talking in his sleep last night, or early this morning. Standing at the window and mumbling. I assume he was asleep.'

'What was he saying?'

'If I've got this right...' Silas thought back. 'He said, "He seeks to take the family name. He means dishonour, he means you shame." And then something in a funny language. Something like "Y'all pay bayat, o Moira potato."'

It meant nothing to Archer, but he sought clarification. 'Take the family name?'

'Yeah. It was a rhyme, apart from that last bit.'

'Which, I assume, is Romanian,' Archer said. 'But my bunica didn't teach me that many words.'

'I thought Fecker might know what it meant.'

'He's Ukrainian.'

'I know that, Archie, but aren't they the same place?'

Behind him, Thomas coughed.

'Not quite,' Archer said, throwing the butler a wide-eyed warning. 'Completely different really, but it's worth asking. Why are you so interested?'

'It's the tattoo,' Silas admitted. 'And the way he's got nothing on him. A Romanian down here in Cornwall, on his own, no luggage, covered in a dragon and talking in his sleep about stealing and dishonour. Smells fishy.'

'I expect his luggage was lost in the crash,' Archer reasoned. 'We have no cause to be suspicious of a traveller just because he has an accent and talks in his sleep.'

'He didn't have luggage,' Thomas said. He dropped the lid on the last cloche and touched the coffee pot to test its warmth. 'Will you require more coffee, gentlemen?'

Archer refused, but Silas took the last from the pot, asking, 'How do you know he had no luggage?'

'I saw him on the platform in Plymouth,' Thomas explained. 'In fact, he came from the London down train, crossed the platform and waited not far from me. He was carrying nothing and had no porter, but instead, appeared to be looking for someone.'

'Did he board with anyone?' Silas asked.

His intrigue was mounting by the second. There was no reason for it apart from the unusual behaviour during the night, yet he was unable to shake off the feeling that Mr Smith was more than an accident victim.

'No,' Thomas said. 'Maybe whoever he was waiting for didn't show up, but I could have sworn he was looking. His head kept going from right to left, first-class to third. When our train pulled in, he boarded last. In fact, the guard had to tell him to close the door and be careful because he was leaning out when we moved off.'

'Nothing strange about that,' Archer said. He finished his kidneys and dabbed his mouth before attending to a pile of correspondence

Barnaby had left beside his place.

'Maybe not,' the butler conceded. 'But on the journey, he stayed away from the window and only went to it when we pulled into a station, as if...'

The other two waited until, prompted by Silas to voice his concerns, Thomas described in detail, how their journey had been spent.

He told them how Smith looked away from other passengers and only engaged with Thomas when pressed. How he looked from the window only when stationary, and how he constantly checked the time. He also told them what Smith had said about being late to his destination and not being exactly sure which train he was on. The man had been vague and nervous, and he wore clothes that didn't fit his style of speech, to which Archer said, 'You're being snobbish,' and Thomas disagreed.

'There was something wrong about him,' he said.

'Which is what I got as well,' Silas agreed. 'Hey, me and Tommy see eye to eye on something at last.'

'I think you're both being unnecessarily distrustful,' Archer chided. 'To me, he seems like a very pleasant man in an unfortunate circumstance. When the doctor has seen him and decided what's best to do, I will invite him to spend a few days with us until fully recovered.'

'You're not being too trusting?'

'Certainly not, Silas. What's wrong with helping someone in need?'

'Nothing,' Silas said. 'It's your hobby, after all.'

'No need for sarcasm,' Archer said with humour. 'And no need for suspicion.'

'Maybe there isn't,' Thomas put in. 'But I did gain the impression that Mr Smith was hiding something. He was...' The word escaped him, even when the viscount prompted him. 'He just didn't feel right,' was the only way Thomas could explain it.

'And now talking in his sleep,' Silas added. 'On top of what Tommy's told us, that makes me trust him even less. I'll look into it.'

'Look into what?' Archer threw down his napkin. 'You are both overreacting.' Pushing back his chair, he stood. Thomas was not fast enough to be there for him, and by the time he reached his master's place, Archer was halfway to the door with the post. 'But you do what you want, Silas,' he said, anger in his voice. 'I have more important things to attend to than misgivings. Just don't embarrass our guest. That's not my way of doing things.'

Archer left and, unusually, slammed the door.

Silas and Thomas looked at each other, concerned, until Thomas said, 'He is very worried about the Easter dinner. It's vital it goes without a hitch.'

'And it will with you in charge, Tommy.' It didn't hurt to pay the man a compliment from time to time, and Thomas appreciated it. 'Now, before that creep Saddle comes and starts fussing around, was there anything else odd about Mr so-called-Smith that you remember?'

Thomas held the back of a chair and closed his eyes. Silas asked if he needed to sit, but he said he was just thinking. All the same, he was worryingly pale, and Silas was worried.

'He wasn't interested in the scenery,' Thomas remembered. 'So I assumed he wasn't on a holiday. Besides, no luggage. He shared my whisky after persuasion and seemed grateful for it as though it settled his nerves. He also knew that Purcari and Mediasch are reds.'

'Which is more than I do,' Silas snorted. 'What's that?'

'Wines from Transylvania. The Mediasch is extremely rare, and apparently, Mr Irving is partial to both.'

'And he's the guest of honour, right?'

'You, I believe, sent out the invitations for His Lordship, Mr Hawkins,' Thomas teased. 'Yes, he is, but I didn't tell Smith that.'

'Did he say anything else?'

'Only that this was his first visit to Cornwall, he hadn't heard of Larkspur or the viscount, didn't travel much, and suffers from motion sickness.'

'Blimey,' Silas said. 'For someone who's been thrown about in a train wreck, you've got a good memory.'

Thomas put his other hand on the chair.

'Why don't you sit, Tommy?'

Thomas shook his head. 'I am fine, honestly, but if you don't need me, I'll ring for Mr Saddle and maybe sit quietly downstairs and attend to my ledger.'

'You go ahead, mate. You look like you need it. Want me to come down with you?'

Thomas appreciated Silas' concern. It wasn't that the two didn't get on, but they were not as close as Silas and James, and the butler was not as easy to talk to as Barnaby. Thinking the name reminded Silas that the footman knew about the library.

'Actually,' he said. 'Could I borrow Barnaby for a while this morning?'

'Yes, as long as he has finished his duties. Can I ask why?'

'You can ask me anything, Tommy.' Silas rose and came to take his arm. 'Here, at least let me go with you to the stairs. You look like a hangover in a suit.'

Surprisingly, Thomas allowed it, and Silas helped him from the breakfast room to the servants' door behind the west staircase.

'I'll be fine from here,' Thomas said. 'Thank you, Mr Hawkins.'

'Ach, Tommy,' Silas tutted. He wished the man would loosen up, but said no more as he watched him go.

Still not convinced that Smith was an innocent traveller, Silas pondered the tattoo. After what Thomas had told him, his suspicions had increased, but was there really a reason for mistrust?

'Why have a dragon painted on his back?' he asked himself as he crossed the hall to the library. 'Who wants to be marked with a symbol of an ancient order of assassins apart from an assassin?'

Perhaps Archer was right. Perhaps Smith was distantly descended from an old family who had, at one time hundreds of years ago, protected the nobility of Romania. If so, what was he doing in Cornwall? It was hardly a place anyone came for a day, and if he had come down on the London train, he must have left the city early in the morning, if not the night before.

'Who travels overnight with no bags?'

The questions stacked up alongside the meaning of the verse and foreign words, but even they paled into insignificance when he heaved open the library door.

'And who the feck collects nearly five thousand books?' he muttered, before returning to the baize door in search of a footman who would know.

Nine

Under the direction of Thomas and Mrs Baker, the morning routine at Larkspur ran like a well-rehearsed theatrical production. The day started early for the maids whose first task it was to clean grates, empty ash buckets, set fires, dust furniture and see to the general tidying. Other work was expertly overseen by Mrs Baker, who was responsible for everything above the ground floor and a lot more besides.

In the kitchens, Mrs Flintwich was also an early riser, especially at times when large dinners were planned. Assisted by two kitchen maids, she lit the ovens, made the bread and planned the day's meals while her assistants fetched milk and eggs, took deliveries from the farms and kitchen garden, and saw to minor cooking tasks. They were, in turn, assisted by the two hall boys. Mark was fifteen and had been at the Hall for two years and was recently joined by a second lad who Mrs Flintwich had trained. He was there to replace Barnaby who, at twenty, had been a servants' servant far too long. Barnaby had turned down the chance to work in other houses because his ambition was to work as a footman at the Hall, and he was given his chance by Mr Payne just after Christmas when Thomas reorganised the staff.

Barnaby's day started early with sweeping the main hall and rooms, brushing the furniture, opening curtains and generally seeing that any rooms used the day before were up to a standard set by the butler. Meanwhile, Robert, or Mr Saddle as he was now called because he had been promoted from the first footman to under-butler, ensured that his senior had everything he needed for the day ahead.

Outside in the stable block, Mr Williams and his two stable boys were responsible for mucking out, feeding and tending to the viscount's horses, while Mr Andrej oversaw the animals' wellbeing, inspected the tack and feed, and ensured the stables and carriages were always in perfect working order. Since Fecker's arrival, Mr Williams had been able to take on more diverse work, something he had always wanted to do, and was now responsible for the machine room that ran the gas lighting and water system. He still tended to the horses because he liked that work, but was happy to be a Jack of all trades, and acted as the coachman when Mr Andrej was busy.

Days started early and often finished late, but with accommodation and, in most cases, uniforms provided by Lord Clearwater, no-one complained.

No-one apart from Mr Saddle, and it was he who on the morning of April the eighteenth, was tasked with attending to the injured visitor, Mr Smith.

Muttering as he took the backstairs to the gentlemen's corridor, he was annoyed that His Lordship had allowed his valet, of all people, to bring the morning tray to the guest. Such tasks were meant for footmen, and as the house was one short, Saddle minded taking on a task that was now beneath his station. Approaching forty years of age, he also minded that Mr Wright and the viscount had so childishly enjoyed playing a prank on Mr Payne by delivering a breakfast tray to the butler and the guest. The butler should not have been sleeping in a guest suite in the first place, let alone one so grand and near to His Lordship.

Saddle kept his thoughts to himself, but since Christmas, and despite his promotion, he was growing increasingly aggravated by the way he had been treated. Some would have said he should be grateful for the increase in salary and responsibility, because he, like the viscount, had recently been elevated, and considering there were so few members of the family living at Larkspur, an under-butler was not particularly needed. Lord Clearwater and Mr Payne had told him it was to reward him for years of loyal service as a footman under Mr Tripp, but Saddle thought it was their way of keeping him quiet.

A Lancastrian by birth, he had found his way to the Hall via a circuitous path that included menial hall-boy service in the city, second footman tedium for a baron in Devon, and at the age of thirty-two, the first footman position at Larkspur. Far from home for most of his life, he had lost touch with his family, and being a man of a gloomy and unwaveringly unhappy disposition, had few friends either outside or in the house. His manner was naturally grumpy, and the act of covering it with politeness and professionalism, instead of helping him through each repetitive day, only served to heighten his dissatisfaction with life.

Entering the gentlemen's corridor, he sneered at Mr Hawkins' bedroom door because that was another thing that angered him. The way this uneducated and untitled Irishman had wheedled his way into the Hall and somehow become part of the Riddington family home. For a nobleman such as Viscount Clearwater to have a private secretary was nothing surprising, the man had many fingers in many pies both philanthropic and commercial, but for such a post to be taken by a snip of a lad, and one from no discernible background, did the respectability of the Hall no favours. Then there was the question of how His Lordship had acquired such an annoying young upstart, and why he had decided to house him in the main suite. Until the death of the previous viscount, whom Saddle held in great esteem, the rooms had been for Lady Clearwater, now dispatched to the dower house even though the viscount showed no signs of marrying. For an immigrant to be using her Ladyship's rooms as though he deserved them, simply added fuel to Saddle's already smouldering fire of discontent, a mood which others might have thought was caused by jealousy, but which he insisted was caused only out of concern for the family.

Growling, and trying to put the negative thoughts from his mind, he came to rest outside the Bosworth second bedroom and adjusted his tails along with his demeanour. The man on the other side of the door was a guest, and it was Saddle's responsibility to make him welcome and see to his needs.

This is what the under-butler was born for, but he would rather the gentleman he was about to serve was a nobleman, a baron at least, if not a viscount, but he was still a guest of Lord Clearwater and thus, must be treated with respect. Saddle didn't live to serve Archer Riddington, as was, he lived to serve His Lordship, no matter who held the title, and he reminded of himself of that as he finally buried his disgruntled thoughts and knocked purposefully on the door.

'Hello?' was the unorthodox reply, and told Saddle that the guest was no nobleman.

He entered, placing a forced semi-smile of greeting on his otherwise withering features, and closed the door.

'Good morning, Sir,' he said, bowing his head to the man sitting up in the bed. 'His Lordship asked me to inform you that the doctor will be here presently, and to ask how you are feeling, and if there is anything I can do for you.'

It was a standard sentence for Saddle, but the guest had trouble putting all the questions together. 'Doctor?' he said, and Saddle immediately noticed his foreign accent.

Bristling, because he was serving a foreigner who didn't know how to say, 'Come in', he said, 'Yes, Sir. His Lordship returned from the village bringing news that Doctor Penhale will be visiting yourself and the other injured we have here at the Hall.'

'Oh,' the man said, pushing himself further upright. 'There are others?'

'One and one staff, Sir. May I ask how you are feeling?'

Saddle was still at the door, but his eyes searched the room for anything out of place. Whoever had attended the man last had not tied back the curtains, nor tidied his clothes. Mr Wright (another upstart who shouldn't have been in the position he was in) might be the viscount's valet by some shortcut route, but he didn't know a footman's duties. Saddle attended to the curtains and cushions, chairs and dressing table.

'I must admit to having the devil of a pain in my leg,' Mr Smith said. 'But Clearwater told me it wasn't broken as I first thought.'

Saddle drew in a sharp breath. '*Lord* Clearwater,' he emphasised, 'is most concerned that you have everything you require.' He wanted to add, 'Including manners,' but it was not seemly.

'I do, I think,' Smith replied. 'Except for information. Clearwater...' (Saddle cleared his throat pointedly.) 'His Lordship told me little about what happened and nothing about what will happen next. Can you tell me?'

'If you wish, Sir.'

One of the things Saddle would miss in his new role were the tips traditionally left by guests for the footmen and valets who had attended them. On his mildly increased salary, he was not expected to receive such gratuities, and Saddle had some habits which needed constant financial fuelling. He doubted this man, with his foreign accent and being unaccustomed to etiquette, would know how things worked, and if Saddle played his cards right, he might be able to squeeze a few pounds from Mr Smith when he left.

'What's your name?' Mr Smith asked.

Seeing it as a chance to break a little ice, Saddle told him. 'Saddle, Sir. I am under-butler but new in this post, so I am more than happy if you care to call me Robert, as that is the name I am more accustomed to hearing.'

Smith shrugged in a continental manner as if he didn't care how a servant was addressed. 'If you want,' he said. 'So, Robert, can you tell me what happened? I'm very glad to be alive, of course, and very grateful to Lord Clearwater for taking me in, but the man who brought that tray didn't tell me much, and Clearwater only asked how I was and told me to stay in bed.'

Wright had not thought to return for the tray, and Saddle wondered why Barnaby hadn't been up to fetch it. Under the young viscount, standards were slipping.

'The train derailed,' he explained, standing at the end of the bed and rearranging the eiderdown. 'You suffered a concussion, I believe, and there was some injury to your leg, but the doctor saw to that, and there is no lasting damage. You were brought here unconscious with Mr Payne and the boy, and given a sleeping draught for the night. Oh, this is the Bosworth suite. The late and noble viscount named the guest rooms after his favourite historical battles.'

'Hang on...'

Hang on? Saddle resisted the temptation to ask what to.

'Mr Payne, the butler, yes?'

'Yes, Sir.'

'Decent fellow. If it wasn't for him, I would surely have perished. Is he alright?'

'He is, Sir, I am pleased to say, but like yourself, was knocked about, and although he is back at work, he has taken lighter duties for the day.'

Another thing which wrangled Saddle. If a man was fit to work, he was fit to work his proper duties. Payne had chosen to direct the preparations for the Easter dinner from his pantry as if he, and not the viscount, was lord of the manor.

'That's good to hear. I will thank him when I see him. And this boy you mentioned. Who is he? Family?'

'Not at all, Sir. In fact, we are still not sure. He is being cared for by the housekeeper and his Lordship's valet.' He wanted to add, 'For a reason no-one has bothered to explain to me,' but held his tongue. 'The child has not yet been claimed, and we wondered if perhaps he wasn't meant to be travelling alone. Either that or those with him were not as fortunate as yourself.'

'Traveling alone?' Smith was interested to know more. 'I saw no lone child. Was he in third class?'

'He was, Sir. He wasn't anything to do with you, I take it?'

'No. I was also travelling alone.'

'No doubt all will be revealed in the fullness of time.' Saddle came around the bed to top up the man's water glass.

'What else?'

'What else, Sir?'

'Yes, Robert. What else do I need to know?'

Being addressed by his Christian name increased Saddle's hopes of a tip at the end of the man's stay.

'Only that you should stay at rest until Doctor Penhale has seen you. I believe he will be first with the boy, but you shouldn't have to wait long. Do you need anything in the meantime?'

'My clothes,' Smith said, looking around the room. 'Are they here?'

Saddle had already noticed and disapproved of the pile of filthy garments the valet had left hanging over the back of a chair.

'They are, Sir,' he said, reaching for them. 'Was there anything in particular?'

'My watch? My jacket?'

Saddle lifted the jacket, ripped and stained with oil among other less discernible things, and held it out by his fingertips. 'I fear it has suffered worse than you.'

Smith laughed. 'I like your attitude, Robert. I could do with a few amusements right now. May I have it?'

Saddle passed it over.

'Sit, if you want.'

'I shan't, Sir, if you don't mind.' That would have been completely against etiquette, tempting though it was to breed familiarity.

Smith examined the gold fob watch closely. Pressing the winder, the cover popped open to reveal the face. 'Still working,' he said. 'Still has all the necessary parts.'

'I am glad to hear it.'

Smith dropped the watch into his pyjama jacket. 'Whose nightclothes am I wearing?'

'They belong to His Lordship's secretary,' Saddle informed him, shuddering at the thought of having to wear an Irishman's pyjamas. 'He being of a similar build to yourself, the housekeeper thought they would make a reasonable fit.'

'I must thank him.' Smith turned his jacket inside out and examined the lining. 'That's still intact,' he said. 'More good news.'

'Still intact?' Saddle asked before had had a chance to check himself. It was unusual enough for a man to examine the stitching of his suit, let alone be concerned for its condition following such a violent accident.

By way of explanation, Smith showed him the inside, and leaning closer, Saddle saw that it contained a hidden pocket fastened by a camouflaged button. From it, Smith produced a bundle of notes, and Saddle's dry heart leapt as much as his interest.

'It's all I have,' Smith said. 'I am so glad the valet didn't throw these away. Will you tell him I am thankful? I'll give him a tip.'

The growl of jealousy as the back of Saddle's throat only went unheard because he covered it with a sycophantic, 'Certainly, Sir.'

'Now then,' Smith said, putting the jacket on the bed beside him. 'Tell me more about this boy. What age is he?'

'Age? I think Mr Wright said he was nine. His name is Jerry O'Sullivan. Does that mean anything to you?'

Smith shook his head defensively. 'Why should it? What does he look like?'

Saddle was keen to know why Smith was taking such an interest, and thinking the man might identify the child, told him all he knew. 'Dark, red-brown hair as they have in Ireland,' he said. 'Speaks as though well educated, or so Mr Wright tells me. Wary of everyone apart from the valet who he thinks rescued him, which is understandable, and likes to read books. Apart from that, nothing.'

Smith considered the information, rubbing the bridge of his steep nose with the back of his finger.

'He still rings no bells for you, Sir?'

'No, Robert,' Smith admitted. 'Will he be staying long?'

'That, I imagine, will be up to the doctor and His Lordship,' Saddle replied, unable to think why Smith was unnaturally interested in the lad. If the boy was related to him or in his charge, it would make sense, but he had hardly asked about Mr Payne, who had, by all accounts, pulled him from the wreck just in time to save his life. Why should he be more interested in a stray child?

'Clearwater said I might stay, but he has someone special happening this week?' Smith probed. 'I must be out of his way by then.'

'Perhaps the doctor will have found room for you at the hospital,' Saddle suggested. 'Again, we will have to wait and see, but I am sure His lordship will be happy for you to rest here for as long as necessary.'

'That's kind of him.'

'Yes.' It was said without emotion, apart from perhaps annoyance, because Saddle considered the viscount charitable to the point of weakness.

'What's the big event?'

'Big…? Oh, the Holy Week dinner.'

'Which is…?'

Remembering Smith's other clothes, Saddle attended to them, holding them up to see if the man wanted them. Apparently, now he had his watch and his money, he wasn't worried about anything else, and he shook his head at each garment.

'The Larkspur Holy Week dinner,' Saddle said, 'was inaugurated by the late viscount some years ago. It was his way of entertaining friends who, like him, were of a devout Christian disposition, the dinner taking place on Good Friday. This year, under the new viscount, the dinner has been arranged by His Lordship for some of his acquaintances from…' He swallowed a little bile. 'The Garrick Club.'

It was unusual to discuss Hall business in this manner, but the man was a guest with money. Saddle had gambling debts to pay in Padstow, and his creditors had, of late, grown impatient. The more he could do for Smith, the more chance he stood of paying those debts, and he had seen the potential in the man's pocket.

Smith was waiting for a further explanation and Saddle was happy to provide it.

'The guests are arriving on Friday afternoon, he said. 'They will stay until Sunday evening when, I believe, Mr Irving has arranged a private railway carriage for those returning to the city.'

'Mr Irving? You'll have to slow down, Robert. My head is not settled, and there is a lot for me to take in.'

'My apologies, Sir.'

'Go on, but slowly. A private carriage? Mr Irving? He must be very special. Who is he?'

'Our guest of honour.' Despite himself, Saddle managed a smile. He wasn't a great lover of the arts, but when the country's leading Shakespearean actor saw fit to grace the county, let alone the corridors of Larkspur Hall, even he succumbed to enthusiasm. 'Henry Irving,' he said. 'You may have heard of him. A great actor and more. He is what they are calling an actor-manager because he not only performs, but also directs and runs the Lyceum Theatre, presenting productions as never before seen.' His words were directly copied from a recent edition of The Times, but he doubted Smith would know. 'There is talk, I understand, that Her Majesty, being so enamoured with the great man, may see fit to award him a knighthood. If so, he will be the first actor to receive one.'

'Really?' Smith was impressed. 'I can see why he is to be a guest of honour.'

'Indeed, Sir. He is currently on his way back from America and is breaking his journey here for a few days. We are all determined to give him a memorable stay.'

'I'm sure you are,' Smith said, reaching for his glass of water. 'Who else is coming?'

The two were establishing a bond, and Saddle did all he could to encourage it. He had never spoken to a guest in this way, but then he had never been in a position to be so intimate with one. The man was intriguing, and not only because of his accent and his looks, which Saddle though rather Eastern European (he had seen pictures in The Illustrated Police News), but also because of his finances.

'The others will include our Poet Laureate, Lord Tennyson,' he said proudly.

Smith was enthralled. 'Clearwater knows some important people.'

'His Lordship does.'

Saddle let the lack of title pass. At that point, he would have allowed Smith anything, he was sipping water with one hand and holding open his pyjama pocket with the other. Saddle had so far counted seven five-pound notes. 'Also in attendance will be Earl Romney and the great composer, Mr Sullivan,' he added. 'Of the Savoy Operas, although I prefer his more serious works.'

'Their wives?'

'No, Sir, I believe not, save for Countess Romney. Mr Sullivan is unmarried. Mr Irving will be attending with his business manager.'

Smith raised his thin eyebrows above the rim of his glass, a prompt for even more information, and Saddle wondered if he was going too far.

Apparently, he wasn't. Smith wanted him to go further and was intentionally tapping the money in his pocket, suggesting without subtlety, that he was willing to reward Saddle for the information.

'His business manager? Who's that?' the man asked before taking a sip from his glass.

'Mr Irving's associate is a man by the name of Stoker,' Saddle said, and Smith spluttered on his drink. 'A towel, Sir?'

The offer was brushed away. 'Sorry, Robert. It went down the wrong way. Stoker? The man who writes those stories?'

'I believe he has published some short stories, yes, and a novel. Apart from that, I know little about him.'

'I must certainly get myself fit and away before then,' Smith offered. 'On which note…' He swung his legs from the bed, and Saddle immediately rushed forward to help. 'No, no, Robert,' Smith said, grimacing. 'Let me see if I can manage.'

He couldn't, and nearly crashed to the floor as he put weight on his leg. Swearing, he offered no resistance when Saddle held his arm and assisted him to the bathroom.

'Thank you,' Smith said. 'Sincerely, thank you. You're the first person who has shown an interest in me since I woke up.'

'Glad to hear it, Sir,' Saddle said, both eyes on the man's pocket.

'You only need to tell me what I can do for you, and it shall be done.'

Smith clutched the doorjamb, and limped into the bathroom, saying, 'I will hold you to that.'

Ten

The reason James hadn't removed the tray from Smith's room was because he was busy with Mrs Baker and Jerry. Firstly, the doctor had called and asked to see the boy, finally declaring him perfectly fit physically, but advising James to keep a close eye on the boy's mental stability. Such a trauma, the doctor said, might well manifest itself in the boy's behaviour rather than his body. With Jerry examined and given permission to leave his bed and be mobile, James' next job was to search for clothes Jerry could wear, and the hall boy, Mark, was dispatched to Mrs Williams to ask for anything she might have, her youngest child being a slight boy of eleven.

Meanwhile, Barnaby was unavailable to clear Smith's tray because Silas had called him to the library to help find any information on the order of Rasnov assassins.

'To be honest with you, Sir,' Barnaby said as they faced the thousands of books on the floor-to-ceiling shelves, 'I've not much been in this room. It's my father's job once a month, and I've spent my life below stairs.'

'Is your dad available to come and see me?' Silas asked, also wondering where he might start.

'Sorry, no, Sir. He's over Marazion way for a few days visiting my uncle.' Barnaby scratched his head, disturbing his earthy-brown hair. He flattened it back into shape and said, 'But he does keep a record. An index, I think he calls it. It should be here somewhere.'

Once Silas realised Barnaby was waiting for permission to find it, he offered him the room with a wave of his hand and followed the footman to the nearest reading table where, opening drawers, they found nothing but writing materials. At the next desk, however, Barnaby found what he was looking for.

Six large volumes stood in a line on the shelf abutting the desk, and each one was titled, 'Larkspur Hall Library' and its volume number. Silas whistled through his teeth when Barnaby opened the first book and showed him the endless lists of titles.

'There be some rare reading in here,' the footman said. 'So me father says. Some date back three hundred years. It was the viscount's great...' He paused to remember, chewing his lip and closing one eye. 'His great-great-great-grandfather who started the collection proper.' Holding the ledger, he swung to make an arc of the room and pointed to a distant bookcase. 'That there should be the oldest books, under glass, see? Over there...' Referring to the list, he counted the number of cases in from the door. 'That's the old legal collection. I believe the fifteenth Viscount Clearwater was in the legal profession, and over there...' Another turn and a decisive indication of more shelves. 'That's the sixteenth viscount's collection. From then on, as we get more modern, the books are arranged by subject, then author.'

'Blimey,' Silas said. 'I never owned one book, let alone this many.'

'Never had a book, Sir?' Barnaby asked. 'Is that true?'

'That's perfectly true, Barney.'

'How did you learn anything, Sir?'

It occurred to Silas that the man, no older than himself, although brought up as a servant, had known a great deal more comforts than Silas, a man brought up in the slums of Westerpool, and for a moment he was reminded of his roots. With the library shelves towering over him, the tall windows overlooking the moor, and the wood and leather furniture, marble fireplace and crystal chandeliers of his current home, the shared room in Canter Wharf seemed an impossible place to have come from.

'I learnt about life in a different way,' he said. 'That's all. So, where d'you think we might find a book about the Rasnov family and their Romanian history?'

'That's interesting,' Barnaby said, replacing the first volume and selecting another. 'Because I'm not sure if that would come under travel, geography, general history or family history. The viscount is descended from the Rasnovs of Romania, did you know?'

'I did, Barney.'

The footman sifted through several pages, grimacing. 'I'm really not sure, Sir.'

'Would Mr Payne know? I could ask him.'

'He was resting, Sir, so I'd leave him a while now. I'll help you find what you want.' Again chewing his lip and thinking, Barnaby eyed the walls, finally deciding on a course of action. 'How about you start there with family history, and I'll look over here in general history. The list here says the fifth shelf from the east wall — that's this one — holds copies of the College of Arms records, and the one between the second and third window holds general. There's a list of titles.'

Silas read the list, which was written in a neat, cursive script and perfectly legible. 'Good idea,' he said and crossed the room, counting his way to the fifth bookcase. 'Let me know if you find anything about Rasnov.'

'Yes, Sir.'

To give Barnaby his credit, he hadn't asked why he was assisting the secretary in his search instead of being downstairs attending to the silver and polishing the plate, and Silas was grateful for the lack of questions. It suggested instant trust. If the footman had asked, he would have had to tell the truth, and to say that he didn't trust the viscount's guest further than he could spit him, was probably not what the man was used to hearing.

Archer's words at the window the previous morning came back to him, his story about how he sensed bad things coming as he had done that night on his ship in the Black Sea. Silas felt the same unease, but only since first laying eyes on the mysterious Mr Smith.

'Is anyone from Romania called Smith?' he muttered, running his fingers along the spines.

The books were a mixed collection. Taking them down one at a time, he found indexes where the names Riddington, Clearwater, Larkspur and others connected with the family were referenced. Turning to the entries in the texts, he found some were single lines, mentions in court circulars and published events, attendees at coronations and royal funerals, and general mentions of all manner of occasions where Archer's family happened to play a part, but there was nothing about the Rasnovs.

After half an hour, and only partly through the first shelf, he was starting to wonder if this was a waste of time when Barnaby called him over to the window.

'Did you find something?'

'No, Sir, but I had an idea.'

'Go on.'

Barnaby was flicking through his ledger, and when he found the page he wanted, he showed it to Silas.

'Bible,' he said as if that was the answer to everything.

'Bible?'

'Family bible, Sir. Here, there's a note from a librarian before my father, probably granddad, and it says…' Holding the heavy volume to the light, he quoted. '"Ancestral records in the Riddington family bibles." It's just a note in the margin beside a book about Larkspur Hall, but it's a place for you to start.'

'Where is it?'

'There's more than one, Sir.' With his head still down over his ledger as if it was a map, Barnaby led Silas to a reading table beside a glass cabinet on the far side of the room. 'In there,' he said. 'There are three. May I?' He pointed to the cabinet, and Silas nodded permission.

The bottom shelf, half-hidden by the wood surrounding the glass panelling of the doors, held three large bibles. Barnaby crouched to examine them, and Silas dragged over two chairs so they could sit.

'This one,' the footman said, checking his list and pointing but not daring to touch, 'is a Geneva Bible. That dates from about fifteen eighty and is probably here as a collector's curio, rather than a working family bible. That one, the second, that's a King James from…' He again checked his notes. 'Seventeen twenty, so not an original, but it may have a family tree in it, and this one…' He indicated the third. 'This is modern. Well, it's also a King James, so my father's notes say, but it was acquired only twenty years ago, and it's one printed with family pages. If you're looking for His Lordship's ancestors, that's a place to start, but I bet there are better records too.'

Silas removed the bible from the shelf. It was large and weighty, bound in a solid cover with brass corners and deeply engraved with a cross beneath the crest and name, 'Riddington' in gold letters.

'Thanks, Barney.' Silas dropped it into his lap where it pressed uncomfortably on his thighs. 'I'll have a look here if you could carry on searching for the Rasnov information.'

'Aye, Sir.'

Barnaby returned to his search as Silas undid the brass clasp and lifted the cover. The spine creaked as he opened the book as if unhappy at being disturbed. The pages smelt of age and damp, and yet had been in the cabinet, suggesting that the book had not been used for some time. He turned through the publisher's pages and the first plates, guarded by tissue paper until he came to what he was looking for.

Except it wasn't what he wanted.

For anyone researching Archer's family tree, it would have been the perfect find; a chart of the parents and grandparents stretching back for generations across several pages, with information written in various colours of unfaded ink, but the only information was names and dates. Silas read the various surnames, which included Rasnov in one branch, and many others in other lines, and the tree ended, or began, with Archer Camoys Riddington and his date of birth, March 26th, 1859, and his older brother, Crispin Henry Riddington, October 25th, 1857.

'Camoys?' Silas said through a grin. 'He kept that quiet.'

Interesting though it was, it was of no help in his search for the history of the Rasnov assassins or Mr Smith and his possible connection. The pressure of the book on his legs was aching them, and he stood, heaving the bible, still open, intending to replace it.

As he rose, the pages rolled back into place, fanning him and ejecting a sheet of thin paper. It spiralled to the rug, coming to rest by his feet, and with the bible back in its place, he picked it up.

The page was a single portfolio from somewhere else, either left by accident or put with the family tree for a reason. Finding it blank, he turned it over to see what might be on the other side.

What he read brought him crashing back into his chair, his mouth open and his mind whirling.

The words were confused and confusing, but within them, he was certain, lay a clue to Mr Smith's intentions. The events of the last twenty-four hours shunted back into place like the cars of a freight train in a siding. There was only one person who could throw any light on the writing.

Archer.

He comes at night on silent wings of betrayal, this father of mine that strips away what was promised. What was once an assured future is now to be denied. I know it. I feel it. And for what? And for who? Not for me as with generations past. Not for me the law of primogeniture. Denied, instead to keep the name of the fraudulent family whose mask he wears. To keep it there in face but not in noble mind.

Stripped, I am. Deprived, misunderstood. It is coming. I anticipate it tonight. I have prepared.

He who is so worthy. He the leader, the King Henry on the eve of my day who rallies his troops with words of dignity signifying nothing. Me, the man-of-war who carried the pennant, tattered now by his cheating. Me, left to carry all I have remaining; anger, revenge, knowledge.

I use all three. Anger to drive my revenge which is itself fuelled by knowledge, knowledge from contacts — but the truth might not be found when I am chained and bound. Lest the madness takes me.

And when time is right, we righteous shall have our revenge. The battle plan is laid. The instructions given. Time will play its part, and I shall learn, one day, of his great falling. Not through the ease of death, but through the birth of shame.

He will be given the family name, but he is nothing but dishonour personified, and there will be nothing but shame until his humiliation is complete.

Dorjan is watching. Dorjan is prepared, and my faithful are watching him, staying close, as duplicitous as a father who no longer cares. Time will bring the pieces together when time is right, and the family will be protected. Rasnov will be mine again, and I will return triumphant protected by my Dorjan.

Archer handed back the piece of paper and said, 'Standard Crispin nonsense. Ramblings of a troubled mind, and, looking at the date, written just before my father had him incarcerated and stripped of his titles.'

'But don't you see a connection?' Silas asked, folding the paper.

'To what?'

'Smith.' He lowered his voice. They were in Archer's private sitting room across the corridor from where Smith was housed, but Silas was not taking any chances.

'You've got this thing about Smith,' Archer said, returning to the letter he was writing. 'You need to let it go. He's a perfectly amiable chap fallen on a difficult time. I've told him he can stay for the dinner if he wants to.'

'But this,' Silas persisted, waving the page. 'It's a threat against you. It's your brother saying he is going to get revenge, and it mentions Rasnov, and Crispin being protected by someone called Dorjan.'

'My brother was, and still is, mad. He would write rubbish like that all the time and rip them from his diary to leave them where I would find them. Intimidation that's all.'

'How many times have you looked in your family bible?'

Archer growled. 'Alright, so I wouldn't never have found it there. But I found similar things inside other books, under my pillows, he even wrote to me when I was in Stonehouse recovering from the slicing he gave me. Actually...' He took the page and reread the date before handing it back. 'I was in hospital when he wrote this. It was just before his worst episode. My parents confronted him about what he had done to me, my father tried to flog him — ridiculous as Crispin was thirty years old — and Crispin attacked him. If it hadn't been for Thomas and Tripp pulling him off, he'd have been hanged for murder. My father disinherited him, had him locked away, passed the titles to me by Lord's Statute, and that was the end of the matter. Except, Doctor Penhale thought that Crispin's behaviour contributed to my father's early death from heart failure, so in a way, he did get his revenge. Now, that's that, and I must get on with this.'

'Don't you see it?' Silas showed him the name, running his thumbnails beneath it. 'Dorjan. It doesn't take much to work out that's one of Jimmy's wordplays on dragon.'

'There is no J in dragon. You are being fanciful. I must finish this letter to my mother, and you must put that away and stop worrying about Mr Smith.'

'All right then, the thing he was talking about in his sleep. The family name, dishonour, shame. In Smith's late-night muttering, and in your brother's twisted diary. There's a connection, Archie.'

'There's a coincidence.'

'"Rasnov will be mine again", Silas quoted. 'The name, the title. It's Crispin writing himself a note, promising himself he'll get his title back.' He rested on Archer's desk, facing him, and causing the viscount to sigh and put own his pen. '"My faithful are watching him." Quill? That other man Thomas saw. Hawley?'

'Hawley was a friend of mine.'

'So was Quill.'

'Hawley is dead.'

'And Quill isn't.'

'And you want me to believe that a man Thomas happened to meet on a train here in Cornwall, is working for Crispin in the Netherlands, via Quill, to cause me harm so that my insane brother who…' With a rustle of papers, he produced an invoice. 'Who is still safely and expensively incarcerated in The Rotterdam Institute, and has no chance of reclaiming his title even if he wasn't criminally insane, has engineered a plot…?' He threw the invoice down. 'Silas, I know you care about me. I know you're bored, but really, you are imagining things.'

'I have a feeling…'

'Why?' Archer stood. 'Why not just send someone to slit my throat in the night,' he said, pacing. 'If Crispin wants me dead, and I don't deny I wouldn't put it past him…'

'You thought he was the Ripper.'

'I did, but we know that's not the case.'

'No, the Ripper is still out there, biding his time and dreaming up who-knows-what. Against you.'

'Mr Smith is an accident victim like the boy. Like Tom. That's all there is to it.'

Silas wasn't going to let the matter lie. The twisting in his stomach was so strong, he was convinced Smith was on the train for a reason; probably heading to Larkspur village to wait for the ideal time to visit the Hall and carry out Crispin's wishes to murder Archer.

Quill was on Crispin's side, they all knew that. Quill had twice failed to kill Archer, so Crispin called in his 'protector', Dorjan, the Romanian in the spare bed with a tattoo of a dragon; an assassin. It made sense to Silas but only to his instinct. If he had asked Thomas for his opinion, he like Archer, would laugh him away. He needed to prove that there was at least cause for concern, and there were only two ways he could think to do it. Beat a confession from Smith, or understand Crispin's ramblings and show Archer that Smith was Dorjan, the Dragon-Order assassin sworn to protect the family name of Rasnov, a name that should be held by Crispin but was, instead, Archer's.

'I'm going to look into this whether you like it or not,' Silas said, unintentionally making it sound like a threat. 'I'm sure that man is a Romanian assassin sent here to kill you.'

'Well he's not going to get very far,' Archer scoffed. 'Doctor Penhale has ordered him to stay in bed and rest his injured leg, he can't walk unassisted yet, and all he's got on him is a pocket watch. What will he do? Count me to death?' Archer sighed, reining in his annoyance. 'But, Silas, as it is you, and as you're so keen to have something to do, then do whatever you want.'

'I will,' Silas shot back, angry at the way he was being patronised. 'Because I care about you even if you don't.'

Archer's face didn't move for a full thirty seconds. His wide, chocolate eyes stared at Silas, his full lips cocked to one side, and an eyebrow raised as if he was caught between outrage and disbelief. The colour drained from his face, and his chest swelled as he drew in a deep, calming breath. Swallowing, his lips reformed into a smile.

'I'm sorry,' he said, reaching for Silas' shoulder and pulling him close. 'I don't mean to be angry with you. Like one of Thomas' clocks, my spring is fully wound because of the Easter dinner, the Foundation, Tom… I shouldn't take it out on you.'

His kiss went a little way to alleviating Silas' anger, but the viscount's next words wrangled him.

'I'll humour you because it's so sweet of you to think I am in danger. Again. You don't know he is Romanian,' he said. 'And you don't know he is an assassin. Just because of his inked skin… I expect there is a reason for that. Why don't you go and ask him?'

'I will.'

'No! Please don't. It would embarrass me.'

This time Silas sighed. Archer was nervous about his dinner

party and the guests who would attend. Their presence meant a great deal to him, and maybe it was wrong of Silas to burden him with his suspicions.

That was all they were. Loose connections put together because he didn't trust a man on sight. He was acting with his heart where his friends would act according to their minds. Perhaps Archer was right. Silas was bored at Larkspur and yearned for the excitement of the city. His way of coping was to look for a distraction, and the dark man in the guest suite was an easy target.

'Alright,' he said, forcing a smile. 'I'm sorry. I didn't mean to upset you either, but being honest, that man scares the bejeebers out of me, and I don't like him. I know!' He raised his hand to prevent Archer interrupting. 'No, I don't know him, but like you, I've got this sense when something's going to go bad, and I reckon there's something rotten about Smith. But, leave it with me. I'll do my own thing, and put my own fears to rest.'

Archer wasn't sure what he meant, and said so.

'Just let me do my own thing,' Silas said, an idea forming. 'I'll stay out of your way for a couple of days. You don't need me.'

'The dinner…!'

'Ain't until Friday, Archie. Tommy will be mended by then. Barnaby's a great worker, Mrs Baker and Old Ma Flintwich are on top of things. You don't want me under your feet.'

'Where are you going?'

'I don't know yet,' Silas admitted. 'But I'm not letting this rest until I've shown myself that I am being doolally about it. Trust me?'

'Of course.'

'Then don't worry about me.'

Silas turned to leave, but Archer caught his arm, swung him around and braced the two together with a long, lingering kiss. His hands wandered to Silas' backside, instantly arousing them both.

'You got me all riled up yesterday,' Archer whispered, his lips brushing Silas' ear. 'And we never got to finish that off.'

'You ain't getting round me that easily.'

'I love you, you do know that?'

'Yeah.'

'I know I am not always…'

'Hey, Archie, shush. I love you, even when you're in a bad mood.'

They kissed again, longer this time, losing themselves in the embrace, hearts racing, cocks stiffening, hands exploring until they were broken apart by a cough.

'Sorry, Sir,' Barnaby said, half in and half out of the room. 'Shall I come back?'

Eleven

Archer, frozen in Silas' arms, had never looked so terrified. He tried to back away, but Silas took charge. 'Leave this to me,' he whispered, still in the embrace, and only releasing Archer's arms when he had looked him up and down. It was inevitable they would be caught one day, and Silas was grateful it was Barnaby who had stumbled upon them. Trying not to blame himself for leaving the doors open, he took a deep breath, gave Archer a wink intended to comfort, but which only shocked the viscount further, and stood to attention.

'My Lord,' he said, tipping his head and turning. 'Ah, Barnaby, come with me, would you?'

He gave the footman no time to reply, but passed him in the doorway, and waited for him to join him next door.

'Right, Barney', he said, stepping up to the man and fixing him with a dispassionate look. 'How long were you there?'

'I just arrived, Sir,' Barnaby said. 'The door was open, but I knocked before I entered.'

'And what did you see?'

'You and his Lordship talking, as I often do.'

'I want you to be honest with me, Barney,' Silas challenged, and Barnaby picked up on the mild threat.

'I didn't see anything that was my business, Sir,' he said, nervously doing his best to maintain a footman's composure.

'Tell me,' Silas said, taking him by the shoulder and leading him through the dressing room to his own suite. 'Do you have many friends?'

'Friends?

'Do you?'

'I get along with Sally and Lucy, and some of the other maids,' Barnaby said, uncertain if that was the correct answer. 'Mark and I worked together fine, but we're not close friends.'

'Anyone else?'

'Nathan in the stables, but I don't think he likes me as I like him. I don't get much time to spend with friends, Sir.'

'I'm sure you don't. So, no-one close you can confide in, tell your secrets to?'

'No, Sir.'

Silas stopped and turned the footman to face him. Equal in height, they stood eye to eye, blue on brown. 'Well, you have now, Barney,' Silas said, adding a cheeky smile and his rougher accent. 'You and I ain't so far apart if you know what I mean.'

'But you're a gentleman, Mr Hawkins,' the footman replied, his brow creasing. 'And I'm just a footman.'

'Yeah, and before that you was a hall boy, washing up after the kitchen staff, shifting boxes, sweeping floors, serving the servants, and now look at you.' He waved his hands up and down the smart uniform. 'Tails, collar, tie, shiny shoes, smart hair and all.'

'I shan't tell anyone what I saw, Sir.'

'I wasn't threatening you,' Silas said. 'How can I? It ain't my job, get it?'

Barnaby bit his bottom lip and glanced to the side. 'Sorry,' he said when he looked back. 'I don't know what you're saying.'

'Okay, Barney, then listen to this.' Silas slouched against the wall and folded his arms. 'Not many at Larkspur know what I'm going to tell you, and I'm trusting you to keep it that way. I'm the son of an Irish immigrant, born and brought up in the slums of Westerpool where me mam died when I was sixteen. With me two sisters to support, Karan and Iona downstairs, I went up to the city and found work in Greychurch. I worked on the streets, Barney, selling this...' He opened his arms, showing his body, before folding them again. 'Did that for four years before His Lordship found me and took me in, gave me a job and a lot more. I've broken into places, I've nicked stuff, I've been a naughty boy in more ways than one. I've even been in prison and up in court, but here I am, right before your eyes, telling you that if you want a mate, you've got me. I know I ain't a lot, but I trust you, else I wouldn't be telling you, and you can trust me. So, if you've got anything to ask me about what you just saw, or if there's something you want to ask and you can't ask

Mr Payne or Saddle or them others, you've got me. You following me there, Barney? I'm your mate if you'll have it.'

Barnaby swallowed and nodded. It was hard to tell if he was shocked by Mr Hawkins' revelation or emboldened by it.

'Thank you, Sir,' he said. 'I am honoured.'

'No, I am,' Silas grinned. 'So, mate, is there anything you want to ask me about what you just saw?'

Barnaby thought for a second, his eyes flicking from side to side and finally settling on Silas. 'I can't think what I'd have to ask about you and His Lordship talking,' he said. 'It wouldn't be any of my business for a start, but, Sir, if I do have a question, I shan't hesitate to come and speak to you.'

'Good man.' Silas winked, and after hesitating, Barnaby did the same, although not as skilfully. 'So, mate, what did you want with His Lordship?'

'What did I...?' Barnaby was suddenly a footman again. 'Oh, I came to deliver a message to you, Mr Hawkins,' he said. 'Mr Payne wonders if he might have a word in his pantry. He would come up, but he's been told not to.'

'Of course he can, Barney. Shall we go?'

They parted at the bottom of the backstairs where Barnaby dutifully went about his business as if nothing had happened, and Silas veered right to the butler's pantry. Thomas, when he found him, was at his desk poring over a ledger, and James was sitting in an armchair.

'How you doing there, Mr Payne?' Silas asked jovially as he swept in, closing the door to the bustle of maids. 'Hello, Jimmy.'

'Mr Hawkins.'

Thomas pushed himself painfully to his feet, but Silas told him to stay seated, for which the butler was grateful.

'To be honest,' he said. 'Everything still aches, apart from my head. I am no longer dizzy, but Doctor Penhale says I should stay at my desk if not my bed, and I can't stay in bed all day, there's too much to do.'

'And what can I help you with?'

Thomas glanced to the closed door before offering Silas a seat and telling him to bring it to the side of the desk so the three could talk quietly. Once they were settled, the butler said, 'Thanks for coming down. I'd have come up to you, but…'

'Yeah, Tommy, just get on with it. You look worried.'

'If I am, it's James' fault.'

'It's the boy,' James admitted. 'There's something he's not telling me.'

'How do you mean?'

'Doctor Penhale came up this morning, and I was with him when he checked Jerry over.'

'That his name?'

'He says it is. Jerry O'Sullivan, but that's all he's telling me, and he won't speak to Lucy or Mrs Baker at all, apart from please and thank you.'

'Jerry O'Sullivan? Sounds Irish to me,' Silas said. 'Does he sound Irish?'

'No, not at all. He's well-spoken and quite literate. If I was a gambling…'

'Hang on,' Silas laughed. 'You mean the Irish don't speak well and can't read? You fecking gobshite.'

'Sorry.' James blushed. 'I didn't mean it like that.'

'Just joshing with you, Jimmy. Go on.'

'I was going to say, if I was a gambling man, I'd say he'd run away from a posh school, but that's only a gut feeling. Anyway, he's fine, the doctor says, and can get out and about tomorrow. He also said, though, that everyone involved in the crash was accounted for. The police have their names and addresses and have contacted their families, or are trying to. The only ones who haven't been claimed or identified are Jerry and Mr Smith.'

'So the kid was travelling alone?'

'Looks like it,' James nodded. 'Sergeant… Who?'

'Lanyon,' Thomas reminded him.

'Thanks. He's sending messages to the stations back down the line to see if he can find out where young Jerry got on. Meanwhile, as he seems to have taken to me, I've been trying to get the information out of him, but he won't talk about it.'

'And you want me to try?' Silas was sceptical. 'He doesn't know me.'

'No,' Thomas said. 'If anyone can find out, it's James.'

'Okay.' Silas wasn't sure why he was there. 'And?'

'Then there's the man in the guest room,' James said.

'Yeah? You don't trust him either?'

'I've told Tom about his inked skin,' James continued. 'But it's more than that. There's something… I don't know. It's just not right. *He* is not right if you get me.'

Silas was nodding.

'And you feel the same?'

'I do, Tommy. In fact, this morning, I was in the library with Barnaby, trying to find out about Mr Smith's tattoo when I came across this.'

He drew Crispin's garbled diary entry from his pocket, unfolded it and placed it before the butler. James rose to lean over Thomas' shoulder and read it as Silas explained his concerns.

'I showed it to Archer,' he said when they had finished reading. 'But he says it's nothing to worry about.'

'His Lordship's brother did write a lot of these things,' Thomas agreed, sitting back. 'It was in the latter stages of his illness. We used to find them everywhere. The dining room was a favourite place, and usually just after we had laid it. He would leave them on the guests' chairs, and Robert and I would have to discretely remove them without upsetting him, but before the guests arrived.'

'I don't see how that…' James indicated the note, 'could have anything to do with Mr Smith. It was written nearly three years ago.'

'Two and seven months,' Thomas muttered rereading the lines. 'Just a madman's jottings, but I can see what you might think, Silas.' He looked up from the desk. 'But you're worried about Mr Smith.'

'I'm worried about who he is, and why he is down here.'

Thomas took a set of keys from his pocket and unlocked the top drawer of his desk. 'I can't yet see anything except a set of coincidences,' he said. 'But James told me about the tattoo, and that made me think more about why Mr Smith was on the train.'

'I'd be interested to hear what you've got to say.' Silas drew his chair closer until his knees pressed against the side of the desk, and rested his chin in his hands, ready to listen.

'There was something intriguing about him at first,' Thomas remembered. 'He went to great lengths to sit opposite me in the

114

middle of the carriage. At every stop, he went to the window and looked out as if he was watching to see who got on and off. Then he would come back and sit opposite me again and play with his watch or stare at his shoes. Very odd behaviour which might have been designed to draw my attention.'

Thomas had withdrawn a book from his desk and began leafing through it, pausing in his search now and then to look up at Silas to make sure he was still listening. Silas nodded, and Thomas continued.

'Smith asked questions about Larkspur,' he said. 'Intimate questions about life here, who visited and who worked where. At first, I thought it was just general conversation, but he asked especially about Easter, and what we did at the Hall. Without thinking, I told him about the dinner on Friday, and he immediately changed the subject. I was grateful for that as I hadn't intended to reveal any details of His Lordship's business. I discussed the wine instead, thinking it innocuous, and he had heard of the Purcari I had been to Plymouth to inspect.'

The page found, he turned the book to face Silas who leant in to look. Among the text was an illustration, large and clear with the words 'Fig 1' beneath it.

'Mr Smith's tattoo,' Silas said, when he saw the drawing. 'Is this the book Archie said he had about the Rasnovs?' He'd not thought to ask Thomas where to find the books and mentally kicked himself.

'It's one of them,' Thomas replied. 'Saddle found it for me. It's about the old families of Romania, Carpathia, Hungary and so on. Read that.'

Thomas pointed to a section of the text, and James came to stand beside Silas so they could read together.

Fig 1
Engraving shows the Râşnov balaur sacru, *the sacred dragon of the family Rasnov. This symbol, used by the Rasnovs, has largely and long thought to be that of the* Protectorul Regalității Râşnov, *the order of protectors of the once royal Rasnov family of central Carpathia.*

Silas pushed the book away. 'Mr Smith's tattooed with the

assassin's mark because his ancestors used to protect Archer's. Is that right?'

'It's what His Lordship said,' Thomas replied. 'And according to this, that's the case. At first sight, Smith's tattoo means he is not an enemy of the Rasnovs, and thus Archer, but is, in fact, a protector, so even if he was an assassin, he's no threat to us. However…' He turned a page. 'Now read this, and look at that.'

Silas did, and saw what at first appeared to be the same illustration, this time marked 'Fig 2.'

Fig 2
Again, the dragon, but note: the image is reversed - to the left, the west. This similar symbol is that of the Protectori ai Szekely. *Unlike the Rasnov balaur sacrcu, this Protectori, an older order, are sworn through their families to protect the Szekelys against whom the Rasnovs fought for land in the 14th century onwards. The* Procectori ai Szekely *are sworn to destroy anyone who seeks to besmirch their proud, conquering ancestors or the Szekely name.*

'That's all getting a bit foreign for me,' Silas said, squeezing his eyes. Reading the text a second time made it no clearer. 'What are Szekelys? Is that how you pronounce it?'

'I think so,' Thomas said. 'There's a chapter on their race later in the book, but the long and short of it is, because the dragon is looking left, Mr Smith is a Procectori ai Szekely, and we can assume from his painted skin, a member of an order of fighting men, or assassins if you will, sworn to protect his Szekely heritage.'

'Two things,' Silas said, still examining the drawing. 'Protect it against what? And why in Cornwall? There's something not right about him. It's too much of a coincidence he was heading this way, and I'm not going to be satisfied until I find out more about these… Szekelys.'

'Likewise,' James agreed. 'Which is why I came to talk to Tom.'

'And I first suggested that maybe he had relatives in the area,' Thomas explained. 'In which case, you are both overreacting to nothing.'

'But if not?' Silas asked, raising his eyebrows.

'If not,' James said, 'our reasoning went like this: If Smith wasn't travelling to visit family, and he's clearly not a tourist, and assuming that he's not here to do harm to Archer because he has no reason…'

'No reason at all,' Thomas interrupted. 'His Lordship is only an Honorary Boyar of the Musat-Rasnovs due to the distance of his lineage, and has never said or done anything against the Szekelys.'

Silas stared at him for a second before rolling his eyes. 'You're not helping, Tommy,' he said with a smirk. 'Smith's no threat to Archer, maybe. I got the point. Go on, Jimmy.'

'We thought that if it's all innocent and circumstantial,' James said. 'Then why was he travelling towards Larkspur village?'

'And the answer is?'

'He wasn't.' Thomas sat back. 'He said he was travelling onwards. He should have changed at Bodmin Road, but we steamed straight through. Which means we have a coincidence and nothing more.'

'You're sure about the tattoo?' Silas asked, trying to remember the image. He could recall words and accents and recreate them without thinking, offering exact replicas of a man's speech, but images were different, particularly ones smeared with blood.

'I asked James to valet the man after lunch,' Thomas said. 'James had told me of his unease, and I thought a closer look would be in order.'

'I helped him undress for a bath while the girls changed his sheets,' James explained. 'And in the drawing of the Rasnov assassins, figure one, the tattoo faces that way, but Mr Smith's definitely faces the other way. He's a Szekely, and only likely to harm someone who tries to hurt his family.'

'And Archer's Rasnovs haven't done that?'

'No,' Thomas said with annoyance. 'I told you. I have never heard it spoken of, and over the years, Archer…. His Lordship has told me all he knows about his past. You have nothing to worry about.'

'Yet you called me down here.'

Thomas and James exchanged glances. 'Yes,' Thomas said, slowly, turning back to Silas. 'The thing is, if I am to understand it correctly, when Smith thought he was going to die, he said he had failed.'

'That's how Archer translated the words,' James agreed before turning to Silas, enthusiasm dancing in his eyes. 'Which made us think, failed what? Or who. So, we did a bit more researching.'

The butler looked at his lover, and the valet reached behind for a newspaper. He threw it onto the desk, already open to a page, and Thomas angled it towards Silas.

'That,' he said, 'is a review of a play that was performed in the city late last year.'

'Blimey,' Silas swore. He was having trouble taking in all the information, and he hadn't even mentioned Smith's sleepwalking ramblings. 'This is getting thicker than me. What's a play got to do with Smith?'

'To save you reading it,' Thomas said, 'this play was a putting-down of the Szekely people. The villain was a nobleman who went around eating women, or something equally as unpleasant and derogatory. It was morbid, to say the least. The critic, George Bernard Shaw, called it "An uneducated man's stab at the Gothic, and a direct attack on an ancient people." Apparently, it was politically charged and very bloody.'

That appeared to be the end of Thomas' case, and when nothing more was said, Silas was more confused than before.

'And what has that got to do with Larkspur Hall?' he asked. 'Come to that, what's it got to do with west of here, if that's where the bloke was going?'

'Not west of here,' Thomas said. 'Here, at Easter.'

'You'll have to do better than that.'

'The dinner.'

'Keep going.'

'The guests.' Thomas leant forward and tapped the newspaper. 'The theatre.'

Silas read the name. 'And?'

'More precisely, the actor-manager of that theatre.' James rested his arms on the table.

Their faces were close, the three were conspiring, but Silas had been left out of the most valuable information. The answer.

'And he is?'

Thomas sighed as if about to tell off a child for the third time, and said, 'His Lordship's guest of honour on Easter Friday is Henry Irving.'

'Currently returning from a tour of America, aboard a steamer and out of contact,' James added. 'Which means he can't be warned that there's a man in the Bosworth suite possibly intent on killing him as soon as he steps ashore.'

'In Cornwall?' Silas smirked. 'I was brought up in Westerpool, mate. I know steamers don't pull into Cornwall. Not even Plymouth. He'll get off at Westerpool, or sail around to Southampton.'

'The liners dock at Westerpool, yes,' Thomas nodded. 'But there are tenders which go out to collect passengers and bring them to the west country, to save the long railway journeys from the north.'

'Which made me think,' James said, 'that Mr Smith might be planning to assassinate Irving when he steps ashore. Think about it; it's quiet here and remote, easier to slip away, and it would take at least a day for the city police to get down and investigate. We've seen how inept the local peelers are.'

That made more sense than Silas' idea that Smith was Crispin's protector and working with Quill, but he still couldn't accept the idea of a man being killed because he appeared in a play,

'So, what are you saying we do?' he asked.

'Smith's going to be here all week,' James said, his hazel eyes twinkling with the thrill of his plan. 'Irving's boat isn't due into Newquay until Friday. Meanwhile, Smith's got limited mobility and isn't in a rush to go anywhere, and that's good for us. We can watch him. I'll dress him if he does get out of bed. Tom has asked Saddle to report his every move on the pretext that he's concerned. We thought you could ask your sisters to do the same when they're in there, but of course, without explaining why.'

'Meanwhile,' Thomas said. 'We need to assume one thing and discover one other.'

'Which is. What are?'

'Because of my lack of discretion on the train,' Thomas frowned, 'Smith knows that Mr Irving will be here for the dinner, thus, he now has direct, but perhaps more public access to his victim. The train crash was a stroke of good fortune for him. I should have left him trapped.'

James took his lover's hand and squeezed. 'You wouldn't do that,' he said. 'And it's not your fault. He would have read about the dinner in the papers.'

Thomas swallowed. 'Either way, we must assume that he will act on the chance that has fallen into his lap. We don't know exactly when that is likely to be, but Mr Irving is due on Friday afternoon and will leave on Sunday after lunch. We must be wary of Smith without embarrassing His Lordship.'

'Have you told Archer all this?' Silas asked, but he received a negative reply. 'Probably for the best.'

When Thomas and James asked him to explain, Silas told them about Smith's strange sleep-talking and how he had, that afternoon, tried to persuade Archer of his suspicions. He also related Archer's throw-away response, and Thomas reminded them all how important the guests and party were to Archer, adding that the viscount was also concerned for the fate of the accident victims and the effect of the crash on his village. Silas knew all this and was fed up with hearing it, but he listened politely.

'Whatever we do to prove ourselves right and prevent an assassination,' James said, when Thomas had finished, 'we have to do it without Archer knowing.'

'Same as the opera house thing,' Silas groaned. Keeping secrets from his lover was painful, but his friends were right. The less Archer knew, the less he would worry, and that could only be for the good.

'So what am I doing?' Silas' eyes were narrow as he looked from one man to the other. 'While you're watching Smith, what am I doing?'

'That's the thing we have to discover,' Thomas said. 'One thing the books don't tell us is how these Protectori dispatch their victims. If we knew that, we could be better prepared.'

'Or we could just tell the police,' Silas countered.

'And bring on Archer the embarrassment and shame Mr Smith talked of in his sleep, by drawing conclusions before we are certain?'

'Good point, Tommy. Okay, so we pass him on to the hospital and don't let him into the house.'

'And lose sight of him? Let him escape to Newquay and kill Mr Irving as he intended? At least if he's here, we have some control.'

Silas hated it when Thomas was right. It happened often, but he had still not numbed to it. 'Or we could cancel the dinner, so Irving isn't here at all,' he suggested.

'I refer to my first point about social embarrassment,' Thomas said. 'And anyway, Archer would never stand for it. The gathering is too important to him and his work.'

'Yes,' James said. 'And Lord Tennyson said he was looking forward to seeing me again.'

'Despite barging into his home, insulting his butler and borrowing two hundred pounds so you could hire Her Majesty's locomotive?' Thomas grinned in admiration. 'Show off.'

'Can't help being popular, Tom.'

'Yeah, alright.' Silas didn't see the same cause for amusement; he had been in a prison cell at the time. 'I get it. The dinner goes ahead, and you two keep watch on Smith. So, you want me to find out how he is likely to kill Irving?' The nodding heads told him he was correct. 'How do I do that if there's nothing in your books?'

'Ah-ha!' Thomas reached to a shelf and pulled down a large ledger from among many. He placed it on the table and opened it to a page marked by a red ribbon.

'What's that?'

'This, Mr Hawkins,' Thomas said, speaking with his butler's voice. 'Is my record of guests, their associations, families, relationship to the family, favoured rooms or suites, wines and meals, whether they hunt or shoot...'

'Yeah, okay,' James interrupted. 'Time's moving on.'

Thomas coughed pointedly, but accepted the interruption. 'It's also where I keep my research,' he said. 'Example, Lord Tennyson is likely to want peace and quiet, and these days prefers to write in his rooms and only comes out to dine. Here, Mr Roxton is likely to ask Lord Clearwater to accompany him in the music room and thus, I need to make sure the correct music is in place so his Lordship can practice in advance and not be caught off guard. Mr Irving's manager, Mr Stoker, prefers to be called Bram rather than Abraham and likes to exercise, thus, I shall introduce him to Danylo and Andrej. Lady Marshall always travels with her lady's maid, and so on. I do my research so that the viscount doesn't have to.'

'Which is how he found out about the Lyceum Theatre,' James said, with more than a little pride.

Silas told them they might as well have been speaking in Romanian for all the sense they were making, and James pointed to a newspaper article glued into Thomas' book.

'The Lyceum is Mr Irving's theatre where he produced and acted in that play,' he said. 'According to the critic, Shaw, Irving amassed research about the Szekelys which contains the information we are looking for. How Smith is likely to assassinate. Where is it…?' Thomas pointed it out, and James quoted, '"From their folklore to their modus operandi for murder, The Lyceum stripped the skeletons from the Szekely cupboards to debase their heritage, and is considering the publication of the research currently held at the theatre." Couldn't get much plainer, and it seems to me as good a place to start as any.'

'We thought you could blag your way in saying you're after background for His Lordship,' Thomas said. 'To brief him before the dinner. You're his secretary, they should believe you. If you can't find anything there, perhaps there will be something or someone to tell you where to find the information, possibly the British Museum Library. You can then telegraph back, and we'll present the evidence to His Lordship and let him decide what to do.'

'We need all the proof we can dig up,' James said, reinforcing the plan. 'Mainly because we are working on my gut feeling and your instincts. We have until Friday, enough time for you to get a train to London, spend two days to find out what Smith is likely to do to Irving and how we can stop it, and get back before the guests arrive. For Archer's sake.'

'You've got this all thought out, ain't you?' Silas said. 'Except one thing. How am I going to get out of the village with a fecking locomotive blocking the tracks?'

He thought he'd won a point in the ingenuity stakes, but he should have known better.

'Fecker's going to drive you to the mainline at Liskeard,' Thomas grinned. 'The night train leaves at eleven. Plenty of time for James to help you pack.'

For a moment, Silas was jealous that he hadn't thought of the plan, and was worried that Thomas and James might care more about Archer than he did. Knowing that to be untrue, he let the anger go. Jealousy would not help Archer. All three men around the table cared for the viscount as much as their master cared about them. They had sworn an oath to look after each other and to do what it took to keep their secrets and their reputations intact. They were, he realised with a proud smile, their own band of *Protectori*.

Twelve

Standing at Silas' bedroom window, James watched the trap leave as he folded away the clothes his friend had chosen not to take. The sun was about to set, and a mist was rising on the moors. Catching the dying rays, it glowed a dusty shade of pink and covered the rolling landscape like a layer of silk. It swirled against the wheels of the trap as Fecker guided the horse towards the far gatehouse with Silas beside him wrapped in a travelling cloak.

The viscount was downstairs with Mr Harrow, the estate manager, and the vicar discussing what could be done to raise funds for the unfortunate families who had lost loved ones in the railway accident. He had told James that although the men would be staying to eat, the viscount was not changing as their dinner would be informal. James had been present when Silas told Lord Clearwater that he was travelling to London and the viscount had taken the news surprisingly well. Apparently, he had already discussed Silas' thoughts on the enigmatic Mr Smith and was prepared to let him go despite the arrival of house guests in three days. As Silas had mentioned at the meeting in the butler's pantry, Archer was disinclined to take an interest in Smith being a possible threat, and that was something that worried the valet. Archer had shown the same lack of concern when Silas had feared for the opera house gala the previous year, but strangely, James didn't find his attitude disturbing. Convinced that Smith posed no personal danger to his master, he judged it would be easier if Archer was kept in the dark about their plan. As Thomas had said, it would only cause him unnecessary worry, and it was in the viscount's nature to think the best of people, not the worst. It also meant that he wouldn't interfere and, should his servants turn out to be wrong in their suspicions, he would be able to convincingly deny he knew much, if anything, about their plot.

His own mind settled, he gave the bedroom a final once-over, and finding everything in order, headed upstairs to see Jerry. Smith and his possible intentions towards Mr Irving were one mystery, the unclaimed boy was another.

James found him sitting up in bed, turning the last pages of his reading book. The fire was aglow, and someone, probably Mrs Baker, had left the lad with a jug of lemonade, now half-finished.

Jerry looked up suddenly as the door opened, and James caught a fleeting look of panic before he was recognised. The lad's concerned face soon morphed into a beaming smile, and he set the book aside.

'Hello, Sir,' he said, tidying his covers. 'I was hoping you would come up.'

'I said I would,' James smiled back. 'How are you feeling?'

'Bored,' was the simple reply.

'Not enjoying the book?'

'Oh, no, Sir,' Jerry replied. 'I enjoyed it very much, but I finished it a while ago and was just rereading the last chapter for something to do. Can I get up now?'

James sat on the end of the bed, aware that the air in the room was stale. 'The doctor said not until tomorrow.'

'But I am not unwell, Sir.'

'I know, but we have to do as we're told, don't we?'

Jerry's shoulders slumped. 'I suppose so.'

The boy's enthusiasm to be free of the room gave James an idea. He needed information and thought of a way to extract it. 'I tell you what,' he said, wriggling his way out of his jacket to appear more human and put the boy at his ease. 'How about a game?'

'Snap? Do you have cards?'

'No, nothing like that,' James laughed. 'You are an intelligent chap, so a grownups' game would suit you better.'

'Bridge? I'm not very good.'

'No, Jerry, not bridge. Let's call it "Payoff".'

Jerry looked sceptical as if he knew what James had in mind. 'Go on, Sir,' he said. 'What's that?'

'Well…' James hoisted a leg onto the bed and tucked it under himself before leaning back on the footboard, moves designed to make him appear relaxed and informal. 'Mrs Baker will be bringing supper before long, and you're keen to be out of bed. I bet you'd rather eat downstairs in the hall with us, wouldn't you?'

'Yes, please, Mr Wright.' The boy's eagerness was apparent, and again his eyes lit up.

'The thing is, Jerry,' James continued more cautiously. 'Before I can defy the doctor and let you get out of bed, and before I can show you more of Larkspur Hall, I need some information. So, I ask a question, and if you answer me honestly, then you get to see more of His Lordship's house. Of course, we have to start by getting you dressed, so answer me a question, and you can get up. That's the payoff, and that's round one. What do you say?'

Jerry said nothing but stared at James blankly.

'Not a good idea?' James prompted, when it was obvious he wasn't to have an answer.

'You're bribing me,' Jerry said and folded his arms petulantly.

'You are far too clever for your age,' James laughed.

'That's what the masters say at...'

It wasn't how James had intended to extract information, but somehow, he had caught the lad off guard.

'Your schoolmasters?' he probed. 'At what school?'

Silence.

'Very well.' James stood and collected his jacket. 'Maybe we'll play tomorrow.'

Silence.

The threat hadn't worked, but James was determined to see it through. It wasn't until he had the door open that he heard a sniffle, and turning back, realised Jerry was crying. Where the viscount found it hard to see the bad in anyone, so did James, and although Jerry could easily have been calling his bluff, he preferred to think he was dealing with a scared and lonely nine-year-old, rather than a calculating and educated gambler. All the same, he wasn't prepared to be too soft on the lad.

'That won't work with me,' he said, his hand on the door handle. 'If you want to be up and about, you have to play fair, Jerry. Have you run away from school?'

A pair of cautious eyes sent their signal across the room as Jerry made up his mind.

'You can trust me, mate,' James said, and the use of the word surprised the lad. 'And the sooner you do it, the sooner we can get you downstairs having fun rather than sleeping in a maid's room watched over...' He crept closer and made a dumb show of glancing behind as if about to impart a horrific secret. Pulling an exaggerated grimace, he said, 'Watched over by a *girl*.'

Jerry giggled at the clowning.

'Although Lucy is a very pretty girl,' James added, instantly feeling guilty because he had been derogatory to the maid. Another idea apparently fell into his head, and he gasped. 'Say! How about, after dinner in the hall, we see if we can't find you a room meant for boys.'

The lad's eyes widened.

'Perhaps next to mine.' There was a daybed in the sitting room he shared with Thomas. 'Would you like that?'

'Yes please, Sir.'

'So, have you run away from school?'

Silence.

James growled. 'I do have better thing to do, Master I N T S.'

The boy's head shot back, and this time, he was the one to gasp.

'I assume the initials sewn into your jacket are yours?' James said, standing over the bed, his face stern. 'I do hope you are not a thief.'

'Certainly not, Sir!'

'Then the jacket belongs to you.'

Jerry's cheeks, until then pallid, flushed pink. It was answer enough for James, and deciding that to gain the boy's trust he needed to show a little on his own part, he said, 'Up you get then.'

'May I?'

'You might not have said anything, but you have answered a question.'

The lad was out of the bed before James had time to collect his dressing gown.

'What's for supper?'

'Wait!' James made himself as grand and grown-up as he could, and his tone halted Jerry in his race for the door. James cleared his throat. 'I am the personal valet to His Lordship,' he said, doing his best impersonation of Thomas in an imperious mood. 'I would be failing in my duties if the young master roamed the Hall in his pyjamas.' He held the gown open, allowing Jerry to back into it. 'And it would not do for you to be seen in this a state in the

126

corridors of such a fine house.' With Jerry doing up his belt, James collected a set of clothes Mrs Williams had donated. 'Follow me, young Sir,' he said and left the room.

Along the passage, he opened the door to the male servants' quarters and ushered the lad through, stopping him when he reached the bathroom.

'In you go,' he said. 'Wash quickly and dress yourself. I'll wait here.'

'Are you going to lock me in?'

'No. Why? Is that what they do at your school?'

'No, they stand and watch.'

'Which tells me you attend a boarding school,' James said and grinned when Jerry stamped his foot. 'I may not have been taught in a place like yours, Jerry, but that doesn't mean I'm stupid. I don't expect you'll tell me the name of your school, not yet, but so far, you have only reached the bathroom. There's a long way to go before we reach the supper table. In you go, wash and change but don't lock the door. You still might have concussion, and I don't want to have to break it down if you pass out.'

Jerry scowled. Beaten, temporarily at least, he let himself into the bathroom.

He was back a couple of minutes later, and James doubted he had washed sufficiently, but an examination of his hands showed them to be clean enough. Leaving the boy's nightclothes on the chair, he nodded to the far end of the corridor.

'It's that way,' he said. 'You're not going to run off, are you?'

'Does that count as a question?'

'Blimey, mate, you're a tricky one ain't you?'

Jerry looked up at him, his mouth twisted in an expression of confused disbelief. 'Why do you speak like that?'

'I'm from London,' James said. 'It's how I speak with me mates, it ain't how I speak with His Lordship, of course.' Not exactly true. James was able to be himself when appropriate. 'Is that where you're from? The city?'

Jerry regarded the door at the end of the corridor behind which lay his chance of a decent supper at a table and all the wonders a great house might offer, considered his options and slowly nodded.

'Then we shall proceed.'

They were nearing the end of the passage when James felt a small, warm hand slip into his own.

'Thank you, Sir,' Jerry said, his voice a whisper.

James was touched, but unnerved to realise he was suddenly a surrogate parent and squeezed that lad's hand gently.

'These stairs lead down to the gentlemen's corridor where his Lordship has his rooms,' he said as they descended the plain backstairs. 'There's the door.'

'Can I see?'

'Not yet. Keep going down, and we will come to the servants' passage that leads to the main backstairs and the green baize door.'

'There is a play by that name,' Jerry said.

'That's an odd thing to say,' James replied. 'Is it one you've done at school?'

'No. I just know it.'

They turned into the servants' passage, a long thoroughfare that connected the east end of the house to the central hall and the west wing beyond. The walls were painted green, and the gas kept at half-light to save the cost. On busy occasions, Thomas had said when showing James around, the lighting was turned up to avoid accidents, and in the days of the late viscount, the passage was like 'Dury Lane when the theatre is turning out,' bustling with maids and footmen going about their masters' business. Tonight it was dull and uninspiring, but Jerry took it all in, his head swinging from one side to the other, his hand never letting go of James.

'And here's the main entrance to the Hall.' James stopped at a door beneath the east staircase where Jerry looked up at him with eager eyes. 'We're only going through there if you answer a very big question,' the valet warned. 'And we're only going down there to eat…' he pointed to the staircase that descended to the servants' hall, 'if you answer another.'

'You mean that you'll make me starve if I don't answer you?'

The boy was not only quick-witted, he was confident. He knew James wouldn't let him starve, but James was prepared to push the idea if it meant gleaning more information.

'No,' he said. 'I wouldn't do that, but you will have to go back to your room and eat off a tray in bed like an invalid.'

Jerry regarded the baize door and then the stairs before finally considering the grown-up beside him. 'I'll tell you what,' he said. 'I'll answer a question, and we'll go down to eat, but you have to give me a piggyback.'

James rolled his eyes and letting go of the boy's hand, crouched to his level.

'You drive a very hard bargain,' he smiled. 'Something tells me you've transacted this kind of contract before.'

'My father is in business,' Jerry said. 'He taught me.'

'And where is your father?'

'Is that your question, Sir?'

James had been about to ask him where he was travelling to when the train crashed, but knowing the whereabouts of the boy's father would be more useful. 'Yes,' he said.

'St Merrynpawth.'

It was a simple reply but meant nothing to James. 'And where's that?' he asked, but Jerry was already scrambling to climb on.

'I answered, you have to carry me to supper.'

Deciding to ask Barnaby or one of the maids, James gave in and hoisted the lad onto his back.

'Hold on tight,' he said, unable to contain a boyish laugh. 'These stairs are steep and winding. And mind your head.'

Jerry was light and no problem at all to carry down to the lower passage. He ducked at all the right places and gave James random directions as if he knew where he was going. By the time they approached the servants' hall, James had given in to the childish game and was having as much fun as his young charge, so much so, that as they ducked and trotted into the hall, he only came to his senses when he saw Thomas glaring from the head of the table, and Mrs Baker standing with her mouth open. Chatter ceased, and in the awkward silence that followed, one of the maids sniggered.

'Ah,' James said, and lifted Jerry over his head to place him on the ground. 'Can I introduce Master Jerry O'Sullivan to those who've not met him?' He was looking directly at Thomas in case he was in trouble. A gaggle of maids descended on the lad and, over their heads, James received a surreptitious wink from the butler along with a wry smile.

'You're both just in time,' Thomas said, before scolding the maids for squawking and cooing over the boy and ordering them to lay a place for him beside Mr Wright.

'You'll not be needing the tray then.' Mrs Baker halted Sally who was on her way to collect it.

'No, thank you,' James replied, leading Jerry to his chair. 'Master O'Sullivan has been good and has answered my questions. We're playing "Payoff", and he has just passed round one.'

'I don't know what that means, Mr Wright,' Thomas said, his usual demeanour of authority once again apparent. 'But we were just about to say grace.'

James knew full well that Thomas, like Archer, had no time for grace or anything overtly religious, but it was traditional, and keen to discover more about Jerry, suggested their guest might like the honour. 'That is if you know one?' he added, pulling Jerry to his feet. 'No-one sits before Mr Payne has taken his place,' he whispered.

'Oops, sorry, Sir, I didn't know.' Jerry aimed his apology at the butler who bowed graciously.

'Would you care to say grace, young man?' Thomas asked. 'I feel it would be appropriate as you have, by the grace of God, Mr Andrej and Mr Wright, escaped a great calamity.'

Jerry looked at James for a translation.

'Just say what you know,' James encouraged. 'I'll explain the rest later.'

'Thank you, Sir Payne,' Jerry said, causing a ripple of laughter from the lowliest hall boy to the housekeeper.

'Mr Payne,' Thomas emphasised, throwing James' a glare as if it was his fault.

'Just say your grace, Jerry, and we can eat.' James nudged him, and the room fell silent.

The lad looked from one servant to the next until he was happy that they each had their heads bowed. Another nudge from James, whose stomach was rumbling, and he spoke up with a clear and practised voice.

'*Quae de tua benignitate sumus percepturi, benedicito per Christum Dominum nostrum. Amen.*'

James was a stunned as everyone else, and glad that Silas was not at the table. Had he been, he would have voiced what was on James' mind; 'What the fuck was that?' Instead, he muttered 'Amen' along with everyone else and sat.

Supper was taken in a semi-formal manner as was the custom, with the hall boys and kitchen maids serving the higher servants, and Thomas and Mrs Baker discussing domestic matters while the maids chatted about anything not to do with work. Jerry ate politely and only spoke when he was spoken to, but failed to answer any questions. Even when asked about the crash, which Mrs Baker thought not an appropriate subject, he said nothing, but shrugged and looked at his plate.

'He's a man of few words, aren't you, Jerry?' James cajoled. 'We'll start on round two after dinner.'

'May I see the Hall, Sir?' Jerry asked, but James directed him to Thomas.

'Not this evening,' Thomas decreed. 'His Lordship has guests.'

The meal was interrupted only once when Mr Saddle was called to attend Mr Smith, and it was finished promptly in time for His Lordship and his company to be served their dinner above stairs.

Before Thomas went up with Barnaby to oversee the meal, James managed to take him to one side, and they agreed that Jerry, if not claimed by the next day, could take up temporary residence in their ground-floor suite. It would be easier for James to keep an eye on him, and promising the move to the men's quarters would, he reasoned, give Jerry an incentive to answer more questions. Thomas agreed, adding in a whispered snigger, 'I always knew you were a family man, Jimmy.'

'Only with you,' James replied. 'Tell you what, when the lad moves in with us, we can pretend we're married.'

'I shouldn't like that!' Thomas feigned horror. 'We would have to hyphenate. People would call us the Wright-Paynes.'

The laughter that followed was unbecoming of men in their stations, and Mrs Baker said so as she bustled past, but it was said with good humour. The boy's presence below stairs had raised everyone's spirits, including Thomas', and the atmosphere was only dampened by the return of Mr Saddle.

Calling James away from the others, he informed him that Mr Smith was keen to see the other survivor of the accident.

'What for?'

'He, like myself and us all, I suspect,' Saddle said, 'is keen to know more about him. He also thought it might help the boy to know that he was not the only survivor. Alleviate any guilt, perhaps?'

After consideration, James agreed that he would take Jerry to see Mr Smith later when he returned him to Lucy's room for the night, and that satisfied Saddle.

'What do we know about him?' the under-butler asked, one of his narrow eyes on where Jerry was shuffling a deck of cards.

'He comes from London, his father's in business, he's probably run away from school, and his father is in St Merrynporth,' James said. 'But I haven't found out yet where that is.'

'The village of St Merryn is adjacent to Padstow,' Saddle said. 'Not far from here, but I've not heard of St Merryn*porth*. Perhaps Barnaby would know.'

Saddle left James to ponder and wait for Barnaby to return from the dining room, but he also left him with an unfounded sense of unease.

He was about to collect Jerry and take him upstairs when Mrs Baker cornered him.

'I was interested in the grace,' she said as Mrs Flintwich spoiled the boy with a leftover slice of lemon cake.

'It was a bit over the top,' James agreed. 'Was it Latin?'

'It was, Mr Wright,' the woman replied, watching Jerry over the valet's shoulder. 'If, as you suspect, the bairn attends a private school, then a Latin grace makes sense. As you know, I am a Christian, and I take an interest in all aspects of my religion, particularly how it is taught to the young. But, what's strange is, if I am not mistaken, that particular grace is peculiar to one institution.'

'Oh? His school, you think?'

'I doubt it, Mr Wright,' the housekeeper said. 'Unless they accept nine-year-olds at University. It is the grace traditionally spoken at Trinity College in Dublin.'

Thirteen

Once His Lordship's dinner guests had retired to the smoking-room to continue their philanthropic discussions, Saddle left Barnaby to close the dining room. Downstairs, he collected a walking cane from the umbrella stand and a fresh jug of water from the scullery, and made his way up the backstairs to attend to Mr Smith.

The Romanian was at the writing-table beside the fire, elegant in one of the viscount's smoking jackets and sipping the last of the wine the under-butler had provided with his supper.

'Robert,' Smith smiled as the servant entered, closing the door delicately behind him. 'You are spoiling me with your attentions.'

'And I intend to spoil you further, Sir,' Robert replied. 'I took the liberty of bringing this.' Placing the jug by the bed, he crossed the room holding the cane before him. 'I thought it might assist you.'

Smith took it, and replacing his empty glass, pushed himself to his feet with one hand on the desk and the other clutching the silver top of the cane.

'You are thoughtful,' he said, testing his weight and grimacing.

'Not at all, Sir. Does it help?'

Smith took a couple of paces, and finding that the pain in his ankle was lessened by its use, realised his frown had been made in false expectation. 'It's perfect,' he said, taking a few more steps towards the bed. 'I shall be able to make my own way about.'

'On which note, His Lordship asks if you would like to dine with him tomorrow,' Saddle said, attending to the bed and straightening the covers. 'He asked me to again send his apologies that he won't be able to visit this evening, but says you are welcome to use his house as yours from the morning onwards.'

'The doctor did say I should try walking as soon as I could,' Smith nodded. 'And I should be very happy if I am not a burden.'

'You are not, Sir.'

'Then maybe, if you are not too busy, you can show me the house in the morning.'

'I will have to clear that with Mr Payne, but I can't see it being a problem, Sir.'

Smith sat on the edge of the bed and removed the smoking jacket. 'Then that's settled,' he said. 'Which is more than I can say for myself.'

'Oh?'

Smith laughed. 'It's this gown.' He threw it onto a chair. 'Far to gaudy for my taste, but I am grateful.'

'Indeed, Sir. His Lordship favours the brighter colours of the Chinese patterns over the new style of the French.' Saddle collected the gown and hung it on a hanger. He was returning from the wardrobe as Smith climbed into bed. 'Let me help you, Sir.'

'Thank you, Robert, but the more I do for myself, the better.'

'As you wish.'

It occurred to Saddle that with the cane affording Mr Smith newfound mobility, and with the way his ankle was healing, he would soon have no need for Saddle. The under-butler would be reduced to his usual menial duties once the man knew the layout of the Hall and where he could go. He would become the viscount's guest rather than Saddle's, and the more distant the pair became, the less chance there was of any tip.

'Did you ask about the unfortunate young man?' Smith asked, swinging his legs onto the bed and pulling over the covers.

'I did, Sir.' Saddle looked at the time. 'Mr Wright will bring him to you in an hour unless you are too tired?'

'No, not tired at all, Robert. My race is known for its stamina, and it's going to take more than a sprained ankle, a few knocks and bruises to keep me from my intentions.'

'Intentions?'

Smith flustered. 'I mean, my intention to be away from Larkspur as soon as I am able, and thus, no further imposition on Clearwater's hospitality.'

'You are invited for the week, Sir,' Saddle said with a mild bow. 'And I am charged to assist you in any way you need. We are quite used to house guests.'

134

'Oh? How so? I'm sorry, Robert, but I am unaccustomed to these great houses, and I am not sure of the etiquette. I've been in your country for many years, I was educated here but only to a middle-class degree.'

Saddle attended to the fire, stoking the logs and adding two more. He was uncomfortably aware that Smith was watching his every move, and when he stood to place the guard, caught the man studying him, deep in thought.

'Your idea of your class surprises me, Sir,' he said.

'Why? Is my accent still strong? The fellows at my university did all they could to knock it out of me.'

'No, Sir.' Saddle wondered if he had insulted the man. If he had, it was by accident. 'What I was ineptly trying to say was that I am surprised you would call yourself middle-class. You behave as though you are quite used to life in a manor house or a hall such as Larkspur, and your accent has nothing to do with it.' It was an outright lie, of course. Saddle had an ingrained mistrust of foreigners simply because they were not from his country. Smith's accent, with its rolling Rs and long vowels pricked him each time he spoke, but Saddle was keen to stay in the man's good books, his mind fixated on the Romanian's money.

His path towards it was about to become a lot easier.

'Ha!' Smith said. 'I can easily show you I am not a man of breeding. Tell me, Robert, do you play cards?'

Saddle's heart missed a beat. He gambled very well, but his good fortune at cards had more to do with sleight of hand than fair play, the gamblers of Padstow could attest to that. During regular games on his nights off, he had amassed a goodly amount of cash which he spent frivolously until his trickery was exposed and he was left under threat of personal injury. A threat that had been hanging over him this past couple of months. The time to repay his debt to the fishermen was fast approaching, and he was nowhere near the total needed to keep his limbs unbroken and his reputation intact.

'It's not something I am permitted to do, Sir,' he said, this time honestly. 'For a servant to gamble with a guest of His Lordship... It's not etiquette.'

'You see? I am not from the upper classes, or I wouldn't have made such a base suggestion. But, we are friends, I believe, Robert and we have an hour, you said. A quick hand of Septica?'

Saddle glanced at the room. There was nothing more for him to do; his guest was in bed, had eaten and was mobile. 'It's time I was downstairs,' he said.

'I would only ring for you if you went.' Smith's eyes were twinkling. 'You are at my beck and call, are you not?'

It was true. Until the man was asleep or declared that he had no more use of a servant, Saddle was on duty, and Mr Payne had made it clear that it was Saddle alone who should keep a close watch on the Romanian.

'What is Septica?' he asked, approaching the bed with growing interest.

'You may have heard it called Sedma?'

Saddle was none the wiser.

'It's a form of whist, then,' Smith said. 'You have a deck?'

'I can fetch one, but…'

'Then fetch away, Robert, and bring your coins.'

Whist was Saddle's game and the one with which he had the most success. Usually, he would play at a table where slipping and changing his cards undetected was difficult, though not impossible, but Smith would be sitting in bed and Robert beside it, lower. This would give him an easy opportunity, when shuffling, to stack the deck, float the ideal cards to the top, and second deal the Romanian. He had success cheating this way with a group of three opponents watching, it would be easy with only one.

'As you command,' he said, and with a bow that concealed his wicked smile, slithered from the room.

Forty-five minutes later, Saddle's fortune had taken a turn for the better. Smith was down several pounds and had no idea that Saddle had been playing him. He had to keep one eye on the clock to be sure they were not caught, and Wright and the boy were expected shortly, but as long as Mr Smith was in the house and calling the shots, Saddle was happy to take his money.

'I fear you've picked up my homeland's favourite card game with ease,' Smith said. 'But I would welcome a chance to claw back my losses.'

'We are expecting your visitor presently, Sir,' Saddle said. 'Perhaps we should continue in the morning.'

'You have had, what? Ten pounds off me?' Smith said, impressed rather than outraged. 'At least give me a chance to reclaim that before we finish. Shall we say, one hand, double or die?'

Twenty pounds would pay off Saddle's debt, but should he, by some unexpected catastrophe, lose, he would owe Smith nearly a whole year's wages, and the same again was already owed to the unfriendly fishermen of Padstow.

'I really think that the morning would be...'

'One five-card round with no danger of a draw.'

'Tomorrow would be...'

'No, Mr Saddle. We play now.'

Up until then, the room had been a place of warm bonhomie and equality. Two card players enjoying the gentlemanly thrill of a harmless gamble, and Smith's tone throughout had been congratulatory. Suddenly, there was a sharper, menacing edge to his voice, and his eyes, previously wide in admiration, were now narrow. His mood had swung from pleasant to threatening in six words.

Saddle swallowed, his heart picking up its pace. It was his turn to deal, and all he needed to do was a reverse shuffle, slip and float, and lay out five cards each. This, he could do beneath the level of the bed where Smith couldn't see; he had been successfully leading the game that way for nearly the last hour.

'As you wish,' he said, his throat dry but his palms slippery.

Watching the cards closely, he shuffled them before raising his head and smiling as though intent on not seeing the pack. Smith also smiled, but this time his lips drew back, revealing the edges of his teeth, and his eyes were none the narrower.

Smith dealt, and the play began.

'There's something else I should have said about Septica as it is played in my homeland,' Smith said, placing a card and losing the first trick. 'It's a word we borrowed from the Hungarians some six centuries ago.'

'How interesting,' Saddle replied, wondering where this was going while he played his next card. 'Why was that?'

'Oh, the usual,' Smith said as he considered his hand. 'Tribes at war, the conquests of lands, one side coming in with its own customs and language and demanding those they left alive adopt them. There was, and still is, much of that in my part of the world.' He placed his card and played straight into Saddle's hands, again losing the trick. One more, and Saddle would win. 'Us Szekelys are very proud. That's my original race from within Romania, you understand.'

'How fascinating,' Saddle's disquiet was worsening. There was intent behind Smith's words, and he was sure it was not pleasant.

His unease increased further when Smith won the next trick.

'More interesting is that the word Septica derives through a route of death and torture from the Hungarian word, zsirozas.'

Saddle played his penultimate card.

'An interesting choice,' Smith said without looking at it. 'And it leaves you only the king of hearts.'

Smith played, and won his second trick.

'And the word, zsirozas, means what?' Robert dared ask, his nervousness apparent in his voice as he laid his final card.

'Literally translated,' Smith said, his teeth glistening through his crooked grin. 'It means "greased". Which is exactly what you have been doing to me since we began.' Putting down the ace of trumps without even looking at what Saddle had played, he added, 'As have I to you.'

Saddle's skin dripped with cold sweat as the realisation landed in his gut like a fallen lead weight.

'I believe your debt is twenty pounds, Mr Saddle,' Smith said with a sigh. 'I shall give you until I leave to pay up, else I will have to ask it from His Lordship.'

At first, Saddle thought the knocking was his heart against his hollow ribcage, but on the third strike, he realised it was someone at the door. Instinct took over, he swept up the cards and had just pocketed the deck and stood, when the door opened, and Mr Wright's boyish face appeared.

'I hope we're not late,' James beamed, stepping into the room.

'Not at all.' Smith was instantly jovial as if he hadn't just ruined Saddle's life, let alone threatened it. 'Where is the poor chap who, like me, owes his survival to the good grace of faithful servants?'

James opened the door further, and looking behind, saw he was alone. 'Jerry,' he said with a sigh that suggested the lad had wandered off more than once. 'Stop gawping and come in. Mr Smith is keen to see you.'

The child entered, his head raised to the ceiling, his eyes wide in awe of the mouldings and chandeliers before they fell on the gilt picture frames and furniture.

'Come in, boy,' Smith said, pushing himself up against his pillows. 'Let us celebrate our luck and get to know each other.'

Jerry was too interested in his surroundings until James yanked his hand gently. 'Jerry,' he said. 'Mr Smith is from Romania.'

The boy's head turned to the bed, but the smile he had placed there lasted only a second. On seeing Smith, it faded, his mouth dropped as wide as his eyes, the colour left his cheeks, and he froze.

'Don't be like that,' James said, crouching to the lad. 'Go and say hello.'

Jerry had other ideas. He wrenched his hand free, turned and fled the room, leaving the three men to gawp at each other in stunned silence.

James reacted first. 'I'm sorry, Sir. We'll try again tomorrow,' he mumbled before hurrying after the boy.

'Perhaps he too doesn't like foreigners,' Smith said, and the threatening tone returned to his voice. 'Close the door, Saddle,' he added, reaching for his pocket watch. 'I have a proposition for you.'

Saddle willed his limbs to cooperate as he did as instructed with the distinct impression that he was sealing his fate along with the room, and when he turned back to the bed to find Smith dangling his watch as if about to hypnotise him, he knew that the Romanian had seen straight through him from the start.

'Sit,' Smith ordered. 'Sit and listen as I have listened to you. You have told me of your difficulty,' he continued when Saddle had lowered himself fearfully into the chair. 'And I have added to it. However, you are not the only man in a predicament, as I, too, need assistance. Give it, and your debt to me shall be forgotten.'

Optimism glimmered in Saddle's tight chest.

'Give it without question and do exactly as I request,' Smith added, lowering his voice, 'and I shall also see to your other debt. Do you agree?'

Hope grew but was tempered by mistrust. 'What are you saying?'

'Simply this, Robert...' Smith adjusted his posture again and spun the watch on its chain until it landed in the palm of his hand. He showed it to Saddle. 'I am offering you this watch for a reason. If you take it, you are binding yourself to an agreement that cannot be broken on pain of a very painful demise. You must do exactly as I say, else, as our proverb says, "One man's breath is another's death".'

The message could not have been clearer.

'What do you want me to do?' Saddle was done with politeness. The foreigner had trapped and tricked him into servitude, but the stakes of refusal were too high. Even so, he was not a man to accept a promise blindly.

'Take the watch, bind yourself to the promise, and I will tell you,' Smith said with more than a hint of finality.

Saddle shook his head. 'Not without knowing what it is you want.'

Smith's thin mouth once again twisted into a grin. 'I can see I am dealing with a man of principle,' he said. 'Which, in this case, is a good thing. I believe that I can trust you, Mr Saddle, and if it turns out that I can't, then... Well, you understand the consequences. I shall tell you what I want you to do, and you will see when I have finished, that you will not suffer in any way for doing it. But first, let me reassure you with another proverb from my homeland. It will absolve you of guilt.'

'You will pay my debts?'

'And write off the one you just accrued.' Smith added temptation to his voice.

Left with no choice, Saddle nodded. Whatever the man wanted, he would do it, and in doing so, ensure his financial worries would be over.

'What's this other proverb?' he scowled.

'*Chiar is tacerea este un raspuns.*'

It was said like an enchantment, and sent a shiver through Saddle's body.

'Which means?'

'It means, "Even silence is an answer."'

Smith dangled the watch as he told Saddle exactly what he was to do.

The under-butler listened with no outward sign of emotion, but

140

inside, his heart churned, and his stomach tightened. What Smith wanted was not impossible, but it was unusual. What the man offered in return was irresistible, and what Saddle stood to lose from carrying out his wishes was nothing compared to the reward.

When Smith had finished, Saddle answered with silence and accepted the watch.

Fourteen

The journey from Liskeard to the city lasted an eternity and Silas couldn't rest. The sleeper car was comfortable enough, and he had a berth to himself, but his mind refused to let go of suspicions. The tattoo, Mr Smith's presence at Larkspur, the link to Archer's ancestry and the gut feeling that everything was connected played inside his head like music from a steam fair calliope. The image of the dragon returned with relentless regularity like the thumping of a bass drum while the words of Smith's night-time mutterings clattered repetitively in strict rhythm until they became one with the rattle of the coach.

Sometimes sitting up and resting his head on the glass to see nothing but the reflection of his tired face, and sometimes lying down to stare at the dark ceiling, he imagined what lay ahead. In his vision of the days to come, he played a leading role in securing the safety of the viscount: returning to Larkspur to find everything in order and his concerns misplaced, with Archer forgiving him for leaving him alone during such an important week. As he turned to seek sleep by facing the wall, he imagined James' face and heard him speaking encouragement, supporting Silas' belief that Mr Smith was not who he pretended to be. A traveller with no luggage, singling out Thomas, asking about the Hall, the note from Archer's demented brother, Dorjan, his protector, the Protectori, too many coincidences, too many possible connections but no proof...

It wasn't until he woke that he realised he had slept, but even while sleeping, his mind had soldiered on and yet still found no answers among fractured dreams. After washing and dressing, he packed his bag and climbed from the carriage just after eleven the following morning to be greeted by air far colder than that which had seen him off from Cornwall. It went some way to revitalising his tired eyes, but his bag was heavy, and his limbs ached as he trudged through the steam and oil-smelling concourse of Paddington Station to hail a cab. On the street, he hoped he would feel more awake after a decent lunch at Clearwater House. He would need his strength to see him through the task he envisaged and the places he had to go, but right then, at the start of a long day after an endless night, not even the sight of clear sky, fogless air and the noisy bustle of the city could lift his spirits.

That job fell to a woman.

As Silas stood to take in the sight and remind himself of how he needed to be more alert and cautious than in the country, he was distracted by the call of his name. More unusually, it was a woman's voice, and stranger still, she was waving at him from beside a familiar trap led by a very familiar horse. Silas approached, taking in the woman's riding outfit and her straw hat from which a feather poked at a jaunty angle, and it wasn't until he was close enough to make out her features that the mystery was explained.

'Mrs Norwood?' He greeted her, unsure whether to shake her hand or hand over his luggage. 'What are you doing driving the trap?'

'Hello, Mr Hawkins,' the retainer replied, reaching for his portmanteau. 'We got your telegram late yesterday evening, but Mr Norwood has to be at the publishing house today, so I thought I would come to collect you.'

'But, you're a...'

She had taken his bag and swung it into the back of the trap before he finished stating the obvious.

'Yes, I know,' she said. 'And a woman who sees no reason why a lady can't drive. Why, if I wasn't teaching most other days, I might even take up being a cabbie. It's quite thrilling. Here you are.'

She was holding the door open for him, and too dumbfounded to refuse, Silas climbed aboard.

Mrs Norwood ignored the whistles and taunts from the male drivers around her as she climbed deftly into the driving seat, picked up the reins and set Emma in motion with her head held high.

'You have a good day for it,' she called back over her shoulder. 'We're expecting rain tomorrow. Two days you said?'

Silas stood to lean on the rail. He would have preferred to sit up front as he did when Fecker was driving, but standing to chat was good enough.

'Aye. I must be back at Larkspur by Friday afternoon,' he said.

'I hope you'll have time to tell us how the season has been,' Mrs Norwood enthused. 'And when you return, you must tell His Lordship that all is well at the house. Mr Norwood has seen to all the jobs Mr Payne required, and the new lighting has been installed. There are a few redecorations in the servants' rooms yet to see to, but Isaac will be attending to them in good time. Now, I've prepared you a lunch, and while you eat, you can tell me all about Christmas. How is His Lordship…?'

She prattled on, asking questions but never allowing time for a reply, and Silas was reminded that at times, she could be as talkative as her husband. It wasn't until they pulled into Clearwater Mews that she finally drew a breath and even then, only to halt the vehicle and jump down to open the gate. She led the horse into the yard, shut the gate, announced that she would stable the animal later, and helping Silas with his bag, explained how she had borrowed Emma back from Lady Marshall's stable where both His Lordship's horses were being regularly exercised and well cared for. By the time Silas entered the house, he was twice as exhausted as when he had stepped from the train, yet he had hardly said a word.

Walking back into Clearwater House brought a myriad of memories forgotten among the mist and magic of the Bodmin moors. He remembered his first visit, scruffy and stinking, emaciated and intrigued by the invitation, with Fecker towering behind. That had been six months ago, and he had not been in his house for the last three of them. It smelt different, and in places, the walls were not as he remembered them. They were in the same place of course, but where there had been gas sconces, now there were modern brass lanterns with reflectors and strange, round glasses within.

'The new electricity,' Mrs Norwood explained proudly as if she had fitted them herself. Silas wouldn't have been surprised if she had. 'You get used to them very quickly. Here…' She demonstrated a switch, and Silas, who had seen larger and more impressive ones at the opera house, feigned ignorance so as not to deflate her ego.

'Thanks,' he said. 'It's a lot quieter, isn't it?'

'It certainly is, Sir, and less smelly. Now, would you like to eat first or take a bath? Your room is ready, and I have heated the water, which, by the way, is still running on gas. After that, if you need taking anywhere, I am free all day, though I should be preparing lessons for after the holiday, and I have Easter Sunday school to think about, and I don't like to leave the house for too long, but...'

'Mrs Norwood!' Silas stopped her with a grand smile but firmly shown palm. 'Please, don't trouble yourself. I know my way around well enough. I'll drop my bags, come down and eat, change and be out of your way in a couple of hours.'

With that, he left her as quickly as he could without appearing rude and scurried up the backstairs to the first floor. Anymore of Mrs Norwood and the last of his strength would be sucked from his bones.

Bones that were decidedly chillier that afternoon as he stepped from a hansom cab and faced Cheap Street Gate and the entrance to Greychurch. He could have taken the cab right to his destination, but something — morbid curiosity perhaps, or nostalgia — compelled him to walk the last half mile. Leaving one area of the city and entering his old stamping ground was as unnerving as leaving Cornwall to return to Clearwater, but both journeys came with a thrill. That of knowing that he was acting to protect his lover, or at least, to allay fears that Archer might be in danger, if not from an assassination, then from the scandal of having one performed in his home.

There were two things for Silas to ascertain, although Thomas had suggested only one. He would act on the butler's suggestion later and return west to the Lyceum to see what he could discover, but before that, he had his own question in need of an answer.

'*Yia buyatul shi uchideh tatal.*' He repeated the words as he had done through the night. They formed the melody against which played another tune, one more easily understood, but far more threatening. 'He seeks to take the family name. He means dishonour, he means you shame.'

The two expressions had to be connected, but until he knew who the 'He' of the English lines meant, the Romanian language could have meant everything or nothing. He'd asked Fecker on the drive to the station last night, but Fecks had simply shrugged.

'I am Ukraine, Banyak,' he said. 'That shit is foreign.'

Able to remember the phrase exactly, he could think of nowhere else in the city to find a translation than among the immigrants of Greychurch. More specifically, at the Cheap Street Mission where, if he was lucky, he would find Doctor Markland in attendance and someone who spoke both English and Romanian.

The street was exactly as he remembered it, but now that he walked it with confidence wearing a tailored suit and a bowler hat, he didn't fear it. The looks he received from the match-seller girls and hawkers came with a deferential nod of the head or touch of a peaked cap not, as before, with scorn or a thumb-to-lips curse. The barrow boys stepped out of his way, their boots splashed with mud from the gutters where he had once searched for dropped coins, and it was he who stepped over piles of rags rather than being the unfortunate beneath them. Policemen paid him no attention, and he no longer needed to fear them. Silas was one of the lucky ones, unlike the renter boys gathered at the entrances to rat runs, their eyes darting to potential customers as the gentlemen passed by.

As he neared the mission building, regret swelled in his heart, pushing tears to the corners of his eyes. Not because he missed his life on the street, nothing good had come from it apart from meeting Fecker and being found by Archer, but because nothing had changed. Boys and women still sold their bodies, children still begged, injured men rattled tin cups, and the wealthy ignored it all. He hadn't decided to walk because of any feeling of nostalgia, he realised, but because he wanted to remind himself of how his life could have been, and the more he saw, the more he appreciated his good fortune. Silas was lucky, but impotent against the depravity and desperation. There was nothing he could do for these people, no amount of money would end their struggle. That could only come with time and determined change from those above, those like Viscount Clearwater whose name was carved in stone above the entrance to the warehouse he had reached.

Silas looked up the forbidding red-brick walls, beyond the iron-framed windows to the gutter. One above to catch the rain, one at his feet to sweep away the detritus of street living, and between them, four floors of help and charity. He had found this building, he

146

had worked with the local traders and authorities, under Archer's guidance, to secure and repair the property. As an advisor and campaigner, he had done something, he had made a difference, but all the same, his eyes still pricked with tears, and he longed to do much more.

'Help you, Sir?'

The voice brought him to his senses and, sniffing, he pulled himself together. A uniformed man stood in the doorway, guarding it against the drunks and the illiterate unable to read the sign, "A mission for destitute men from the street."

'Yes, hello,' Silas replied, pulling a business card from his pocket. 'Silas Hawkins. Is Doctor Markland here?'

The doorkeeper took the card and read it aloud as if he was used to being tricked by charlatans wanting a free bed and a decent meal. 'Private secretary to Viscount... Oh! My apologies, Sir.' The man stepped aside. 'The Superintendent is in his office. I'll direct you.'

'No need,' Silas said whipping back the card. 'I designed the place.'

That was not exactly true, but he had suggested what the Mission should have within its walls, and he knew the layout.

Entering the hall, the first thing that struck him was the smell. Unlike Molly's dosshouse less than one hundred yards away where the entrance stank of piss and sweat, the air held the tang of antiseptic. The floor tiles were clean, the paint on the walls was as fresh as when it was applied, and the lighting lent warmth. The corridor to Markland's office was no less meticulous and was being swept and mopped by a pair of boys no older than fifteen.

'Afternoon, lads,' Silas chirped as he passed, his heels clicking on the tiles. 'Good work.'

They thanked him with beaming, clean faces, while Silas shut out thoughts of what their lives would have been like before they were rescued. Instead, he turned his thoughts to his purpose, and on reaching the superintendent's office, found the door open.

Markland sat behind his desk, his head down, his sleeves rolled and his pen scribbling furiously over paperwork.

Silas knocked and received a gruff, 'Yes?' but no visual acknowledgement. That gave him an idea, and he stepped back into the passage out of sight. Clearing his throat and trying not to snigger, he projected his imitation of Archer's voice loudly enough for Markland and the boys to hear.

'Damn it, Philip! There's a tart here saying you owe her five guineas.'

One of the boys dropped his mop, the other gasped but both covered their mouths when Silas winked and placed a finger on his lips.

Markland was at the door in a flash, his moustached face red, his eyes darting. 'Lord Clearwater?' he blustered searching the passage but finding only Silas. Realisation dawned. 'Oh, very funny, Hawkins.' The complaint came through a smile and an offered hand which Silas shook. 'I didn't know you were coming. Are you alone? Come in, come in.'

'Didn't have time to warn you,' Silas said, following the doctor into his office. 'And I'm not staying long. How's it going?'

'Oh, fine, fine.' Markland busied himself at a cabinet, opening and closing drawers, fruitlessly searching for something. 'Clearwater with you?'

'No, just me. You look busy, sorry.'

'Not at all, not at all.' Markland was still rummaging, crouching now to reach into the back of a bottom drawer, and Silas watched with amusement.

'All the beds full?'

'Everything's full,' Markland said. 'Completely oversubscribed, but it's working. We've had a good run of successful cases. Found a boy a kitchen position in a decent household only yesterday. Completely back on his feet, free of disease and keen to make a fresh start. Four more last week, five the... Ah!' He stood clutching a bottle of rum, and holding the cabinet while his blood found its natural course. 'Will you?'

'Won't say no.'

As the doctor carried out another foray, this time into a cupboard to locate glasses, Silas admired the office. Despite Markland's apparent absentmindedness — something which had increased since his run-in with Quill's brother, the murdering Miss Arnold — his office showed him to be organised. One wall was papered with charts listing names, dates and the progress of his clients, another held basic medical records. Not intimate details but a checklist of

148

who had been treated successfully, as if Markland worked his way through every unfortunate man, giving them a thorough check for everything from lice to V.D., two things from which Silas had never suffered, he was pleased to note. The wall behind the desk was a window that looked onto what had once been the warehouse floor but was now a dormitory. Four rows of beds, separated by low walls, but otherwise open, were neatly lined and made. Youths rested on some while others swept and tidied around them. There was no noise, none of the shouted threats Silas had experienced in Molly's rope room, and no-one was marauding with a blade, robbing or attacking.

The harsh memories were pushed from his mind when he was offered a measuring beaker.

'It usually holds a solution of iodine and hydrogen peroxide,' Markland announced. 'But it's been washed.'

Silas took the rum and swilled it in the beaker, sniffing it and finding only the smell of alcohol. 'Cheers,' he said, thrusting it towards Markland's glass.

The doctor pulled his away sharply. 'Better not, dear chap,' he said. 'These specimen jars are damned delicate.' He retook his seat behind his desk. 'Now, what can I do for you, Mr Hawkins?'

'Call me Silas, for a start,' Silas said. He sipped his drink, and the liquid burned the back of his throat. 'You sure this is safe?'

'Oh, yes.' Markland waved the concern away with a laugh. 'I can't vouch for the rum, mind you. So, what do you need?'

Markland was keen on coming to the point, and understandably so. With over sixty homeless men in his care, plus his staff, the building and his role on the charity's committee, his time was always limited. Silas appreciated that and also came straight to the point.

'I want a Romanian,' he said. 'Preferably one who speaks English. Got any?'

'You make us sound like a knocking shop,' Markland said, his bushy moustache twitching.

'Sorry. Are any of our residents Romanian, do you know?'

'I can easily find out.' The doctor rose, and Silas feared there would be another expedition into a cabinet or cupboard, but he walked to the wall displaying the largest chart. 'Can I ask why?'

'Need some words translated.'

'Ah, of course,' Markland said, tapping a name on his chart. 'Young Mr Popescu. Been with us three weeks, already turned himself around, cleaned up and now...' He traced a line across the chart, tapped there, and turned to the door. 'Conveniently sweeping the ground floor. Dragos!'

The clatter of a bucket and the scurrying of feet heralded the arrival of one of the lads who had been cleaning the corridor. He skidded to a halt in the doorway, brushing the front of his apron and standing to attention.

'Come in, would you, Dragos?' Markland returned to his desk while Silas stood to greet the young man. 'This is Mr Hawkins. He works for Lord Clearwater and has something to ask you.'

'Yes, Sir?'

Perhaps he was still smiling because of Silas' practical joke, or maybe he was simply pleased to be called to assist, but the youth's face was a picture of enthusiasm. His features were not unlike those of Mr Smith; dark hair, deep brown eyes beneath bushy, black eyebrows and a long, narrow nose. His mouth, when the smile faded to seriousness, was thin, and his brow set with concentration.

'Mr Popescu,' Silas began, returning the smile to the boy's face with the respect in his voice. 'I have a strange request, but the doctor thinks you can help. You speak Romanian, I understand.'

The lad rattled off a sentence which could have been any language, but Dragos was so keen to please, Silas doubted deception was involved.

'Good. I heard something the other day and was interested to know what it meant. If I repeat it, will you be able to overlook my bad accent and tell me it's meaning?'

'Yes, Sir.'

'Thank you. There were two things actually. First, what does Am eşuat mean?'

'Easy, Sir. I failed, or I have failed.'

Archer had been correct. At the moment Smith thought he was going to die in the train wreck, he said that he had failed, presumably in his duty to assassinate Henry Irving. Silas hoped his sleep-talking words would offer more clues.

'The second thing was longer,' he said. Closing his eyes for a moment to aid his memory, he pictured Smith standing in the moonlight, recalled his accent, and repeated the words.

Dragos' expression changed. His brow knitted further and he dropped his chin to stare at Silas with eyes that now pierced.

'I did warn you about my accent,' Silas apologised.

'It's not that, Sir. Your accent is very good. Are you sure of the words?'

'As sure as I can be. Why? What do they mean?'

The youth looked from Silas to Markland, who nodded permission for him to speak. 'Go on, Dragos,' he encouraged. 'You shan't offend either of us if it's rude.'

'It ain't rude, Doctor,' Dragos said, returning his glare to Silas. 'But it's not very nice.'

'Go on, mate,' Silas said. 'You'll be doing myself and His Lordship a great service.'

'It's the Szekely dialect, Sir. Not much used, but good enough known.'

'And it means?'

The lad swallowed, shrugged his shoulders and said, 'I can't imagine where you heard it, Sir, but I suppose you heard it right. *Yia buyatul shi uchideh tatal.* Well, it means…' He hesitated. 'It means, Sir, Take the child and kill the father.'

Fifteen

The journey back to the West End was easier to make than the journey into the East End. The cab trundled through Cheap Street Gate and entered the financial area of the city, leaving behind the smells of tanning workshops and sweat factories. Not only did the air become cleaner, so did the people walking the pavements, which gradually became less cluttered. The sight of immigrant workers, slaughterers and labourers was replaced by businessmen, well-dressed ladies and, later as the carriage took him along the river road and through Temple, hurrying members of the legal profession, their gowns flapping.

The scenery transformed along with those ignoring it and heading home in the dusk after their day's labours. The stark red-brick factories and tenements gave way to classical buildings which were eventually replaced by the varied architecture of the Strand. As the cab crawled in the worsening traffic past King's College and the magnificent frontage of Somerset House, the cab driver yelled down his apologies for the delay.

'Should have taken the Aldwych,' the man called. 'Sorry about that, Sir. I can put you off here if you don't mind crossing the road.'

Leaning from the window, Silas told him that here would do fine, he could see the street he needed, and it wasn't far. He was silently glad they hadn't taken the Aldwych route as that would have taken him past the bottom of Bow Street, and he had no desire to relive his experiences there.

Paying the man, he weaved through the traffic to reach Wellington Street, a road of five-storey houses, some with shops beneath, that ran north towards Covent Garden, and on the corner stood his next destination in all its grandeur.

The entrance to the Lyceum Theatre was possibly the most impressive theatre he had seen. Behind the porch, the façade rose high into the night sky and curved around the corner to run for many yards. The side of the building was beautifully structured and proportioned, but the front was something else entirely. Six slender columns crowned by intricate swirls supported the portico, its apex gilded and crafted in white stone, embossed with carvings Silas couldn't make out at that height. Behind the columns, three high arches housed oak and brass doors, their glass glinting in the lanterns that burned either side. Silas didn't know much about architecture, but he knew that when he stood beneath the entrance, he felt small and yet privileged. Walking through those three doors would transport him into a theatrical world far removed from Greychurch, even from Larkspur Hall, and not wanting to be put off from his cause by the splendour, he took a moment to remind himself of his intentions.

'Henry Irving's play about the Szekelys,' he whispered to himself. 'Lord Clearwater, entertaining the great actor, needs as much background as he can get, would like me to see his research...' He broke off, suddenly aware that although the sun had set, and the porch was lit, he was the only person there. Strangers passed by out on the pavement, but no-one was heading towards the entrance and, as he approached, he realised that despite the time of day, the theatre was closed.

'Well, that's a fecking good start,' he mumbled, trying one of the doors. Pressing his face to the glass and shielding it with his hand was no help; all he saw was a dark, empty foyer. Even the box office grilles were down.

Sighing, he retreated to the pavement and followed the building's curve towards Covent Garden looking for the stage door. Dodging ladies in fine dresses heading for the cafes, and men in suits hurrying for their trains, he weaved through the crowds searching the side of the theatre until he spied a lantern ahead. Its yellow glass threw just enough light for him to read the sign painted on the stonework beneath it, and he approached the stage door only to find his way partly blocked by a bundle of blankets. Beggars were not only to be found in Greychurch, it seemed. This one sat against the wall with his head bowed, his legs out and his hands clasped around a tin mug. There was nothing in the man's begging bowl, and Silas resolved to drop a coin or two in it once he had finished

153

his business inside the theatre. The man was the only unfortunate on the street, and although Silas couldn't help all those he saw in Greychurch, he could at least make himself feel happier by donating a few shillings to this one.

The stage door was set back into the kind of alcove Silas once used to turn tricks in, another reminder of his past and how far he had come thanks to Archer. There was no bell or knocker, but the door was half-open, and a light within gave him hope that people were still at work even if there was no performance taking place. He stepped down into a small room to the left of which was a grilled counter, and behind that, a middle-aged man in shirtsleeves and waistcoat. He looked up as Silas entered, peered at a pocket watch, and wrote a note in a ledger before addressing the visitor.

'Help you, Sir?' he said, his accent unmistakably west country and not unlike the accent Silas heard in Larkspur village.

'Evening,' Silas nodded, reaching for his business card. 'I've come on behalf of Lord Clearwater or Riverside and Larkspur.' He pushed the card through the grille where the doorkeeper was attaching round spectacles to the bridge of his nose. 'I know that Mr Irving is currently returning from a tour,' he continued, applying his best impersonation of Archer. 'However, he is breaking his journey at Larkspur Hall, and His Lordship is keen to make him as welcome as possible. For that reason...'

'Sorry, Sir,' the man said, pushing the card back to him. 'But there's no-one 'ere abouts 'part from me, and you've already talked of things far beyond me understanding. Who is it you be wanting?'

'More like what,' Silas said, hope fading fast. 'His Lordship wants me to access Mr Irving's work on his plays, and is of the opinion that there would be research here in his offices.'

'Aye,' the man said, staring blankly. 'So?'

'I'd like to see it, so I can forewarn His Lordship with information and thus enable the two men to discuss, intelligently, the great actor's work.' He was repeating, more or less, what Thomas had suggested he say, and doing it in Archer's public-school voice was impressing the doorkeeper who now nodded thoughtfully. It wasn't, however, helping Silas progress any further towards his goal.

'Quite understand, Sir,' the man replied 'And I'd be more than 'appy to assist, but I can't let you into Mr Irving's office without

154

either 'is say so or that of Mr Stoker, and as Mr Stoker be with Mr Irving and the company in America...' He referred to a calendar hung on the wall beside him. 'Or, more rightly, aboard the SS Britannic on the way back, there be not a lot I can do for you. Can you come back next week?'

'No,' Silas sighed with apparent helplessness. 'Their meeting is this weekend, and Lord Clearwater is rather embarrassed that, although he is a member of the Garrick Club, the same as Mr Irving, this will be their first chance for an in-depth discussion of the work of your great theatre...' Having gone off the script Thomas had outlined, he was starting to lose himself. 'You see my problem?'

Thankfully, the doorkeeper did and was keen to help. 'What is it exactly you was looking for, Sir? Perhaps I know something about it.'

'In particular, any papers he has regarding the Szekely people. His research on the subject of the Romanians, and the play he performed here last year.'

'Oh, that.' The man obviously wasn't a fan of that particular piece because he screwed up his nose. 'No disrespect to Mr Irving,' he said. 'A great man, very great, but that wasn't my favourite of his plays. You should see him as Shylock, Sir, incredible. And his Macbeth! Well, now there's a play where the blood and witchery made sense, unlike...' He leant forward to whisper. 'Last year's production. Mad foreigners devouring children, throwing babies to wolves, biting flesh and...' He shivered. 'Not me cup of tea.'

'That's all well and good,' Silas said, impatient to move the discussion along. 'But do you know where Mr Irving kept his background work? I would only need half an hour to make some notes for His Lordship.'

'House be dark, offices locked up, even the carpenters are taking an Easter break, Sir. You can't get no further into the theatre than 'ere. No-one goes in when the 'ouse be dark.'

'But there are notes and things here?' Silas indicated the theatre generally when, in fact, he was making a mental note of how many doors and whether they had locks.

'Books, mainly,' the doorkeeper said. 'And copies of the draft script, but they be top floor in the offices. Mr Irving, whether he directs or just appears in, always does his research, and Mr Stoker is very keen to keep all his notes. There were a great load of them Mr Stoker found, so the clerk told me. Always coming in and out through 'ere carrying another new set of papers on the Szekely play. Mind you, that were nothing compared to The Merchant.'

'Had to carry all this paperwork a long way, did he? The clerk, I mean?'

'That 'e did, Sir. Six floors up to Mr Stoker's office where it all be kept. I'd like to 'elp you, Sir, but the doors be locked and I ain't able to leave me post anyway. Sorry.'

'No, no, I understand,' Silas played at being reasonable while his mind worked on other theories. 'One last thing, though. As you are so knowledgeable, would you know where this work, the research on the Romanians, came from? I mean, would I be able to find it elsewhere?'

'I wouldn't know that, Sir,' the man said, scratching his nose with a pencil. 'Libraries I expect, that's where Mr Stoker gets his from.'

Silas was getting nowhere. It was a spurious notion of Thomas' that he would find out how the assassin might operate by seeing the background reading of an actor, and the doorkeeper's suggestion of a library made much more sense.

'I'll let you get on,' he said. 'Thanks for your help.'

'Welcome, Sir. Always willing to pass the time of day, not a lot else 'appens round 'ere when the theatre be dark. If you'd close the door on your way out. I be off 'ome soon.'

Silas left him and stood outside in the alcove to consider his options. Somewhere among the mass of resources the capital offered was the answer he was looking for, but he was suddenly overwhelmed with a desire to head to Paddington and take the first train to Cornwall. He needed to be with Archer. He was alone in his house and potentially in danger, and Silas should have been by his side. Someone with more intelligence, Thomas perhaps, or James, should have been doing this. They were educated, they'd been to school and would know where to look.

The darkness was oppressive, as was the loneliness that crushed as he watched flames flicker in the grimy streetlamps all the way to Covent Garden. They formed parallel lines that met as one diffused glow at their vanishing point, murky in the mist that had started to cloud the street. He wished he'd worn a cloak over his topcoat to

156

keep out the cold that crept in with the oncoming rain, and a lonely evening by the fire in Archer's study was all he had to look forward to. Perhaps the library at Clearwater House would offer him the chance to discover more about the Protectori. Then again, maybe it wouldn't.

'It's all fecking ridiculous,' he muttered, pulling his bowler tighter over his head and scanning the street for a cab.

'Got any change, Sir?'

The clatter of a tin mug on the pavement reminded him of his self-promise, and he searched his pocket to find a shilling. Taking two, he crouched to drop them into the cup.

'I know what it's like, mate,' he said to the bowed head. 'Good luck to you.'

The head rose slowly and turned to him at eye level. It was a young face, unshaven, grubby and gaunt, with eyes that sagged through exhaustion. Silas knew how the lad felt; he'd hardly slept for the last two days, but at least he had a home to go back to.

'Mr Silas?'

It took a moment, but when Silas realised who had spoken, he couldn't help but swear.

'Feck me! What are you doing here?'

'Hoping to beg something to eat, Sir.'

Silas gawped at the youth, unable to comprehend the chance meeting. The man was in the wrong place, and he wasn't dashing from here to there carrying props and announcing calls.

'Jake?'

'Hello, Sir.'

'What...? I don't understand.'

Silas looked back towards Covent Garden where he had last seen Jake at the opera house. The young man had played his part in saving Cadwell Roxton and protecting Archer's reputation. Then, he had been active and cheeky, fast and loyal, and yet here he was begging for his supper on a pavement in the drizzle.

'What happened to you, Jake?' he asked, lowering himself to sit beside the teenager.

'Bad fortune. How have you been, Mr Silas, Sir?'

'Fine, fine, yes... But you? Why aren't you at the opera house?'

'Ah, granddad died, Sir. Just after Christmas last. Sudden like.

Bad heart, they said. Course, they got another doorman in, and I had to go. It was granddad who kept me in work and lodgings. Still, Mr Bursnall did pay for his funeral, so I was grateful for that.'

'Jake, I'm sorry, man.' Silas gripped his shoulder. 'And you've been on the street since?'

'I have, Sir. All I could do. I tried getting other work, but there's none about, not for someone no-skilled like me. I sit here in the hope the Lyceum might find a use for me. It used to be the opera house, did you know that, Sir? Long time ago mind, and before the fire, but all I know is the inside of a theatre, and one's very much like another. Anyway, thanks for the shillings, I'll push on over to Southwark. I can get a room there with sixpence, and a pound of sausage with the rest.'

'No you bloody won't,' Silas said, standing. 'Get up. Can you stand? Sorry, let me help you.'

'I'm alright, Sir,' Jake said. 'Bit hungry, maybe, but...' He heaved himself to his feet and stood on thin legs, the filthy blanket hanging from him like a shroud. 'Good to see you again.' He started to walk away.

'Where are you going?'

'Southwark.'

Silas was not going to let that happen and made it clear by hailing a hansom. 'You're coming with me,' he said, and despite the protestations of the cabbie, bundled the homeless man into the back. 'Bucks Row,' he barked. 'Clearwater House. Front door.'

For the first time that day, Mrs Norwood was speechless when she answered the bell and saw the collection of rags Mr Hawkins had brought home. Her shocked silence gave Silas the opportunity to slip by her while giving his orders.

'My friend needs a hot bath, warm food and some decent clothes,' he said, leading Jake towards the staircase. 'He can stay in my suite with me, save you making up another room. I'll see to his bath if you could make us both supper. And thank you!'

'Wait!' Mrs Norwood ordered as she closed the door. Seeing Silas' shock, she tempered her tone. 'I am sorry, Sir, school ma'am's habit. A telegram arrived for you in the early afternoon.'

She handed it to him on a silver salver, which caused Jake to raise his eyebrows and Silas to blush. He took it, thanked her and continued on his way.

Jake was no weight, and Silas had no trouble helping him upstairs. As he had said, he wasn't unwell but had sat in stunned silence on the ride home as if everything that had happened to him since Christmas had suddenly hit him at once. It wasn't until Silas showed him into his rooms that he came out of his reverie and realised where he was.

'I can't put you out, Mr Silas,' he said, his voice, once so chirpy, was hushed and tentative.

'You can, and you're not,' Silas said, closing the door. 'We'll get you fed soon. Meanwhile, I'll put water in the bath and find you a dressing gown or something. Looks like Mrs Norwood's made up the fire, so I'll light it first.'

'I can do that,' Jake offered. 'I'm really okay, Sir, just hungry. Maybe I can eat and then be on my way.'

'You ain't going anywhere apart from the bath, supper tray and bed. You look like something from the knacker's yard.'

'Just cold, Sir.'

'And for fuck's sake, stop calling me Sir.' Realising that had come out as if he was telling the man off, Silas said, 'Sorry, don't mean to yap like that. I'm just annoyed that they turned you out on the street. Lord Clearwater won't be happy when I tell him.' He knelt at the fire and struck a match. 'You should have come to us. I promised you nothing bad would happen to you after that fuss at the opera.'

Jake hadn't moved. He stood like a grubby statue in the centre of the room, his hair, long and straggly, falling to his shoulders, his dark eyes the only thing about him with movement.

'Sit down, mate,' Silas said once the kindling was alight.

'I'm dirty.'

'You're alright.' Silas didn't look nor care as he opened the telegram. 'Sit on that dust sheet if you're worried. The house hasn't been used for a few months, and they've not uncovered everything. Just sit, here, near the fire while I sort the bathroom.'

'Okay, Sir.'

'Silas.'

'Okay, Sir Silas.'

'Oh, for fuck's…' Silas laughed. Ever since they had met, Jake hadn't been able to call him by his first name. He had put up with Mr Silas, but Sir was a step too far. 'Just Silas, Jake. Can you manage that?'

'I'll try, Sir.'

Silas gave up and went to run the bath. He read the message as it was filling.

Jerry O run away. Thinks father in mortal danger. Am with Fecks going north to search. Investigate 'INTS' and Smith link if possible. YBM Jimmy.

The telegram raised more questions than Silas was able to cope with. Was Jerry a runaway, or had he run away from Larkspur? Who was his father, and what danger? Why were Jimmy and Fecks going north, and how far north? INTS were the initial's in the boy's jacket, but what did that have to do with Smith, and how could he find a link? The only thing Silas understood was the signature, and he smiled. *YBM* stood for 'Your Best Mate.' The thought that he and James were once again working together to protect Archer sent a warm shiver of comradeship that helped dispel the last of his earlier mood of unhappiness.

'I dunno,' he tutted. 'Can't leave them alone for one day.'

Putting the telegram in his pocket and deciding to ponder it later, he popped back to the bedroom and rifled through his wardrobe. Jake was only a couple of inches shorter, but he was much thinner.

'I doubt my clothes will fit you,' he said as he pulled out a dressing gown, trousers and underclothes.

'I can take them in if you've got thread and needles.'

'That's right, you wanted to make costumes, didn't you? Hey...' A memory returned. 'Archer was going to have a word with Lady Marshall about hiring you, wasn't he? Yes, he said he would.'

'I never heard anything,' Jake said. 'And I didn't like to ask.'

'We can think about that later.' Silas handed him the gown. 'I'll call you when the bath's ready. Put this on for now.'

By the time Mrs Norwood delivered their dinner, Jake was clean, warm and dressed. He was also on the verge of sleep, and by the time they had eaten, Silas too was fit to drop.

'Go to bed when you want,' he said, putting the tray outside.

'I'll be fine on the floor, Sir.'

'No. The bed's big enough for the two of us.'

Returning, Silas found Jake standing at the foot staring at the headboard. 'Why are you being so good to me?' he asked.

Silas thought back to last year, trying to remember what Jake knew of him. Was he worried that there was a dubious motive behind Silas' actions? How much did he know about the relationship between Archer and Silas, Thomas and James? With everything else cluttering his mind, it was difficult to recall, but it made no difference, Silas had no intentions other than helping a man who had helped him.

'Nothing to worry about, Jake,' he said. 'I'm just passing on kindness that was once shown to me, and you deserve it. You'll be safe. My side, your side.'

'Oh!' Jake understood what the Irishman was insinuating. 'I wasn't bothered about that, Sir. I worked around queers all the time.'

It was a mild insult but not meant as one, and at least it told Silas how much Jake knew.

'No,' Jake continued. 'I was wondering what you were doing at the Lyceum and thinking how fortunate it was you were there.'

'Long story, mate,' Silas said, sinking into the armchair and picking up the glass of wine Mrs Norwood had brought with his supper. 'I was trying to get hold of some background on a play Mr Irving did. It was Thomas' idea, and it's a bad one if you ask me.'

'Thomas?' Jake turned to him. 'Was that the footman? No, that was Jimmy. The butler I costumed for the gala?'

'That's him. You sitting, drinking, sleeping, what?'

Jake sat and lifted his glass. 'What does he want with Mr Irving?'

Without giving too much away, Silas explained what he was doing in the city, and told Jake that Thomas suspected Irving would have kept notes that could be useful for the viscount.

'The theatre's locked up and I can't get in,' he concluded. 'So tomorrow, I'll take a look at libraries or something. I've got to be back by Friday, so I've only got one day.'

'I'll be out of your way in the morning,' Jake said.

He raised his glass to Silas and, as before Silas was struck by the man's resemblance to his sisters; black hair, bright blue eyes, the same shaped nose. He could well have been a cousin.

'We'll deal with tomorrow when it hits us.' Silas yawned. 'Cheers.'

Jake fixed him with a look of sadness. It might have been the fire flames flickering in his eyes, or it could have been exhaustion, but they were glassy, as though he was on the verge of tears.

'Thank you… Silas.' His pale mouth curved into a smile. 'You're a good man.'

'And so are you, Jake. You deserve better than a life on the streets.'

Jake's glass was at his lips when he stopped and drew it away, staring at its contents. 'The blood of the dead,' he said as if he had just realised what it was.

'No, just red wine.'

'The name of Mr Irving's play. "The Blood of the Dead, or The Mystery of the Szekely." It wasn't his biggest success. If it hadn't been for his manager, he would have lost a fortune. In writing it, Mr Stoker was trying to recreate something like Mr Irving's first big play, "The Bells." That's where he found his fame, as I remember Granddad telling me. If I got this right, that one was based around a thing called "The Polish Jew." All about a man's bad deeds coming back to haunt him, and him getting his comeuppance. Irving likes stuff like Faust and all that.'

'You know your theatre.' Silas was impressed.

'It's been my life. What does Lord Clearwater want to know about that play for anyhow?'

'Like I said, a long story.' Silas was impressed with Jake's memory and enthusiasm for the theatre. He could be a handy ally in the search for knowledge, but he doubted he knew anything about the Protectori and how they killed their victims. 'I'll tell you more tomorrow. You must be knackered.'

'No, I'm alright.' Jake smiled again, and it was good to see. 'Does His Lordship want Mr Irving's play really bad?'

'His play, his notes, anything about the Szekely people, so when they meet on Friday, he's got something to talk about. Between you and me, I think he's a bit in awe of Mr Irving. He wants him to back the mission we have in Cheap Street, and put on another gala night to raise money.'

'Oh, Mr Stoker's the one you want for that,' Jake said. 'He's good at publicity. But he needs this stuff bad?'

Silas nodded.

'And Mr Thomas thinks it's in his office?'

'Just Thomas, and yes.'

'And the stage doorman won't let you in to look?'

'Not even in the name of Viscount Clearwater.'

'Oh, well then…' Jake put down his glass, sat back in his chair and put his hands behind his head. As he thought, his eyes remained on Silas, but he blew out his cheeks one after the other, made a tutting noise and cracked his knuckles. Leaning forward, he scratched his recently shaved chin and said, 'I suppose we could break in.'

The idea had occurred to Silas at the stage door, but he hadn't seen an obvious way to do it. The windows were too high and opened directly onto a busy street, and the building abutted others with no back alley.

'Break into the Lyceum?' he queried, a smile growing.

'No,' Jake said. 'Not the Lyceum. The Opera House.'

Sixteen

At about the time Silas had been drifting into troubled sleep on the night train to London, James was lying in bed watching Thomas dress. That morning, he moved slowly as his body was still stiff, but he was more mobile than the day before.

'Don't put them on,' James said, leering as Tom stood naked, turning his underclothes the right way around. 'I love it just as you are.'

'Go back to sleep,' Thomas replied, smiling. 'You've got an hour yet.'

It was six-thirty, the maids would already be at the fireplaces and sweeping the floors. Barnaby would be opening the main hall, and Saddle would be setting the breakfast room before collecting the post and bringing the newspapers to Thomas or Barnaby for ironing.

'I'm awake now,' James said. 'I think I'll have a bath. How are you feeling?'

'A bit stiff, but otherwise fine.'

'I know what you mean.' James threw back the cover to reveal his naked erection. 'Want to give me a hand?'

'You're incorrigible, Mr Wright,' Thomas said, stepping into his trousers. 'And there'll be none of that with your young friend staying down here.'

'No, of course not.'

They had arranged that Saddle would bring down some of the viscount's old games to keep Jerry occupied, and once James had finished his morning duties, he was to show the lad around the Hall and move him into the butler's suite. James was keen to discover more about the boy, and Lucy was more than keen to have her room back to herself.

Thomas had just finished dressing, and James was considering how he might coerce him back to bed when a knock on the sitting room door took them by surprise.

'Who's that?' Thomas complained, hurriedly buttoning his shirt.

No-one disturbed the butler unless it was an emergency, and James' first thought was that Mr Smith had done something dreadful to the viscount.

'Wait!' he hissed as Thomas headed for the next room.

James scurried from the bed, grabbed his dressing gown and hurtled through into his own bedroom where he stood behind the door as he dressed.

'Who is it?' Thomas called.

The reply was muffled, but the mild Scottish accent told James it was the housekeeper. Listening, he made out two words, 'Jerry' and 'missing', and two minutes later was dressed and on his way to the servants' hall.

He was met by an unusual amount of chatter, with Lucy in nightclothes, Iona and Karan without their aprons, and Barnaby looking as though he'd just crawled in from a night on the town with his dressing gown badly tied. Mrs Baker was also in her nightclothes, a sight that suggested everyone had been called immediately the disappearance was discovered. The only two people properly turned out were Thomas and James.

'Young Jerry's gone, Sir,' Lucy said, her eyes red-ringed and her cheeks wet. 'He was fast asleep when I turned in at eleven and gone when I woke at six.'

'We've searched the top corridors. He's not there,' Saddle announced hurrying into the room and fixing his wing collar. 'Sally's looked in the women's half, I've covered the men's. No sign.'

'Maybe he's gone exploring,' Barnaby suggested, scratching his chest and yawning. 'You want me to look on the main floor, Mr Payne?'

'Was the back door open?' Mrs Baker asked the dairymaid, but she reported that it was closed and locked when she came in.

Others made suggestions, and the chatter became a clamour.

'Enough!' Thomas's voice echoed around the vaulted ceiling and brought everyone to a standstill. 'The boy is Mr Wright's concern, he can decide what to do and where to look. Lucy, you've done nothing wrong, so calm down. All of you, go and dress properly and be about your duties. He's a nine-year-old boy. They take themselves on adventures. I expect we will find him in the library, reading Shakespeare out of sheer boredom.'

'Well said, Mr Payne,' Mrs Baker agreed. 'Off you go.' She directed her words at her maids who left, picking up their chatter as they did so.

'Can I go back to bed?'

'No, Barnaby, you're up now.'

'But I've still got half an hour, Mr Payne,' the footman complained.

'Then you will have more than the usual time to prepare His Lordship's tray. Mr Wright is properly turned out a whole hour before he is needed. You should take a lesson from him.'

'I will be back directly,' Mrs Baker said, and hurried after her girls.

'Which leaves us men to search for the lad,' Thomas decided. 'And that will be done quietly and discreetly. We don't want to wake His Lordship nor his other guest. Mr Saddle, did Mr Smith ask for a wake up at any particular time?'

'No, Mr Payne. Though he has told me he is not generally an early riser.'

James wanted to suggest Saddle go and check the man's rooms now, but it wasn't up to him to order the under-butler around, much as he would have enjoyed doing so. The only time he had authority over him was in matters concerning the Viscount's clothes and footwear.

Thomas, however, was thinking the same thing and told Saddle to check on the house guest. 'I suggest you enter quietly through the adjoining suite so as not to disturb him. If Jerry got in there for any reason, Mr Smith would probably have rung, so it's unlikely, but please go and look.'

Saddle obeyed readily, something he rarely did when ordered by his superior, he usually made at least one counter suggestion, and, James thought, only for the sake of it. He was impressed by the way Thomas let the annoyance drift over his head and never took the bait.

'Barnaby?' James said. 'When you're dressed, come back via the ladies' corridor.'

'Good idea,' Thomas agreed. 'All the doors are locked, but check

166

the alcoves and call into the backstairs when you pass.

'What do you want me to do?' James asked, once they were alone.

'I don't know,' Thomas admitted. 'I have no experience with children. What would you do if it was your sister?'

'Be grateful I didn't have to listen to her whining,' James joked, but Tom was not in a joking mood. 'Sorry. I'd assume the lad's wandering the corridors somewhere,' he said. 'Probably lost like I was those three times when I first got here. Shall I wake His Lordship?'

'No, I'll do that if we haven't found the boy half an hour after everyone's dressed. You and I can search the ground floor, and when the others are back, they can get on with their work. If that's alright with you?'

'Of course,' James said, keeping his tone formal.

Mark was in the scullery, and when James called for him, the cheerful and obedient fifteen-year-old popped his head around the door.

'Yes, Mr Wright?'

'Will you listen out for the bells? As soon as one of the maids or Barnaby gets back, tell them to carry on as normal.'

'Yes, Sir.'

'And if His Lordship rings down,' Thomas added, 'send someone to find me. I will be the one to tell him if Mr O'Sullivan has run away.'

Forty minutes later, the servants were back in the hall, giving their reports. No-one had found Jerry, and every room had been searched apart from the cellar, which was locked and had been all night, Thomas being the only one with a key.

'Well done everyone,' Thomas said. 'But now we must get on with our day. I will speak with His Lordship, and we will leave Mr Wright to deal with this, he is, after all, the one who has the boy's confidence.'

He and James had decided this while searching the ground floor. There hadn't been time for a thorough search, and James suggested he return and continue once they knew for sure the boy wasn't simply lost in the house. Thomas was expecting his wine order delivery and had other important matters to see to concerning the dinner party, and like the viscount, had things on his mind.

James kept an eye on him from a distance, keen that he didn't overwork himself. It wasn't that Tom was delicate or highly strung — though he could be both on occasions — but James couldn't help but be protective.

Household order was restored just as the master bedroom bell rang. Barnaby had the viscount's tray prepared, but Thomas insisted he and Mr Wright take it up.

'You can help Mr Saddle this morning.'

'I can manage quite well on my own, Mr Payne,' Saddle complained.

'I would like Barnaby to attend Mr Smith today,' the butler insisted. 'You can observe and correct if necessary. Barnaby is still learning, and I trust you to ensure he does everything correctly.'

Flattery never worked on Saddle even if it was meant, and in this case, it wasn't. Thomas didn't care for the man at all, but the under-butler agreed as if he had a choice, and James couldn't help but feel he was jealous that someone else should attend to the Romanian.

Putting that thought from his mind, he followed Thomas upstairs to the master bedroom, where they found Archer in bed reading a book.

The situation was explained, and Archer was concerned but thankful that Thomas had done the right thing. 'Do you think he's run off?' he asked as James poured his coffee.

'Hard to say,' James replied. 'I can't see any reason unless I was asking him too many questions and he got the jitters.'

'Why should he?'

'He took a strange reaction to meeting Mr Smith. I assumed he was shy, but when they were introduced to each other, he looked horrified more than embarrassed.'

'Perhaps the man reminded him of the accident,' Thomas reasoned. 'Maybe it came back to him in a flash, and he went to pieces.'

'How was he afterwards?' Archer asked.

'It took me a while to settle him into bed.' James replaced the coffee pot on the tray and moved it to the table. 'He wouldn't say why he had run away from the man. I told him I thought he was being rude, but he said nothing, so I tried asking him gently if he was still upset about the accident.'

'And?'

'Just shook his head. I read to him for a while, and he fell straight to sleep.'

'You're a natural-born father, Jimmy,' Archer said through a smile, and Thomas laughed.

It was a good-natured jibe and made James flush with pride, but only for an instant. 'I'd like to go looking for him,' he said. 'If that's alright with you, Sir? Once you're up and running, that is.'

'Of course,' Archer agreed. 'Can't have a house guest, particularly a young one, lost in the grounds. You go and search, I can see you're worried. Tom can dress me, it will be like old times and give us a chance to catch up. We never get enough time alone, Tom.'

'As you wish,' Tom said. 'I have the wine arriving and a few other things to make ready, but that's later this morning.'

'Excellent. Have you heard from Silas?'

'Not yet.' Thomas noticed the time. 'He will still be on the train.'

'Ah, yes. So, that's that then, I had best get up.'

With a growing feeling of anxiety, James left to go in search of the enigmatic Jerry O'Sullivan.

It was not until an hour later that he made the discovery.

After looking in every room on the ground floor, calling the boy's name and receiving no reply, he made his way to the first floor, trying every door and looking in every unlocked room. The maids were busy preparing the guest bedrooms, airing them and dusting everything from the picture frames to the curtains, and no-one reported seeing the lad. His concern grew as he trudged to the top floor to take one more sweep of the servant's quarters. He had no qualms about entering the viscount's suite and Silas' rooms, it was part of his job to be in there at various times of the day, but when he approached Barnaby's room, he was worried that he was being too intrusive. He knocked, called and reluctantly entered telling himself that he had to be thorough, and Barnaby would understand.

The room was like the others on the top floor with its sloping ceiling, small gas fire, a sink and basic but sturdy furniture, and, as expected, there was no sign of Jerry. Considering Barnaby's appearance earlier, the room was surprisingly tidy.

Mr Saddle's room displayed the same level of fastidiousness, and there was nothing out of place, but as he was leaving, something on the dressing table caught James' eye. Among Saddle's collars and studs, one item of jewellery stood out, a gold pocket watch that James had never seen the under-butler wear. Thomas carried a watch, and it was reasonable to assume that his deputy did the same, but if that was the case, why wasn't Saddle wearing it? Hearing no sound from the corridor, he inspected the timepiece more closely, uncertain why he found it so intriguing. It was a simple fob watch with a chain and carried no inscription. It was also lighter than he expected when he lifted it to press the winder and release the catch on the cover. Inside was where the watch became curious. The face was white with black, Roman numerals, but there was no maker's mark. He could find none on the outer casing either, or inside the lid. What it did tell him, however, was the reason Saddle wasn't wearing it.

The watch wasn't working. There was no ticking, the second hand was static, and the mechanism had stopped with all three hands pointing directly to twelve.

Resisting the temptation to wind it, because that would alert Saddle to his nosiness, he put it back as he had found it and moved onto the maid's quarters, knocking on doors and calling.

Lucy's room was as he expected to find it, the bed made and a faint scent of femininity hanging in the air. Jerry's bed had been made, and his pyjamas were neatly folded on the end. The copy of 'Kidnapped' was on the locker, and James sat as he picked it up. It was the only connection he had with the boy, and as he touched it, his concern for Jerry grew. It was hard to explain how he knew, but something was wrong. Something bad was happening and the feeling transferred to him from the book.

'Why would he run away?' he asked as if the novel would reply. 'Where would he go?'

Jerry was not in the house, but he might be in the grounds, perhaps even helping Fecker with the horses. There were still plenty of places he could be, it was a calm day and not cold, perhaps he was playing in the abbey ruins, or chatting to Danylo at the smallholding. James pictured the lad playing with the Ukrainian's practice foils, learning to fence, but no matter how much he tried to imagine a happy outcome, he simply could not.

'You've got to think logically, Jimmy,' he muttered, flicking the pages. 'The lad's run from his boarding school, he's probably still running.'

The question was, where? It was one among many.

Who was I N T S? Was the jacket borrowed, stolen or Jerry's? Was his name really Jerry? Who was his father? Where was St Merrynporth? The most difficult question came last. Why was James concerned about a child he didn't know?

Assuming it was a natural, fatherly instinct even men like him were born with, he slapped his thighs and stood. Instead of befuddling his mind with questions he couldn't answer, he should have been looking for the boy and was about to replace the book when he found himself compelled to open it. The novel wouldn't let him go without demanding more attention.

Opening the cover, he understood why.

Five minutes later, he found Archer in the drawing-room with Mr Smith. They were being attended by Saddle and had just come in from breakfast. Leaning on a cane, Smith was in the process of sitting, aided by the under-butler, and Archer was sipping coffee at the window.

'My apologies, My Lord,' James said at the doorway. 'May I have a word?'

'Come in, Wright,' Archer said, distracted by the view. 'What is it?'

James waited for Archer to realise he wanted to talk alone, but the viscount didn't pick up on the hint.

'In private, My Lord?'

Saddle's ears pricked up and he threw James an inquisitive look as he collected coffee for Mr Smith. James ignored him and stepped out into the hall.

'What is it?' Archer asked when he joined him.

James showed him the novel and opened the cover in silence, hoping not to attract Smith's attention.

'Who's done that?' Archer said. 'That's a first edition!'

'I'm sorry,' James said. 'But it can only have been Master O'Sullivan.'

'What do you intend to do about it?'

'With your permission…' James glanced over Archer's shoulder, ignoring his bluster and keeping an eye on Saddle. This was one of those times he needed to be Jimmy talking to Archer, not a valet talking to his master, but Saddle was hovering near the door, and Smith's interest had also been aroused by the viscount's mild outrage. James whispered. 'I need to take Fecker and go after the boy. No matter who he belongs to, we can't let him run off and not do anything about it.'

'Where has he gone?' Archer reread the scrawled writing on the title page. 'We don't know who his father is.'

'True, Sir. But I do know *where* his father is, and that's where Jerry has gone. Merrynporth.'

'Never heard of it.'

'Me neither, but I've got to find out where it is and get him back.'

Archer rolled his eyes, forced a smile, and having checked that Saddle was now walking away from the door and was out of earshot, he said, 'Go with my blessing, comrade, and do what you do best.'

Archer was taking the situation too lightly, but now was not the time to pull him up on the matter. The boy's life was in danger.

'What's this shit, Jimmy?'

Fecker was brushing Lightning when James found him in the stables. Nathan, the stable lad, was nearby doing the same to Thunder, and David, the second hand was mucking out. James pulled Fecker aside and repeated what he had just told him.

'And we go now?'

'Yes.'

'You want me? Why? You think trouble?'

'I don't know what to expect, Fecks,' James said. 'But I'd feel happier if you were with me. Can you do it?'

'How long we go?'

'I don't know. We need to find St Merrynporth, and I've got no clue where that is. But look, the boy can't have got far. The chances are he's in the village, and the sooner we leave, the sooner we find him and bring him back.'

'Why?'

'I'll explain all that on the way.'

'Ha!' Fecker scoffed. 'Geroy did that in the snow and see what

172

happen.' He held up the remaining fingers on his left hand.

'Yeah, well… Just get two horses ready. I'll change and be back in fifteen minutes, yeah?'

'Da, if is what you want. Ivan!'

Nathan came hurrying up, nodded to James and stood cowering beneath his Ukrainian master. 'Aye, Sir?'

'Saddle these two. I come back.'

'That be with panniers, Mr Andrej?'

'Ask him,' Fecker said as he left to make ready.

'Can I ask how you want your 'ourses, Mis'r Wright, Sir?'

Nathan's heavy, local accent gave James an idea.

'Nate,' he said, knowing that was how Nathan liked to be known. 'You're from 'round here aren't you?'

'Aye, Sir. Born 'n' bred in Larkspur village. On the estate, in truth.'

'Do you know the county well?'

'Cornwall be a country not a county, ask me, Sir,' Nathan smiled as he brushed his straggly, strawberry-blond hair from his brow with the back of his hand. 'Aye, knows it well as any true Cornishman.'

'Thought so. Have you heard of a place called Saint Merrynporth?'

'I knows St Merryn,' the stable lad offered. 'Small village up over Padstow, 'bout twenty-five mile.'

'But not St Merrynporth?'

Nathan thought harder but shook his head. 'Sorry, Mis'r Wright. I can tell 'e that the word *porth* in Cornish means *port* in English, Mis'r Wright, if that 'elps. But I don't know as St Merryn 'as a port, being a little inland. Harlyn or Padstow would be its port, if you follow.'

James understood. 'Thanks,' he said. 'Will these two horses make that distance easily?'

'Take you 'bout six 'ours walking, Sir, but Thunder and Lightning be strong enough a canter long time, and Mis'r Andrej knows 'em well. Be near on nine now, so I'd say you'd be there 'round one this afternoon.'

'We'll be riding on roads and maybe across country, if you can prepare the horses for both, and add bags with feed or whatever they need in case we don't make it back today.'

Thanking Nate again, he left the smell of manure and straw behind and hurried back to the Hall to change. Without knowing what time Jerry had left, he had no way of calculating how far he might have travelled or which way he might have gone, and without any other leads to go on, the only thing he could think to do was ride to St Merryn and start there. It seemed the most logical place to go, and with Jerry on foot, they would probably see him on the way.

What he didn't know then, was that Jerry O'Sullivan was heading in a completely different direction.

Seventeen

James thought quickly as he changed his clothes, and Thomas packed a bag. Only one thing mattered, and that was finding the runaway and bringing him safely back to the Hall. The boy was James' responsibility, and James had come to like him. Apart from that, he was a vulnerable child alone on the moors.

'*Would* he be on the moors?' he asked as he tucked his breeches into his boots.

'He could be anywhere,' Thomas replied. 'But we're now certain he is not in the house, and Mr Harrow's men have searched the estate.'

'It annoys me that Archer isn't bothered,' James complained. 'I know he's got this big dinner and important guests, but he's not taking anything seriously these days. We're worried about Mr Smith, and now Jerry's vanished, and it's my fault.'

'It's no-one's fault,' Thomas reassured as he passed James a shirt. 'What you need to ask yourself, is where's he gone, and why has he run away?'

'I've been doing that and have come up with nothing. What if he's fallen and hurt himself out there? He doesn't know where he's going.'

'Slow down.' Thomas was behind him and wrapped James in his arms. They stared at each other in the full-length mirror, the butler resting his chin on the valet's shoulder. 'You are not to blame, and you're not alone. Yes, Archer is distracted, and yes, he has this cavalier attitude to problems and laughs them away. It's just how he is, but that doesn't mean he doesn't care. He's letting you go, and he's doing that because he trusts you.' He kissed James' cheek and held him tighter. 'And I love you. You've got me behind you, literally. So, let's think sensibly. Wherever he's gone, he is on foot. You will be riding, so you'll catch him easily, but there's no point racing off without consideration. Take a minute now, and you'll save time later.'

James took a deep breath, leant his head into Thomas', kissed him and broke away to continue dressing.

'Thanks,' he said.

'So, what *do* we know?' Thomas took a riding jacket from the wardrobe. 'Go through it piece by piece.'

'Well, we know that he was on the train, in third class and didn't have a ticket, and I've found out that he ran away, probably from his boarding school. But we don't know where that is, so we can't even guess where he boarded the train.'

'Irrelevant,' Thomas said. 'He left you a note. What did it say?'

'"Sorry, Mr Wright, but I have to go to my father because he is in danger".' James recited the message from memory.

'Who is his father?'

'We don't know.'

'But you do know where he is.' Thomas began buttoning James' shirt, standing before him and looking him directly in the eye.

'St Merrynporth,' James said. 'A place no-one has heard of, but which Nate said might be the port at St Merryn.'

'And St Merryn is north of here, about twenty-five miles, next to Padstow.'

'Yes.'

'Keep thinking,' Thomas said, reaching for the jacket as James tucked in his shirt.

'Padstow is at the end of the line. The train was heading that way.'

'Thus, it's reasonable to assume that's where Jerry was going when the accident happened. It's the end of the branch line, and there's only one train per day, the one he was on.'

'Makes sense that he was heading to St Merryn then.'

'Quite. What else do you have?'

Thomas held the jacket open, and James slipped his arms into it. 'I'm convinced his name isn't Jerry O'Sullivan.'

'Why?'

'Because his clothes carried a label reading INTS. My mum used to sew my initials into mine when I went to school, and that was only down the road.'

'Agreed. It's a common practice. Some of the valets and servants who stay here during the season do the same thing to avoid confusion when their shirts are laundered. Right, we are fairly certain that Jerry will be heading for the coast, and his father's surname may or may not be O'Sullivan. Go to St Merryn, or the nearest port if there isn't one there, in this case, Padstow, and ask after a Mr O'Sullivan.'

James turned to his lover, who had been brushing the yoke of his jacket. Tom's eyes glittered, and his soft lips broke into a smile.

'You know something, Mr Payne,' James said. 'I fucking love you.'

'You feel better now?'

By way of a reply, James kissed him and ran his fingers through Tom's auburn hair.

'I wish you wouldn't do that,' Thomas tutted playfully as they broke apart.

James smiled as the butler fussed at the mirror to straighten his appearance. 'I must go,' he said. 'Fecks will be waiting. I'll message you when we get there whether there's news or not.'

'I doubt you will be back tonight,' Thomas said. 'I will valet His Lordship and keep an eye on Mr Smith. Let me know where you end up so that I can send word if the boy returns.'

'Always practical.'

'Talking of which, they say there's a storm coming, so pick up your cape on the way out. Here.' Thomas handed him his bag. 'I asked the kitchen to prepare sandwiches, get them on your way through.'

'What would I do without you, Mr Payne?'

'Oh, you'd find someone else to clear up after you. Go on, Fecker will be waiting.'

A farewell kiss lasted a full minute until Thomas, laughing, pushed James away and told him to, 'Go and be a hero. But be a careful one.'

James kept his promise to Fecker. As soon as they left the stable, he explained the purpose of their journey. Fecker listened with interest, and when James said he thought Jerry might have headed directly to St Merryn, and why, the Ukrainian nodded.

'And you think he takes road?' he asked.

'I have to admit I am guessing,' James replied. 'We don't know what time he left the Hall, but it was after dark. As far as we could tell, no lanterns were missing, and as far as I know, the boy isn't familiar with the area. If he is heading north, it makes sense that he took the road.'

'He has long legs?' Fecker asked, sitting up in his saddle and scanning the horizon.

'No. He's only nine, Fecks.'

'I had long legs.'

'Yeah, well, you've got long everything. Why?'

'Longer legs, faster walk. Five miles for short legs like Banyak, it take maybe two hours. Me, I do it in one.'

It was an interesting point. 'He's shorter than Silas, about Mrs Flintwich's height, but slim. Probably plays sports at school, and I know he can run because he ran from Smith last night and was a bugger to catch. How fast do you think he would travel?'

'On this road,' Fecker said, 'he goes at four miles the hour. Over fields, two. This place is twenty-five?'

'From Larkspur, yeah. Roughly.'

'Seven hours he takes by road, or maybe more than twelve over hills.'

It was nearing eleven o'clock, and James realised with a groan that if Jerry had left at midnight, he could have reached St Merryn before James was even out of bed.

'We ask first in the village,' Fecker decided.

That had always been James' intention, and he wasted no time in his enquiries, stopping first at the telegraph office to dispatch a message to Silas. The postmaster had not seen any strangers in the village that morning and had been working since six o'clock. The lamplighter hadn't seen anyone either, but suggested James ask the repair workers taking lunch at the pub.

Riding through the High Street, they stopped at the police station to alert the on-duty constable to the missing boy, saying that they were sure they would find him tramping the road or wandering the fields, but should he be found, would the policeman take him to Larkspur? That agreed, they continued to the inn, and stopping there, discovered there had been no sightings of the boy. They did learn that the men assigned to clear the railway line were working in shifts through the night, and the route would be reopened by the next morning. That was good news for Archer and his dinner guests who were due to arrive by train, but not useful for the search.

Riding on, they passed through hamlets and open farmland, waving down anyone they saw to ask the same question and receive the same negative reply. The horses' hooves clattered on the stone bridge as they crossed the River Camel while beneath, the water flowed without a care. Sparrows twittered in the copses and hedgerows, and hawks wheeled overhead. The late-spring sun warmed them through their jackets, and it would have made for a pleasant ride had it not been for the guilt James suffered at losing his charge. He kept an eye on the weather, but it showed no signs of worsening, and he hoped to be back at Larkspur, with Jerry, well before the predicted storm hit.

Once the landscape offered no more settlements or farmsteads, they took to the open moorland, galloping the horses where they could until they finally approached the village of St Merryn from the east. The horses took the ride well, even enjoyed it, but Fecker insisted they walk at times to save the animals, and it wasn't until later in the afternoon that they crested a low hill and saw the village.

The sea was spread out to their right, glittering into the distance beneath the cloudless sky, and a wide, sandy bay opened up on the shoreline. Above it stood a collection of houses which looked out of place among an endless vista of undulating hills. It wasn't the remoteness of the village that worried James, it was the lack of boats on the beach. If, as Nathan had said, porth meant port, there was no sign of one here.

'I have an idea, Fecks,' he said, pulling his horse to a standstill. Twisting in his saddle, he strained his eyes towards Padstow as Fecker drew up alongside. 'I can't see how St Merryn has anything but a beach, but Padstow is just there, and I wonder if it used to be called St Merrynporth.'

'You the boss,' Fecker said. 'We go.'

They arrived at the quayside as a thin layer of white cloud damped the sun's warmth and brought a cool breeze from the sea. The harbour was a hive of activity with returning fishing boats, men transferring their catch to the quay, and women sitting on the stone, mending nets draped over their knees. The air smelt of sea salt and fish, voices carried through it calling prices, while people haggled over the landed catch that flapped in the final throes of death. James and Fecker weaved carefully through the crowd, eyes peeled for the small boy with the red-brown hair until they came to a coaching inn.

As Fecker stabled the horses, James secured a room and asked if anyone had reported finding a lone, lost child. As expected, he received no information about Jerry, but the landlord told him that the fishermen had been out since dawn, and if any lost young man had stumbled into the village in the early morning, they would have noticed. Once they had emptied their boats, many would pour into the inn, because, as the landlord proudly declared, 'The Old Ship Inn serves the best Cornish ales.'

James intended to test that theory, but not before he had located the telegraph office and sent a message to let Thomas know where they were. On the way back, he stopped at every pub and shop along the harbour to ask if anyone knew a Mr O'Sullivan who had a son called Jerry, and put out word that should a lost boy turn up, he was to be informed. When locals were sceptical of his motives, he used Lord Clearwater's name, and when others were reluctant to engage, he offered a reward. Returning to The Old Ship, he met Fecker coming from the opposite direction.

'Man says you went to ask around,' Fecker said. 'So I started other end and worked back. Nothing.'

It was touching that the Ukrainian had thought to widen the search without being asked, and James thanked him. Fecker simply shrugged and stomped his way into the public bar saying, 'Getting dark now. We stay here.'

Where the bar had earlier been empty, it was now teaming with men. Heavily accented voices spoke over each other, pipe smoke hung in the air but did nothing to dampen the noise of chatter, laughter and occasional swearing which rose and fell like a swelling tide. The two men occupying the adjacent table were playing dominoes, slapping their tiles down and growling through their beards. The younger of the two, no more than twenty years old, spoke more aggressively than the older, and when the other drinkers complained, his replies were not exactly courteous.

James fanned away smoke as he ordered two tankards from the barmaid, and she brought them to their table, fending off the unwanted advances of fishermen, old and young alike.

'Can I ask you something?' James had to raise his voice.

'Not if it be about nothing other than ale or supper,' the woman shouted back as she placed their drinks.

'Do you know of St Merrynporth?'

'No, me duck. You mean St Merryn?'

'There's no port there, is there?'

'Eh?'

He was about to repeat the question, but she turned and fought her way back to work. At the next table, the game of dominoes had boiled over into an argument.

'I'll ask around the tables,' James said.

'What?' Fecker put his hand to his ear.

'I said, I'll go around...'

A man slammed into Fecker's shoulder, knocking his tankard and sloshing beer into his face, before rolling off him and landing on his back on the table. James' drink was sent flying, and he leapt away. The younger fisherman was on his feet, bearing down on the older whose face was as white as his beard, and the attack was accompanied by a barrage of swearing and a look of hate from the youth. Before James could remonstrate, the attacker pulled the old man towards him and was aiming his fist directly at his terrified face.

'You cheating dobek, you bain't even a jacker!' the youth roared and threw his punch.

Fecker caught the incoming fist in the palm of his hand, saving the old man a broken nose. The youth screamed as his fingers were crushed and his arm twisted, and James was on his feet in a second, ready to defend himself. They were strangers, they'd been in the bar less than ten minutes and wouldn't stand a chance if this turned ugly.

'Ye be the cheater you knack-kneed lather.' Seeing his chance to escape, the old man struggled from the table, but the youth was not letting him off lightly. He kicked, sending his victim staggering towards James, who caught him just in time to prevent him falling face-first into a table littered with glasses.

'Get your filth away a me.'

The attacker turned his rage on Fecker, lifting his leg to kick him in the groin, but Fecker twisted his arm harder, spun the lout around and pushed him away.

The bar had fallen silent, and all eyes were on the fight. James righted the white-haired gentleman and helped him sit, hoping that would take some of the heat from the situation, but he was no longer the problem. The problem now was Fecker.

'What be he, some Polish emmet?'

'Be like a girl with them locks.'

Other insults were thrown, but the Ukrainian was impervious. His attention was once again on the youth who, having been freed, turned with newfound determination and raised both fists, ready to punch.

'Ah, get ye 'ome a your wet nurse,' the old man spat at his assailant. 'Waste a space if you can't even fight a yarnigoat.'

That brought some laughs from the men nearby, but it drew the youth's attention from Fecker and back to his original victim. Before James could step between them, he had grabbed the man by his collar and was about to drag him from the chair when he gasped. The insults faded as he rose into the air as if lifted on invisible wires. He let go of the old man, his legs kicked, and he cried out in panic.

'Door!' Fecker barked as he carried the youth towards the exit at arm's length.

Stunned, the fishermen stood back to give him a path, and one opened the door, letting in a rush of cold air. The smoke swirled around the struggling attacker, now turned victim, and his friends ignored his cries for help. Worried that the crowd would now turn on him, James hurried after them, but found he was the last in the queue as the fishermen followed Fecker from the inn and onto the quayside. By the time James pushed his way through, Fecker was holding the lout over the sea wall.

'He swims?' he shouted, and someone yelled back that the lad could.

Shrugging, Fecker released his victim, and the unfortunate youth vanished into the harbour. Turning back to the crowd, now open-mouthed in either horror or admiration, he said, 'He spill my beer,' and walked back into the inn through stunned silence. He was still holding his tankard.

'Good job the tide be in,' someone said. 'Be a ten-foot drop a the mud elsewise.'

'Had that coming a while,' said another. 'Still, better get him 'ome.'

Having checked that the unfortunate youth was being helped from the water, James was convinced he would be lynched on his return to the table, but he entered a bar that hummed with quieter conversation, the punters chatting as if nothing had happened. Two fresh tankards had appeared on their table along with a bottle of rum and the white-haired man. Fecker was sipping as he had done before, and the barmaid was wiping away the last of the spilt beer.

'Them be from Branok,' she said, nodding at the tankards and thumbing towards the old man. 'The rum be from the bar as we be grateful you got that stink out a here without breaking the windows. You'll have no more trouble from these men.'

'Thanking you for your assistance, Mis'r...?'

'Wright,' James said, taking his seat dubiously, one eye on Fecker who was contentedly sipping his fresh ale and leering at the barmaid.

'And ye, Sir? What be your name so I can thank ye?'

'Andrej Borysko Yakiv Kolisnychenko,' Fecker replied.

Mr Branok's grey eyebrows raised in momentary confusion but quickly settled. 'Then thank ye, Mis'r Kolisnychenko,' he said and raised his glass. 'Sorry 'bout the quarrel, and I be thankin' ye fur your assistance.'

It was the first time James had heard anyone other than Fecker or Archer pronounce the Ukrainian surname with ease, and he was more impressed than surprised.

'What ye be doing 'ere,' Mr Branok asked. 'You emmets?'

'Are we what?'

'Emmets, Mis'r Wright. Visitors. Only I not seen ye in Padstow afore and I been 'ere longer than me teeth.'

'We're looking for someone,' James said. 'A man by the name of O'Sullivan who may have a son called Jerry. Do you know of him?'

'I can tell ye plain there be no-one of that name in Padstow,' the man replied.

James had no reason to doubt him, and his heart sank. Now that the fuss had died down and he could observe the man more closely, he put his age at sixty at least, and judging by his calloused fingers and weather-worn face, guessed that he was a fisherman.

'I be that now, Mr Branok said when James asked. 'But only these past twenty year.'

'But you've lived here all your life you say?'

'Aye.'

'Then can I ask you, Sir, do you know if St Merrynporth is nearby?'

'Not right now, I don't, lad,' Branok said. 'But wait a day or so and I will.'

Fecker and James exchanged confused glances.

'I don't understand.' James put down his tankard. Branok hadn't said no, and that gave him hope that he might be getting somewhere. 'A day or so?'

'Aye.' Branok took a leisurely drink of rum and wiped his mouth. 'I first went a sea on me fader's skiff,' he said as he folded his arms. 'Only a small thing she were. Used to fish off the shore, close in mind. Fader taught me, and later I started on the gigs, they be larger boats, but it weren't the life fur me. Not then and not that I were soft nor anything, just weren't exciting enough. Often said that, and that's another reason them tegs like the one you dunked, Mis'r Kolisnychenko, don't take a me.'

He fumbled in his pocket for his pipe, and James waited while he stuffed leaf into it, happy to let the man take his time. The beer was warming, his pulse had returned to its usual pace, and his eyes were stinging with tiredness after the ride. The wind had risen, and through the leaded glass of the small windows, the pub sign was swinging. The only thing marring the pleasure of good ale and a warm hearth was the thought that Jerry might be lost in the worsening weather.

The pipe alight and fuming, Branok continued his story.

'I found another life but still on the sea,' he said. 'Once you agree to be 'er slave, see, she don't let you go. Salt in your blood, the mysteries in your bones and the fear always in your 'eart. You can't turn your back on 'er, not once she's your mistress. All the same, the skiffing weren't fur me, and the gig boats only took family crews. Me fader had only his skiff, so there were no work fur me. This were back in forty-seven when Elizabeth came in, see? I found me

184

place with 'er, and I learnt me trade.'

He offered the pipe to Fecker who, to James' surprise, accepted and took two long draws before handing it back. When it was offered to James, he declined and was about to ask who Elizabeth was, when Branok continued.

'Moved on, later, a Jessie Munn and spent five year content with 'er afore they sent me a Tayleur.'

Fecker's smoke rolled across the table, and looking up, James could tell he was just as confused. Branok gazed to the window, lost in his memories.

'Sad it were, Tayleur. Never took us where she were going, and on our first time too. We was brought back by Defence, and I were 'ome a while, but I missed me life, as you do when you abandon your mistress.'

James was starting to think that they had befriended an alcohol-coddled soak, when things fell into place.

'I always reckon it was cos a that time away from me mistress that I got the bad luck.' Branok sucked on his pipe, his mouth turning down at the corners. 'First they didn't want me for Emma, then the work with Annie Wilson didn't pay off, so I ended up wrecked with the Blue Jacket. Shame that were. Was a good post, and I saw much a the world.' Pointing his pipe at Fecker, he added, 'That's how come I get your name, Sir. I saw your surprise.'

'One moment,' James interrupted. 'Were these all ships?'

'Did I not say that, nipper? Me sorries a you. Aye. Merchant ships. I made me way up a purser in the end, but there always be a final straw, and it were Golden Sunset. Ha!' He spat. 'Nothing golden 'bout being wrecked fur the first time, let alone me fifth. Jonah, I must 'ave been. That were the sunset of me days on steamers, and so I came back 'ome and picked up from me fader, long in his suicide's grave be then.'

That appeared to be the end of Branok's reminiscences, but James waited a polite amount of time in case the old man remembered to explain his initial mysterious remark.

'And you said that you know of a place called St Merrynporth?' James prompted when it was clear he hadn't.

'Aye. I still follows the fleet, you see.'

'Fleet?'

'White Star Line, nipper. Best liners a be working on. Well, them as didn't sink, blow boilers or vanish. It were early day of steamers, see. Exciting, but you weren't always guaranteed a make it 'ome.'

'And when you were working aboard their ships you went to St Merrynporth?'

'It ain't a place,' Branok said, emptying his pipe onto the floor. 'It be a boat.'

'A boat?'

Fecker had been examining his fingernails, but his head shot up, and James caught his eye.

'In harbour now?' the Ukrainian asked.

'Not as yet.' Branok refilled his pipe. 'She be the tender as meets the liners coming in from America. Them toffs as don't want a travel on a Westerpool afore coming down west can change onto 'er in the Irish Sea, see? She went out yesterday af'noon, due back a'morrow, less storm blows up bad. What do you want with that old tub anyhow?'

James didn't answer, his mind was pumping like a steamer's pistons.

'What liner does she serve?' he asked, suspecting he knew the answer.

'The Britannic. Fine ship that one. Fifteen year old, had a few bumps, but when you be five-thousand tonnes and...'

'Sorry,' James butted in. 'I need to be clear. The St Merrynporth is collecting passengers from the Britannic and bringing them here?'

'No, nipper, she don't come in a Padstow. Needs deeper water, see? She'll be docking miles west at Newquay. Least, she will if this storm blows in and out afore then.'

Eighteen

That Wednesday night, having delivered a message to the stables on behalf of His Lordship, Saddle was the last servant to retire. He shared the locking-up and closing-down duties with Mr Payne, but due to the butler's recent accident, volunteered to take on the duty even though it was not his turn. Mr Payne was thankful and returned to his rooms as soon as Lord Clearwater was settled into his suite.

With the smoking room cleared, Saddle roamed the ground floor ensuring the windows and internal shutters were closed, and the gas was turned off before taking the backstairs to the gentlemen's corridor. There, he knocked lightly on the door to the Bosworth bedroom and when called, entered.

Mr Smith was at the window gazing into the night with the light turned low and the fire dying.

'Your carriage has been ordered for the morning, Sir,' Saddle said. 'Mr Williams will drive you to Lostwithiel for your onward connection to Newquay.'

Smith turned to face him. He had prepared himself for bed with no assistance and crossed the room without the use of the cane, a slight limp now the only signs that he had suffered any injury.

'Thank you, Robert.'

'Will there be anything else, Sir?' the under-butler enquired. Scanning the room, he saw nothing that needed his attention.

'Only your assurance that you will carry out my orders.'

Saddle took a deep breath and closed the door silently. 'If I may, Sir,' he said, tension rising in his stomach. 'You have asked me to do something with which I am not comfortable, but I have agreed because you gave your word to offer a, er...' The man's intense glare was terrifying. 'A reward.'

'And you now want an assurance that I will make good my word.'

'If I may make such a request without showing distrust, yes.'

'I don't see how I can prove to you that the money will come your way,' Smith said, opening the wardrobe. 'And I don't see how you can trust me, a stranger who has asked a great deal from you. But bear this in mind. I am trusting you as much as you must trust me, but you are correct, and I promised you a sign of my good faith.' Smith's long-fingered hand reached into the wardrobe to remove his battered jacket. 'Remember that the only person who will suffer from what you are to do is your superior, Mr Payne, you said so yourself. You also said that he had treated you poorly, sending you back to live on the top floor in one room where before you had the suite, and the one by the plate safe at that. Having managed the Hall, you were degraded from a position of responsibility and good accommodation to a position little higher than that of a footman. There is your motivation, and that was one of the reasons you so readily agreed. The other, I know, is the large debt you owe to men who have threatened to expose and injure you within the next week, should you not make good on your debts. You have been honest with me, and in return, I have given you the chance to settle all your matters, and should you wish, begin a new life elsewhere.'

'Yes, you have promised much generosity, Sir,' Saddle said. His nervousness was gnawing, but he stood his ground. If he was caught carrying out this man's demands, he would lose his job; if he failed, he would suffer far more than a beating by a couple of unruly fishermen.

'Allow me to demonstrate my resolve to keep my word,' Smith said, drawing an envelope from the secret pocket. 'I apologise for the condition of this, but I was not expecting to be turned upside down at great speed. I was on my way to visit a great friend at Prideaux Place when my plans were, quite literally, derailed. The purpose of my visit was to deliver this on behalf of another friend who lives in Ireland. I am so well recovered now, thanks to you, that I will continue my journey in the morning. However, after being so well attended by yourself, I changed the name on the envelope and have addressed it to you, because I can think of no-one better to fill the post it offers.' Bushy, raised eyebrows approached Saddle, fixing him to the carpet and seemingly sucking the breath from his chest. 'This is my sign of good faith, for our contract requires trust between strangers, and this will seal it. It is an invitation from the Duke of Wexford, a personal friend and a far more generous employer than Clearwater. Should you wish, you may leave Larkspur on Saturday morning, travel to Wexford, and in reply to this invitation, take up employment as His Grace's butler as soon as you arrive. You will see the salary is double what you currently earn. Money to travel to Ireland is included. This is the best I can do.'

Saddle took the unsealed envelope, and having read its contents, swallowed hard. His nervousness vanished and was replaced by pride that Mr Smith should think so highly of him. There was a fair amount of greed coursing through his veins too, but he pretended it was excitement at the offer which had been made on the Duke's embossed, personal notepaper.

'I don't know what to say,' he said, folding the letter away.

'Say nothing, but repeat your oath that you will do exactly as I have asked. I may then retire to bed, satisfied that my best man is ready to carry out my wishes. When I hear of your success, which I will undoubtedly do through various publications, and when His Grace tells me you are safe with him in Ireland, I will send the promised money. This is the hour, Robert. Do you swear your loyalty?'

Believing Smith to be a man of honour, and hungry for the position and financial reward a few duplicitous acts would bring him, and innocently believing that no-one would be harmed by what Mr Smith had described as a prank, Saddle once again agreed to carry out his wishes.

'I do, Sir,' he said with a solemn bow.

The deal was done, and being a man of his word, Saddle had no intention of going back on it. After all, he thought, it was only a jape. No-one was going to die.

He was, of course, quite wrong.

Nineteen

After the drizzle of the previous evening, Thursday offered the city a fine spring day as Silas stood sipping coffee at the window. Jake was sprawled on the bed, still asleep, though to watch him you would never know it. Silas had been kept awake most of the night by the young man's fidgeting and mumbling. Jake kicked and turned as he suffered unsettled dreams, and at one point, called out indecipherable words. Silas was forced to cross the passage to Archer's room, but it was cold and musty, the bed unmade and the furniture, covered in white sheets, loomed over him in the moonlight like spectres waiting to pounce. Instead, he returned to his suite, threw coats on his dressing room floor and slept there.

Not only did Jake sleep as though he was running a foot race, he also slept for hours, and Silas envied him his ability not to wake at his own snoring and physical activity.

The poor man had been exhausted, and Silas knew all too well the stress and labour of sleeping rough. He sympathised with Jake's plight and admired him for enduring it, and during the night, resolved to do everything he could to help the younger man. The attraction was not physical, but he had liked Jake since he met him at the Opera House the previous year, and something less tangible than physical attraction drew him to Jake's character rather than his looks. It was something he couldn't explain and yet was undeniably present. Sometimes when Silas met a person for the first time, he knew not to trust them, or in a similarly mysterious way, took against them, as he had with Smith. With Jake, it was the opposite, but his magnetic quality aside, he had slept for twelve hours, and there was much to do that day. Silas woke him just after ten and rang for Mrs Norwood to bring more coffee.

She had just left, when Jake appeared from the bathroom wearing one of Silas' suits and smelling of Penhaligon's Blenheim Bouquet, one of his more expensive scents.

'First thing we've got to do,' Silas said, 'is get you a haircut and some clothes that fit.'

'I can alter these.'

'I'm sure you can, mate, but we haven't got time for you to start doing all that. We'll go out and buy some. I've got to get some gear anyway.'

'Gear?' Jake hitched up the trousers and sat in the armchair to pour himself coffee. Mrs Norwood had thoughtfully provided bread rolls with jam, the first of which he devoured in two mouthfuls.

'You gave me a lot of detail last night, Jake,' Silas said, sitting in the opposite chair 'And if what you said is accurate, we're going to need a few bits and pieces. I'm good with most locks, but we don't know what we're up against until we get to Irving's offices.'

'If they're like the Opera House, they'll be heavy locks with long keys. But like I said, if there's a night-watchman on, then the clerks get careless with locking rooms inside the building, 'cos no-one can get in. I expect the Lyceum's the same.'

'Yeah, but we don't know, so I need to be prepared. And you're sure about the tunnel?'

'More than sure, I've been in it.'

'And it leads to the Lyceum?'

'Trust me, mate,' Jake said slurping his coffee. 'Them tunnels lead everywhere, even into the sewers, and you can tell that from the stink. I know me way around the opera, and I know me way around theatres, especially them put up by Mr Beazley. I ain't been to school, but I know theatres.'

'Alright, Jake, don't get funny about it. Drink up, and we'll go into town.'

'We've got all day. The House won't close up until midnight.'

'You said, but I want to get everything sorted and send a message to Larkspur to keep Jimmy and Tom up to date, then get back and have a kip. It's going to be a long night.'

'I ain't got any money for clothes, though.'

'Don't worry about that. I've got an account at Simpsons where they sell things ready-made. While you're being fitted and kitted, I can call into Chubbs for the stuff I need. Oh, and remind me to get a couple of black jumpers and hats too.'

The rest of the day went according to Silas' plan, and he didn't care about the cost. True to his word, Archer had invested the money Silas was awarded for his false imprisonment and turned it into an impressive quarterly income. That was on top of the wage Silas was paid by the Clearwater Foundation which, Archer had said, was not only useful to put against his taxable income for a reason Silas didn't understand, but also misdirected prying eyes away from the true nature of their relationship for a reason Silas understood only too well.

Having had his hair cut, Jake followed him into Simpsons looking like a circus clown with his sleeves hanging and his shoes flapping at the toes, and left the shop an hour later as a respectable, middle-class gentleman. Silas' man, as they told Mr Simpson, was the assistant to Lord Clearwater's private secretary. Archer didn't have an account with Simpsons, he only wore tailormade clothes and even bought his underwear in the Row, but the shop owner lived in hope that one day the viscount would patronise his emporium of "Off the peg suits, shirts and collars for the discerning gentlemen of average means", as his signage described the Regent's Street shop. He was always happy to have Mr Hawkins' purchases delivered to Clearwater House, and usually included a pair of free cufflinks or a spare collar as an incentive for Silas to recommend him to His Lordship. Silas never did, because Archer wouldn't be interested, but he thanked Mr Simpson on His Lordship's behalf, adding, 'He sends his best wishes,' and making the man's sagging eyes light up with pound signs.

Silas left Jake at Sparkes-Hall to try on boots and shoes while he called into two haberdashery shops, Chubbs, the locksmith, and Kingston's, the glove makers. The items he bought couldn't be delivered to the house, not because he didn't want them to be, but because he wanted no suspicion to fall that way should they be caught.

'That'd be caught breaking into not one theatre but two,' he mumbled as he crossed Piccadilly avoiding the carriages and horse shit. 'You're outdoing yourself, Banyak.'

Having met Jake back at Sparkes-Hall where he approved of and paid for the footwear, he took him back to Piccadilly.

'What now?' Jake asked as they stood at the junction.

'Lunch.'

'Back at your house?'

'No, Jake. I think we can do better than that, but first, you've got to tell me something about yourself that I don't know.' He stepped away from the noise of the traffic and throng of pedestrians to find privacy beneath the arches, and Jake dutifully followed.

'What can I tell you?' Jake asked with concern tainting his voice. 'You know I ain't got no family, not now granddad's dead. I think I told you I was from the West End, seventeen last October and they used to call me Tricky. What else is there?'

'For a start,' Silas replied glancing across the junction. 'Your surname?'

'Oh.' Jake was taken aback. 'Didn't you know it?'

'No,' Silas admitted. 'When we first met you told me everything there was to know about the Opera House and the way it worked, you gave me your thoughts on life and said how lucky you were to live there, and you rabbited on about all kinds of costume stuff, but you never told me your full name. Mind you, mate, I probably didn't have a chance to get a word in.'

Jake pulled a face. 'Sorry if I talk on. I know I goes too fast as well, but that's because Mr Keys never let me speak much, and when I were backstage, I had to stay silent, so when I get the chance...'

'Yeah, okay,' Silas chuckled. 'Slow it down. I know Keys isn't your last name like Tricky isn't your first.

'Happy to tell you of course, but why d'you need to know?'

'Because we are going to lunch over there.' Silas pointed across the busy intersection to the opposite building, and when Jake understood his intentions, his mouth fell open.

'The Criterion? You're flipping joking, ain't you?'

'No, Mr Tricky, I'm not. Now, listen. I'm fine with it. I've been with Archer long enough to know how to behave, and I'm good at mimicking how posh people talk, but if you're going to be my assistant, you'll have to play-act a bit. Can you do that?'

'I can play-act, for sure. Not so confident about keeping quiet.'

'Yeah, I guessed that. So...' Silas put down his shopping and adjusted his tie. 'You think you can pass off as a gent now you're dressed like one.'

'Will they let us in?'

'Why not? We're old enough, we're dressed well, we're just a man and his assistant taking a rest from shopping, and I have my business cards on me. I'll put it on Lord Clearwater's account as an expense. We'll take a private banquette away from everyone else so we can talk through the details of tonight's break-in, and afterwards, full up and laughing at how we duped the waiters into thinking we're respectable, we can rest until after nightfall. But, to get past the Maître d', we've got to be convincing, and that means I have to know your surname if they ask.'

'I get you...' Jake coughed. 'I mean, I quite understand, Sir.' His city accent was still present, but along with the more considered words came a change in his posture as he pulled back his shoulders and lifted his head. 'My surname, Sir, is O'Hara.'

'Get out of here!'

The sea-blue eyes, black hair, the similar nose to Silas' sisters which bore a strong resemblance to Silas' own, the short stature...

'O'Hara. Why? What's wrong with that?'

'Was your dad Irish?'

'He was born there, outside Dublin. Came over to Westerpool when he was eighteen. Left his brother behind. Twins, they were. He moved down to the city, met my mum, had me, both died of cholera when I was little... You do look pale, Mr Silas, Sir.'

Silas' legs were suddenly weak, and his heart was racing.

'Was he a dockworker before he came over?' he asked, dreading the answer but too intrigued to leave the subject alone.

'Well, he worked in the Harland and Wolff yards as a lad, then the Westerpool dock. That's how he got work at the city river wharves.'

'His first name?'

'You and your names,' Jake laughed. 'William, why?'

'And his brother? Your uncle?'

'Martin, I think. Don't know what happened to him,' Jake said, frowning. 'All I know is what Granddad told me, and he was my mum's dad, so not totally sure, but my dad's name was William. Mind you, they all called him Billy.'

'Billy O'Hara?'

'That's it. Why? Blimey, Silas, you ain't half looking ill.'

'I need to sit down,' Silas said. 'If I can pull myself together by the time we get to the Criterion, you and me have a lot more to talk about than the simple job of breaking into the Opera House.'

At first light, James and Fecker set out to ride inland to the main road between Lostwithiel and Newquay. There, they made their way west and coastwards, stopping at each farm and settlement to ask after Jerry, always, as the day before, receiving the same answer. No-one had seen him, and prospects for finding Jerry, like the weather, worsened through the day.

At the time Silas was successfully blagging his way into a swanky, West End café and securing a private banquette in gilded surroundings, James and Fecker were saddle sore, wet with drizzle, and panting after a hard morning's ride. The incoming storm blackened the western skies and turned the sea to a seething mass of grey and white, jabbed at by lightning and frothing against the rocky coast. The rising gale bit at their ears as they surveyed the scene from the brow of the hill above Newquay.

'He's got to be down there somewhere,' James shouted over the wind.

'Da. If he not dead in ditch.'

'Thanks, Fecks,' James muttered, and urged his horse onwards.

The irony of their horses' names was not lost on him. Fecker rode Thunder, and James was on Lightning, two elements of the bad weather evident in the near distance. The thought played on his mind as they descended towards the port, but as it came closer, he was only able to think about Jerry. He was a determined lad, that was for sure. The boy had run away from school, stowed away on the train, survived a horrific crash and fled Larkspur all while keeping his identity a secret. Why did he fear for his father's safety if he knew he was aboard the St Merrynporth sailing to meet the SS Britannic?

The more he considered the facts, the more the questions piled up. Would a crew member on a tender be able to afford a public school for his son? What danger was the man in? Not the storm, no-one could predict when that might have hit, and presumably, the father had been to sea before, so Jerry wasn't rushing to save him from the weather. Then there was his reaction to Mr Smith. Perhaps the sight of the man *had* brought back memories of the accident, and Jerry had run from him, so he didn't have to face them. If that was the case, James would have expected him to burst into tears or show some other signs of trauma, when all he had done was run to his room and demand another story before falling straight to sleep. Or at least, pretending to.

These were questions that would have to wait, and when James found the boy, he would demand answers, but before then, they had to find him, and Newquay was larger than Padstow. There were hundreds of places Jerry could be hiding if he had, in fact, made it safely to the town.

They slowed their approach as the hillside met a lane. Fecker overtook, pointing ahead to a fence. James understood, and both horses took the jump easily. Once in the lane, they slowed to a trot. The drizzle had turned to rain and was running in rivulets about the horses' hooves, and the clouds were so dense it was like riding at dusk. The lane became a better-made road with scattered cottages either side which thickened as they made their way into the town.

'You think the harbour?' Fecker called across.

'Seems logical.'

The road narrowed and twisted as it was joined by others and weaved its way downwards. They rode with eyes peeled but not hopeful until they came to the harbour, lined with houses, nets piled outside beside lobster pots, and tackle secured with ropes against the wind. Fishing boats rocked on the sea, the swell reaching in between the harbour arms to crash against the quayside. Few people were out, and as before, James suggested they find an inn, stable the animals and begin their enquiries.

'First, we get dry,' Fecker said as they dismounted. 'I stable horse, you find food.'

'He could be on the streets, Fecks. In trouble. He needs us right now.'

'Da. Or he dead on moors, stolen away, or in father's house being warm. We won't know if we kill ourselves in shit storm.'

Fecker was a man of few words, but when he spoke, he usual spoke sense, and James took his point.

The inn was warm and quiet, and run by a busty woman in her fifties. She showed no anger as a young man walked into her bar and shook the water from his cape. Instead, she rushed to help.

'What you been doing out in this, young Sir?' she asked in an accent lighter than that of the Padstow fisherman yet just as lyrical. 'Get yourself by that fire.'

She mothered him across the bar and didn't stop fussing until he insisted he was comfortable, and ordered two tankards of ale.

'Thirsty ride were it?' she asked, looking back to the door.

'My friend is with your stableman,' James explained.

'Ah, right y'are.'

She waddled off, returning a while later with two ales and two towels, apologising that they weren't really suitable but better than nothing, and James, recovering from the journey, asked if anyone had reported a lost child.

'I expect so,' she said, folding a towel over the second chair. 'Children are always running off. Why, have you lost yours, me duck?'

'In a way. And can I ask you, does the Britannic tender dock near here?'

'The Merrynporth? Aye, not far, Sir. At the western end of the harbour arm, but it ain't due until tomorrow.'

'I know. Are you very friendly with the crew?'

Her chubby face, until then friendly, dropped, and she glared, insulted. Her stubby arms flew to her sides, fists balled, where they were planted heavily against the summit of her hips.

'I don't know what you be suggesting, young man, but I run a tavern of repute.'

James tried not to laugh and covered it with remorse. 'I am so sorry,' he said. 'I didn't mean to imply... I don't mean in that way. But, I take it you are local and wondered if you knew the crew by name. Particularly a Mr O'Sullivan who has a son called Jerry.'

Accepting the misunderstanding, the landlady dropped her threatening stance. 'Can't say I do,' she said, twisting her mouth as she thought. 'And I knows most of the men as they be from round 'ere. That name don't ring no clanger with me. Sorry, you be out a luck with your questions, Sir. Now, will you want some pie with your ale?'

'That sounds fine. Two, please. Actually, you'd better make that three.'

Mildly confused, she nodded, turned and screamed.

Fecker leapt back in surprise, and James rushed to his feet.

'He's with me,' he exclaimed.

'Sorry, Sir, you gave me such a fright.' The landlady turned to James and whispered, 'Big bugger, ain't he?' before returning to Fecker. 'After work at the dock, are you?'

Fecker shrugged and looked at James for advice.

'No, we're not. But we are looking for something to eat,' he said, smiling sweetly. 'And a room for the night if you have it.'

'I do, Sir, but I might not have a big enough bed.'

She shuffled away as Fecker sat.

'Stable is good,' he declared. 'Man knows his job. Horses safe.'

'That's good to hear, Fecks. Did you ask the cost? Only I didn't bring much money with me.'

'Nyet. Geroy will pay.'

'Lord Clearwater doesn't have an account at every inn in the county,' James smiled. 'We'll see how we get on.'

They removed as much of their wet clothing as was acceptable, putting their boots to dry by the hearth and hanging their jackets over the fireguard. When she returned, the landlady didn't seem in the least surprised to see them half-dressed, and James guessed the inn was used to weathered sailors and fishermen returning from sea in a similar state.

The storm intensified as they ate, the wind moaning over the chimney and lightning crackling beyond the windows. The sound was underscored by the repetitive boom of the tide against the sea wall as it vibrated through the low-ceilinged bar and into James' chest. The food and fire were luxuries after two days of riding, but it also reminded him of Jerry. He tried not to think of the boy struggling against the storm, lost and crying, while he and Fecker were warm and sheltered. The horses were safer than the lad, but there was nothing they could do until the weather eased. As Fecker had said, there was no point them risking injury or worse. What use would they be then?

He did, however, express his concerns to the Ukrainian, and asked how he had survived his great walk from his homeland to Italy when he was younger.

'You just survive,' Fecker said. 'Or you die.'

'That's hardly the reassurance I was after, mate.'

'We will find him, Tato.' Fecker rested a hand on James' knee. 'I know this.' Sitting back, he drained his tankard.

'Tato? What's that mean?'

Fecker twisted to hail the landlady and wave his tankard in her direction. When he turned back, his white teeth were glinting in the lamplight, his mouth a cheerful gash across his chiselled face.

'Tato,' he repeated, nodding. 'Da, your *prisvisko* found you.'

'Come on, man, I had enough of Silas going on about Mr Smith's funny language, what are you talking about?'

'Few men have real *prisvisko*,' Fecker said. 'It finds you. I don't invent. You call it... I don't remember. Like Banyak.'

'A nickname?'

'Da. Nicked name.'

'What does Banyak mean, anyway?'

Fecker's grin widened, and he did something James had never seen him do. He giggled. It was short-lived, and he fell serious. 'The Master I call Geroy because it means honourable,' he said, covering his childishness.

'Yes, I know that. What is Banyak?'

'Alright, I tell you because you are Tato.' He wiped the last of his gravy from his plate with his fingers and sucked them clean before continuing. 'Banyak in my village is for cooking. Small pot. Everything goes in, bones, flesh, good things, bad things, out comes dinner.'

'So, your best mate is a cooking pot?' It was a ludicrous thing to ask.

'Nyet.' Fecker shook his head. 'Banyak also mean something else.' Shuffling closer on his chair, he touched the side of his nose with a finger, and said, 'Is also secret for two men. What we know and don't say. If you have friend like this, you have banyak to keep secrets in, good things, bad things, but nothing comes out. No-one else learns secrets.'

James recalled what he knew about Silas and Andrej before he met them. They had shared a difficult past and experienced much together that was best not disclosed. When he thought of it from that perspective, the explanation made sense.

'But a Tato?' he asked. 'What am I, a King Edward's or something?'

Fecker let loose a raucous belly laugh that caused the landlady to shriek and duck behind the beer pumps in panic.

'Nyet,' he said, once everyone had recovered. 'You with your boy, Jerry. You make fuss, you worry, you read him books, take his hand, you care. Not just this boy, but Banyak, Geroy, Bolshoydick, even woman in black and my Lucy. You look before them.'

'You mean, I look *after* them.'

'Da. Is it? You, Jimmy, you always do right thing. You care like a Tato.'

'Thank you, but what the fuck *is* a Tato?'

Fecker sighed heavily, his eyes boring into James, his face still displaying good humour. 'You are, Jimmy. It means you are a...'

A deafening rumble of thunder accompanied the crashing of the inn door against its hinges. The landlady shrieked again, louder this time, and James shot from his chair. Rain hurtled in behind a man in oilskins, a hurricane lamp swinging from his hand. He flicked back his cowl and searched the bar with eyes that dripped water and burned with panic. They landed on James and Fecker.

'You'll do.'

'Whatever is it, Petroc?' The landlady shouted against the cacophony of the elements.

'There be a child putting a sea in Jack Corney's skiff of west pier.'

James' heart froze, and Fecker gripped his arm.

'No time a fetch me crew,' the man yelled, pulling up his cowl. 'Lads, get out 'ere afore the pup kills himself.'

Twenty

The storm attacked James as soon as he ran from the inn, but panic blocked the cold and stabbing rain. There was no time to pull on his boots, but his feet were already wet, and the puddles meant nothing as he followed the man, trying to see ahead through the downpour.

'There!' the fisherman shouted against the screaming wind.

Twenty yards ahead, a figure, tiny against the harbour wall, was hanging from a ladder by one hand, pulling in a small boat by its painter with the other. It was Jerry being beaten by the spray from waves as the gale sliced across the foaming surface.

'Boy's an idiot.' Fecker was on James' heels. 'What's he do?'

There was no time for discussion and no time to think about the consequences. James didn't need to, If Jerry pushed off from the safety of the mooring and into the swell, the boat would be swamped. Other craft nearby were listing, some were half-filled and sinking, while along the harbour, those badly moored were slamming into the wall.

A flash of light accompanied a second later by a crash of thunder revealed another man, not far from Jerry. He was doing nothing to stop the boy but was standing at the opening of a narrow alleyway, his head flying from side to side as if he was searching.

For a split second, James was convinced he knew the face, but it was quickly enveloped by darkness, and when the lightning struck again, the man had gone.

The sweep of the lighthouse brought the scene into sharp focus just as Jerry threw the rope into the boat and jumped in after it. By the time James arrived at the ladder, the boy was wrestling with an oar far too big for him, and the skiff was being buffeted against the quay.

'Oi!' the fisherman screamed, skidding to a halt. 'What the

buggery d'you think you be playing at?'

Jerry took no notice, or he couldn't hear. He heaved the oar to the wall and pushed, desperate to send the boat into the maelstrom.

James screamed his name, but it was snatched by the wind and swallowed by the tempest. A second shout met the same fate.

Fecker threw himself on his belly and reached over the quayside, but the boy was too far below and being dragged further along the wall by the current. He was sliding his legs over the edge to lower himself down when James stopped him.

'No Fecks,' he roared, pulling him back. 'You can't swim.'

'He drowns.'

'Yeah, and so do you.'

'Quick, lads or he be done for!'

The fisherman's yell diverted their attention and, as the lighthouse beam swept past, James watched, horrified, as a massive wave rolled across the surface, the skiff smashed into the wall and Jerry tumbled backwards into the water.

'Where's the lifeboat?' the fisherman yelled to the others along the quay. None heard. They were too busy saving their own livelihoods.

Instinctively, James pulled his shirt over his head, threw it away and dived.

The storm was suddenly gone, and all he could hear was the rush and gurgle of the turbulent sea. Freezing water impacted on his skull and stole his breath until he broke the surface a second later, but he might just as well have stayed beneath. Salt spray slashed his eyes and choked his throat as he thrashed, gaining his bearings. Above him, the fisherman's lantern gave him a light to steer by, and he located the boat five yards distant. There was no sign of Jerry.

Kicking his legs and pumping his arms, James swam. Coming up for air as the light raced overhead, he saw a small hand reaching from the teaming water and trying to grab the gunwale. The current pulled the boy under, and James swam harder, fighting the swell and bending his head to his shoulder to avoid inhaling spray.

His hand met the side of the boat, and he grabbed it, holding himself steady against the raging waves.

'There!'

Fecker's voice, the fisherman's lantern close by, both men

pointing a few feet in front of James' face, but he could see no-one in the water. Taking a deep breath, he dived. The boom-crash of the waves against the wall invaded his ears, as his hands thrashed and twisted, finding nothing. Coming up for air, he swallowed saltwater, and choking it out, took another breath and crashed back into the madness.

This time he was lucky, and his fingers touched flesh. Clutching Jerry, he heaved and kicked himself to the surface dragging the boy up with one hand. His other found the sea wall and stabilising himself, he pulled Jerry until he could hold him around his chest. Jerry wailed and fought against his rescuer.

'You're all right,' James spluttered. 'You're okay.'

Using the cracks and rough stones, he dragged himself towards the ladder where Fecker was hanging perilously from the three fingers of his left hand and reaching down. The closer he came, the more Jerry protested, and as soon as he was close enough, James passed Jerry to safety, and clung to the ladder to catch his breath.

Angry at being robbed of its prey, the tide slammed the skiff against the wall, forcing James to catch the bow to prevent himself being crushed. Gasping and shaking, he secured the rope, pushed the boat out from the wall and climbed, his arms weak and his lungs burning.

A rough hand took his and hauled him onto the quay. 'You be alright, lad?' the fisherman asked, holding his hood to his head, his old eyes mere slits against the rain.

James nodded, he was more concerned for Jerry, but when he saw him, he became more concerned for Fecker. The Ukrainian had him firmly by the collar, but Jerry was pumping his fists into Fecker's stomach and kicking his shins, shouting hysterically.

'I throw him back?' Fecker bellowed, but the threat made no difference to the boy, he was determined to get away.

'No, Fecks.' James nearly laughed, not sure if he was serious. 'Get him to the inn.'

'You done well, mate,' the fisherman said, landing a hand on James' shoulder.

'Everything alright, Sam?' A constable had arrived, holding a lantern to the fisherman's face as thunder rolled overhead.

'Aye, Bert. This nipper got in trouble.'

Jerry's hysterics had not abated.

'Who's this?' the policeman asked, shining his light directly at the lad's face.

'He's with me.' James stepped in. 'I don't know what came over him.'

As soon as James laid a hand on Jerry's arm, the boy's head swung around, he saw who it was and stopped attacking Fecker. Instead, he clawed away from him, and clung to James, sobbing into his chest.

'Aye, well better get him inside,' the officer hollered. 'Any damage, Stan?'

'Opposite. This man saved Corney's skiff.'

'We're going back to the...'

James froze. The lighthouse beam had skimmed the alley again, and in a burst of lighting, he saw the man was back. This time there was no mistaking who it was.

Smith.

Jerry clung to James tighter, whimpering.

'You see that?' Fecker pointed to the alley, but Smith was gone. 'That Smith.'

At the mention of the same, Jerry began thrashing again, terrified.

'Son,' the policeman shouted in Jerry's ear. 'Was that man after you?'

Jerry nodded violently.

'Has he hurt you?'

Jerry whimpered.

'Why we still in this rain shit?' Fecker demanded with his usual bluntness, poking the policeman in the chest. 'You and me, we find that man.' Pushing James towards the inn, he said, 'You get crazy boy inside.' Leaving no room for debate, he took the startled officer by the arm and ran.

'Aye, get dry, lad,' the fisherman yelled. 'And my thanks for your help.'

By the time James had carried Jerry back to the clammy warmth of the inn, his legs were buckling and he could hardly feel his arms, but at least Jerry's hysterics had calmed to a gentle sob.

'Oh, my word! The landlady exclaimed, rushing to close the door. 'What's happened to this little mite?'

'Exactly what I want to know,' James stammered.

'Sir, you're shaking with cold.' She tried to take the boy from him, but Jerry wasn't having it and buried his head harder into James.

'You said you had a room, Mrs…?'

'Just Mary. Aye, I do. Come with me.'

Dripping, and trying not to slip on the flagstones, James followed her across the bar towards a door. 'Jerry,' he said. 'I'm going to have to put you down, or I'll drop you. Can I do that?'

Jerry shook his head.

'One moment, Mary.' James sank into a chair with the boy still wrapped around him. It was awkward, and James was shivering to the point where he could barely control his teeth, but he cradled that lad's head and spoke softly. 'Jerry, I'm not angry with you, but I am very worried. We've been looking for you for two days. Everyone's concerned, and I need to know what you were thinking. But first, we need to get you dry and warm.'

Mary hung a towel over James' shoulders and crouched beside them. When she tried to take Jerry's hand, he pulled away.

'The boy's been on an adventure,' she said, winking. 'And like a proper explorer back from his travels, what he wants now is a hot bath and some of my beef stew. Doctor Livingstone always asked for it when he called on his way back from an expedition.'

James raised an eyebrow, and Mary shrugged.

'Does that sound like a good idea, Jerry?' James asked, his voice was no more than a whisper; it was all his frozen lungs could manage.

A nervous nod of the young head brought a smile to the landlady's lips.

'Well then,' she said, standing. 'I'll get my Victoria to bring up hot water for the tub while your…' She pulled a questioning face at James.

'Uncle.' It was the first thing that came into his head.

'While your uncle here gets you ready for a bath. There are towels in the cupboard on the landing, Sir,' she added. 'And I'd get one of the bed blankets around the both of you soon as you can.'

'Okay, Jerry. I need you to walk on your own now. Can you do that?'

Jerry nodded and slithered from James' lap. Taking his hand,

James led the boy to the door, his head light and his insides a block of ice. Mary called for her girl with a bark that challenged the thunder for volume and took her guests up a narrow flight of steep stairs where she showed James a low-ceilinged room at the front of the inn. Two beds stood either side of a small fireplace, already made up and with spare logs lined across its mantlepiece. Apart from one chair and some hooks on the walls, a tin bath leaning up in a corner and a shelf that needed fixing, the room was empty.

'It's my best suite,' the landlady said, beaming. 'I'll just light the fire.'

Sitting Jerry on the chair, James finally had a chance to examine him. His eyes were bloodshot and puffy from the salt of tears and seawater, and his clothes were a sorry state, but the lad himself looked unharmed.

'I'm sorry, Uncle Jimmy.' His words were barely audible, and they were broken through his shivering.

James followed Mary's advice and wrapped Jerry in a blanket before taking the other for himself.

'I'll bring your clothes up presently, Sir,' she said. 'Where's your...? Where's the tall one?'

'He'll be back later,' James replied, wondering the same thing. 'He's, er, helping the constable with...' Throwing a sideways glance at Jerry, he decided it was best not to mention Smith at that moment. 'He's helping in the harbour.'

'Right, me duck. You two stay warm, and I'll be back with what you need.'

The landlady's daughter brought buckets of hot water, soap and towels, the tub was filled, and when they were finally alone, James turned his back while Jerry undressed and stepped into the water. As the lad was washing, he took off his own wet clothes and rewrapped the blanket tightly before hanging his trousers and long johns on the back of the chair. The storm rattled on, but had just started to fade when the landlady returned carrying a bundle.

'Old Jack Corney's missus brought these over,' she said, offering an assortment of clothes. 'Wanted to say thank you for saving his boat. They're a bit old but might fit you and your nephew. You can keep them.' She put them on the bed. 'Now I'll just go and get you that stew.' She smiled at Jerry, rolled her eyes at James, said,

206

'Nippers, eh? Who'd have them?' and shuffled away.

'You're very lucky to have people looking after you, Jerry,' James said, sorting through the pile. Are you ready to tell me what's been happening? Why you ran away from Larkspur, and why you are so scared of that man?'

Those were only the first three questions on James' list.

'Will I be in trouble, Uncle Jimmy?'

'You will be if you don't wash your face,' James admonished with a playful wag of his finger. There was no point being angry with the lad, not if he wanted to gain his trust and learn some truths. 'As long as you're honest, you won't be told off, not by me, but I expect your parents and teachers are very worried. I tell you what, you get washed and dressed, and we'll play Payoff over our supper, yeah?'

'You don't need to bribe me again,' Jerry said. 'I realise now I have to tell you everything I know. I have found myself in something of a predicament, and have to admit defeat. I need help.'

They were the words of an adult, spoken by a nine-year-old in a bathtub who had tried to put to sea in a storm as though it was a game. Jerry was a young man of many surprises, and James wondered how many more would come his way before the night was over.

'And I am here to give you that help,' he said. 'As is His Lordship's coachman, the man you were kicking earlier.'

'Sorry about that. I thought he was Mrs Shelly's monster.'

'Ha!' James huffed a laugh. 'I doubt you're the first to think that. But he's not, he's a very nice man. It was him who found you under the railway carriage, and he will help you again as long as you are honest with us.'

'He's scary. What's his name?'

'Mr Andrej.'

'Oh, is he Russian?'

Another intelligent comment.

'He is from Ukraine, and it's safest for all of us to remember that. Come on, out you get. If the water's not too dirty, I could do with washing my face.'

Jerry climbed from the bath and backed into the towel James held open for him. The valet-turned-guardian knelt and washed as his charge dressed in silence.

The landlady delivered their supper, and they ate their shares quickly. James's intention of learning the truth from the boy as they ate was pointless, Jerry spooned in the stew as if he hadn't eaten in two days. They had just finished, and James was about to repeat his questions, when heavy footsteps approached in the passageway.

'Who's that?' Jerry's nervousness returned in a flash, and he hurried to stand behind James as the door latch rattled.

Fecker ducked into the room wearing a triple-cape greatcoat to his ankles with brass buttons and wide cuffs. His wet hair hung in strands from beneath a tricorn hat. Water dripped from his nose and ran into the corners of his mouth as it spread wide in a grin.

'Tato,' he laughed. 'Why you look like man in lighthouse?'

Wearing a white, woollen jumper rolled at the neck, and dark trousers tucked into his boots, James had to admit that he did look like a lighthouse keeper, but the jest went both ways.

'Why do you look like a highwayman?' he retorted. 'Get in, you're letting the heat out.' Jerry was tugging at his sleeve. 'It's alright,' he reassured the boy. 'It's only Mr Andrej.'

'Police give me from station,' Fecker said, taking off the hat that was being crushed by the ceiling. 'Their horses are shit.'

'Oi! Not in front of the boy.'

Fecker closed the door and undid his coat as he took in the scene. 'We chased Smith,' he explained. 'Police had horses, so did he. Man got ahead, and police idiot fell off at first jump.' Hanging the coat on a hook and placing his hat over it, he came to stand by the fire. 'Cold, dark, wet, mud, my horse tired. They not feed them right. I caught man on fields.'

'You caught him?'

'Da. I reach across as we gallop, but he slippery like *riba*.' His hand weaved like a fish. 'And laughing.'

'Laughing?'

'Don't know why. Is also idiot. "What you do?" I shout. "Why you scare Jimmy's boy?" He only laugh and whip horse. Police horse not fast. I can't catch him. Horse was shit.'

Jerry laughed.

'This isn't funny,' James snapped, his patience worn down by concern and exhaustion. 'It's your fault we're here and Mr Andrej had to go riding into the night.' Jerry appeared about to burst into

208

tears, and James relented. 'I'm sorry, but it's time you told us exactly what this is about.'

Jerry's bottom lip quivered, and his eyes grew large.

'And you can forget that. My sister pulls the same act when she's in trouble, and it...'

Jerry really was crying. Genuine tears of remorse ran from his eyes, his shoulders slumped, and he sat on the bed staring forlornly at the floor.

James and Fecker looked at each other, neither knowing what they should do. Fecker thumbed at Jerry and shooed James towards him before sitting to devour the remains of the stew. James mouthed, 'Thanks,' with a fake sneer and sat beside the boy who immediately leant into him and pulled James' arm around his shoulder.

'Okay, mate,' James sighed. 'Here's where you come clean. Start by telling us what you were doing on that train. You didn't have a ticket, did you?'

Jerry shook his head and looked up with dewy eyes. 'You won't be angry?'

'No, I promise.'

The boy looked nervously at Fecker ripping bread with his teeth and grinning.

'I told you, Jerry. You don't need to fear Mr Andrej. Think of him as a cuddly, toy bear.'

Fecker threw an untrusting glance his way.

'He's a big old softie really, aren't you, Andrej?'

When Fecker didn't answer, James nodded violently behind Jerry's back, and finally understanding, Fecker raised his undamaged hand, and curling his fingers, growled softly, bringing a smile to the boy's face.

'So, off you go, Jerry. Take your time, but you *must* tell me everything. How come you were on the train with no ticket.'

'It was that man,' the lad began. 'He came to my school and told them he was a relative there to collect me for a day out. I refused to go with him, of course, and he left, but he came back on Sunday morning.' He hesitated, pouting up at James who squeezed him gently and told him to go on. 'We were returning from church, and I saw him watching. I told my housemaster, and the masters took me seriously, but there wasn't anyone in the grounds. They told me he had gone, but if I saw him again, they would tell the police.'

'You didn't recognise him?'

'No. I should know if I had met him before, with those eyes and that long nose. His hair too, all black and swept backwards. Not at all in the manner of a gentleman.'

'This was the same man you saw at Larkspur? The one His Lordship allowed to stay after the accident?'

'Yes. Definitely.'

'Okay. And how did you end up on the train?'

Jerry took a breath before continuing. 'I had a gate pass... That's when we can go to the village, and I was going for tuck with Bradshaw and Elphinstone. They're in my dorm, and some boys are allowed out on Sundays after church. Last Sunday it was the turn of dorm two, that's ours. The housemaster had told Bradshaw and Elphinstone to stay with me, but they ran ahead because they thought the shop was closing as it was Sunday, but I knew it wasn't. Bernard Harcourt said that it never closes early because...'

'Yes, alright, Jerry,' James interrupted. Now the boy was finally speaking, the words were gushing like water from a tap. 'I don't need all the details. What happened next?'

'Sorry. The man leapt out from nowhere, behind me. He grabbed me, dragged me away, behind the houses where he had a carriage waiting. Don't mind admitting I was frightened, but when he tried to get me into the carriage, I kicked him in the... You know, like Bradshaw did to Harcourt once when he wasn't wearing a cricket box, and got a caning from...'

'Just the important things.'

'It was important to Harcourt.' Jerry seemed surprised James didn't agree with him, and then noticed his warning expression. 'Oh, yes. He let go of me, and I made a run for it. The nearest place to go was the railway cut. I was very upset, as you can imagine, and I ran the wrong way. Just ran and ran until I was lost, but I followed the tracks and came to the shunting yard. I thought he wouldn't be able to find me there, but I was so worried, I stayed until it got dark, thinking the school would come looking for me. I stayed the whole night wondering what to do. As soon as it got light, he was there again, still searching for me, and the only thing I could do was run into the station where there was a train. I hid in third, because in third you can hide under the benches, and no-one in third is going to tell the attendant. Then the train pulled out. I looked around and thought I'd lost him.'

'And you stayed on the train?'

'No, I changed later to get on the one going to Plymouth.'

'Why?'

'So I could get the train to Newquay.'

'To meet your father?'

'That's right.' Jerry was pleasantly surprised. 'How do you know that?'

'I'm asking the questions, mate,' James frowned. 'Why didn't you call for help or tell someone?'

'Because of what the man was saying when I kicked him.'

James waited, but when no explanation came, prompted with, 'Which was what?'

'That if I didn't go with him, he was going to kill my father.'

'Mr O'Sullivan who works on the St Merrynporth, and who is due to arrive here tomorrow afternoon. Yes?'

'No. Well, no and yes.'

'Jerry.' The warning tone in James' voice made the boy cower.

'Father doesn't work on the boat,' he admitted. 'He is a passenger on the Britannic.'

'A passenger?'

The Britannic. The initials in Jerry's jacket. The tattoo on Smith's back. The Lyceum theatre. Realisation hit James like the blinding beam of the lighthouse, except he was no longer blind, he could see clearly.

'Oh, shit!'

'Oi, Tato!' Fecker complained. 'Not in front of the boy.'

James ignored him, took Jerry by the shoulders and forced him to look into his eyes.

'Your name's not Jerry O'Sullivan, is it?'

Shamefaced, Jerry shook his head. His eyes were watering again, and his bottom lip had turned out.

'Who is Jerry O'Sullivan?' James demanded. It was the only piece of the puzzle he couldn't fit into place.

'One of father's characters,' Jerry admitted, and burst into tears.

Twenty-One

While James, Fecker and Jerry slept the sleep of the dead in Newquay, the storm passed overhead and gradually travelled north-east through the night. It hadn't reached the city by the time Silas and Jake left Clearwater House dressed in black, wearing gloves and with Silas carrying a lantern and small leather pouch in his overcoat pocket. The night was clear save for a light smog that rolled in on a gathering breeze.

Silas walked in high spirits thanks to Thomas Payne and a chance meeting. Thomas because he had remembered the theatre review and made the connections which led to Silas now preparing to break into a building, something he hadn't done since his desperate days starving in Greychurch. Although he wouldn't admit it publicly, he missed the thrill of a break-in and the possibility of being caught, and he was wound by nervous excitement as he and Jake made their way into the West End.

Jake was the chance meeting, and Silas was still trying to make sense of how it came about. Fate was the only word to use after they worked out their unlikely connection over lunch.

Silas had asked Jake for every detail of his parents, and once Jake had told him, he knew the connection was complicated and couldn't be proved, but it was too unlikely to be anything but the truth.

'Why do you want to know all this?' Jake asked, relishing the half bottle of wine they had ordered.

'Your dad was called Billy O'Hara.' Silas wanted to double-check the facts. 'Came

to Westerpool when? Sixty-six?'

'That's right. Westerpool in the late sixties then down here. Came looking for work, met my mum, went back and forth for a few years, married my mum and settled in town in seventy-two, year after I was born. We went through this just now, and you still ain't told me why.'

'That's because I am still trying to make sense of it.' Silas had finished his steak, and he pushed his plate away. 'Jake, you know what I used to do in Greychurch.'

Jake nodded.

'Well, when I was renting and stuff, I called myself Billy O'Hara.'

Jake's eye opened wide. 'That's a coincidence.'

'Well, maybe not. See, the thing is, I never knew my dad. To be honest, I'm not sure my mam ever knew who he was either, and she left Dublin a few months before I was born. When I was about three, my mam had a boyfriend in Westerpool. My earliest memories are of being in the room with just us, and him playing a guitar and singing to me. We had our own room in the block then because this man had a regular wage from the docks. Then there was this time when he wasn't there so much, he'd come and go, you know, and when my mam was pregnant with the twins, he vanished. Least, that's what she said when we had to move into spare rooms. "Can't afford our own with no Billy," she said. When mam died, and I had to come to the city to earn a living for Karan and Iona, I used the name Billy O'Hara because it was a name I remembered from when I was little. Me mam's boyfriend. Do you see where I'm going with this Jake?'

Jake's fork had been halfway to his mouth for the last minute, and gravy was dripping from the piece of beef suspended there. He nodded again, this time slowly.

'Coincidence maybe,' Silas said. 'If it weren't for the fact that you've got the same hair, same eyes and same kind of face as Iona and Karan. Okay, so I've got my mam's black hair and blue eyes the same as them and hundreds of other Micks, but that time I first saw you, I couldn't get over how much you looked like them. You get me?'

Jake gave up on the idea of food and put down the fork. Instead, he picked up his wine and drained the glass.

'Granddad did tell me that my dad liked to play around,' Jake said, thinking hard. 'That's why he was happy to go up and down to Westerpool even after he was married. His boss here used to send him up there regular to work at their yard in… Where was it?

Something to do with horses? Gallop Wharf?'

'Canter Wharf?'

'That's it! How d'you know that?'

Silas' heart was racing. That was the link in the chain that surely proved him right.

'Because that's where we lived,' he said.

'This is weird.' Jake shook his head in disbelief. 'So, you think my dad was your sisters' dad? No way. That would make you and me... what?'

'I don't know,' Silas admitted. 'That's what I've been trying to work out. If I'm right and your dad was mam's boyfriend back then, you're half-brother to my half-sisters which makes us... Two halves of no relation, really.'

'Or quarter-brothers,' Jake said, grinning. 'Not by blood, though.'

'Man. I'd be happy to have a quarter of a brother like you.'

'And I've got two sisters?' Jake was too dumbfounded to notice the compliment.

'You have, and you'll meet them when we get to Larkspur.'

'Larkspur?'

'I'm not sending you back to the streets,' Silas said. 'We've got a job to do tonight, and when that's done, it's straight back to Cornwall. That's if you want to come.'

The waiter had arrived at that point, fussing over the table and ending the conversation.

They took it up again through the afternoon, and by nightfall, had decided they were to consider themselves as brothers-by-accident because most things in Silas' life had happened by accident. It pleased him that fate was on his side. It was a good omen for the night ahead.

High spirits became focused determination as they weaved silently through the side streets to Covent Garden, their way lit by yellow gas lamps and Silas' oil lantern. There were few people about, the market stallholders wouldn't arrive to set up for a couple more hours, but when someone approached, they talked about the weather, appearing as respectable young men on their way home after an evening's entertainment. They fell silent again as the back of the Opera House came into view, murky through the veil of fog.

'There's the stables,' Jake said, pointing. 'People live above them,

214

but by this time of night, the downstairs will be empty. I'll go in first, though, just in case.'

Coming to a pair of tall wooden gates, Jake let himself in through a smaller, built-in door while Silas waited outside, pretending to read the bill posters that advertised coming attractions. When Jake's hand appeared and beckoned him through, he checked that he wasn't being watched, and followed.

The stables were lined either side with stalls, and the floor was covered by straw which muffled their footsteps. A solitary lamp threw little light at the horses, asleep on their feet. The creak of floorboards overhead warned them of the presence of the stable hands, and they crept cautiously towards the far end and another door built into the plastered wall. Jake stood with his back to it to keep watch while Silas crouched to the lock and took the leather pouch from his pocket. Unrolling it on the straw, he examined the lock and selected a Chubb's master key, and picked a thin strip of steel from a ring of several.

Nudging Jake, he passed him the lantern and directed it towards the keyhole before inserting both the steel and the key. Pressing his ear to the wood, he listened as metal slid over metal until he found resistance. The picks pressed firmly together in place, he turned them clockwise until the deadbolt began to move. When he judged it to be free of its housing, he leant his head against the wood, applied pressure and the door opened a fraction. Standing, he replaced his tools and cautiously opened the door further, expecting to hear the hinges creak. The door opened silently, however, and they slipped inside with ease.

'Blimey, you're good at that,' Jake whispered, once the door was closed.

'There's a bloody key on the inside,' Silas hissed, taking it from a nail hammered into the frame. 'What's the point of that?'

Jake put his finger to his lips while he took the key and relocked the door.

'Just in case,' he said, replacing the key on its hook. Holding the lantern over his head, he revealed a space no bigger than Silas' dressing room. A few paces ahead of them, another pair of doors barred their way, and Silas' heart sank when he realised there was no keyhole and no visible hinges. He shrugged helplessly at Jake, but Jake grinned, stepped over to the wall and took hold of a rusty lantern hook jutting from the plaster. He pulled it downwards, and the doors slowly parted to reveal a void, black and uninviting. The smell of sewage seeped out, and Silas wished he'd brought a scarf to cover his nose.

The lamp lit stone steps leading down to an arched opening, and beyond that was nothing but darkness.

'Welcome to the world of the theatre,' Jake said. 'We're okay to talk from here on, but still, keep your voice down.'

'Why the secret mechanism?' Silas asked, impressed but confused. 'And why a key on the inside?'

'They say that necessity is the mother of invention,' Jake replied, taking a lantern from the wall. 'But really it's the theatre. This way.'

He descended the steps as he lit a lamp, and with two lights, the way ahead became clearer.

'You remember those clouds for Aeneas?' Jake asked, referring to the gala night the previous October. 'Well, they were made for the original production. The script called for descending angels on clouds, so someone had to invent it. The smoke that came up through the stage? Invented for something unpronounceable by Wagner. There's men work in the building above us who come up with all manner of clever stuff like hidden doors, traps and the like. And then there's this…'

The lamps threw light into a tunnel. High enough for them to stand, it was tiled in a perfect arch, with parallel tracks on the floor and candle sconces tapering off as far as the light would let them see.

'A spare key's on the inside,' Jake continued, walking ahead. 'In case anyone gets locked in by accident. There's the same arrangement at the other end. You've always got to have safety in mind when you're around a theatre. Especially as so many of them burn down.'

'Makes sense,' Silas said. His voice echoed briefly, but strangely the sound seemed to travel only as far as the light. It was an eerie effect. 'What are the tracks for?'

'Ah, now that's just laziness. Oh, mind where you walk, there's rats. There are some side tunnels ahead. Inspection ways into the sewer, and some of their doors are rotten. I used to play down here with the kids from the stables until one got rat-bitten and nearly died from the spirally fever. Anyhow, the tracks… The House was rebuilt after burning down eighty years ago. As they were designing the new one, the owners did a deal with a place called Casby's Worldwide Emporium in Wellington Street. That place provided everything for the new House from the booze to the canvas, including stuff for the restaurant, material for the costumes, the gas, the plush, you name it. So, rather than trundle all this expensive stuff up Bow Street in all weathers, they dug this tunnel and ran carts on these tracks from the warehouse to the opera house. Simple.'

'Blimey, Jake, you know some shit.' Silas was happy to let Jake prattle on, it took his mind off disease-carrying vermin and the thousands of tons of buildings and roads above their heads.

'You know me and theatres, Brother,' Jake said, 'You mind me calling you that?'

'I don't.' Silas answered with a smile that was impossible to see in the gloom. 'But where does this come out? What's on Wellington Street?'

'Ah, now that's the thing, see.' Jake was off again, his words bouncing back to him a second after he spoke. 'Casby's was right next to a performance hall what it did business with, but like loads of other places with gas stage lighting, it caught fire in eighteen thirty. The fire damaged a lot of Casby's too, so they had to stop trading and went bust. So, the theatre bought the Casby building and moved there, right next door.'

'The Lyceum?'

'You're getting it. The tunnel was left, and these days only gets used by Mr Bursnal the house manager when he wants to sneak his mistress about, and maybe Mr Irving and his mates, when they want to do the same. Dirty lot, these actors. We'll be there in a moment. Best go quiet, as I don't know if they've got a nightwatchman or not.'

The tunnel, having sloped down and levelled out, now rose beneath their feet, and several paces further on, a second set of steps came into view.

'It comes out behind the kitchens of the Beef Steak room, Jake said. 'Mr Irving's posh dinner club. Theatre's dark while they're on tour, there won't be anyone working, so we should be okay.'

'That's good to hear. And how do we get from there to the offices?'

They reached the steps, and Jake hung his lamp on a hook. Turning to Silas, he said, 'I don't know. I've never been inside. Ain't you got a plan or nothing?'

Silas had taken it for granted that Jake knew everything about every theatre in the city, but his concerned expression told a different story.

'No. But the doorman said the office is six floors up. I was hoping you'd know the rest.'

Jake thought for a second and shrugged. 'Well, I do know that theatre managers like their offices facing back, away from the noise of the street, but I don't know Irving, so who can tell? Anyway, before we go and find out, ain't it about time you told me what we're looking for?'

'Information.'

'Yeah, you said that, but being honest, Brother, if I'm going to get done for breaking and entering, I'd like to know why I was doing it. Are you thieving?'

'Only information.' Silas sighed. He'd known he would have to explain his purpose to Jake at some point, but hadn't yet found a way of doing so. He decided it would be best to tell him the whole dubious story.

'Look, Jake, if I told you that the butler you dressed up in royal livery thinks that a Romanian assassin is planning to kill Henry Irving because of a play he wrote about the Szekely people, and we think we can prevent the murder if I can find out how he plans to do it, and then get that information to Tom and Jimmy by tomorrow evening before Lord Clearwater's got a scandal on his hands… would you believe me?'

Jake's eyes glinted in the lamp spill as he looked Silas up and down. He took off his bowler ran his gloved hand through his new haircut, replaced his hat and said, 'Yeah, wouldn't surprise me in the least, mate.' Shaking his head, he collected his lantern. 'Better whisper from here on,' he said, and mounted the stairs.

The door into the Lyceum was the same as the one out of the Opera House, and beside it hung a similar key, making their entry easier. Jake led the way, listening intently before signalling for Silas to follow. Silas stopped him by putting his hand on his shoulder, and pointed to his shoes. Having taken them off and left them inside the tunnel entrance, they found themselves in a storeroom among crates and boxes. It led to a kitchen fitted with stoves and plate racks, tables and utensils. The lantern light threw shadows that loomed and fell as they scanned the walls searching for the way forward. It was a kitchen Mrs Flintwich would have been proud to work in with its immaculately ordered shelves, dressers and perfectly polished, hanging pans. It even boasted an ice room and a dumb waiter, or as she called it when Barnaby was dithering with service, a 'dumb footman.'

Jake moved the lantern around the walls until he located an opening leading to a brick staircase, and looking up, Silas nodded. They climbed in silence, their stockinged feet making no sound until they had risen two storeys and Silas was beginning to sweat beneath his jumper. He was wishing he had left his coat in the tunnel when Jake yanked him down by the collar. Covering his lamp, he held his ear before pointing towards an open doorway beyond which a dull light glowed as keys jangled. The sound and light faded as it ascended stairs, and crouched on their haunches, they scuttled upwards until, out of breath, they arrived at the top floor.

'Right,' Jake breathed. 'If the watchman is doing a proper round, it will take him ages to get up here, but still, we got to be quick.'

Through another door which creaked as it closed and caused them to wince, they found themselves in a corridor. Carpeted and smelling faintly of old cigar smoke and wood polish, a window at the opposite end let in a vague amount of diffused streetlight, as did one at the end of a passage to their left. Once their eyes had adjusted, they made out dark recesses of office doorways, and hearing no noise apart from a distant clatter of hooves on the Strand, they set about examining each one. Although the rooms had nameplates, none of them was Irving's. Doubling back, they took the other passage and here, at the far end, two oak doors, larger and grander than the others, stood facing each other. They also displayed far more important nameplates.

'Mr Stoker.' Jake read the one at the rear of the building.

'Here.'

Opposite, the streetlight picked out a brass plate announcing

'Mr Irving', and Silas dropped to his knees. He had taken out his kit, examined the keyhole, and was preparing his picks when the door opened.

'Didn't think so,' Jake said, shining the light into the room. 'No point locking it if there's a watchman and the house is dark.'

The room was large and dominated by a desk piled high with books and manuscripts. Shelves were lined with more, and plush leather armchairs sagged beneath the weight of the actor's reading material.

'We'll never find anything in this,' Silas whispered.

'What we looking for?'

'Anything about that play, "The Blood of the…." whatever it was.'

Jake put his lantern on a cabinet pointing away from the windows in case anyone in the street happened to look up, and it gave them just enough illumination to see by. White papers were picked out well enough, but Silas had to bring darker documents to the lamp to read.

'It's all bloody Shakespeare and stuff,' he muttered, toing and froing from the desk to the lamp while Jake squinted at the bookshelves.

Flicking through handwritten manuscripts and finding nothing, he was wondering if Thomas' reasoning had for once been off the mark, when he came across a piece of paper that gave him an idea. At first glance, it appeared to be nothing more than scribbled notes, but the words 'The Blood' and 'Stoker's cabinet 2' leapt out. Calling Jake, he showed him, and they looked across to the opposite office.

A minute later, having left Irving's room as they had found it, they crossed the passage.

This time, Silas tried the door but found it locked. As he set about picking the lock, Jake tiptoed back to the stairs to listen, and returned just in time to find Silas packing his tools with the door open.

'He's three floors below,' Jake whispered. 'Got to hurry.'

In stark contrast to Irving's study, his manager's was organised and tidy. There was only one window, high up and round so the lantern would be no problem, and Jake left the door open. By way of explanation, he cupped his ear and pointed to the corridor.

'Good idea,' Silas mouthed. 'Cabinet two.'

One wall was lined with wooden filing cabinets, their uniform row interrupted by a square-framed, sliding door, possibly concealing a large safe, another was a mass of bookcases. The third displayed framed posters, one of which was the billboard for 'The Blood of the Dead', and it hung in the place of honour over a dining table and chairs.

None of the cabinets were numbered, but instinctively, as if they had worked together before, Silas started at one end and Jake at the other. Taking the most logical approach, they counted two cabinets in and began their search. Lifting files and papers to the light, they worked quickly and silently. Having found nothing, Jake closed the top drawer and returned to the passage to listen. Giving Silas a thumbs up, he resumed his task.

Silas had no luck with the first three drawers, but in the fourth, he finally found what he was looking for. He beckoned Jake with a hiss before laying the folder on the desk.

'Szekelys, Transylvania and the Lore of the Undead,' was handwritten across the top in bold lettering and beneath it was the title of the play. Inside a stack of papers was arranged in seemingly random order. There were far too many to read through, and all Silas could do was look for certain words as he scanned the titles. 'History of the Region' was followed by 'Character Outlines.' The next set of pages were to do with 'Plot, Synopsis and Intent', whatever that meant.

These weren't papers about an order of Romanian assassins, they were to do with Irving's play, he thought, but what he read on the next page made his heart stop beating.

'Got it!' The words were out of his mouth before he realised, he'd said them aloud.

Jake gripped his arm urgently, and looking up from the page, Silas saw lamplight growing stronger beyond the door.

'Close it,' Silas hissed, sending Jake scuttling across the room to silently shut them in.

Silas took the section of pages, rolled them and shoved them into his coat, dashed to the cabinet, replaced the folder and thought frantically.

There was only one place to hide, and that was beneath the desk. Silas dragged Jake into the well, and cramped and balled, they extinguished the lamp and held their breath.

The turn of the door handle was followed by the brush of wood on carpet. Light swung around the room in an arc raising and dropping shadows, a man coughed, and the light faded as the door closed.

'Bloody close,' Jake whispered. 'We'll have to wait a while before we go.'

'No,' Silas said. 'We have to leave now. He'll be back in about thirty seconds.'

Egerton Sandfield hadn't been born to be a nightwatchman, he had been born to act. His father always said he had the name for it, so why not try the profession. Encouraged by an over-ambitious mother and a father with ideas above his son's ability, Egerton followed the dramatic arts from an early age. By the time he was nine, he could recite Shakespeare sonnets, and monologues by the time he was ten. Marlow held no mysteries for him, and he had even dabbled with 'The Duchess of Malfi' in his early teens.

Sadly, the closest he had ever come to the stage was pacing the corridors of the Lyceum nightly since the age of eighteen. The manager then had promised him auditions and had even heard him recite in his study, the room he now stood in aged fifty-two with nothing to look forward to but a low wage and a few more years of humiliation before he shuffled off the mortal coil.

He shone his lantern on the poster of Mr Irving's Hamlet as he did every night, and sighed.

'That could have been you, Egerton,' he said. 'Hear that, Mr Irving? That could have been me if they'd given me a chance.'

The windows were locked just as he expected, not that anyone would climb six storeys and crawl the parapet to break into an actor's office, but men had done more dangerous things in the name of burglary. No-one had been in or around the theatre for weeks now. The company was away enjoying the high life, first on a steamer, then touring America and now heading back on the Britannic no less, pumped with success and no doubt looking forward to the new season. He imagined the fine dining, the cast and managers enjoying camaraderie at the first-class tables while the crew sweated out the voyage in steerage. He would have been happy with even that, but his potential had been ignored.

'Should have been me,' he sighed, scanning the desk and shelves. 'What you heard was a rat.' Bending beneath the desk, he looked for signs of vermin.

His was a pointless job when the theatre was dark, it was one of the most secure buildings on the street. There wasn't much worth stealing apart from Mr Irving's personal effects, there had been no takings, so there was no cash. Irving knew this and never bothered locking his door.

'All the same, Sir,' Egerton said as he returned to the passage. 'I do think you should be more secure-minded like...'

He stopped in his tracks before he completed the sentence.

Mr Stoker always locked his office. He insisted on it. Even when the room had been decorated last spring, it had to be kept locked when he wasn't in there.

His adrenaline was suddenly pumping. Egerton had just checked that room, and the door had been unlocked.

'That was no rat.'

Throwing the door wide, he shouted, 'Oi! Who's there?' and braced himself for a burglar's swipe.

None came.

Window? Unbroken and closed. Behind the coat stand? Empty space. Beneath the desk? No-one.

Egerton stood scratching his head. 'You're getting too old for this,' he said. 'Your mind's going.' Locking Mr Stoker's study, he wondered if it was time he retired.

Six flights below, Silas and Jake tumbled from the dumb waiter, their hands sore from lowering themselves with the ropes.

'Good job it wasn't a safe,' Silas snorted as they hurried back to the tunnel.

'What now?'

'Now we get these back to Tom and Jimmy as quick as we can, and hope they can make sense of them before Smith kills Henry Irving.'

Twenty-Two

Having cadged a ride on the back of a milk cart from Covent Garden to South Riverside, Silas and Jake crept into Clearwater House in the early hours and headed straight for bed. After a few hours of unsettled sleep, they washed and changed, packed a case and were back on the streets, leaving a note for the Norwoods to let them know they were gone.

The sun had just risen by the time they arrived at Paddington Station where Silas secured two tickets on the Flying Dutchman while Jake searched out the telegraph office to send a dispatch Silas had prepared.

They met outside the café, where Silas paced, chewing the edge of a fingernail.

'Send it okay?' he asked as Jake hurried towards him.

'Yeah. Got an odd look from the man at the counter. I didn't think they were meant to read your messages, only count the words. Still, it was sent, and they said it would get to His Lordship pronto.'

'That's the good news,' Silas said as he collected his case. 'You want the next bit?'

Jake was distracted by the arching roof and the scale of the railway station, tipping back his head and gawping.

'Oi, Jake!' Silas nudged him with his luggage. 'You want the next bit of good news?'

'Blimey, I thought the Opera was big. Sorry, what?'

'You not been here before?'

'Never been on a train. Is it safe?'

Silas laughed. 'You can ask Thomas that when you meet him,' he said. 'Yes, Jake, it's as safe as it can be. But you've never been on a train?'

'No. Never been able to afford it. Will you look at that!'

He was pointing, still agape, at a first-class Pullman carriage being coupled to another. The cream and brown paintwork gleamed beneath electric lights, and the lettering of 'First Class' was painted in gold. Inside, a steward polished the picture windows being careful not to disturb the lamps on the linen-covered tablecloths.

'That's the next bit of good news,' Silas said, enjoying the younger man's wonder. 'You're riding in it.'

'Get out of here!' Jake wasn't sure if Silas was joking. 'And you can eat in it?'

'The bloke at the ticket office said they've only been doing it a week, trying out this American idea. Says it won't catch on, but sounded too good to miss to me. I got us special tickets so we can stuff our faces all the way to Cornwall if we want.'

'Bloody hell.'

'Yeah, whatever next, eh? Now, you want the bad news?'

Jake's face fell. 'What?'

'It doesn't leave until a quarter-on-twelve, which means we won't get to Plymouth until a quarter-on-six. Only a fifteen-minute wait for the connection, but it's another hour from there to Bodmin and that one don't stop at Larkspur. Assuming we can get a cab at Bodmin, we won't get to the Hall until around half seven when I'm expected to be turned out smart and talking to toffs.'

'Look on the bright side,' Jake enthused. 'We'll get there in the end, and after they get your message, someone will sort things out, and everything'll come right. You've stopped Irving from being murdered, you said so.'

'No, I've confirmed he's in danger, but we suspected that. They still don't know how or when he's going to do it.'

'We'll figure it out while we're eating posh,' Jake beamed. 'Good ideas always follow a hearty meal.'

The young man's eyes had gone from wide and wondering to kind and smiling, and Silas couldn't help but grin.

'That's what I like about you, mate,' he said. 'You're always so cheerful.'

'The way I see it, you get one chance on this earth, so there's no point not making the most of it. Like my granddad used to say, you only go around once, and then you get tucked in with a spade. What we doing until the train leaves?'

Silas threw his arm around Jake's shoulder and turned him to the etched glass and fancy brass lamps of the café. 'Eating posh?'

'Nice,' Jake said. 'I could do with the practice.'

Jake had been amazed by the size of the station, he was awestruck by the café, but later, when he stepped into the dining car and took a seat opposite Silas, it took him until Ealing before he could speak.

'You with us yet, Jake?' Silas grinned as the express rattled through the station, its whistle blowing.

Jake tore his eyes from the crystal glasses, the silver cutlery and the bone china decorated with 'GWR' and fixed Silas with unblinking, sad eyes.

'A couple of days ago I had no home,' he said. 'No family neither. No hope if I'm to be honest, and now look at me.' He swallowed, and a thin, trembling hand reached across the table to rest on Silas' arm. 'I can't pay you back, ever.'

'You don't need to,' Silas replied. Lowering his glass, he placed his hand on Jake's. 'And if you feel you do have to, let me tell you, you already have. Without you, I'd not have got hold of these...' The stolen notes lay face down on the empty chair beside him. 'Without them, I wouldn't have known what's going to happen at Larkspur tonight, and if I'd not been able to warn Thomas, His Lordship would have suffered a load of scandal and bad-mouthing. A death... No, a *murder* in his home is unthinkable. His reputation would go down the pan, not to mention his Foundation. Couldn't have done it without you.'

'Cheers for that,' Jake said, blushing. 'But you're sure the message will get to His Lordship?'

'For sure. Whatever servant takes the telegrams off the boy gives them to the butler no matter who they're addressed to, and Tommy'll know what to do for the best. He's devoted to Archer. Most of the servants are.'

Jake suddenly pulled his hand free, and Silas was worried he'd been too forward by holding it.

'Sorry, mate,' he said. 'That's just how I am. Didn't mean anything dodgy.'

'It's not that. I used to get all kinds of weird attention backstage. Everyone from the baritone to the dressers were at it, but I know where we stand, you and me. No, I just got this feeling...' His

226

brow furrowed and he peered over the table to papers. 'You told me something about all this last night, it's a right queer tale, ask me, and I didn't take it all in, but…' Again he broke off, this time sighing before clenching his bottom lip with his top.

'What is it?'

'Can I have another look?'

Jake cleared a space while Silas lifted the notes onto the table. They were held together by a string fed through a hole in the top left corner of each one, every page was the same size, the handwriting neat, and the various sections were divided by thin sheets of card. Jake turned the pages to face him, glancing at the other diners in the car to make sure they weren't being overheard. The other passengers were too interested in the novelty of menus to notice two respectably dressed young men who, to the outside world, appeared to be having a business meeting.

'Can you go through it again?' Jake asked, leafing through the various sections. 'What you said about this Mr Smith character.'

'Yeah, why?'

'I don't know, but I thought I saw something. Can't explain it. Go on. There was this train crash?'

'Best not think about that,' Silas said. They were puffing through the Berkshire countryside, the fields wide and verdant, the afternoon sky clouding and threatening rain. 'But yeah. Ended up with Archer taking Mr Smith and this lad to the house because the hospital was overrun.'

'And Smith had a tattoo that made you not trust him?'

'That's it. Archer thought it was something to do with his old family who were Rasnovs, but we looked it up, and it's not. The drawing on Smith's back was what they used to ink themselves with if they were protectors of the Szekelys.'

'"The Szekelys… Their heart's blood and their swords boast a record like the Hapsburgs, and the Romanovs cannot reach",' Jake quoted from a page.

'Yeah, proud race and all that, I read that bit. So, Smith's tattoo gave me the creeps, and I didn't trust him. I did some digging, looking for a book like I said, but Saddle had already found it for Tommy and… What is it you want to know?'

'Who's Saddle?' Jake wasn't looking at Silas as he asked his questions, he was flicking pages, turning some back and forth, checking one against the other.

'He's the under-butler, one down from Thomas.'

'Loyal?'

'To Tommy? He has to be if he wasn't to keep his job.'

'To Lord Clearwater?'

'I suppose so. He was put in charge of looking after this Smith character, but it's difficult to tell anything with Saddle.'

Jake looked up, opened his mouth and returned to his reading. 'You had this gut feeling?'

'Yeah. Jimmy felt it too.'

'That's the footman who went up the fly tower with you and got thumped by a man in a dress?'

'Yeah,' Silas said, recalling the incident vividly. 'But he got up and saved me from falling sixty feet.'

'Is he loyal too?'

'Jimmy? He's everyone's best mate. Hey, Jake.' Silas banged his hand on the paper to distract the young man. 'We're all good mates, and that includes Archer, but you never call him that. When we get to the Hall, it's His Lordship, and you don't discuss our relationship with anyone, right?'

'Of course.'

'Good. Now, what were you getting at?'

'You said something about the language Smith was talking in his sleep?'

'Translated as "Take the boy and kill the father",' Silas said. 'And he was muttering about taking the family name too, dishonour and shame.'

'That was it!' Jake turned the papers to Silas and pointed to a section. 'Read this note.'

Chpt/2; Count's speech: "For when the good name of the Szekely people is besmirched by the Turk or tainted by the Hungarian, we retaliate with force."

Note: They killed at even the threat of such insult else allow dishonour upon the family. The Protectori (R1 paragraph 3) never allowed such shame (still do not). Cunning, they tricked a comprimario to unknowingly kill their enemy. (C/04)

'No idea what it means, mate,' Silas said. 'What you saying?'

Jake took back the notes and continued his search as he spoke. 'These are notes for Mr Irving's play, right? Background, ideas, some speeches, but they're all based on truth. It says so here...' He indicated a reference but had moved on before Silas could read it clearly. 'That speech basically says that the Romanian assassins are still in existence... Yeah, here.' He indicated the corner of a page. 'R one. Research page one, paragraph three. "The *Protectori* are still active. Ensure Irving knows the risks." Is that the tattoo?'

Jake's eyes were darting from line to line as Silas leant in to look at a sketch. 'That's it,' he said. 'Looking to the left. What are you getting at?'

'Do you know what a comprimario is?'

'Not a clue, Jake. But I'm guessing you do.'

'Only 'cos I worked in the theatre. In Italian opera, the comprimario is like a supporting role, the master's faithful servant kind of thing. In the orchestra, the musicians call the one who sits behind the leader the same thing. He's usually a violinist.'

'Playing second fiddle?'

'Exactly.'

'All very interesting, Jake, but still means nothing to me.'

'Here!' Jake had turned to a page headed with the letter C. 'Character ideas. Character number four...' He followed a list to the fourth name and read the note. '"A man, possibly a madman, duped into assisting the Count to carry out his plan. Perhaps greed. Greed for life. Greed for revenge?" Are you seeing what I'm seeing, Silas?'

'I'm seeing that this train is going slow,' Silas said, looking at the gloom beyond the window. 'But I'm not seeing how this is going to help Tommy understand how Smith is going to kill Irving.' He looked at his watch. 'Who should be arriving at Larkspur anytime now.'

'Why Irving?'

'Because he wrote that play. The one based on those notes. You just said so with that stuff about "Even at the threat of dishonour." From what I understand, Irving's play has upset the Szekelys, and they've sent their assassin to kill him because he dared write it. Smith was on his way to wait for Irving or meet him off the boat when the accident landed him at Larkspur. Lucky for him, bad for Mr Irving, but at least Tommy now knows for sure and can convince Archer. As for how he's going to kill Irving, we still don't know.'

The waiter was taking orders at the next table, and Jake lowered his voice. 'Do the words Golden Mediasch mean anything to you?'

'Not a thing, why?'

'I might have this all arse about face,' Jake whispered. 'But there's two things you should know. One, according to these notes, the Protectori send their faithful, but usually tricked servant, their comprimario, to do their dirty work, so they never get caught themselves if the plan goes wrong. Secondly, they do it with something called a Golden Mediasch. If I'm right, that's what your Mr Smith is going to use for his murder if he hasn't done it already.'

The thought that they were too late chilled Silas, but he comforted himself with the knowledge that his message would, by now, have arrived with Thomas. His friends would know what to do. They were, as Archer insisted, comrades bound together for the common good.

'So we know the victim,' Silas said, thinking aloud. 'Irving. We know when — sometime between this afternoon and Monday, and we suspect Smith won't do it himself. I can't think who he might have tricked into doing his dirty work, but then I still don't know everyone at the Hall. What we *don't* know is how. Anything there say what a Golden Mediasch might be?'

'I'm afraid we don't have that on the menu, Sir.'

Silas looked up sharply to find the steward scribbling on his pad. Jake flipped the notes face down.

'It's extremely rare, as I am sure you appreciate.' The waiter finished writing the table number and smiled. 'We do have a rather fine claret.'

'It's a wine?'

'Claret? Yes, of course, Sir.'

'No,' Silas tutted. 'Golden, er… The gold one.'

The waiter looked from one man to the other as if he suspected they were stowaways from second-class. 'Both the claret and the Mediasch are reds, Sir. The Mediasch comes from the Medias region of Transylvania. At least, it did until production was halted. There are very few bottles left in existence. Perhaps if you would care to place an order, I can advise you on the wine?'

Silas stumbled through the menu and placed an order for beef and potatoes, and accepted the wine the waiter suggested. He'd never heard of it but was anxious for the man to go away.

'So I reckon we know how,' he said, once the man had gone.

'Wine? What, poison?'

'Stella,' Silas said, staring at Jake. 'Poisoned chalice. Quill's brother. Same style?' His mind was racing, thinking back, picking up ideas from previous events and trying to shuffle them into the current puzzle.

'You'll have to explain,' Jake said.

'I will, mate, but let me think a minute.'

The train rattled as it sped through a tunnel, the sound of pistons and wheels churning in the background against images of Quill, his twisted form hunched over a bottle of red wine, grinning as he tipped poison into the neck.

'No,' he muttered to his reflection. 'Thomas decants the wine. Always. He never lets it out of his sight until it reaches the dining room.'

'Silas.'

'Tommy wouldn't do it. Don't be stupid, man.'

'Silas?'

'But it's left on the sideboard during the dinner. Barnaby? Get away. You trust him.'

'Oi, Silas?'

Jake was tapping his knee under the table, but Silas ignored it. The last piece of the puzzle clicked into place as the train screamed from the tunnel, the sound fell way, and his reflection was drowned by the sunset.

'Unless he's busy,' he said, turning back to Jake.

'Who?'

'Thomas. He's going to be busy. It's Archer's first big event, and Tom's. He'll get his under-butler to do stuff, and even if he doesn't, Saddle's at the sideboard through dinner.'

'I don't know what you're getting at,' Jake said, 'but you need to see this.'

'Saddle has spent the last couple of days with Smith. He hates Thomas, but would he agree to put poison in the wine?'

'If he's a comprimario, he might not know he was doing it,' Jake suggested, flicking to the note he had read earlier. 'If he's greedy for life, blood or revenge, he might, but there's something else you need to know.' He clicked his fingers in Silas' face to draw his focus.

'I bet it's that creep, Saddle.'

'Yeah, okay, Silas, but look.' Jake waved the bundle of papers. 'These notes aren't just about the play. They refer to chapters, not acts. What's more, they talk about Mr Irving in the third person. "Ensure Irving knows the risks." Irving didn't write this.'

'It was his play, wasn't it?'

'He was *in* it,' Jake said. 'But he didn't write it.' He shook his head and offered the last page of notes as his evidence. 'These are notes for a book about a blood-thirsty Szekely Count that someone else is planning to write. See? It says here, "End of outline chapters", and it's dated February this year. *After* the play was performed. Henry Irving ain't the author. He ain't the one to be murdered.'

'Then who is?'

'Bram Stoker.'

At Paddington Station that morning, Silas' message had been expertly translated into a series of dots and dashes by a man fluent in Morse code. After eight years working the Cooke and Wheatstone transmitter, the operator was so accustomed to converting letters to signals that his mind didn't need to absorb the words, it instinctively knew how many taps of the key represented each letter. Had he been reading Silas' message, he might have wondered at words such as *Protectori* and *Szekely*. If he had a mind to be inquisitive, he might have become concerned at certain phrases, in particular, *Definitely assassin, Contain Smith,* and T*ake the boy and kill the father,* and if he had been interested in celebrity business, he might have picked up on Henry Irving's name. He was none of those things, simply a well-trained man doing his job and doing it efficiently before the telegraph office closed early for Easter Friday.

Each press of the key caused the attached metal stylus to complete an electrical circuit producing a charge which pulsed through the copper wire. The dots and dashes followed each other along the cable overtaking locomotives steaming through towns and cities, and arrived in Cornwall a few seconds later. There, the code woke an electromagnet, shocking it into action and compelling it to jolt a small lever into life. The lever was pulled down for the brief lifetime of either a dot or a dash, and as its other end rose, an inked wheel made contact with a strip of paper which automatically rolled out when the Paddington machine connected to the Larkspur receiver two hundred and twelve miles away.

The paper tape flowed until the message was complete, and was torn from the reel by the postmaster's eldest son, a barrel of a man who was due to be married in a month. Noting that the message was marked as urgent and that it was for Larkspur Hall, he swung his legs from the fireside stool and heaved himself upright to set about translating the code and writing it on the delivery slip. Had it been for anyone else, he would have finished his tea first, but His Lordship had personally pulled the man's fiancée from the wreckage of the Plymouth train, and in doing so, had saved her life. The postmaster's son was so grateful to the viscount that he didn't dwell on the message or search for gossip, and instead, sealed it in an envelope and bellowed the name of his younger brother, instantly and professionally forgetting what he had just read.

The brother, summoned from his reading of 'The Primrose Path' in the parlour, sauntered into the room, stretching. A minute later, he was furiously pedalling the two miles to the Hall.

Arriving out of breath and sweating, he rang the back doorbell and, as soon as the maid appeared, flustered and backed by a cloud of steam, passed the envelope across. The messenger waited, hoping for an invitation to rest with a glass of beer, but the crashing of pans and chopping of cleavers told him the kitchen was busy and he didn't stand a chance.

The kitchen-maid closed the door on the pushy lad from the village, and bustled her way through the vapours and fervour of the kitchen, along the passage, through the servants' hall and down the corridor to the under-butler's pantry. There, she found the door open and Mr Saddle nervously examining a pocket watch.

'Another message for Mr Payne,' she announced.

She had lost count of how many had been delivered and passed to the under-butler in the last two days. With Mr Payne managing the dinner and guest arrangements, it was currently Saddle's job to filter the post, and so the proof of impending murder was placed in

Saddle's hand, and he dismissed the maid. As soon as she had left, he hid the message in his inside pocket with the other unopened communications Mr Smith had bribed him not to deliver, and still believing this was part of some humorous prank that would humiliate Mr Payne, he returned to readying the decanters for the evening wine.

Twenty-Three

Easter Friday morning had dawned over Newquay with a westerly breeze that cleared the last of the storm clouds from the north coast and left a pale sky. It brought with it the smell of the sea and the sound of waves lapping at the quay. James woke late to hear sails flapping and men calling as the fishermen left on the tide, while seagulls squawked overhead in irregular counterpoint. His limbs ached from yesterday's exertions, and the pleasant numbness told him he had slept well and long.

Refreshed, he sat up in bed and blinked against the sunlight. Jerry lay curled in the other cot, and Fecker, wrapped in his new coat and lying on extra blankets supplied by the motherly landlady, snored lightly across the door, a precaution in case Jerry decided to run away, or Smith returned. Neither had happened, and that gave James hope that the day ahead would be a simple one. Checking the time, he found it was ten o'clock and decided to put his thoughts in order before waking the others.

As well as hearing Jerry's story the previous evening, he had also learnt his proper name, or rather, names. His father had christened him Irving, after his friend and colleague, Henry Irving, but, Jerry said, he was known by his second name, Noel, so as not to cause confusion at home. He was also named after his uncle Thornley, and although he had no objections to that, he thought to have three first names was, 'Perhaps something of a confusion.'

'You should ask Mr Andrej his full name,' James had said, and Jerry did.

'Andrej Borysko Yakiv Kolisnychenko.' The words rolled proudly in Fecker's native accent, as they did when he added his title, 'Master of the Horse.'

Jerry looked at him curiously. 'I would say, that in English, you would be Andrew Boris Jacob,' he said. 'Fine and noble names, Sir.

I am pleased to properly make your acquaintance.'

For a nine-year-old, he was articulate, and he certainly knew his own mind. He declared that his 'Uncle Jimmy' and Mr Andrej were fine friends to have, and he formerly thanked them for their assistance, adding that they could call him what they wanted. James decided it would be easier and raise fewer questions locally if they stuck with Jerry for now, aware that after reuniting the lad with his father, he would probably never see him again.

It was a sad thought. He had come to like the boy, despite his precociousness which, James assumed, came from his schooling. That thought had prompted him to discover the name of Jerry's school, and remembering the name as he yawned, reminded him that there were tasks to see to and a timetable to keep, and he slipped from the bed with the day planned.

It was nearly twelve by the time he and the others had washed, dressed and tidied the room. The landlady prepared them a fine feast as an early lunch, fussed over Jerry a while, and left them alone. They were the only customers in the inn, but they took the table furthest from the door for privacy should anyone else arrive.

'Right,' James said, once they were served and eating. 'I have a couple of messages to send, but there's nothing else we can do until the boat comes in at…?'

'Between half-past one and a quarter-to,' Jerry announced. 'I had a timetable in my dorm, so I knew when father would be back in the country.'

'I don't suppose you had a railway timetable too?' James asked, and when Jerry told him that he did, he was not in the least surprised.

'Not in my dorm, but I found one on the floor of the third-class truck when I was hiding. That was when I had to change trains at Plymouth. I was very bored until then, so it was good to have something to read. There are two afternoon trains from Newquay to the line change at Liskeard on a Friday,' he said. 'One that leaves before my father arrives, and one that leaves at thirteen minutes past two o'clock. There is an evening train which terminates at Lostwithiel, but only on a Sunday.' He beamed, pleased with himself.

James ruffled the lad's hair. 'Clever chap. So, in order to escort Mr

236

Irving and your father to Larkspur, we must catch the two thirteen.'
Turning to Fecker, he asked, 'You'll be able to take both horses back across country, won't you?'

'Da.'

'But before that, I must send the messages.'

'Can I come?' Jerry sat up, eager and smiling.

'Best not,' James said, and the boys' face fell. 'We don't know where Mr Smith might be, but we do know he is determined to snatch you away. You must stay here with Mr Andrej.'

'Da,' Fecker nodded as he poured tea into a tin mug.

'But I will be bored,' Jerry complained, pouting.

'Nyet. We play clobyosh.'

Jerry giggled. 'What's that?'

'With cards,' Fecker explained. 'Good game from Ukraine.'

'But not for money,' James warned. 'Which reminds me, how much have you got on you, Fecks? I'm down to a few shillings.'

Fecker had more in his wallet which he extracted from his socks, making James grimace and Jerry laugh.

'I have sixpence left over from my shillings,' Jerry offered. 'I had to use the rest to get here.'

'That's kind of you, Jerry,' James said. 'But you keep it.'

Having paid the landlady, there was enough left for a couple of succinct telegrams, train tickets, and some change for Fecker in case he needed to rest on his way overland to Larkspur.

With that matter dealt with, James left to send his messages. Walking along the quay, past women mending lobster pots and old men in their coats playing dominos, sailors' caps pulled about their ears, it was hard to imagine that the events of last night had taken place. The fishing port was picturesque with its white-painted cottages, swinging tavern signs and window boxes displaying spring flowers. Strangers nodded their heads in greeting, and he replied with a cheerful 'Good morning', stopping the first one he met to ask for directions which were willingly and pleasantly given along with good wishes and the hope that he would enjoy his visit in the town.

The pleasantries aside, he was wary and on the lookout for Mr Smith. Jerry had given him no indication of why Smith wanted to kidnap the boy. Presumably as a way of drawing Stoker to him.

Why anyone would want to kill a theatre critic and manager, was anyone's guess. As far as James knew, Stoker had only written a handful of short stories and one novel. 'The Primrose Path' was where Jerry had found his name. It wasn't a book that James knew, and not one that featured on Thomas' shelves either. James' lover preferred romantic novels that Archer called mind-numbing, while James had recently been reading the works of Tennyson, having met the man, works which were far more romantic than Thomas' romances, and far more exciting that Silas' penny dreadfuls. Considering both Lord Tennyson and Mr Stoker were to be guests at that evening's dinner, James thought Thomas would have been more interested in the works of those men than 'Seduce Me At Sunrise.'

His mind was wandering, but at least it was wandering towards Larkspur, and picturing Tom lying next to him in bed, reading and idly stroking James' thigh, put a smile on his lips. They would be doing that again before long, but in the meantime, he needed to send the good news that Jerry was safe.

Finding the telegraph office, he entered and approached the counter. The office was identical to the one he had worked in until last October, it even smelt of the same floor polish, but the permanent background tang of male sweat that pervaded that Riverside depot wasn't so pronounced. Fewer boys worked here and, considering the size of the fishing port against the city, that made sense.

The large clock behind the counter read one thirty as James stepped up to the clerk. The man raised his head from where he had been writing, and smiled.

'Aye, Sir. Help you?'

'Need to send two urgents,' James said, slipping easily into telegraph-boy dialect. 'But I'd like to be sure the receiving offices are open before I leave.'

The clerk turned to the clock, pushing himself by the counter with one hand and gripping his high stool with the other, groaning as if his back pained him.

'Aye, Sir,' he said, coming back to James with just as much discomfort. 'Only open for another hour today, but your messages will be delivered.'

238

'Good.'

James had composed the telegrams in his head during the walk, but he stepped aside to write them on the telegraph form. The first was to Thomas and it was as short as he could make it.

Jerry safe. Smith missing. Beware! Stoker is target. Meeting party from boat. Escorting to Larkspur. On schedule.

Thomas would be busy, but would ensure the relevant parts of the message reached Archer. If he telegraphed the viscount directly, the envelope wouldn't be opened until it was handed to His Lordship who would be distracted by the arrival of guests. Thomas would also inform Archer that James would be returning that afternoon in time to valet His Lordship and any gentlemen who hadn't brought their own servant.

Having reread the message and handed it to the clerk, he took another form and wrote to Jerry's headmaster at Summerhill.

Sir. Irving NT Stoker safe/well. Reuniting with father this pm. Explanation on his return. As yet unsure of date/time. Will inform. Irving sends abject apologies.

He signed it, 'JJ Wright, Assistant to Viscount Clearwater' because although he wasn't Archer's assistant, 'Valet to', wouldn't have carried as much weight.

When the clerk handed the forms back for James to check and agree the price, he reread both, found everything in order and paid. Most customers would have left to go about their business, but it was James' business to ensure the messages were sent, and he had paid extra for them to be treated as a priority. He waited at the end of the counter, listening for the click of the telegraph machine in the room behind reception, and only left the building once he had heard both receiving agencies accept the messages which, he was pleased to note, had been correctly coded.

The walk back to the inn was only marred by concerns for Thomas. It was the first time Tom would oversee the famous Larkspur Easter dinner. There had been other dinners, but only with local men and then only small parties. Tonight, James would return to find the Hall in all its glory, and a glittering table suitably laid for lords and ladies. Etiquette was paramount, as was discreet and silent service, and he imagined Mr Saddle taking a trembling Barnaby through his role as Thomas looked on. It wasn't merely a simple case of proper entertaining, Archer also had to impress his guests with flawless hospitality before turning their gratitude into financial reward for his foundation. On top of that there was his reputation as the new Viscount Clearwater, and beyond even that, his own ambition. Where his father had held his Easter dinner as a Christian and political event, Archer wanted to make his mark from the outset by inviting poets, actors and patrons of the arts. The servants knew this, and the only ones James could remember grumbling about the change of tradition were Mrs Baker (but only momentarily because she had enjoyed meeting the wives of bishops), and Mr Saddle who complained about everything.

'You've got it all sorted, Jimmy,' he told himself as he mounted the steps to the police station. 'One last thing and you're done.'

'Hello again, Sir.' The constable stood behind a desk sipping a cup of tea.

'Ah, Constable…' James slipped back into his refined, working voice. 'I wondered if there was any news of the abductor?'

''Fraid not, Sir.' The policeman put his cup back in its saucer and dabbed his moustache with his sleeve. 'Your man, the Russian, saw him off as far as Trencreek, far as I can tell. Ain't much after that until Burngullow depot. Probably hopped it on the night freight to Plymouth most likely.'

James wasn't so sure.

'Possibly,' he said. 'But whoever he was, he was very determined to do harm to the boy, and we shan't be leaving here until this afternoon. Will your men keep a lookout for him?'

'Already doing that, Sir. Got a description of the man going around town.'

'That's reassuring, thank you.'

'Can I ask why he was chasing the young gentleman?'

'No idea,' James lied. 'But it was with enough menace to force Jerry to flee into a boat in panic.'

'Aye. Nasty business. One thing's for sure, he won't be from 'round these parts.'

'No, of course not.' James considered whether he should inform the police of Smith's real purpose, but decided against it. To bring the Romanian Protectori into the equation would only complicate matters and require more explanation than he was willing to give. As long as the local constabulary was still alert, he doubted Smith would try again. The boat would be arriving soon, there would be a crowd of people, and all he and Fecker needed to do was escort Mr Stoker and his son to the train where they could be easily guarded. If Smith had doubled back to the Hall, Archer and Danylo were expert swordsmen.

'Thank you, Constable,' he said. 'I'll leave it in your hands.'

He left the police station with an air of confidence that covered nervousness brought on by a series of questions. What if there were no crowds at the boat? The town wasn't that big, and he doubted many people took the tender, so there might not be that many passengers disembarking; Smith could easily single out Stoker. Perhaps the customs officers would be busy and distracted by the arrival. What if Smith was lying in wait, ready to shoot Stoker from a distance? What if there was a crowd and Smith was able to sneak among them, grab Jerry and flee?

Checking the time, he decided to take a look at the landing stage at the far end of the harbour and speak to the customs officials, making it clear that he was concerned for a young boy's safety, and reinforcing the police's warning.

The boat was due in half an hour, and he called into the inn as he passed to discover Jerry and Fecker calmly playing cards at the table. It was comforting to see the lad laughing and relaxed, though Fecker looked annoyed, as if he was losing.

'Just going to see if I can see the boat,' he said. 'Get the things ready, Fecks, yeah?'

Without waiting for an answer, he continued on to the customs house where a uniformed man sat smoking a pipe and reading a newspaper. Beside him, two elderly men sat drinking beer from bottles. Another pleasant sight, perhaps but what worried James was the lack of anybody else.

'Good afternoon,' he greeted the man affably while scanning the quayside for signs of activity. 'Are you the harbour master?'

'That I am, Sir. Be helping you?'

'Yes, please. I am meeting some people off the St Merrynporth. Can you confirm its arrival time?'

'I can, Sir.' The man knocked his pipe to empty it. 'Landed at ten thirty this morning.'

At first, James thought he had misheard. 'Ten thirty? I didn't see it.' At that time, he had been standing at the window admiring the view while Jerry dressed and Fecker used the bathroom.

'No, you wouldn't have done,' the harbourmaster said. 'Not unless you got telescopes for eyes.' He began filling his pipe. 'The Britannic tender were forced to land at Penzance on account of the storm. Passengers would have got off there. St Merrynporth will be back 'ere in a day or so.'

James' mind shifted gears, out of shock and into logic. He thanked the man and hurried back to the inn, calculating time and distance and wishing Jerry had kept the railway timetable. The only comforting thoughts were that Smith wouldn't have known the information either, and Thomas would soon be aware that Stoker was in danger and from whom. There was a chance that Silas had found the answer they needed and was back at the Hall, had convinced Archer and alerted the authorities, but with no way of knowing, he had to assume he was on his own.

For all he knew, Smith might be there now, wheedling his way back in and preparing to murder the man as soon as he arrived.

Forcing himself to calm down and think more clearly, he walked into the inn to find Fecker and Jerry ready with their bags.

'Well?' Jerry said, his eyes wide and eager. 'Is it coming?'

'No.'

The clock behind the bar struck two.

'We've got thirteen minutes to get to the station,' James said before calling for the landlady. 'Your father's already on his way to the Hall, Jerry. We can catch the train and be there in three hours. You'll be okay with the horses on your own, Fecks?'

'Da. I tell you this. Only six hours, I be there for supper.'

'What's up, me duck?' Mary appeared from upstairs.

'Where's the railway station?'

'Up into town, along East Street. About a mile. Why?'

'Will we make it in thirteen minutes?'

'You will if you run, love,' she replied. 'But there ain't no point.

Be Easter Friday, and there ain't no more trains leaving Newquay today.'

Jerry took hold of James' hand. 'What are we going to do, Uncle Jimmy?'

'Da,' Fecker snorted. 'What we do, Tato?'

'We'll have to ride,' James groaned. 'And you still haven't told me what Tato means.'

Fecker laughed as he made for the door. 'I saddle horses,' he said, adding pointedly, '*Daddy*.'

Twenty-Four

Larkspur was alive with activity as Thomas met Mrs Baker in the servants' passage outside his pantry. She bustled towards him trailed by two maids he didn't recognise, and they were followed by Lady Marshall's footman, Oleg. Lucy and Sally came from the other direction carrying towels fresh from the laundry. The Larkspur maids veered off to the backstairs as the housekeeper brought her party to a halt.

'This is Mr Payne,' she explained to the two women behind her before introducing them to Thomas. 'Lady Marshall's lady's maid, Mrs Sweet you may know, and the Countess', Mrs Beeton.'

The women, both in their mid-thirties, Thomas guessed, made a small curtsey.

'Any relation?' Thomas asked.

'My aunt,' Mrs Beeton replied.

'I am sure Mrs Baker is looking after you. I won't keep you.' Turning to Oleg, he greeted him with a handshake which surprised the Russian. 'Welcome, Oleg. Mr Andrej will be pleased to see you when he gets back.'

'Any news?' Mrs Baker asked, her attention on the servants' hall at the end of the passage.

'Not yet,' Thomas replied. 'We've not had word from either Mr Wright or Mr Hawkins.'

'Her Ladyship brought me to help, Mr Payne,' Oleg said, his long face drooping from a head held high above his tall frame. 'Use me in any way you want.'

Thomas thanked him, relief flowing through his veins. 'Earl Romney has his man, but Lord Tennyson is visiting alone. I will valet Lord Clearwater if his valet doesn't return soon, but perhaps you could assist Lord Tennyson?'

'A pleasure.'

'Good man. The other gentlemen had said they didn't require a valet, but best be prepared. Is everything alright, Mrs Baker?'

'It will be in a minute,' she said. 'I must get on.'

She led her party towards the servants' hall barking at gossiping maids and scattering them like geese, and Thomas returned to his pantry, noting the time and running through his mental checklist. The most important task was to finish decanting the wine, currently on his desk. Sitting, he draped a clean muslin over the decanter and carefully lifted the open bottle of Mediasch. Holding it steady, he let it trickle slowly through the muslin until the decanter was full and the bottle nearly empty.

He had just placed the decanted wine on the sideboard with the others when the sounds of activity in the servants' hall ground to a halt and the scraping of chairs told him that someone from above stairs had come down. A second later, Archer appeared in the doorway in his trousers and a shirt, holding a cravat in one hand.

'My Lord,' Thomas stood.

Archer glanced back along the corridor where the sounds of industrious work had resumed, and then looked the other way before stepping in and closing the door. Having made sure they were alone, his shoulders slumped, and he said, 'Tom, I'm in a mess.'

'What can I do to help, Sir?'

Archer threw himself into the armchair, and his arms flopped either side as if he was a rag doll.

'I don't understand myself,' he said, staring straight ahead. 'I can make speeches in the House of Lords, I can fight Quill on the top of a moving train, I have trapped a judge in his own net in open court, and I've entertained more than nine people many times. Why then do I feel so out of my depth? My apprehension is starting to show. I just tore a strip off poor Barnaby for no reason other than saying aye instead of yes, and it's all because of Silas. Please tell me you've heard from him? He must be here to give his view on the Foundation and show these people how they can change young men's lives. Half the Garrick Club are here to meet him, and he's buggering about somewhere trying to prove the delightful Mr Smith is an assassin. Bloody idiot. Have you had any news?'

Having let the viscount vent with words he didn't mean, Thomas adopted a calming tone. 'No, My Lord, we have not had any messages for the last two days.'

'Damn odd, and it's not helping my state of mind. Where the hell is he?'

'Clearwater House.'

'I know that!'

Archer's nervousness was manifesting itself as anger. It might have been unfair on Barnaby, but perhaps it was justified towards Silas. Thomas, too, was annoyed with the secretary and concerned about the lack of communication from James.

'I've not heard from Mr Wright or Mr Andrej either,' he said. 'Mr Williams was very helpful collecting guests from the railway station this afternoon, but I have had to ask Lady Marshall's footman to valet Lord Tennyson. Luckily, Mr Roxton and the other… theatricals are happy to look after themselves.'

'It's going to be a shambles, I can feel it. I don't know what's wrong with me.'

Thomas did.

'Stand up, Sir,' he said as he came around the desk.

Archer obeyed, and Thomas led him to the full-length mirror. Standing behind, he straightened the viscount's collar and clicked the back stud properly into place before taking his cravat. 'You are without Silas,' he said. 'You're worried about him, and it's affecting you. He knows to be here in time for the dinner, and I am sure he will be. Likewise, James will be back before long, and all will be well.'

Thomas laid the cravat over Archer's shoulders, and working from his reflection, began to fold it into shape.

'We almost had a row,' Archer said. His words came more quietly than before, a sign that he was calming. 'Maybe he's staying away on purpose.'

'On purpose?'

'To get his own back.'

Thomas stopped in his work and raised his eyes to his master's. 'Is this a Thomas and Archer moment?' he asked. 'Or viscount and butler?'

'Tom and Archer.'

'Then, Archie, don't be so bloody stupid,' Thomas tutted as he continued to tie the cravat. 'Of course Silas isn't staying away on purpose. I expect he is on the train right now, or even in a cab from the station. You know why he went away, don't you?'

'Chasing after some notion that the amiable fellow, Smith, was a danger to me.'

'Quite.'

'But, Tom…'

Thomas put a finger on Archer's lips, and their reflected eyes met.

'Whatever Silas is doing, there's nothing you can do about it now. The same goes for James. Of course, I'm worried about them both, Jimmy more so for obvious reasons, but I know, as do you, that whatever they are doing, they are doing it for your good. There.' The cravat was neatly in place. 'Do you have your pin?'

Archer handed it to him, and coming to stand facing his friend, Thomas carefully pinned the centre of the cravat. 'You look splendid,' he said. 'Or you will when you put on your jacket.'

'Should I have worn the bow tie?' Archer was fussing again. 'I mean, what's the norm in the city doesn't have to be the norm here, does it? Will the cravat offend anyone?'

Thomas rolled his eyes. 'Deep breath,' he said. 'Now, would you like to sample the wine? I've decanted the Purcari which travelled from Plymouth better than I did, I have to say, and the Mediasch is just settling.'

Thomas stepped away, but Archer took his arm. 'Thank you, Tom,' he said, radiating sincerity. 'Really, thank you.'

For a moment, Thomas thought they were going to kiss, and his heart skipped a beat, but instead, the viscount smiled sadly. Whether they wanted to or not, they both knew it couldn't happen.

'Not at all, Sir. Now, will you taste the Mediasch?'

'Ah, that wine,' Archer said, a smile trying to break on his lips. 'They are going to be so impressed.'

'I should think so. Will one bottle be enough? I can bring up more. For something so rare, there is rather a lot of it in your cellar.'

The smile grew. 'My grandfather,' Archer said. 'Avid collector and connoisseur, and made the wise investment of buying as many crates as he could before the vineyard was blighted.'

'Which is why it's so difficult to come by, I assume,' Thomas said.

'Unless, of course, one has access to the Larkspur cellar.'

'Quite.' The smile was complete, and Archer pointed to the decanter. 'It will follow well after the Purcari. Do you know, the Mediasch has not been drunk by any members of the Garrick for well over thirty years. Do you think I should sell them some?'

'I should see how it has aged first. Are you sure you don't want to taste? It should have breathed by now.'

'No, Tom. That honour is for our guests.' Archer saw the time. 'Hell, I must finish dressing.'

'I'll come and help before I inspect the dining room,' Thomas said.

'No, it's fine, Tom, honestly. You have enough to do, and I saw the dining room. It looks superb.'

'All the same, I will check. Mr Saddle is as nervous as the rest of us. Very unlike him. I doubt he has made any mistakes, but still, I had better be safe.'

'I'll get out of your way.'

'Very good, Sir, and don't worry about Silas, I am sure all is well.'

It wasn't.

At that moment, Silas was pacing the platform of Plymouth railway station waiting for news of the connection to Larkspur. The carriage was there and connected to the locomotive, which was ready to leave, but no-one had provided the passengers with an explanation for the delay.

'What is it?' he asked as Jake came running back from the engine where he had gone to speak with the driver.

'They say it's not going to go,' Jake reported, out of breath. 'Something about the fireman walking out on account it's a holy day, and he doesn't agree with the line being sold to Great Western, or something.'

'Shit! We've been here half an hour, the other passengers are turning nasty, and the telegraph office is shut. I can't even let Archer know I'm going to be late, let alone how Stoker is going to be killed.'

'Can we get a cab?'

'It's thirty miles, mate. We'd never get there in time.'

At the front of the train, the guard threw up his hands and raised his voice.

'Hang on,' Silas said, a thought landing in his mind as the hands of the station clock clunked into place at seven. 'It's the fireman, you say?'

'Yeah. And there ain't another one. Everything's shutting down for the night.'

'The fireman just shovels coal, right?'

'I don't know. I suppose. What you doing?'

Silas was taking off his coat. He handed it to Jake and removed his jacket. 'Get the bags,' he said, 'and meet me down the front.'

'There's only one carriage. Front of what?'

'The train, what else?'

Jake realised Silas' intention and gasped. 'Will they let you?'

'If they don't want an angry mob on their hands, they will,' Silas said, rolling his sleeves. 'And it ain't going to be just me. From now on, Jake, we're two workers from the... I don't know, from the Eastern Railway Company, and we're anxious to get the service running. Leave the taking to me, and I'll meet you there in a minute.' He marched to the locomotive, shouting, 'Oi! Driver. I heard you need a fireman.'

The dining room was, as Archer had said, splendid, and between them, Saddle and Barnaby had done a good job. Ten places had been laid with settings for five courses, each piece of cutlery was the exact distance from the table edge, and the various wine glasses were perfectly placed.

At seven fifteen, Thomas used his pocket ruler to double-check the settings as he circled the table, Saddle following silently in his wake. In the centre, a row of fresh flowers was interspersed with silver cruet sets at equal distances, and among them, candelabras stood tall and elegant, the candlewicks trimmed and ready for lighting. Thomas would do that just before the dinner gong sounded, but before then, there was the sideboard to inspect.

The mirrors reflected the dazzle of the chandeliers, and the line of decanters, stoppered now and given one final wipe with a soft cloth, reflected the light from the wall sconces where the gas hissed quietly. They would have to be turned down before long, to bring a warmer atmosphere to the room, but one no less glittering. Beside the wine, the long sideboard was correctly prepared with the serving spoons and mats for the hot dishes, the footmen's white gloves and towels.

'You have done well, Mr Saddle,' Thomas said, viewing the table from a distance. 'I am very grateful.'

Saddle was distracted and didn't reply. The man's face was pale and his brow tight in thought.

'Is something the matter?' Thomas asked. 'You're not unwell, are you?'

'No, Mr Payne,' Saddle replied, his voice hoarse as if his throat was dry. 'I'm glad you like it. I suppose I should say thank you for giving me the chance to show my abilities.'

That sounded like sarcasm to Thomas, who decided not to honour the statement with a reply. Saddle's attitude grated; it always had done, and he could make even a thank you sound as if the recipient should be grateful he'd spoken to them at all.

'It's nearly time,' Thomas said. 'I will light the table candelabras and then attend the library. You can light the sideboard.'

'Yes, Mr Payne.'

Even that sounded like an insult, and Thomas' skin prickled. Lighting a taper, he carried it to the table and began setting the flame to each trimmed wick in turn, his back to the sideboard. Starting at Lord Clearwater's chair at the head of the table, he had just reached Lady Marshall's place at the other end, when the taper died. Turning back to the sideboard for a match, he was surprised to see Saddle still at the decanters fiddling with his pocket watch.

'Get a move on,' Thomas yapped.

'Yes, sorry,' Saddle flustered, stepping back and closing the watch.

'And why have you put your gloves on to light candles?'

'Oh, yes... Sorry, Mr Payne.'

'What's got into you, Saddle?'

Thomas was losing his patience. First Archer in a panic and now his under-butler looking as though he was unable to cope with the simple task of setting the flames. He tutted, and had just lit the last candle when the dinner gong sounded from the hall, its deep, medallic boom reverberating through the ground floor.

'Right. Saddle, go down and start bringing up the first course.'

Barnaby appeared between the double doors. 'I rang the gong, Mr Payne.'

'Yes, Barnaby, I think they heard it in Bodmin. Assist Mr Saddle with the dishes.'

'Right you are, Sir.'

'And don't call me Sir.'

'No, Sir.'

'Dear God! I am surrounded by fools,' Thomas muttered as he left them to it.

He reached the library door just as Archer opened it from the inside. 'Ah, there you are Payne,' he said. 'Are we ready?'

'We are, My Lord.'

Archer stepped aside, allowing Thomas to enter the room where he caught Lady Marshall's eye. As she was the hostess in place of Archer's mother, it was her duty to invite the guests to the table which she did in her usual unorthodox way.

'The feast is upon us,' she announced. 'Overture and beginners, Mr Irving. Half a league onwards, Lord Tennyson.'

Thomas hurried as sedately as possible back across the hall and was at the dining room doors as the party began to arrive. It was an impressive procession. Lady Marshall led Countess Romney at the head, their sparkling full-length gowns rustling, and their Parisian perfumes following obediently in waves. Earl Romney, wearing his military dress uniform, was deep in conversation with Cadwell Roxton, but the opera singer was clearly not impressed with the man.

'So you're a singer?' The earl asked as he passed, ignoring Thomas. 'Not music hall, I hope?'

'No, Your Lordship, opera. You heard me at Covent Garden last year at the Foundation's gala?' He rolled his eyes at Thomas as he passed, but the butler made no reaction.

Behind them came Henry Irving and his manager, both men tall and strapping, the actor talking to Arthur Sullivan on his other side. Thomas breathed deeply and silently, calming his excitement at being in the presence of a great composer and even greater actor, and quelling a rush of anxiety.

The sight of Archer assisting Lord Tennyson by the elbow as the old man walked with a cane, reassured him that the viscount had recovered from his earlier skittishness and was thinking of his guests. That would take his mind from the absent Silas.

Thomas followed the party into the dining room and closed the doors. Barnaby and Saddle stood behind the ladies' chairs, ready to seat them, while Thomas took up his place at a discreet distance behind Archer and his two guests of honour, one either side of the viscount with the actor on his right and Stoker on his left.

It was during the dinner that Archer intended to gently persuade Irving to assist with the Foundation, and having his business manager on his other side, would allow him to deal with any questions as to the benefit of such involvement. The conversation would later open up to the other guests, Tennyson and Sullivan in particular as they, along with Mr Roxton, were members of the Garrick Club, Archer's reasoning being that if he had such illustrious men on his side, others would follow. It was all for the good of the young men of the East End who had no option but to resort to prostitution as a way to survive, and that was not the easiest of subjects to bring up to any man, let alone men acutely aware of their public standing and reputations.

The dinner was being held for the benefit of men like Silas who should have been here to represent the success of Archer's foundation, and Silas knew that. Something bad must have happened for his place to remain empty, but Thomas hid his concern as he turned his attention to the service. Whatever was taking place beyond Larkspur's walls, nothing must go wrong within them.

Knowing Silas as he did, Thomas would not have been surprised to learn that he was, at that moment, ankle-deep in coal amid smoke and steam, shovelling fuel to Jake below. Jake, in turn, heaved it into the boiler as the delayed service from Plymouth to Bodmin steamed through Liskeard with its whistle screaming.

Twenty-Five

The first course had passed without a hitch, and the second was coming to a close. Only three more wines remained to be served, the Purcari, the Mediasch and the dessert wine. Barnaby had behaved exactly as Thomas had trained him to, and at times, had outshone Saddle who continued to show signs of tension or illness, it was hard say which. Although the under-butler hadn't done anything to embarrass the viscount and had been surreptitious when mopping his brow, Thomas kept a close eye as he stood to the side just within Archer's line of sight.

The conversation had gone exactly as Archer wanted. After some initial pleasantries and general chat about the Hall and its history, something which particularly interested Lord Tennyson, the viscount turned to Mr Irving, asking about his tour and his journey home.

'Bit of storm during the night,' the actor informed the party. 'Blew up south-west of Cork. At first, I thought it would carry us towards the channel with speed, but the swell was too great. I feared we might be washed up on a shore as if Prospero himself had conjured the elements. Am I right, Stoker?'

'That you are, and that it was, to be sure,' Mr Stoker agreed in his clipped, Irish brogue. 'We had some luck, and it passed quickly, but left the women fairly shaken.'

'Which is why we ended up in Penzance,' Irving continued. 'And again, Lord Clearwater my apologies for our early arrival.'

'Not at all, Sir,' Archer smiled. 'I am glad the extra time ashore has rested you.' Turning to Mr Stoker, he said, 'I understand you are a keen sportsman, Sir. Tell me, do you fence?'

'I have done,' the Irishman replied, nodding. 'Not for some time now. Why d'you ask?'

'My assistant gamekeeper is from the Ukraine and served

alongside the British before moving here,' Archer said. 'He has been teaching my secretary the skill, and I wondered if you might like to take some sport during your stay. I am sure Mr Danylo would be honoured to oblige.'

'Very fine of you,' Stoker said, dabbing his red beard with his napkin to ensure it was clear of debris. 'Perhaps I may think on it.'

'You should do it, Bram,' Irving encouraged. 'You could give me some practice for the stage by parrying with me in the office.'

At the other end of the table, Lady Marshall engaged the Earl and Countess Romney in conversations about fashion for her, and the theatre for him as a way of bringing her nephew, Roxton, into the discussion, while Lord Tennyson, opposite the composer, asked what Sullivan was currently writing.

'Another as good as The Yeomen, I hope?' the old man enquired.

'It will be better,' Sullivan replied. 'We are working on a piece set in Italy on the canals, but Gilbert can't resist knocking on about the divisions in our own class system. I will be having words when I return.'

Thomas listened to the chatter while ensuring the wine glasses were topped to respectable levels and making sure Barnaby didn't slouch. Noting who had finished and who was dawdling, he also kept eye contact with Archer ready to bow his head gently when the last guest had finished their course. It happened to be Lady Marshall, which didn't surprise him as she was the most talkative, and having given Archer a nearly invisible nod, the viscount made a more obvious one by reply.

'Thank you, Payne,' he said, and the servants stepped forward to clear the plates.

Saddle and Barnaby removed them to the sideboard and from there to the servery behind the servants' door where, out of sight, the maids took them below stairs. Meanwhile, Thomas supervised, on hand should his master require anything, and ensuring that no guest was left unattended.

It was as the third course was served and the Purcari poured, that, picking up on what Sullivan had said about class distinctions, Archer made his move on Irving and turned the conversation to the charity. At first, the actor was wary and appeared uninterested, but when Earl Romney heard what was being discussed and joined

254

in with enthusiasm, followed by Lady Marshall, the actor was more convinced.

'I was hoping that Mr Hawkins would be here to discuss this with us,' Archer said.

'Yes, where is he, Clearwater?' Roxton asked from along the table. 'I should like to see him again. Remarkable little fellow, if unconventional.'

'He is away on an important errand,' Archer said, but when it became obvious his guests were waiting for a further explanation, he dried and looked at Thomas. 'You know, don't you, Payne?' he asked hopefully.

'The work of the Foundation must continue even at Easter, My Lord,' Thomas answered. 'Mr Hawkins did say he would not leave the Foundation until all your matters were seen to. He is, as you know, very conscientious.'

'Sounds like a decent fellow,' Stoker said. 'As decent as this wine, Your Lordship. Do I recognise it?'

'Mr Hawkins is, as Mr Roxton says, sometimes unorthodox,' Archer replied, after a grateful nod to his butler. 'I think you will like him, he is from the Emerald Isle like you.'

'Is he? Where?'

'Near Dublin, I believe. Well...' Archer corrected himself before he misled his guest. 'That is, his mother was from there, and Mr Hawkins was conceived in Ireland, but was born in the Canter Wharf area of Westerpool.'

'Fashionably called the slums,' Lady Marshall threw down the table to add some colour. 'Though to see the way Clearwater has raised him up from that pit to his current station, you wouldn't believe it. And that, Mr Irving, is exactly how the Foundation works. It takes unfortunates and gives them a stab at success.'

'We could all do with some of that,' Irving said. 'I'll get my man here to talk to yours when he arrives. The work sounds interesting, eh, Stoker?'

'Certainly, Henry. But the wine, Sir?'

'Ah. Apologies,' Archer said raising his glass. 'I have a victualler in Plymouth who imports from Carpathia. My ancestry comes down through the region, in part at least, and my grandfather had a love of Romanian wines. This is a Purcari-Dragasani that Payne found for us. What I have next is a surprise from the cellar.'

'Well, it's very fine,' Stoker enthused. 'I'm currently researching that area for a novel I have in me which is going to take some years to come out. I want to get the story correct in detail, and there's a stack load of history to research. Would you be willing to talk further sometime?'

'Of course,' Archer said. 'We could also discuss ways in which the Lyceum could help the Foundation. I have always believed that one good deed deserves another.'

'Of course, Sir,' Stoker said, chuckling at Archer's cheek. 'If it's not impertinent, may I ask how you're descended through Romania?'

'The Rasnov line. It is centuries old,' Archer explained. 'And I am only on the outskirts of it as it dies away. Rasnov is near Brasov, south of Bran where Her Ladyship is currently still holidaying. I must admit, I am no expert on the matter, but here's a connection which might interest you. There was an accident with the railway line on Monday...'

'Oh, don't!' Lady Marshall complained. 'We had a most difficult journey to our rest stop in Plymouth last night, didn't we, Tennyson?'

'I found it rather entertaining,' the old man said, cocking his head to hear Her Ladyship more clearly. 'Difficult, was it?'

'Only in that we took The Cornishman, and it travels at a horrifying speed. One was quite unable to relax.'

'Talking of railways,' Tennyson said. 'Where's that handy fellow of yours, Clearwater? James Joseph, the one who charged my home in need of transport?'

'Mr Wright is my valet,' Archer explained to the company. 'His absence is another connection to the train incident I was trying to relate.' He raised his eyebrows to his godmother at the other end of the table, and suitably abashed, she mouthed, 'Sorry.'

'To answer your question, Sir,' Archer continued, addressing the poet. 'The unfortunate accident occurred on Monday last when the driver of the locomotive suffered what our doctor diagnosed as an attack of the heart. Apparently, the poor man must have fallen directly onto the regulating lever, thus taking the engine to its maximum speed. We assume the fireman rushed to his aid when he should have applied the brakes. People reported hearing the whistle and the brakes were applied, probably by the guard, but by then, it was too late. The train hurtled through a station, approached a bend, and came free of the tracks. Payne here was aboard.'

The moment flashed through Thomas' mind faster than the locomotive had sped through Bodmin Road, and he closed his eyes momentarily. When he opened them, the entire party was looking at him aghast, expecting him to continue the story.

'It was a tragic event,' he said. 'I was one of the lucky survivors.'

'Indeed,' Archer continued, seeing Thomas' controlled distress. 'Several were not as fortunate. However, two of those who were, wound up here at Larkspur. One was a man Payne saved from the wreckage just before it exploded, a fascinating man called Smith.'

'Fascinating?' Countess Romney questioned. 'In what way?'

'He bore the mark — and this is what will interest you, Stoker — of what I thought was the *Protectorul regalității Râșnov*, the protectors of Rasnov royalty. My secretary, the absent Mr Hawkins, undertook some research and discovered that in fact, it was the mark of the *Protectori ai Szekely*.'

'The protectors of the Szekely people,' Stoker said, pointing his fork at Irving. 'The ones I warned you about. Devilish fellows still bent on upholding the good name of the race no matter what.'

'No matter what?' Countess Romney again sought clarification.

'Anyone who crossed them got murdered,' was Stoker's blunt reply.

Thomas' attention was suddenly drawn to a clattering at the sideboard, and looking across, he saw Saddle gripping its edge, trying unsuccessfully to steady himself. He had knocked over the sugar shakers on the dessert tray. Thomas flashed him a furious stare, and with a twitch of his finger, held Barnaby back from running to assist. Saddle righted himself, but had blanched to the colour of his gloves. Thomas was wondering whether he should fetch Oleg to replace the man when the under-butler indicated he was well and regained his upright posture.

Irving had politely ignored the interruption and pointed a long, perfectly placed finger to his manager. 'Good job they're extinct, Bram,' he said. 'Considering how your main character for the "Un-Dead" is a blood-sucking nobleman of the Szekely tribe.'

'They are a race, Henry.' Stoker was more interested in what the viscount had to say. 'And this man bore the ink mark of the Protectori, Your Lordship?'

'He did, or so I was informed. I asked him about it over dinner, and he assured me it was now merely tradition in the way that sailors mark themselves with anchors and names of ports visited. You have nothing to fear, Mr Stoker. The Protectori no longer operate their subversive practices.'

'Where is this chap now? I should like to speak with him.'

'Sadly, he had to leave us,' Archer replied. 'He was on business when the accident occurred and, despite an injury to his leg, needed to continue his journey.'

'Ah, shame.'

'And, to answer *your* question, My Lord…' Archer turned his attention to Tennyson. 'Also aboard the train was a boy of no more than nine years. The only survivor of the third-class wreckage, he was pulled free by Mr Wright and my horse master, Mr Andrej.'

'You see,' Tennyson said, raising his glass. 'I knew it. The man is Sir Galahad, Clearwater. You seem to have a stable full of 'em.'

Thomas inspected the sideboard to hide his smile, picturing James clunking about in armour and saving distressed damsels.

'I think Mr Wright would be the first to disagree,' Archer said. 'Only because he is modest. We had the boy here for a while but, as young people do, he took himself off in the night for no reason. Mr Wright went in search of him, and that's why he is absent.'

'Are you able to control any of your staff, Clearwater?' Earl Romney said with a laugh.

'Me? No, not a chance,' Archer replied in good humour. 'Luckily I have Payne for that.'

'Well, they sound like a very chivalrous lot,' Tennyson said. 'Bravo, Mr Payne.'

Thomas spun on his heels to receive the compliment and gave a gracious bow.

'So, Sir,' Stoker said. 'You and I have an interest in that region of the world known for its mystery and rather violent history. Can you tell me more of your Rasnov ancestors?'

The conversation returned to Archer's family and the novel Stoker was planning, but the viscount was able to bring it back to the Foundation by the time they had finished eating.

258

'And now I must ambush you, Mr Irving,' he said, as the third course was cleared. 'We spoke briefly in the library about the possibility of the Lyceum hosting a gala performance in aid of the Clearwater Foundation. We had a huge success with our first event last year, and we...' he offered his hand to Lady Marshall and the Earl, 'would be most honoured to have you patronise the organisation in some way. You too, Mr Sullivan, Mr Stoker.'

'Trying to get the entire Garrick Club onboard, are we, Clearwater?' The Earl grinned. 'Artists and actors much more likely to help the young men of the streets in return for the adoration, eh?' His grey moustache twitched at what he thought was a joke.

It fell flat when Lady Marshall said, 'Yes, Dickie, and why not?'

Irving rescued the Earl from embarrassment by asking for more details of Archer's proposal, and the viscount guided the conversation effortlessly back to the work of the charity. It continued as the plates were taken, the used wine glasses removed, and the next course was brought to the sideboard.

By the time the fourth course was being served, Irving had heard enough and was persuaded to Archer's cause.

'Up to you,' he said across the table to Stoker. 'Sounds like a simple one-off event to me. Easy to pencil in between performances, or when we're dark for a day or so. Could bring extra publicity, not that we need it. I'll let you decide if we're going to do this. Have a think on it, but I say we go ahead with caution. Don't want to send the wrong signals.'

'The gala last year was held at the Opera House,' Roxton said, winking at Archer. 'I am sure the Lyceum could do better than they did.'

'Damn right, Sir,' Irving agreed fiercely, the ridge of his eyebrows raising before they came crashing together above his imposing nose. 'Over to you, Bram.'

Archer had done what he could, and to force their interest would be to overplay his hand.

'I would like to take a short break,' he said, between the courses. 'I have a treat for our guests newly returned from America.' He nodded to Irving and then Stoker before turning to Thomas. 'Payne, would you?'

This was Archer's moment, the jewel in the crown, the serving of one of the rarest wines available, and one from Carpathia to honour Irving and Stoker and clinch his deal. Assured and proud, Thomas strode to the sideboard and, under the quizzical gaze of His Lordship's guests, reached for the decanter.

Saddle gripped his wrist. The under-butler was paler than ever, and his glove was wet with sweat.

Glaring, Thomas struggled to free himself. 'What are you doing?' he hissed, but Saddle only held him more tightly.

'This isn't in any way a bribe,' Archer, behind him, was saying, 'but hearing of your success with your play about the Szekely people last year, Mr Irving, I thought I might indulge you.'

'Let go.' Thomas' words were spat through clenched teeth.

Saddle said nothing, his eyes were wide, but his mouth firmly closed.

'It wasn't actually mine.' Irving's naturally powerful voice covered the sound of Thomas' struggle. 'Stoker should have the credit for the writing. It was more an introduction to his work on "The Un-Dead." Am I right, Abraham?'

'You are, and thank you for the credit.'

Seeing the altercation, Barnaby positioned himself at Thomas' other side and removed a glove. He was attempting to silently prise Saddle's fingers, when the viscount asked, 'Everything alright, Payne?'

'Yes, My Lord.'

Barnaby's dug his fingernails into Saddle's flesh until he drew blood and Thomas was freed.

'We will have words, Saddle.' Furious, he composed himself and took the decanter across to the table under the expectant eyes of the entire party.

'What's this?' Irving asked, intrigued.

The wine was placed before the viscount, and Thomas stood back, ready to pour when called upon.

'We will all taste it,' the viscount said. 'But if my other friends would indulge me, I would like Mr Irving and Mr Stoker to try it first. I think you will find it of particular interest, Stoker, as it hails from the region of Transylvania in which you are so interested.'

'Another one?' Stoker said, his beard rising with his smile. 'The Purcari was fair-fine enough, Sir, but you intend to spoil us further?'

'Of course, and with one of the last remaining bottles of Golden Mediasch.'

'Good Lord!' Irving gasped. 'Lord Clearwater, I have already agreed to back your charity, there really is no need.'

'As I said, Henry, it is not a bribe. My grandfather laid down several crates in the cellar, and because you were both returning from what I knew would be a triumphant tour of your Romanian play, I simply thought it appropriate. Payne, would you pour?'

'My Lord.'

Thomas lifted the decanter aware that Saddle was whispering to Barnaby. With the viscount's glass filled, he walked to the far end of the table to serve Lady Marshall, as was the etiquette, and glared at Barnaby. Understanding, the footman carefully pushed Saddle away, ignored him, and faced the room.

'If I might indulge you, Sir,' Stoker said. 'Perhaps I might make a toast when the time is right.'

'Of course,' Archer replied.

Thomas returned to fill Irving's glass next, as he was the guest of honour, and then attended to the Earl and Countess, working around the table in order of seniority until every glass was filled.

When he was done, Stoker rose to his feet. An imposing figure, he bore down on the table with his intelligent features composed and serious. 'My Lords, Ladies and gentlemen,' he began. 'After a gruelling tour of America and a storm at sea, what more could a man ask than hospitality such as this? I have only been at Larkspur a few hours, but already I find it a place of tranquillity, beauty and most of all, generosity such as I have never known. I am honoured, Sir.' He tipped his head to Archer. 'To be invited, me, an immigrant myself from the shores of Ireland to be accepted among such company... Well, a privilege. I also find myself swayed to your cause to assist the unfortunates of our capital city, not by the work or because it's a charity, but because a man in your position has considered such kindness in the first place. It is a rare thing indeed to find in our higher classes the compassion needed to help those less fortunate, and I find it in all those present this evening. That said, I would like us to raise our glasses to our host, a man whose nobility and compassion outshines us all through his dedication to those in need.'

Stoker lifted his glass, and the men stood.

'Let us drink a toast,' Stoker concluded. 'To a collaboration between the Lyceum Theatre and the Clearwater Foundation, and to the mastermind behind it, Lord...'

The double doors crashed open, and mayhem ensued.

Twenty-Six

A figure dressed entirely in black stumbled into the room and took stock of the scene. Seeing Stoker lifting his glass to his lips, the intruder yelled 'No!', and threw himself at the author. The countess screamed, the Earl swore, and Tennyson fell back into his chair. Luckily, Thomas had just replaced the decanter, had he not, it would have fallen from his hand in shock as the scene unfolded in shards of images and snatches of sound, much as it had done when the railway carriage rolled over.

The intruder flew through the air and connected with Stoker, knocking his glass from his hand as he fell sideways with the impact.

'What the blazes?' Archer leapt one way while Irving jumped back, tripped on his chair and stumbled.

Another glass smashed, Thomas' heart pounded, and he dashed forward to put himself between the viscount and the assailant. A mass of pitch-black clothing writhed on the floor amid grunts and swearwords before the assassin rolled from Stoker and scrambled towards the sideboard. Thomas intercepted him, kicked the back of his knees and brought the man to the ground. Grabbing the filthy coat, he spun him around.

'Don't drink the wine!'

Thomas realised with horror, it was Silas.

Letting him go, he turned to face to the bemused guests. 'My Lord...' he began, an apology leaping instinctively to his throat.

'What the hell are you doing, Hawkins?' Archer roared.

'Don't touch the wine,' Silas yelled again, as he clambered to his feet.

Those guests holding a glass immediately put them on the table, and Barnaby helped Stoker to stand.

'I'm alright,' the author complained. 'Who is this banshee?'

Had it not been for his voice, it would have been impossible to recognise Silas. His face was black, making his teeth and eyes shine wildly, and his clothes were similarly covered. Clouds of soot rose as he brushed himself down with filthy hands.

'You had better explain yourself,' Archer barked before addressing his guests. 'My abject apologies, I have no idea…'

'It's poisoned,' Silas gasped, wiping some of the sweaty soot from his face. 'Your Golden wine stuff, Smith's poisoned it.'

A moment of stunned silence allowed him time to whip out a handkerchief and reveal more of his skin. Beneath the coal black, it glowed red as if he had run a mile.

'Don't be ridiculous.' Archer was the first to recover. 'Get out, Hawkins. We will discuss this later.'

'You and your staff, Clearwater,' the Earl muttered, as he comforted his wife.

'You were right', Silas pointed at Thomas. 'We found it. I sent a message. Is that it?'

Silas was clearly drunk or had been driven mad, but he had drawn Thomas into his madness, and all eyes were now turning to the butler.

'Is that the wine?' Silas insisted.

'What wine?' Thomas stammered.

'The Golden… Whatever.'

'Yes.'

'Has anyone drunk it?'

'We haven't had a bloody chance.' Archer's face was red and his fists were clenched. He took two strides towards Silas, reaching for his lapels, intent on hurling him from the room.

'Hold on, Clearwater.' It was Stoker's voice, and it drew Archer up short. 'You had better take a look at this.'

Attention focused on the broken glass. The rug was smoking and silently disintegrating where the wine had been spilt.

'Good Lord,' Irving said, looking to where his glass had landed. 'And here.'

Thinking quickly, Thomas took the water pitcher from the sideboard and tipped it onto the steaming mess where it hissed as if dousing a fire. Across the room, Barnaby did the same to the other spillage.

'I warned you,' Silas said as the guests looked on in stunned silence. 'Why did you serve it? I sent a telegram.'

'We have had no telegrams,' Thomas replied, the anger in his voice obvious. 'May I suggest,' he added with great restraint, 'that I take you to your rooms, and we make you more presentable.'

'No,' Irving cut him off as he took long strides around the table, bearing down on the viscount's secretary. 'I think I would like Mr Hawkins to explain the meaning of this display.'

'I would also be fascinated,' Tennyson said, with interest more than shock. 'A dramatic entertainment, Clearwater, but certainly one that needs clarification.'

'Well...' Archer couldn't find his words. 'Of course...'

'Mr Stoker, are you harmed?' Thomas took over.

'Takes a lot more than a rugby tackle to harm me,' Stoker said, brushing black dust from his dinner jacket. 'I'm fine, Payne.'

'Your Ladyship?'

'I think the countess is sufficiently recovered for an explanation,' Lady Marshall said, and the countess nodded. 'But some water would be appreciated.'

'Just don't drink the wine,' Silas repeated, dropping his coat over the damaged rug.

'Barnaby, serve Their Ladyships with water,' Thomas instructed. 'And Mr Saddle...? Where's Mr Saddle?'

'Said he had to go below stairs, Mr Payne,' Barnaby replied.

'Never mind him,' Archer fumed, red in the face with angry embarrassment. 'Barnaby, water. Everyone else sit, and we will get to the bottom of this. Hawkins, why are you covered in soot?'

'Been playing Othello?' Irving quipped. It may have been a release of tension, or he might have had a dark sense of humour, but it lightened the mood.

'Aye, well I'll explain, Sir,' Silas said. 'And I'll apologise for my appearance and what just happened, but first, if you don't mind, I'll get these glasses safely away.' He began collecting them from the table. 'Just in case anyone forgets and takes a mouthful.'

'By God, yes,' Sullivan said. 'One touch of that, and we'd all have been screaming in agony if not dead.'

'I'd never have sung again,' Roxton wailed, pale and trembling.

Silas was right. If the wine was poisoned with something so

corrosive, it was dangerous to leave it anywhere, and Thomas helped him move the glasses and decanter to the sideboard while the guests adjusted their clothing and accepted water from Barnaby.

'No wonder the Golden Mediasch is so rare,' Lady Marshall joked. 'One can only wonder how it is aged. In iron barrels, I assume.'

Surprisingly, the other guests thought it a witty remark; unsurprisingly, Archer did not. He had not yet taken his seat. Still angry, his eyes remained fixed on Silas, and it was difficult to know what he would say or do next.

Thomas held the viscount's chair saying, 'Sir?' with an expression that made it clear Archer should sit and be patient.

Clearing his throat with a growl, Archer sat and instinctively reached for a glass. It was halfway to his lips when he realised what he was doing. Luckily it was empty.

'This is safe, My Lord.' Barnaby filled the glass with water. 'I tested it.'

'It would have only been in the wine,' Silas said, glaring at Archer. 'I won't sit, Sir, if you don't mind, on account of the state of my clothes. I'll change when I've explained myself, and then if you think it necessary, will pack myself off to somewhere else and cause you no further embarrassment.' Matching Archer's glower, he added, 'My Lord.'

Only Thomas noticed the look that passed from one to the other, but in it, he saw the conflict between their love and Silas' behaviour, between the stately way Archer needed to be seen by the world and Silas' hot-headedness; the difference in their classes. The distance between them was huge, a gaping chasm forged by education, privilege and background. If Archer remained angry and said, 'Yes, go,' Silas would leave, and for the viscount's sake, never return, he loved the man that much. The chasm, however, could be bridged if Archer was able to see beyond his upbringing. If he was secure in his love for Silas, he would tell him to stay.

The viscount sighed deeply and swallowed.

'Your leaving won't be necessary, Hawkins,' he said. 'We can plainly see what might have happened had you not made your enthusiastic entrance, but what we need to know, is why was it necessary?'

'Heavens! Who on earth are you?'

Attention was suddenly drawn to Lady Marshall and another black-clad young man hovering in the doorway. The figure turned a bowler hat in his hands, and his feet shuffled from side to side beside a suitcase. Like Silas, he was dripping with sweat, and his face was streaked with lines of filth.

'Are you here to beg?' Lady Marshall asked, fixing lorgnettes to the bridge of her nose and giving the man a thorough inspection.

'I've done my share of begging, Your Ladyship,' the man said. 'But no.'

'He's with me.' Silas beckoned Jake into the room. 'Actually, it was Jake who figured out most of this.'

'Don't I know you?'

'Oh, hello, Mr Roxton, Sir!' Jake smiled, showing uneven teeth and the sparkling whites of his eyes picked out from the grime. 'Pleasure to see you again. It's Jake, Sir. You probably knew me as Tricky. Runner from the Opera House.' His offered hand caused Roxton to withdraw in horror.

'We'll get to that,' Silas said, leading Jake to stand with him at the head of the table. 'If you'd rather, My Lord, we can wash up and explain ourselves later.'

'Now.' Archer's anger was calming, but he was still not the mild-mannered host he had been. 'And quickly.'

Silas related his story as succinctly as possible. He told the party how he had suspected Mr Smith was not to be trusted, how he had gone to the city to find more information and while there, discovered that he was right. Mr Smith was, in fact, Protectori. What he wasn't sure about was why he should be at Larkspur, but when he uncovered more information, he realised with horror that Mr Stoker was the target because of a novel he was planning to publish. A message was sent to warn the viscount, he said, and Jake was of great help, but they were delayed on their return. It was only while on the train and out of communication that the penny dropped, and he knew how Mr Smith was to carry out the murder.

'By poisoning the wine?' Archer clarified.

'Yes, Sir,' Jake put in. 'Because that's how they used to do it in the past.'

'But Mr Smith left us days ago,' Archer countered. 'He is not here, and Payne only opened the bottle this evening.'

Silas continued his story and told them how the Protectori duped a follower, usually a servant, into doing their bidding.

'Unthinkable,' Archer said. 'A fantastic story, Mr Hawkins. Clearly, something was put in the wine at some point, but if you are casting aspersions on Payne…'

'I'm not, Sir,' Silas said, holding Thomas' worried gaze. 'Because I know Mr Payne is nothing but loyal to you and your house. Nor would I imagine Barnaby had anything to do with it as he helped me track down some information before I left.'

'One moment,' Irving interrupted. 'I am fascinated by all of this, but I have questions. Means, yes, by the involvement of a tricked fool, but motive? Opportunity? That is to say, how would anyone get poison into the wine, and why Mr Stoker?'

'For a reason we didn't discover,' Silas said, 'they usually did it by a watch or ring. Something that could contain the substance and not look suspicious.'

'A watch?' Thomas couldn't help but speak up. 'Barnaby, fetch Mr Saddle immediately and bring him here. Have Oleg help you if necessary. Quickly.'

Barnaby nodded once and slipped away through the servery.

'You suspect Saddle?' Archer asked, his brows raised.

'Strange behaviour all day, Sir. Constantly inspecting a pocket watch I have never seen before. He was fiddling with the decanters when he should have been lighting the candles. Of course, I had no reason to think…'

'No one is blaming you, Payne,' Stoker reassured him. 'Mr Hawkins has his facts correct, and that's something which interests me greatly.' He fixed his intense stare on Silas with all the authority his powerful frame possessed. 'Young man it took me weeks in the British Museum Library to research for last year's production, and a great many more to research the Szekely for my novel, and there is yet more to do. How did you come by this information so rapidly?'

Silas and Jake exchanged uneasy glances before Silas held his head high and answered.

'I went to London on the suggestion of my friends, Sir,' he began, his eyes darting to Thomas. 'He reasoned that your play, Mr Irving, was based on fact. The critic, Mr Shaw, had said so in the newspaper, so Mr Payne thought you must have had information.'

'And you were quite right, Payne,' Stoker said with a sideways glance at the butler. 'It's in my office.' Returning his suspicious attention to Silas, he said, 'So how…?'

'Cabinet two, wasn't it, Jake?'

'That's right, Mr Silas, Sir.'

'The theatre is dark. Who let you in?'

'Um, that would be me, Sir,' Jake said.

'Now *I* am confused.' It was Irving's turn to be drawn further into the mystery. 'You said you work at the Opera House.'

'I did, Sir, yes.'

'And I don't know you from the Lyceum. He's not one of ours, is he, Stoker?'

Stoker shook his head, but as he thought, a smile began to grow between his beard and his moustache.

'You may have seen him outside it, though.' Silas had a hint of annoyance in his voice. 'Begging by the stage door after the opera fired him when his granddad died.'

'Oh, you poor child,' Lady Marshall sympathised. 'Clearwater, we must help this young man.'

'My fault.' Silas looked directly at Archer. 'I was meant to ask Lady Marshall if she had a place for young Jake in her fashion house. He's excellent at sewing, Your Ladyship. Studies costume and fashion, and was a great help to me during last year's gala. I felt I owed him a returned favour, but failed to act on it.'

Thomas knew the full story. It was Archer who had promised to help Jake, not Silas. The fault was his, but Silas had again rescued the viscount from embarrassment.

'I've got it!' Stoker clapped his hands and pointed to Jake. 'Casby's Worldwide Emporium?'

''Fraid so, Sir,' Jake said, unable to hold back a grin. Reaching into his coat pocket, he drew out Stoker's rolled up notes and handed them over. 'We took nothing else, honest, and without them, you might not be here now. Sorry about the soot and stuff.'

'I don't follow.'

'I will explain later, Irving,' Stoker said. 'You know, Lord Clearwater, when your man flew at me just now, I was in a good mind to tell you what to do with your Foundation, excuse my manners, ladies. But these boys have shown such ingenuity…' The man was trembling as the enormity of what might have happened dawned on him.

Thomas was about to offer him more water when the sounds of a scuffle turned heads to the doors.

'I say, Clearwater,' Irving laughed. 'Now a highwayman to boot. This evening is turning into a Molière.'

Fecker had appeared at the door dressed in his new trench coat and tricorn hat. Oleg stood tall and stoic beside him, and between them, Saddle writhed in their iron grip. Barnaby appeared from behind, out of breath.

'Allow me to see if I was right.' Silas marched up to the under-butler and removed his pocket watch. Returning to the table, he handed it to Archer.

'If I am correct,' Stoker said. 'One press of the pin releases the cover, a second pops open the face, and behind it… No, Sir!' He gripped Archer's arm. 'It is obviously corrosive. Don't do it over your lap.'

Archer followed the instructions, and when the face opened, a small amount of white powder trickled onto his plate before he snapped the watch closed.

'How horribly ingenious,' he said, raising his eyes accusingly to Saddle. 'Well? What have you to say for yourself?'

'I didn't know, Sir, honestly,' Saddle snivelled. 'He told me it was harmless. It's meant to turn your teeth red. He said it was a joke you would appreciate.'

'A joke?' Archer roared. 'You thought poisoning my guests would be a joke?'

'I didn't know, Sir. Please, he made me.'

'Made you? How?'

'Promised me a position, Sir, and money. I owe money, and I owed some to Mr Smith by then. If I'd known…'

'What position?'

'It's in my pocket, Sir. Proof that he tricked me. A letter for His Grace.'

'Oh, I am enjoying this no end,' Lady Marshall chuckled.

'Search his pockets, Mr Andrej,' Archer ordered, ignoring his godmother's mirth.

Thomas was glad of it. Rather than being outraged, the guests, including Tennyson and the countess, were now finding the scene amusing. The previous outrage and tension were evaporating from everyone apart from Archer who still glowed a deep crimson.

Oleg held Saddle by the elbows while Fecker rummaged in the under-butler's inside pockets from which he withdrew several letters and unopened telegrams.

'What position, Saddle, would make you want to turn your back on my house?' Archer demanded. 'Have we not been fair to you?'

'You have, Sir,' Saddle grovelled. 'But butler to a Duke, no disrespect... The letter introduced me to the Duke of Wexford. I couldn't turn down the opportunity. Once in a lifetime, away from those I owe money. I had no choice.'

Thomas collected the envelopes from Fecker and brought them to the table, reading the sender addresses. 'This would explain your missing telegram, Mr Hawkins,' he said. 'And there appear to be one or two from Mr Wright.'

He handed them to Archer, but instead of opening them, the viscount threw them on the table.

'It's there, Sir,' Saddle protested. 'Proof that he tricked me.'

'Oh, he tricked you alright,' Archer said. 'There *is* no Duke of Wexford.'

'I hope you're writing this down, Stoker,' Irving whispered through a smile.

'I am glad you are finding this of interest, Irving,' Archer said. 'And I mean that truly because I am so embarrassed by the whole charade I am mortified.'

'We very nearly all were,' Irving chuckled, before adopting an expression of seriousness. 'Sorry. Don't be embarrassed, Sir,' he said as if delivering the final speech of a tragedy. 'Your man has acted admirably to save you and us all. Besides...' His sincerity transformed back into humour. 'It is bound to be material for one of Abraham's stories, or perhaps one of Lord Tennyson's idylls.'

'Thank you for your understanding.' Archer's words were clipped, but there was a faint hint of amusement behind his eyes. 'I think the best thing to do is have Mr Saddle put in the hands of Sergeant Lanyon. Payne? Paper and pen, if you would.'

Thomas nodded to Barnaby who hurried away.

'We shall let the authorities decide what to do with you, Saddle,'

Archer continued. 'But whatever they decide, you are no longer employed at Larkspur Hall. You agree, Payne?'

'I do, My Lord.'

'A shame we are forced to air our domestic laundry before such honoured guests, and once again, I apologise. I hope this shambles has no bearing on your decision to aid the Foundation, Sirs.'

'None whatsoever, Clearwater,' Tennyson said. 'I am not sure how I can be of use, but you may use my name, for what it be worth.'

'Mine too,' Sullivan added. 'And I expect Gilbert will be chomping at his wit to produce a libretto on the matter when I give him the details. Perhaps I can persuade D'Oyly Carte to give some backing. After all, if your Foundation can take a young man like this one...' he waved a hand towards Jake, 'and turn him into a man of life-saving ingenuity such as Mr Hawkins, well... There's an opera in there somewhere, eh, Roxton?'

Roxton, fanning himself with Countess Romney's fan, could only nod.

'Thank you, Arthur,' Archer bowed his head in deference and finally smiled.

Barnaby returned with headed notepaper and a pen, and gave them to Thomas who passed them on to the viscount.

'Mr Andrej,' Archer said as he wrote. 'Would you and Oleg please escort this man and his timepiece to the police station? I know he stands no chance of wriggling away from you.'

'Da.' Fecker said, and after a nudge from Oleg, added, 'Lord.'

Archer finished his note and handed it and the watch to Thomas to give to Fecker. That done, he ran his fingers through his hair, brushing it away from his forehead. 'Mr Hawkins, take your friend and change. Join us later so we can hear anything else we might need to know. Payne...?' He broke off. Fecker was still filling the doorway. 'Yes, Mr Andrej? Was there something else?'

Fecker shrugged. 'Da, Geroy,' he said. 'There's this.'

Standing aside, he revealed James with Jerry wrapped around him, asleep with his head on James' shoulder.

'And there's more!' Irving slapped the table in joy as Archer groaned.

'Mr Stoker,' Tennyson reached across the table. 'Will you pass the pen? At least one of us should be taking notes.'

Stoker wasn't listening, he was rising slowly to his feet in disbelief.

'Sorry about this, My Lord,' James said, stepping into the room as Fecker and Oleg dragged away the unfortunate Mr Saddle. 'It's been a long ride, and the lad is very tired, but I thought he should be returned to his father immediately.'

'Father?' Archer looked at Thomas for an explanation, but he was as dumbfounded as everyone else; everyone apart from Stoker.

'Noel?'

'He has been calling himself Jerry,' James explained as he approached.

Jerry stirred at the mention of his name and lifted his head. 'Are we there, Uncle Jimmy?'

'Uncle Jimmy?'

'Bit of a long story, Sir,' James said, lifting Jerry to the floor. 'Your father's here. You're safe now.'

'Noel?' Stoker repeated, his tone hardening. 'Why aren't you in school. What on earth…?'

Jerry burst into tearful apologies which only calmed when James comforted him. 'Your father won't be angry when I explain,' he said, ushering the boy forward.

'It's an evening for explanations,' Silas said, and James noticed his state. 'Hello, Mr Wright.'

'Mr Hawkins.'

'James Joseph, what an honour.'

'The honour is mine, Your Lordship,' James said, bowing to Tennyson.

'Sir Galahad returned from another quest?'

'"To strive, to seek, to find, and not to yield",' James quoted, and the poet, beaming, stood to shake his hand.

'This is all very intriguing,' Lady Marshall announced. 'But listen.' She rose elegantly to her feet. 'I admit to being as confused as the next man, but also as joyous not to be writhing in agony on the carpet. May I suggest that we forgo the next course and donate it to these young men who have, judging from their appearance, suffered great pains to ensure we didn't. We could take our dessert in the drawing-room, with or without wine. What do you say, Clearwater? It hasn't exactly been a conventional evening thus far.'

Archer's head moved from side to side as he took it all in, his mouth agape, but offering no reply.

'That's that then,' her Ladyship declared. 'You don't mind, do you? Countess? Your Lordships?' When no-one objected, she continued. 'Would that cause huge domestic upheaval, Payne?'

'Not at all, Your Ladyship, but I will, with His Lordship's permission, open a new bottle of Mediasch in your presence, just to be sure.'

'Yes,' Archer said, rising and pulling himself together. 'Good idea, and when you two are clean, and you, Mr Wright, have eaten, join us. We are not people who stand too much on ceremony, and I am keen to hear the details of this… This…'

'Full-bodied mystery?' Stoker suggested.

'Sounds like a splendid idea,' the Earl enthused to a chorus of approval. 'Lost me appetite anyway, too much entertainment, but bloody good fun, Clearwater.'

The party rose, each chatting to those nearest, and Lady Marshall led them from the room.

Among the hubbub, a small voice was heard, sleepy but insistent. 'Father? Can I stay with Uncle Jimmy?'

Thomas chuckled at the name, covering it with a cough as Archer approached.

'I don't know what I would do without you, Tom,' he whispered.

'Sir,' Thomas said, stopping the viscount with his tone. 'It's not me you should be thanking. And, if you'll forgive me, you should not only be thanking Mr Hawkins, but also apologising.'

Archer glared for a second, but his anger soon seeped away, replaced by an appreciative smile. 'You always know what's best, eh, Tom? Always do right by me.'

'We all do, Sir. Especially Mr Hawkins.'

Another long sigh. 'I know,' Archer nodded and squeezed Thomas' shoulder. 'I don't deserve any of you.' He changed the subject before Thomas could argue. 'Make sure Silas and his friend have what they need. Better ask Mrs Baker to prepare two more bedrooms, though perhaps the boy should be with his father tonight, if you can tear him away from Uncle Jimmy.'

They sniggered secretly like schoolboys before adjusting their demeanour, and Archer followed his guests.

'Mr Hawkins,' Thomas said, when the others had left. 'Would

you mind changing before you dine? Jake too, if you have anything that will fit him. What on earth are you covered in?'

'The seven fifteen from Plymouth.'

Silas threw an arm around Jake, producing a cloud, and Thomas groaned as it settled on the nearby furniture.

With Stoker's blessing, Jerry was allowed to stay and help James who offered to clear the dining room, but Thomas refused.

'I suggest that you also change your clothes, Mr Wright,' he said. 'You look like a lighthouse keeper in need of a shave. Master Stoker can stay in here with me until we go through to explain where you've been.'

'Very well,' James said glancing over his shoulder to make sure the room was clear before crouching to Jerry. 'I'll be back soon. You stay here...' He winked up at Thomas. 'With Uncle Tommy.'

Twenty-Seven

The storm that had buffeted the county returned after sweeping a full circle across the West Country, and thunder rolled across the moors on a wind that blew sudden squalls against trees and houses alike. As lightning cracked over rocky crags and ponds boiled with pelting rain, Larkspur Hall stood unmoved by the weather as it had for centuries. A warm glow emanated from its tall windows in defiance of the storm, the light a beacon of safety and comfort.

Inside, the drawing-room had never seen such a gathering as the one witnessed that Easter Friday evening. The poet laureate sat on a sofa beside James, a young, working-class man from South Riverside, who, while discussing poetry, entertained Noel Stoker, the son of a Trinity College author. The country's most famous actor accepted a glass of brandy from the son of a dairy farmer and held Thomas in conversation about his role in the events leading up to the attempted assassination. In another part of the room, an earl, a countess, a viscountess and a viscount chatted to a teenager from the streets of the West End dressed in borrowed clothes, and listened intently as he described how he intended to alter the sleeves by the shoulder seams. One of the country's foremost composers discussed arias with one of its foremost countertenors, while the scene was watched by the son of an Irish immigrant who had just explained the connection between a bottle of wine and a runaway child.

Silas had grabbed his audience's attention with the words, '*Yia buyatul shi uchideh tatal.*' After a suitable pause, he continued. 'Those were the words I heard Mr Smith speak in his sleep, and Lord Clearwater said it sounded Romanian. It was them and what he said after that made me not trust him. He repeatedly muttered about taking the family name, dishonour and shame, but Smith said "*He* means dishonour, *he* means you shame" obviously talking about someone else. Then there was the thing with the tattoo on his back which His Lordship said was to do with an old organisation of assassins. Of course, you put those kind of weird things together, and you can't help but be nosey.'

Some of the guests laughed politely while others were too intrigued to do anything but listen.

'The only thing I was sure of,' Silas continued, 'was that Mr Payne and Mr Wright had made a connection between Smith and Mr Irving. That was what they'd found in the newspaper, and it was to do with your play, Sir. We thought that Smith was after you because of what you'd said about his people in your speeches, and Mr Payne suggested that I go and ask if I could see your notes or the script, thinking it would give us an idea of what Smith had planned, and how he was going to do it. He reckoned you must still have them, but as you were out of the country, we couldn't go directly to you.'

'And you were right, lad,' Stoker said. 'Except it wasn't Mr Irving who did the work on it, it was me.'

'Which we now know,' Silas agreed. 'So, the only place I could think of to find someone who could speak Romanian was the East End where we have the Foundation's hostel, so I went to see Doctor Markland. Oh, he sends his regards to you, Sir.'

'He's the superintendent,' Archer explained, watching Silas with a look of admiration.

'Anyway, I found a man who translated the words. *Yia buyatul shi uchideh tatal*, it turned out, means "Take the child and kill the father".'

The countess gasped and clutched her diamond necklace, while Lady Marshall licked her lips, leaning forward and listening closely.

'Now then,' Silas said. 'That didn't mean anything to me either, and it still didn't when we found Mr Stoker's research and were bringing it back. It was because of your notes, Mr Stoker, that Jake worked out that Smith was going to use a lackey to poison the wine, and the notes also told us how. I knew His Lordship was planning to let the two of you taste the wine first, so Jake and I had to do whatever we could to get back before you did. I think you know the rest.'

'Apart from what my son was doing nearly getting himself killed in a railway accident when he should have been at school,' Stoker blustered, giving his boy a fierce look of reproach.

'If I may, Sir?' When Archer nodded, James came to stand with Silas. 'Your son was running away from Mr Smith because the man had tried to abduct him,' he explained. 'He knew that you were returning on the Britannic tender service into Newquay, and with masterful courage, made his way there. Smith, we now know, followed him. It's my theory that he intended to come down to Newquay and carry out the assassination there, the fishing port being a quieter place than, say, London. I can only guess at that, but it seems obvious to me that his instructions were to take Noel and use him as a hostage if he was unable to get to you directly, as a way of getting your attention. When Noel saw he was in the same house as the man who tried to kidnap him, he was terrified and ran away. I don't blame him.'

'And I shall reimburse you any financial deficit the boy incurred,' Stoker said.

'No need, Sir,' James smiled back. 'He's a good lad and very clever if I might say so.'

'And Mr Smith?' Archer asked. 'Which I doubt is his real name. Where is he?'

'Mr Andrej and the police at Newquay went after him on horseback, but the policeman's horses were too slow.'

'Fecker said they were shit.'

'I beg your pardon!' Stoker's face turned as red as his hair, the countess clutched her jewellery tighter, and Lady Marshall had to slap her hand across her mouth to stop herself from laughing.

'No, Noel,' James said, struggling to keep his composure. 'He said they should be shot.' He moved on quickly. 'So, I am afraid the assassin got away from us. You still need to be cautious, Sir.'

'I shan't worry,' Stoker dismissed the danger. 'If they only do away with people via this particular wine, he will have a hard job finding more. As I understand it, there's hardly any about.'

'I shan't be selling any to the Garrick after all,' Archer said looking at Thomas. 'And Mr Payne keeps a very secure guard of the cellars.'

'Still,' the author continued. 'I have no intentions of halting my work on "The Un-Dead." Why, I shall even mention the wine in it somewhere.'

'What exactly is "Un-Dead"?' Lady Marshall enquired. 'Are not all the living un-dead?'

'Ha! Good point,' Irving laughed. 'Stoker, you'll have to find a better title.'

'In good time, Irving. I have barely started on the research.'

The actor returned his attention to Silas. 'So all's well that ends well with young Noel,' he said. 'As for you and Master Jake, I still don't understand how you got into Abraham's office. He's the only person I know who locks his door when the theatre is empty and unlocks it when it's full.'

'There's a tunnel from the Opera to the Lyceum,' Stoker said, and Jake nodded. 'You do know about it, Henry.'

'Do I?'

'I think you've answered all our questions, Mr Hawkins, Mr Wright,' Archer said, before anyone asked how his secretary was able to break into a locked room. 'Unless anyone else has any?' No-one had, so he continued. 'Then sit, gentlemen, I have a few words I would like to say.'

Silas and James sat as Archer broke from his group and stood by the fireplace, his favourite place from which to make speeches.

'My friends,' he said when he had everyone's attention. 'I would like to thank you for indulging me and sharing my drawing room with men of such diverse, and dare I say it, class-divided backgrounds. There aren't many in your position who would agree to be part of such an informal gathering.'

'No need to thank us,' Earl Romney said. 'I think we are all philanthropic here.'

When the murmurs of agreement had died, Archer said, 'Actually, I was talking to my staff,' and raised a laugh. 'But seriously,' he continued. 'This has been a most unusual evening, and Mr Hawkins and Mr O'Hara have told us a remarkable tale, the facts of which have been proved by the actions of a dismissed servant, and the knowledgeable mind of Mr Stoker. Excuse the informality, but a toast to Silas and Jake.'

A toast was drunk with glasses of unpolluted Golden Mediasch, the company laughing in the face of the Protectori ai Szekely.

'You have a very loyal team, Clearwater,' Tennyson said. 'Your men are a credit to you, but also you to them. How should those not born to privilege ever aspire to success if no-one leads from above. To invite your valet and the homeless to be in our company is an act of forward-thinking at which many men of my acquaintance would baulk. I say the honour is ours.'

'Hear, hear,' Lady Marshall agreed, raising her glass to James and winking inappropriately.

'Thank you, My Lord.' Archer bowed. 'I agree with you.' He smiled at Silas with a twinkle in his eye. 'I apologise for my previous anger, Mr Hawkins, it was misplaced and unfair.'

'Ah, away with you,' Silas laughed. 'You're making me scarlet you bowsie.'

'A fellow Dubliner?' Stoker raised his inquisitive gaze to Silas.

'My mother was from Ballymun.'

'Good heavens! Just down the road from me. We must talk, Sir.'

'And you have the Hall at your disposal in which to exchange stories,' Archer said. 'I hope the weather improves, and we can get in some riding. Mr Andrej and Williams will be on hand on Sunday if anyone requires a carriage to the village for the church service. As well as the usual Easter Sunday, er, routine, it will also be a memorial to those who lost their lives in the accident, so I shall be attending. In the meantime, I have, I believe, not only the most loyal and attentive of staff, and the most extraordinary of secretaries, but the best cook in the county. Larkspur Hall is yours.' A sweep of his hand encompassed the entire party. 'You are all welcome to my house. Come freely. Go safely; and leave behind some of the happiness you bring.'

Stoker spluttered on his wine.

'Damn fine words, Sir,' he said, putting down his glass and searching his pockets for a notebook. 'I shall use that line.'

'Use anything you want,' Archer said.

'Thank you, My Lord.' Stoker pushed himself to his feet. 'But for now, if the ladies will excuse me, I will take my boy to his room.' He waved his book. 'It is late, and I have inspiration upon me. Come, Noel.'

'Can Uncle Jimmy read to me?' the boy pleaded. 'We're reading "Kidnapped", Father.'

'I think the fellow has done enough for you already,' Stoker insisted.

'Just one chapter?'

'I expect Mr Wright is exhausted,' Stoker replied, knowing he was fighting a losing battle.

'I don't mind, Sir.' James stood, and Jerry took his hand. 'If His Lordship has no objection.'

'None at all,' Archer smiled. 'After all, it's better to read "Kidnapped" than to actually *be* kidnapped.'

Two days later, as the guests were leaving Larkspur Hall, Mr Smith entered a small, sterile room in a distant sanitorium. His journey from Newquay had been a laborious one. His clothes were crumpled, and his eyes were ringed by dark circles, but mainly it was his failure that had worn him down. Watched by a twisted man in a pigskin mask, he wearily pulled a chair to the bedside and hung his head.

'Am esuat,' he said to the man lying prone beneath the leather straps and white sheets. 'I failed, My Lord. We have lost this battle, but we will win the war.'

'He can't hear you,' Quill said, his voice rasping. 'They had to sedate him after I broke the news.'

'We will try again,' Smith said. 'The man will not have been deterred from writing his book.'

Quill's head turned painfully from side to side. 'No, Dorjan.' A scarred hand dabbed his mouth as he sucked saliva. 'We have a more pressing matter than your feud.'

'He intends to call it "The Un-dead",' Smith protested. 'My heritage shall be reduced to a sickening tale in which we are portrayed as blood-sucking monsters.' His eyes flared and he bared his teeth. 'My ancestors will not forgive me if I fail...'

'No!' The word was spat with a venomous growl that made Smith flinch. 'We have time enough for Stoker and others who take your noble Szekely name for their own glory. While you have been failing in the simplest of tasks, I have worked to put in place a series of puzzles not even Clearwater's drove of asses will be able to piece together.' The words were followed by the sucking sounds and a deep swallow. 'And in this venture, we must not fail. We must return the rightful viscount to his title.' He placed his hand on the chest of the unconscious madman. 'I have sworn my oath to him, and he to me. Mark my words, Dorjan, between us, we will see Crispin restored if it takes years. Our game is not yet at an end. When, finally, it is, I will facilitate any revenge you desire against those who sully your bitter bloodline.'

'You will trust me, even after this failure?'

Quill huffed a short laugh as he lay his hand on Crispin's chest. 'If I didn't *need* you, you would both be dead by now.'

Smith regarded Archer's brother. Serene and untroubled in sleep, he rested peacefully, but the Romanian had witnessed him unhinged, and shivered at the memory. Raising his head to look directly into Quill's watery eye, he said, 'Tell me what you need.'

Look out for book six in the series, coming soon

If you have enjoyed this story, here is a list of my other novels to date. With them, I've put my own heat rating according to how sexually graphic they are. They are all romantic in some way apart from the short stories.

References to sex (*) A little sex (**) A couple of times (***) Quite a bit, actually (****) Cold shower required (*****)

Short erotic stories

In School & Out *****
13 erotic short stories, winner of the European Gay Porn Awards (best erotic fiction). Boarding schools and sex on a Greek island.

Older/younger MM romances

The Mentor of Wildhill Farm ****
Older writer mentors four young gay guys in more than just verbs and adjectives. Isolated setting. Teens coming out. Sex parties. And a twist.

The Mentor of Barrenmoor Ridge ***
It takes a brave man to climb a mountain, but it takes a braver lad to show him the way. Mountain rescue. Coming to terms with love, loss and sexuality.

The Mentor of Lonemarsh House ***
I love you enough to let you run, but too much to see you fall Folk music. Hidden secrets. Family acceptance.

The Mentor of Lostwood Hall ***
A man with a future he can't accept and a lad with a past he can't escape. A castle. A road accident. Youth and desire.

Other People's Dreams ***
Screenwriter seeks four gay youths to crew his yacht in the Greek islands. Certain strings attached.
Dreams come true. Coming of age. Youth friendships and love.

The Blake Inheritance **
Let us go then you and I to the place where the wild thyme grows
Family mystery. School crush. A treasure hunt romance.

The Stoker Connection ***
What if you could prove the greatest Gothic novel of all time was a true story? Literary conspiracy. Teen boy romance. First love. Mystery and adventure.

Curious Moonlight *
He's back. He's angry and I am fleeing for my life.
A haunted house. A mystery to solve. A slow-burn romance.
Straight to gay.

Deviant Desire ***
Book 1. A mashup of mystery, romance and adventure, Deviant Desire is set in an imaginary London of 1888. The first in an on-going series in a world where homosexuality is a crime.

Twisted Tracks **
Book 2. An intercepted telegram, a coded invitation and the threat of exposure. Viscount Clearwater must put his life on the line to protect his reputation.

Unspeakable Acts *
Book 3. A murder will take place unless Clearwater's homosexuality is made public; can his lover stop the killing and save his reputation?

Fallen Splendour *
Book 4. A kidnapping, a court case and a poem by Tennyson. What is the connection? James has four days to find out.

Bitter Bloodline *
Book 5. What do a runaway boy and an assassin have to do with Clearwater's famed Easter dinner party and its guest of honour, the actor, Henry Irving? Silas suspects assassination.

All these can all be found on my Amazon Author page.
Please leave a review if you can. Thanks again for reading. If you keep reading, I'll keep writing.
Jackson

Made in United States
Orlando, FL
16 June 2024

47940147R10171